THE
SCARECROW
QUEEN

THE SCARECROW QUEEN

❖ *A Sin Eater's Daughter* Novel ❖

MELINDA SALISBURY

SCHOLASTIC PRESS / NEW YORK

S

Copyright © 2017 Melinda Salisbury
Map by Maxime Plasse

All rights reserved. Published by Scholastic Press, an imprint of Scholastic Inc., *Publishers since 1920*, by arrangement with Scholastic Children's Books, an imprint of Scholastic Ltd., London. SCHOLASTIC, SCHOLASTIC PRESS, and associated logos are trademarks and/or registered trademarks of Scholastic Inc.

The publisher does not have any control over and does not assume any responsibility for author or third-party websites or their content.

No part of this publication may be reproduced, stored in a retrieval system, or transmitted in any form or by any means, electronic, mechanical, photocopying, recording, or otherwise, without written permission of the publisher. For information regarding permission, write to Scholastic Inc., Attention: Permissions Department, 557 Broadway, New York, NY 10012.

Library of Congress Cataloging-in-Publication Data available

ISBN 978-1-338-19295-7

10 9 8 7 6 5 4 3 2 1   17 18 19 20 21

Printed in the U.S.A.   40
First American edition, November 2017

Book design by Christopher Stengel

For my best friend, Emilie Lyons
Bem, bem, bem

God hates happy children.

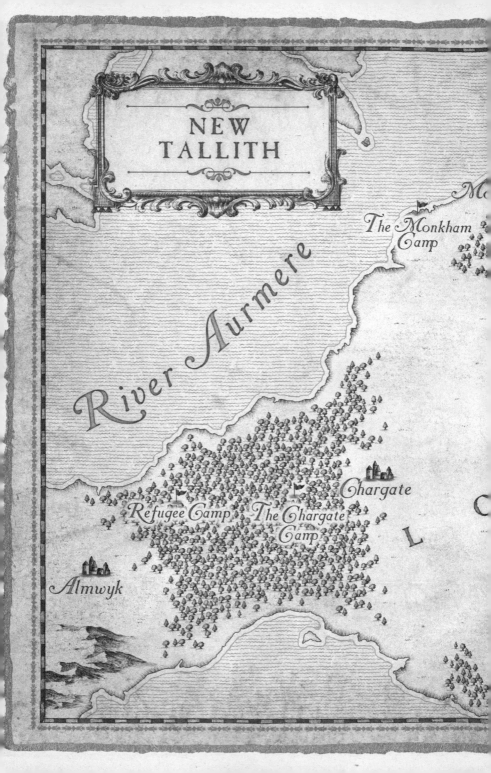

Rising Dawn Base
The Lormere Camp
ham
Lormere Castle
The Salt Miners Cottages
The Salt Mill
L O R M E R E
Haga
The Haga Camp

The Tower of Wisdom

The apothecary sits in the lap of the prince. Her hands are in his hair, her fingers working meticulously, filling his silken locks with dozens of braids. She'd like to put bells on the ends, she thinks. Silver bells to match the silver tresses. His hair reminds her of water, the softness and coldness of a stream flowing over her palms. The prince's eyes are closed as she works; white lashes brush his cheeks, a sleek smile on his full lips, his breathing deep and even. As her knuckles brush against his neck, a low rumbling sounds in the back of his throat: a purr, or perhaps a growl. The apothecary swallows.

The dancing light from the candles makes the prince's eyes look the color of topaz when he opens them and turns his gaze on the apothecary. She feels something inside her stomach twist: a snake inside her, coiled and waiting. Then a rattling, warning her. The prince raises a hand and she flinches, but he only tilts her chin upward, his smile widening.

1

"This brings back old, old memories, sweetling. I used to have girls do this, in Tallith," he says. His voice is musical, soothing, and as he speaks, the apothecary continues braiding. "I liked very much to bathe, and I'd have the girls braid my hair to keep it out of the water. In the Tower of Honor, the entire lower floor was one large, grand bath carved out of marble, and at its deepest, twice my height. We held gatherings in there sometimes, when we had very important guests. The water was pumped in from the springs beneath the ground. It smelled a little strange, sulfurous, but it wasn't unpleasant. Though it would turn my and my sister's hair an unbecoming yellow tint if we soaked our hair in it."

He pauses and leans forward, lifting a glass of wine to his mouth. He offers none to the apothecary, instead draining it and dropping it to the floor carelessly, smiling at her with purple-stained lips.

"I believe there's a pool with the same properties in the mountains here. Perhaps I shall take you, when the weather warms. You can braid my hair there, and we can swim together. If you are good."

The apothecary's fingers are deft in the prince's hair; years of plucking leaves and pinching powders make her movements sure. But the room is cold, the stone walls bare, and the fire burning in the grate is small. When she exhales, her breath lingers on the air before her, and there is a dull ache in her bones that never seems to fade. The prince doesn't seem to feel the cold, but the apothecary does. It's colder in this land than in her home. Her hands tremble, and the prince pulls her closer, stroking her back through her hand-me-down gown. She's no warmer pressed against him; his form does not seem to hold any heat.

2

"There were private baths, too, on the second floor," the prince continues softly. "More intimate ones, for those who desired them. Did I ever tell you about the towers of Tallith castle?" The prince does not pause to allow the apothecary to answer. "Seven in total. Each one named for a virtue. My own was the Tower of Love. Perhaps I should rename the towers here, to honor them. What do you think?" He caresses the side of her face, and her jaw tightens. "Oh, Errin . . ." he begins.

But he's interrupted by a knock at the door.

"Enter," he calls.

A servant with salt-and-pepper hair and a grizzled face pushes the door open. Like the apothecary, he appears to be cold, wrapped in a fur-lined cloak even inside the castle walls. Indifferent blue eyes skim over the apothecary, paying her no more mind than he would the other furniture in the room, before he bows to the prince.

"Well?" the prince says.

"Word from the Silver Knight, my liege," the servant says, his head still lowered as he pulls a roll of sealed parchment from inside his cloak.

The prince holds out a hand for it, and then the servant raises his head, just a fraction, to step forward and hand it over. The prince waves him back once he has the message, and breaks the seal.

The apothecary tries to look at what her brother has written to the prince. But the prince shifts, moving the parchment so she cannot see.

The apothecary is still plaiting his hair, now twining the ends that are still within her reach. Her fingers are numb with cold and stiff from the small, repetitive movements, but she cannot stop.

3

Without warning the prince rises with a jubilant shout, upending the apothecary onto the floor at the foot of his chair. He steps over her, turning back briefly. "Your brother is a miracle, sweetling. An absolute miracle." Then, to the servant: "Have someone saddle my horse and those of four men. We're going into Lortune."

With that, he strides from the room, the servant scurrying after him, leaving the apothecary where she has fallen, lying on her side, her left cheek and ear against the frigid stone floor. She has landed badly, one arm caught beneath her, one knee pressing into the leg of the chair. She feels her fingers still moving, even those crushed beneath her own weight. Still seeking invisible locks of moonlight hair, still trying to cross them over each other. If she had bells for them, she'd hear him coming, she thinks. She'd be warned.

Not that it would help her at all.

Hours pass and the prince does not return. The apothecary's bladder fills, paining her. Her legs and arms cramp, and release, and cramp again. She feels bruises begin to bloom along her body from the fall; the edges of her lips and the skin beneath her fingernails turn blue from the cold. Tears leak unchecked from her eyes, pooling on the floor beneath her ear, and when the meager flames in the fireplace finally die, her body begins to tremble almost immediately. The room grows darker as the daylight fades.

And all the while her fingers still work, work, work at hair that is not there.

Finally the pressure in her bladder is too much and she lets go, soaking herself and the floor beneath her. The initial warmth is a grim moment of respite from the relentless cold, but soon the pool of urine cools, too, and soaks into her thin gown. She wonders if she will die there.

But then the prince returns.

He glances down at the apothecary, his brows rising. He appears puzzled for a moment; then realization causes his features to slacken. He steps past the apothecary and to a table by his chair. He lifts the small clay doll that lies there, a twist of brown hair over its head, two green glass beads to approximate eyes. Around its waist is a strip of paper, and he peels it away from the clay.

At once the girl can move. She feels the supernatural hold over her body vanish and she rolls onto her back.

The prince stands over her, his beautiful face warped by the disgust now etched upon it.

"Did you piss yourself? You little beast. I was barely gone a few hours."

When the apothecary doesn't answer, he nudges her shoulder with the tip of a boot.

"I'm talking to you. Answer me." She does not, and he kicks her again, harder this time. "You're disgusting."

He calls for a servant to come and collect her, and a man enters the room, different from the one who came before. This man's shoulders are slumped, and his dark-eyed gaze stays fixed on the floor; everything about him begs to be ignored. The prince obliges, barely glancing at him as he demands the apothecary be removed from his sight, and that someone else come and clean the mess she's made. The servant says nothing, not flinching when he helps the apothecary to her feet. He might as well be one of the prince's clay creatures for all the expression he betrays as he supports the wet and weeping apothecary from the prince's chamber.

The prince watches them leave, sinking into his chair. He peers down at the doll of the girl he still holds. A vicious scowl flashes across his features and he crushes the doll in his hand, dropping it to the ground. But as soon as he's done so, he bends to pick it up. He pulls the hair out from the mess and finds the glass beads, too, setting them aside. Then his fingers are the ones to move swiftly, teasing the clay out into the form of a girl once more. He wraps the hair back around her head, refits the eyes, and rises, striding from the room.

He finds the apothecary and the servant at the foot of the tower he's assigned to her, starting up the stairs. The servant steps away as he hears his master's boots approaching, and the girl staggers. She turns in time to see the prince draw his knife and reach for her hand. He slashes her palm, waiting till the second her blood spills, and then presses the doll into the wound.

The apothecary cries out and tries to pull away, but it's too late. The clay has absorbed the drops of her blood. She watches as the prince pricks his own finger with the same knife and allows a drop of his own blood to fall onto the simulacrum's form. It, too, is absorbed, and the prince smiles. He strokes the clay poppet before placing it gently inside his pocket. Then, without a word, he turns and walks away, leaving the girl bleeding and sobbing, and the servant staring after him.

❖ PART ONE ❖
Twylla

Chapter 1

Somewhere to the left of the alcove I'm still crammed inside, water drips steadily to the floor. Other than those rhythmic taps, the bone temple is silent. I've counted over three thousand drops, when I hear something out in the passageway. I tense, my already stiff muscles aching as I strain to catch any other sound: muffled footfalls, soft sighs, the whispering of fabric. Moments pass like lifetimes, the dripping continues, and I hold my breath until my lungs burn.

I hear a thud, then another, and then a sort of rustling, and I exhale with a dizzying rush. I know those sounds: just more debris falling from the ceiling. Really, that alone should be enough to make me move, the realization the roof could cave in and bury me. The echoes of boots have long since faded, and the lanterns on the walls are burning low. I need to go.

I start counting again.

When I get to four thousand, I pause, shifting my weight. My foot immediately cramps and I flex it, squeezing my eyes shut at the pain. When I open them, the room seems darker, and I peer out through a sliver of a gap in the screen that conceals me, trying to determine if any of the torches have blown out. Through that small gap I watched Errin scream at the Sleeping Prince, saw her look him in the eye and lie to his face. I watched him stroke her, bend his head to her hair and *smell* her, threaten to murder her, and still she held her nerve. Even when she knelt to him, she did it with the air of someone granting a favor, not someone obeying a command. I have to wonder if Errin would have hidden from him at all if our situations had been reversed. I can't imagine she would have stayed wedged in a crevice, her fist stuffed in her mouth, the taste of her own blood on her tongue.

No, I decide. She's not the hiding type. Even if she had at first agreed to hide, she would have emerged and tried to fight. She could never have stayed concealed. Or if she had managed it, it would have been because she was thinking of the bigger picture, and she'd have left the moment they did. Stalked them through the passageways, eavesdropping to learn what she could, forming a plan. Either way, she wouldn't still be here, counting water droplets.

I thought I'd left my cowardice in Lormere.

Along with all my feelings for Lief. All I can see is the cold look in his eyes when he told me to hide. The grudging way he offered me safety, as though to repay a debt. Calling what we had a *friendship* . . .

I push it away, clenching my jaw, my hands curling into fists. I know exactly what kind of man he is; I know what he did to me, to Merek, to Lormere. To his own sister, while I watched. And yet the first thing I felt when I saw him there was joy. I forgot everything, all the death, all the pain; instead, I remembered the way he smelled when I pressed my face into his neck, the feel of muscle beneath his skin as my fingers clutched his back. His hair falling into my face. The taste of his mouth. As though moons hadn't passed, as though nothing had changed.

All it took was my name on his lips to bring me to my knees again. Gods, I want so much to hate him. No—not even that. I want to think of him and feel nothing. I want him to be a stranger to me.

Enough, Twylla, I tell myself, wishing I could score him from my heart. *Go, now.*

Then one of the torches flickers and dies, adding a new patch of shadow to the room, and I realize it won't be long until the others do the same. And it's that—the thought of being alone here, deep underground, in the dark, surrounded by the dead—that finally makes me unlock my muscles, my legs trembling when I move. Even then I wait, staring into the darkness for any sign of life.

The first step I take is a roll of thunder splitting apart the stillness. The crunching of bone and wood beneath my foot ricochets around the temple, echoing around me. In the shadows something falls, and all of the hairs on the back of my neck stand up. And when another torch splutters and dies, I pick up my skirts and run, stumbling over femurs and ribs and broken struts, terrified of being trapped here in the dark.

As I push through the curtain into the passage, I trip over something large and soft, and fly forward, raising my hands to

11

break my fall. My hands sting as they strike the stone floor and I swear loudly, rolling immediately to stand.

I see a figure, facedown, white hair bloodied on one side. I can't tell if it's male or female until I crouch beside it—*her*—to press my fingers to her neck. I know immediately, from the coldness, from the way the skin feels unyielding, that she's dead. When I gently roll her over, the only injury I can see is a wound to her left temple; it looks small, as though it ought not to have been enough to kill. But it did; her golden eyes are dull and staring, mouth open, all life well and truly fled. I close both eyes and mouth, and cross her arms over her chest.

I've seen plenty of dead people in my life, and I know, deep in my soul, or my gut, that before this night is out I'm going to see a lot more.

The next two hours of my life are the closest to hell that I've ever come. The corridors of the Conclave are a warren and there are no markings or signs to tell me where I am, or where to go. At first I'm cautious, still loosely gripped by the fear that kept me in the bone temple for so long, but with each dead end, each wrong turn, the panic rises, the terror I'll never find my way out, that I'll die down here in the dark, and eventually I'm running, dodging obstacles and vaulting over smashed furniture.

On and on I go, stumbling past body after body, my whimpers reflected by the walls, haunting me with every step. In the back of my mind I know this means I'm truly alone down here. I'm making more than enough noise to give myself away, but I can't stop. I sob and gasp; every single person I come across is a corpse, battered, broken, and splayed. Clothing is askew where they've fallen, exposing breasts and groins, the owners oblivious. Limbs are bent backward, or sometimes not there at all. There has been no mercy here.

I'm in a mass grave, I think, and laugh, immediately clapping my hands over my mouth at the sound. But it's still there, the urge to giggle, bubbling up even as I tell myself this isn't funny. *I'm hysterical,* I realize, but it doesn't mean anything. I keep going, around and around.

After a while I stop running, walking through the tunnels and rooms in a dreamlike state. I drift through chambers carpeted with the charred pages of books; I pick my way through smashed glass and ceramics, cross caverns where the air reeks of herbs and sulfur and myriad other things that litter the ground, crushed beneath the heels of boots. Mattresses have been shredded, bookcases overturned. Like Tremayne above, the Conclave has been explored, stripped, and destroyed.

I pass ever more bodies: alchemists with their luminous hair, normal men, women, even children, and now I stop beside each one, checking first to make sure they are truly dead before I close their eyes and mouths if they're open, neaten their limbs if they're sprawled without dignity.

This is new to me, this kind of death. The corpses I've seen before have been neatly laid out, their hair brushed, wearing their smartest clothes; sometimes even powders and pastes have been added to mask death. They lie in neat repose, waiting to be absolved. Not so down here.

I rearrange clothing. I smooth hair back from foreheads. I find no survivors.

I feel like a wraith, a Valkyrie, wandering a battlefield and counting the dead. Most of them have been stabbed, or had their throats cut, and my thoughts keep fighting their way back to Lief, in his suit of silver armor, his sword hanging at his side, and I keep wondering if any of these lives are on his conscience.

Horribly, it's the bodies that eventually begin to guide me. After a while I can tell where I've been, and where is new, based on how they lie. If I can see they've been tended, I turn back and walk the other way; if not, I see to them, then walk on. The dead become my map.

And that is how they lead me to my mother, as they always have; wherever the dead are, there she will eventually be.

The Sin Eater of Lormere lies in the middle of the great hall, with three other corpses nearby. Feeling oddly numb, I ignore her for the time being, tending to the others. Sister Hope isn't here, and neither is Nia or Sister Courage, which allows me a flicker of hope that they at least escaped. But one of the Sisters has fallen, Sister Peace, a sword useless beside her. I tidy her body and those of the other two, all dead so that Errin and I could run. I arrange them as best I can, wiping the blood from their faces, tidying their clothes.

Then, and only then, do I approach my mother.

At Eatings, I heard people say things about how the dead seem smaller than they did in life, how they look as though they're sleeping. But I can see neither of those things when I look at my mother. I grew in that body; I came from it. It gave me life. And now it's empty. Visibly and unmistakably empty.

She's on her front, and I turn her over, feeling sick at the dull thud of flesh as she rolls back. Mercifully, her eyes are shut, and as with the first body I found, she has only the smallest wound to

14

the side of her head. Her dark hair is oily, and I stroke it gently. I've never been able to see my face in my mother's and I still can't now, can't find who I am in her strong nose, her rosebud mouth. Her skin is clear of my freckles, her eyelids hooded. I could see a little of her in my sister, Maryl, the same bow lips, the same small hands. But not me. I might as well have been a changeling. I wonder for a moment where my brothers are, whether they live, whether they care about the Sleeping Prince's reign. Whether they'd care that our mother is dead. But then, she neglected them even more than she'd neglected me. I at least had a use. A purpose, as it now seems.

Less than a day has passed since I stood in this room and vowed to fight the Sleeping Prince. How sure of myself I was then, with Errin and Silas beside me; how righteous my anger was. It seemed so possible then, so simple. Silas would train the alchemists and their kin to fight and we'd all march on Lormere and defeat the Sleeping Prince. I thought we'd be like an avenging army in a story. I imagined people rallying to our cry, and that the fact we were on the side of good would assure our victory.

And then Aurek came, with my lover at his side, and proved that I am not only still a coward but still a naive, stupid fool, too. And I'm supposed to save us from the Sleeping Prince.

I loosen my mother's hair from its binding and arrange it around her shoulders. I fold her arms over her chest and straighten her robes. But I can feel something missing, something I've forgotten to do. An itch to be scratched. A debt to be paid.

Then I see the table, see the bread and the flagon of ale that have somehow, miraculously, survived the fighting, as if for this very moment. And I know what I need to do.

15

I bring the bread and the flagon from the table and place them beside my mother, reaching for a tumbler that's lying nearby and filling it with ale.

I begin the Eating.

The bread is white and rich, not unlike the bread I ate at Lormere castle, though this is flecked with small seeds that taste rich like liquorice when I chew them. They keep getting caught in my teeth and I have to pause to fish them out. As I do, I begin to catalogue my mother's sins.

Pride, certainly. Some vanity. Lust? Perhaps; apart from the twins, we all had different fathers. Though it's hard to imagine my mother seeking out a man—it's hard to imagine her with an appetite for anything other than her role, and I've always assumed that's why she had us. Duty. I'll never know for sure now. I'll never be able to ask. I push that thought aside and concentrate on the sins; she could be wrathful at times. Spiteful, too.

But I really can't focus. My mind keeps pulling me back to the talk we had before the attack. Of her saying she tried to save Maryl in the only way she knew how. The fear she felt of refusing the queen when she came for me.

Her saying she loved me, as best she could.

The bread sticks in my throat, and I have to take a sip of the ale to force it past the lump that's formed there.

I'm not even performing the Eating correctly; I'm not weighing each sin and taking it on myself. This isn't how you do an Eating.

I set down my cup of ale and lean over to kiss my mother's cold forehead.

"Good night," I say softly. "I give easement and rest to thee now, dear lady. Come not down our lanes or in our meadows. And for thy peace I——" I can't bring myself to say it. I can't. I sit back on my haunches and close my eyes, breathing deeply.

I'm tired of taking people's sins on myself.

I'm tired of running away from everything.

I want to be like Errin. Like Nia. Like Sister Hope. I want to be the girl who fought a golem, the girl who slammed her hands on a table and told a room full of powerful women that I was going to fight, and to hell with them.

I survived the court of Lormere. I survived the journey to Scarron. I survived the Sleeping Prince's raid on the Conclave. I am a survivor.

Then I speak, the words coming from deep, deep inside me. "I give easement and rest to thee now, dear lady. Come not down our lanes or in our meadows. And for thy peace I will put Aurek back to sleep. For good. That's what I'll do for your soul. That's what I'll do for my own soul."

A slow clap begins from the doorway, and I knock the ale over as I fly to my feet. Nia stands there, bloodied, bruises patterning her dark skin, but very much alive. I throw myself across the room, hugging her as hard as I can. To my surprise, her grip on me is just as strong, and we clasp each other, relief coursing through me, until she pulls away.

"I thought I was the only one still down here. Are you alone?" I ask, and she shakes her head.

"Sister Hope lives and is aboveground; they're hiding outside the town walls in an abandoned barn."

"They? Who else is with her?"

"Sister Courage, but she's injured. A few others managed to get out, too."

"Silas?" I ask, and Nia shakes her head, causing dread to fan out through my stomach. There's something I have to tell her as well. "Errin was taken, too."

Nia's jaw tightens. "He took all the alchemists he didn't kill. We have to rescue them. We can't leave Silas and Errin there with him. Or Kata." Her voice cracks as she says her wife's name.

"We will," I promise. "We'll get them all back. And we'll stop him, the Sleeping Prince. We'll stop him."

"How?" She looks at me with wide, hopeless eyes.

"Take me to Sister Hope. Then we can talk."

She nods and turns, and I make to follow. Then I stop and turn back, walking to where Sister Peace lies. I pick up the sword that has fallen beside her and heft it in my grip, testing the weight, the sensation of it in my hand. It's heavier than I thought it would be, and I bring my left hand to join the right on the pommel. I take a tentative swing with it, almost knocking myself over, and feel immediately foolish. But I don't put it down. If a Sister could learn to hold it, to use it, then I can. I tuck the blade through my belt and give the room one final look.

I nod at my mother as if she can see me, then I follow Nia, my new sword banging against my hip. I like the feeling of it.

Chapter 2

We move through the tunnels quickly, and Nia keeps her eyes fixed firmly ahead; not once do I see her turn toward any of the fallen, though she must have known them. It reminds me of Errin, in Tremayne above, and how she wouldn't look at the dead, either. They come from a world where the dead aren't part of life.

"I tried to give them some dignity, but should we do something more?" I say as we walk past the bodies.

"They're already buried," Nia says flatly. "This is their grave."

We walk on in silence, stepping over pools of blood and abandoned possessions, until I feel the ground begin to incline under my feet and we reach a set of stairs carved out of rock. I remember them from the journey here. Soon we're passing through doors, and Nia closes each one behind us with finality. When we reach the last door, she pushes it into place and then rests both hands on it, her back to me, head bowed.

"We will never come here again. My only wish," she says in a low, spiked voice, "is that I hadn't had to leave *his* people down there with them." I reach out, squeezing her shoulder gently, and she turns. "You know what I mean."

She's right. As I tended the dead, I steered clear of everyone who I thought was our enemy, leaving them as they lay. I judged them, refused to touch them. A Sin Eater wouldn't do that; a Sin Eater would do her duty.

But then, I'm not a Sin Eater.

"I do," I say to Nia. "And I hope their souls, if they had them, never rest for what they have done."

When we emerge onto the street, I'm astonished to find it's daylight outside, the sun low in the sky; somehow I thought it would be night still. After so long in the near-darkness of the tunnels, the daylight tints everything blue, and I rub at my eyes, black spots exploding across my vision as they adjust.

"Is it safe?" I ask, blinking rapidly. "Have Aurek's people gone?"

Nia shrugs. "I saw no sign of life as I came through. If anyone is still here, I expect we'll find out in the next few moments." Though her words are bold, she looks around, her fingers moving to the knives on her belt. "He'll have taken Silas and the alchemists to Lormere castle." She pauses. "Where did you hide?"

"In the bone temple."

"Surely they looked in there?"

I nod. "Errin told them I'd already run."

"And they believed her?"

"They must have. I was . . . fortunate." Something warns me not to tell her it was Lief's idea for me to hide, nor that he helped cover for me. Not yet, anyway. But from the way she looks at me, eyes narrowed, I get the creeping feeling she knows I'm leaving parts of the story out. "It's foolish to remain here; come," I say before she can ask more questions, moving out into the street, watching every shadow for movement.

She falls in step beside me, staying close, both of us flinching in tandem at the slightest noise: falling plaster in the shell of a home, a cat dislodging rubble as it streaks through the streets, the rustling of wings above me. My lungs feel full before I've taken a breath, each one shallow. Beside me Nia is quiet, ghosting through the dust and debris, a frown darkening her expression.

Her words, when she finally speaks, surprise me. "You talk funny."

"I—what?" I blink. "Well, I'm from Lormere."

"Silas is from Lormere. He doesn't talk like you do."

"I grew up in a court. They have particular ways of doing things, saying things, and I suppose I picked up some of it. I was born a commoner. I didn't always speak like this."

After a moment she nods. "My brothers always say I sound different whenever they come back. I never thought about it before. You do what you have to, to fit in with where you are."

"Exactly," I say. "Talking of where you are, you still haven't told me where it is we're going."

"There's a farm, around three miles from here, the Prythewells—"

"Yes . . . I know it. We passed it on the way here. It was on fire then."

"One of the barns is more or less intact. Sister Hope and the others are waiting for us there."

"How many got away?" I ask.

A shadow passes over her face. "Five alchemists, three civilians, including me. All of the Sisters, bar Sister Peace."

Eleven people. I think of the bodies I tended, and remember how many people were gathered in the Great Hall the first time we went there. Less than a quarter could have escaped.

"We'll make for Tressalyn tomorrow, or the day after," Nia continues as we pass through the winding streets. "We'll be safe there."

I can't help but look at the devastation around us. The walls of Tremayne did not protect anyone.

As though she's heard my thoughts, she replies, "Tressalyn is a fortress compared to here. City walls, and beyond them a castle with huge walls, and a moat . . . That's where the Council is, so I'm willing to bet there's a higher contingent of soldiers. And, of course, they'll step up their security once they learn what happened here." She smiles bitterly.

When we emerge into the town square, Nia heads straight for the ruins of a tall building opposite us, her eyes fixed on where she's heading, not looking left or right.

But I look. I can't help myself. So much worse in the daytime, the gaping holes in rows of shops that look like teeth punched out of a mouth. The smoke that still lingers, spiraling lazily along the rooftops. A crow lands on the remains of the golem I downed, eyeing me curiously; others pick through the clothes that lie strewn around as though hastily discarded by newlyweds. Buildings have been razed efficiently; the destruction is deliberate, that much is clear. The Sleeping Prince did not want Tremayne to still stand after he was through with it, and I wonder now whether it was because he knew, or guessed, that the Conclave was here. Is this the town's punishment for concealing his descendants from him, or does he leave everywhere he conquers like this?

And Lief did his bidding. This was his home. He grew up here. How could he have run rampant through here, allowed the golems and so-called soldiers to do what they've done?

Nia stops in front of a gilded building and waits for me to catch up. I look at the black maw of the doorway, the actual door nowhere in sight, the sign missing from the bracket above it.

"This is—*was*—the apothecary," Nia says. "Any equipment you see—pots, spoons, knives, bandages—take them. Any texts to do with alchemy, we'll take those, too. We need food, water especially, and cloaks. Just don't touch any plants or herbs, or powders. Leave those to me."

I hesitate and she takes my arm. "Sister Courage is badly hurt. She needs help now. And we have nothing. It's a long, cold road to Tressalyn." With that, she disappears inside.

I smell the body straightaway, an unmistakable odor: metallic, sour, and overpowering. Nia is frozen ahead of me, and I follow her gaze to the dead man at her feet.

There is a dark hole in the center of his chest.

"Master Pendie," Nia says softly. "He was Errin's mentor . . ." Then she turns and runs from the house and I hear the sound of retching from outside. I give her a moment, then follow her out. She stands with her hands braced on her knees, eyes closed, a sheen of sweat on her ashen face.

"Sorry," she says, opening her eyes as I reach her, though she won't meet my gaze. "I've known him all my life. Before the alchemists, before any of that. We used to supply him with salt. Not Sal

Salis, just regular sea salt. He taught me to sprinkle it on toffee. Just a bit. To bring out the flavor." Her face crumples and she bites her lip, shaking her head.

The effort she's going to in an attempt to master herself breaks my heart, and I rest a hand on her shoulder. She stiffens, then relaxes, taking a deep breath.

"I've walked past the bodies of so many people I knew, today," she says quietly, wiping her face on her sleeve. "People from above, and below. I lived in both worlds. I never thought they'd meet like this. My family's been helping the Conclave for generations, since it was settled here. Because the cellars under our house ran into the Conclave, it was either tell us and let us help, or move us. We ate with them, laughed with them. They spent so much of their time underground, for their safety. Kata hated it. She wanted to feel the sun on her face. When my father was away on business, she would come up and we would sit in the garden. I don't want . . ." Her voice breaks. "I don't want to lose her, too. I don't want to think of her like that—with that . . ."

"Oh, Nia . . ." I move to hold her but she shakes her head.

"I'm all right. I can't . . ." She takes a deep breath and pulls herself upright. "I won't get her back by crying. It won't help anyone. Come on. We'll see what we can find elsewhere."

"Wait . . ." I say, bracing myself. "What do we need?"

"You don't have to . . ." She pauses, then nods. "Bandages. Anything you can find on the shop floor. He kept the poisons locked away, so don't worry about accidentally coming across those."

As if I would.

"I'll be only moments," I say. And I am. Any bottles or jars that are intact get thrown in a sack I find behind a consulting desk. I

24

don't stop to read the spidery writing on the labels, taking whatever I can find: bandages, tweezers, a few ceramic bowls, a set of spoons, all tossed in. I work around the body, taking a moment to find another sack to cover it, but even so, I'm back outside in under three minutes.

Nia looks at me, and the sack, then wipes her face again roughly, her eyes bloodshot but determined. She holds a hand out for it and I hand it over, following as she leads us from the apothecary toward a street leading off the square.

We continue to scavenge; in one cottage we find a set of water skins and fill them from a rain barrel in a narrow yard; in another we find a loaf of bread wrapped in cloth, and a bag of apples. Nia raids a wardrobe in the tailors' district and finds us some cloaks, and a large sack to carry our things in. In another home I empty a drawer of all its knives, not caring if they're blunt, and add them to a second sack.

We venture into the butcher's and Nia goes to look upstairs while I check the lower rooms. I'm peering through a door when a sharp gasp from behind me makes me whirl around.

There is a man at the entrance.

I reach for my sword, holding it out before me as he crosses the threshold, brown eyes following my movements. The hood of his plain cloak is pushed back, revealing a handsome, proud young man, his skin darker than Nia's, the shadow of a beard at his jaw. He looks to be my age, perhaps a little older. The set of his chin is determined. And furious. He draws his own weapon, and points it at me. Mine shakes noticeably. His does not.

"Who are you?" he says, his accent Tregellian. Overhead the floorboards creak, and he looks up. "Who else is with you?"

I'm frozen, staring at the sword, preparing to move if he lunges. I hear Nia on the stairs, each step bringing her closer, and the man looks between me and the doorway behind me.

"Twylla, have you—" Nia begins, but she doesn't finish. Instead, she makes a sound of surprise and barrels past me, into the open arms of the man, who is now beaming.

"Nia!" he says, holding her at arm's length before pulling her back into his embrace. "I thought everyone was dead."

"They mostly are," she says into his shoulder and, despite herself, starts to cry again.

He strokes her hair until her sobs die away. "Is your family?" he asks her.

"No. They're at the coast with my brother. His wife just had her baby. I was here with . . . I was here. I hid."

They're silent for a moment, and I notice she hasn't said she was here with Kata and the alchemists. So whoever he is, this man isn't part of the Conclave.

"What about Lirys?" the man says. "Do you know anything? Have you seen anything? I went to the dairy, but the place is destroyed and they're gone . . ." He trails off, looking at Nia hopefully.

"I don't know," Nia replies. "I'm sorry."

The man nods, then his gaze falls on me. "So who are you, then?"

"Twylla, meet Kirin. And Kirin, this is Twylla—she's a friend of Errin's," Nia says to him before I have a chance to speak.

His attention snaps back to Nia at the mention of Errin's name. "Is Errin here?"

"She was . . ." Nia looks at me helplessly, and the man follows her gaze.

"What?" he asks. "What's going on?"

Nia takes a shaky breath. "Listen, maybe you should come with us. We can talk on the way."

"On the way to where?" Kirin asks.

"You'll see when we get there. Which needs to be soon; the sun is setting."

He looks at me once more, his eyes narrowed with suspicion.

"Do you have somewhere better to go?" I ask.

He shakes his head.

"Then we should leave."

As he leaves the shop, I notice he has a limp; he favors his left leg much more than his right.

"You trust him?" I ask quietly as Nia makes to follow him.

"Yes. I've known Kirin since we were children. He was friendly with my brothers. He . . . liked me, for a while, when he was about thirteen." She smiles. "He was three years younger than me, but that didn't stop him following me around, him and . . ." Her smile fades, and I wait for her to continue. "Anyway, it's forgotten now."

She ducks out of the shop to where Kirin waits, and I follow, staying behind them as they walk, my fingers on the hilt of my sword, ever watchful for attack. They talk softly, too softly for me to hear, and then Kirin drops back, falling in step with me.

"So, you're Lormerian?" Kirin says, and I nod. "Did you meet Errin in Almwyk?"

"No. I came to Tregellan before all this."

"Did you live in Tremayne?"

"Scarron."

He whistles softly. "Why Scarron? There's nothing there."

"That was the appeal."

We leave Tremayne through the Water Gate, retracing the route Errin and I took to get to the town. We stick close to the side of the road, Nia leading, then me, with Kirin bringing up the rear. The countryside is eerily quiet, the path muddy from the rain, and the air smells washed clean. Miles pass in trudging silence, and I fight off wave after wave of tiredness. As the night draws in, the temperature drops, and I begin to shiver, wrapping my arms around myself, beneath my cloak, the sack of salvaged knives clinking faintly with each step.

Then finally, to the left, I see shapes hulking in the shadows, and the acrid smell of smoke hits me, and I recognize the farm buildings Errin and I passed on our way to Tremayne. The Prythewells' farm.

Nia steps off the path and into the fields approaching the barns and sheds, and I follow, the long grass whipping against my skirts. We pass the worst of the damaged buildings, now nothing more than skeletons, beams jagged and jutting like snapped ribs, the walls burned away, the scent of smoke still on the air. Nia leads us deeper into the complex of buildings, until we come across a barn that has fared better than its neighbors. One half is blackened, the roof burned away, but the other half looks much sturdier.

As soon as Nia pulls open a small door and ushers us inside, I see Sister Hope, hunched like a crow over a small fire at the back of the space. She stands as we approach, and it looks as though she's aged a thousand years since I last saw her. Her face is waxen, the skin taut over her bones, making her appear more hawk-like than ever. Her attention passes from Nia to me, finally resting on Kirin, and something changes in her eyes. "No one else?"

"No." Nia's voice is the gentlest I've ever heard it, but Sister Hope flinches as though she's been punched. "I'm sorry."

Sister Hope shakes her head, discarding the apology. "You found Twylla."

"Where are the others?" Nia asks after a moment.

"I sent Terra, Glin, and the alchemists on to Tressalyn, with Sisters Honor and Wisdom. There was no sense in them waiting here, and smaller groups will be less conspicuous on the road. Who's this?" She looks at Kirin.

"Kirin Doglass. He's from Tremayne. Used to be the blacksmith's apprentice."

Sister Hope's gaze sweeps over Kirin briefly before she looks back at Nia. "Did you salvage anything from the Conclave?"

"It's all destroyed. We scavenged what we could," Nia continues. "It's not much." She kneels down beside the fire and begins to pull items from the sack: bread, the apples, some grubby-looking bandages, and an almost full bottle of brandy. Sister Hope kneels, too, and tears off chunks of the bread, adding it to a bowl she unearths from inside the sack.

I sink down next to her. "Thank you for waiting for us," I say, wanting to say something.

She doesn't reply; instead, she pours a little of the brandy over the scraps of bread, soaking them, before moving back, and I see for the first time the prone outline of someone lying on straw away from the fire. Sister Courage.

"How is she?" I ask softly.

Sister Hope still doesn't reply, but she shakes her head.

Nia reaches for the bread and helps herself before offering the loaf to me. I take a piece and pass it on to Kirin, then move closer to the fire, grateful for the warmth. Kirin sits beside me as Nia tosses us both an apple and reaches for the brandy. I refuse it when it comes to me, tiredness already clouding my mind, but Kirin takes it and drinks deeply. We sit in silence, listening to each other crunching our apples, the occasional slosh of liquid in a bottle, and Sister Hope gently murmuring to Sister Courage. When she moves back to the fire, the bowl is still full of bread.

"She's asleep," she says quietly. "I don't expect her to wake again." We let the words settle on the air, the weight of them, of everything we've seen tonight, heavy on us. "As soon as she's at rest, we'll leave for Tressalyn."

"What about Kata? And Silas and Errin?" Nia says instantly.

A dark look passes over Sister Hope's face. "We will find them," she says. "But first, Tressalyn."

"But Kata—"

"My son—my only son—was taken, too," Sister Hope snaps, then collects herself. "If I thought we could get him—get them all—back just like that, we would be on the road to Lormere by now. But we can't. Twylla is our only hope of defeating Aurek for good. For the greater good of all of us, getting Twylla to Tressalyn has to be the priority. We need a strategy; we need a plan." She pauses. "Silas and Kata would tell you the same thing."

I feel a spike of annoyance at the way she talks as though I'm not there.

But as I begin to ask what her plan is once we get to Tressalyn, Kirin speaks. "I don't understand. Who are you people? Where's Errin?"

Sister Hope looks between us, finally settling on Kirin, causing another spear of anger, sharp in my chest. "You're from Tremayne. Were you there during the attack?" she asks.

"No, ma'am. I was conscripted, and stationed with the army in Almwyk, but I escaped after the Sleeping Prince attacked and made my way home, to Tremayne. My fiancée and her family live there, too. Or they did. I don't know if they got out . . ."

Sister Hope ignores the plea in his voice and continues. "And you know Errin Vastel?"

"Yes, ma'am. I grew up with Errin and her brother. In fact, Lief is my best friend."

I turn to him, openmouthed, my anger temporarily forgotten. So that's why Nia stopped talking about Lief earlier.

Kirin frowns. "What?" he says. "Why are you looking at me like that?"

I shake my head as Sister Hope and Nia exchange a glance. "So Almwyk has been taken?" Sister Hope asks, drawing his attention back to her.

"Yes, ma'am," Kirin says. "Four nights ago. The Silver Knight came through with an army and sacked the town. Thankfully, all of the civilians had already been evacuated; it was just the soldiers and the town Justice left. They slaughtered him, and I . . . well, I ran." He looks defiant. "It was that or die, too."

"What of the other towns? Tyrwhitt? Newtown?" Sister Hope asks.

31

"I don't know. I avoided them, just in case—kept to the fields and byways. Headed straight here, as fast as possible. I wanted to get back to Lirys—my fiancée—and put as much space between me and the Silver Knight as possible."

We all remain silent, none of us wanting to be the one to tell him.

"What?" Kirin says again. "Why do you all look like that?"

I lick my lips, and swallow. "You say the Silver Knight was the one who led the invasion?"

Kirin nods. "He did. I fought him. He almost had me."

There is a pause. "Lief is the Silver Knight," I say finally.

He looks at me, eyebrows knitting together, blinking slowly. "No." He shakes his head, then swigs from the brandy bottle again. "No. No, I just told you, I fought him. He nearly—he nearly killed me. Lief wouldn't have fought me. We're practically brothers." He puts the bottle down and looks at us all in turn. "He wouldn't. He wouldn't have anything to do with the Sleeping Prince, not Lief. You're mistaken. You don't know him."

"I fought him, too. While he was standing next to the Sleeping Prince. In my home." Nia reaches over and takes the bottle. "I've known him almost all my life, too, remember."

Kirin gapes at her, then stands, wobbling before he finds his balance. He turns and walks away from us, out of the barn.

Nia moves as if to go after him, but Sister Hope shakes her head. "Leave him."

Then I remember something. "So you knew, when Silas healed Errin, that she was Lief's sister?" I say to Nia, and she nods. "But you were angry he wanted to help. Why, if you knew her?"

Behind us Sister Courage whimpers, and Sister Hope moves quickly to her side. "We just didn't know . . ." Nia drinks again. "We knew Lief was the Silver Knight. That's part of why Silas was watching her."

"Part of?"

"You were the main reason. Lief was your only Tregellian connection. We thought eventually you'd seek him out." I say nothing, and after a moment Nia continues. "But we weren't sure whether Errin was with them or not."

"I'm still not sure." Sister Hope joins us again.

"Still?" I begin, but she holds up a hand.

"The attack on the Conclave came just hours after her arrival—"

"She was with me. And by the time we reached Tremayne, it had already been ravaged. We had no idea what we were heading into. Don't forget she had her spine broken by one of his golems."

"What if that was part of a plot to draw out the philtersmith?"

"You think she planned to have her back broken?" I scoff. "Quite a risk to take."

"No riskier than searching for a job at the castle in Lormere, and working for mad Queen Helewys . . ."

The back of my neck prickles uncomfortably as I remember Lief and his first betrayal. Errin was looking for me, though she didn't know it was me. Was it for him? Was it only that my identity was revealed when we were already in the Conclave that saved me?

"No," I say, my voice like a whip. "She had the chance in the ossuary to hand me over. She could have easily told him where I was hiding." Again something stops me from saying it was Lief's idea that both Vastels sought to hide me from the Sleeping Prince. "It could have all ended down there. She could have told him I was hiding, and he could have killed me and guaranteed his safety. But because of Errin, it didn't happen."

Sister Hope stares into the fire. "Well, I hope you're right," she says finally. Then she, too, stands, following Kirin out into the night.

Chapter 3

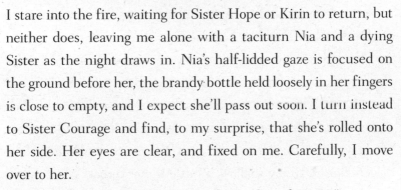

I stare into the fire, waiting for Sister Hope or Kirin to return, but neither does, leaving me alone with a taciturn Nia and a dying Sister as the night draws in. Nia's half-lidded gaze is focused on the ground before her, the brandy bottle held loosely in her fingers is close to empty, and I expect she'll pass out soon. I turn instead to Sister Courage and find, to my surprise, that she's rolled onto her side. Her eyes are clear, and fixed on me. Carefully, I move over to her.

"Can I help you?" I ask. "Can I do anything for you?"

She doesn't speak for a moment. "No, child. You can't."

"I'm sorry," I say.

"As am I. I'm not ready, if I'm truthful. I wanted so much more."

The bleak, sparse honesty in her words makes me look at her closely, and with a start I see she's not old at all; she's younger than my mother, and Sister Hope. She still has her triple-peaked hood on, and I think how uncomfortable it looks.

"Shall I remove your hood?"

Her lips quirk. "Why not?"

I reach gently for the covering and pull it from her head, revealing hair as red as mine, though shorter, darker where it's sweat-slicked to her head.

"Gods, that's better," she says, tilting her chin to the air. "Thank you." She falls quiet for a moment. "You're all so young," she murmurs, then coughs, a choking, wet hack that leaves her body spasming with the violence of it. She tries to turn away but I see red on her lips, coating her teeth. I lean over, gently lifting her head, so the blood does not drown her. When she's finished, I wipe her mouth with my sleeve.

"Water," she rasps.

A hand appears before my face, holding a goblet, and I turn to find Sister Hope standing over me.

I take the goblet and hold it to Sister Courage's lips. She gulps the liquid down, finally shaking her head to tell me she's had enough, and I lower her back to the straw. She smiles again, then her eyes flutter shut and I slip my hand from beneath her neck. We stay still, Sister Hope and I, watching as Sister Courage falls asleep, her breathing shallow, a rattle in her throat. When I look away I see Nia curled on her side by the fire, the bottle still clutched in her hands.

"We must talk, Sin Eater," Sister Hope says.

"I'm no Sin Eater."

"Amara is dead and you are her eldest and only living daughter. You *are* the Sin Eater. I suspect you are the last Sin Eater."

Every hair on my body stands up at her words.

"So we must talk," Sister Hope continues. "I must know your intentions. Will you flee again? Or will you do your duty?"

My duty. A lifetime of expectation weighs down on me: I could be back in my mother's hut; I could be in Rulf's chamber. I could be singing for King Terryn. I could be in the ossuary, feeling the strands of my life knit together like the tapestries I used to stitch in a tower in Lormere. Sin Eater. Daunen Embodied. Poisoner.

All I have ever been, all I will ever be.

"I'll stop him, if that's what you mean," I say finally, holding her gaze. She is the first to blink.

"How?"

"Poison, of course. My specialty. I need an alchemist, and I need Errin. Errin can deconstruct the potion—the Opus Magnum—and, with my blood, reverse it to create the only poison that can be used on the Sleeping Prince. With my blood added to that poison, we'll have a replica of the original one used on him. We can poison him again."

"But you understand he'll have been taking the Elixir? That's why he needs my son. As long as he drinks a little a day, he's immortal. He can't be stabbed, or crushed, or killed. Or even mortally poisoned, I expect."

"The Elixir stopped the poison from killing him outright last time, but it still put him to sleep. Whatever is in my blood is strong enough to incapacitate him, at the very least."

Sister Hope looks thoughtful. "And there's no Bringer to collect hearts and wake him again this time. No fail-safe for him."

"No," I say, my voice low. "But that won't matter anyway, because I'm going to kill him while he sleeps. To the best of my knowledge, you can't survive a beheading, no matter how many potions you drink or how magical your blood is." I sound much braver than I feel. "So we'll take off his head, and send it far away from his body. We'll brick it into something, hide it in the mountains. Bury it at sea. Whatever it takes."

Sister Hope gazes at me with wide eyes. "You can't."

"Yes, I can. And you should have done it years ago. The girls who lost their hearts and lives to him over the centuries, Merek, everyone in Lormere, Almwyk, Tremayne. Everyone in the Conclave. Their deaths are on your conscience, too. My ancestor may have placed the original curse on him, but your people are the ones who perpetuated it: hiding him away in Tallith, protecting him, even when he ate the hearts of innocent girls."

She opens her mouth, but I don't let her speak. "It ends. Now. It has to. Otherwise, what's stopping him from coming back again?"

"And Lief Vastel?" Sister Hope spits. "What of him?"

I look away from her, into the fire. "He has to pay, too," I say finally. I think of his arms around me, his laughing eyes, the musical lilt of his voice when he whispered in my ear.

"Could you take a sword to his neck?" she asks.

I don't hesitate. "Yes."

For the first time, Sister Hope looks at me with approval.

When Sister Hope returns to Sister Courage's side, I check on Nia, finding her unconscious. I pry the bottle from her hands and cover her with a cloak; I don't envy the headache she'll have in the morning. As I move the bottle so she can't accidentally knock it over, I catch the scent of the brandy and have an unexpected flashback to being in Lormere, to Merek holding a cup of it to my

38

lips while Lief glowered behind him. The memory takes my breath away for a moment, the strength of it overpowering. I set the bottle down and sit back, staring into the darkness, thinking of Lormere, of Merek, of all the things he'd hoped for once the throne was finally his.

Kirin returns, drawing me out of my thoughts, but his expression forbids conversation and he picks the bottle up as he passes me, skulking off with it into the shadowy corner of the barn. I end up sitting back with Sister Hope, each of us on either side of Sister Courage, listening to her labored breaths, counting the seconds between each one. More than once I think she's passed on and look down, only for her to rasp again as she clings to life. Again it strikes me how young she is, perhaps too young to be ensconced in a religious order. But then, the Sisters of Næht aren't a religious order, not really.

"May I ask something?" I say, my voice barely a whisper, when the fire has burned low enough to keep most of our faces concealed.

Sister Hope nods.

"None of the Sisters are alchemists, are they?"

"No. If we were alchemists, we couldn't perform our public role as a religious order."

"You're not a religious order, are you? Not truly," I say. She shakes her head, so I continue. "But as you say, the Sisters had a public role, so surely people approached you to join. How did you manage it, in a place like Lormere, without being completely hidden like the Conclave?"

Again she dips her head in acknowledgment. "We hid in plain sight. There's nothing suspicious about what's right in front of you;

Helewys had no reason to be interested in us. We were nuns, quiet and devout, nothing more. Of no threat or bother to her. On the rare occasions we were approached, we either pleaded illness or insisted there was simply no room. Besides, we were based in the East Mountains, difficult to get to, difficult to find."

My lips part as I remember something Merek told me moons ago. "There's a closed order of women at the base of the East Mountains. She can spend her days there . . ." Helewys would have been delighted to find herself in the midst of all those alchemists; she'd have been back on her throne in days, and Merek's whole plan would have backfired. I wonder briefly where Helewys is now, before turning my attention back to Sister Hope.

"May I ask how you joined the Sisters?"

She remains quiet for a moment. "Through my husband—Silas's father. He was an alchemist, of course. I gave up my life to live in the commune, with him. I took orders after his death; I was fortunate that a place had become available."

"A place?"

"There are only seven Sisters of Næht at any one time: Sisters Courage, Wisdom, Peace, Love, Truth, Honor, and Hope. Each of us is named for one of the seven towers of Tallith castle."

I mull this over. "So, have there been many Sister Hopes?"

"According to our records, I am the twenty-ninth. When I am dead, the title will go to another. Or at least it will should the Sisterhood survive this. You have to understand, the commune of the Sisters is—was—much smaller than the Conclave. We had just twenty-two people living there, including the Sisters, and only nine were alchemists. The Conclave housed seventy souls; though less than half were alchemists. They're a dying people."

Fewer than fifty alchemists in all the world.

"Nia said only five escaped. Is that true?"

Sister Hope lowers her head. "Hence the need to get them to Tressalyn as soon as possible."

I'm still not convinced that Tressalyn can be any safer than Tremayne was, and my face must once again betray my thoughts, because Sister Hope arches a brow before saying firmly: "The alchemists of Tregellan pay well for their privacy, and secrecy. A good amount of Tregellan's coffers are filled with alchemic gold. The Council will want to protect their investment, especially with war here. They'll be safe there. So will you."

I frown. "What do you mean?"

"Only that you'll be protected there by the finest guards we can muster, until it is safe."

"No," I say loudly, causing Nia to mutter something and roll over. "No. I am not hiding."

"Sin— Twylla, you are our most valuable weapon against Aurek. Our only hope of stopping him."

For the third time I think of Lormere. Of my tower. My prison. "I said no—I won't be shut away. If you want me to be safe, teach me how to protect myself. Teach me to fight. But I'm not going to sit in a room, quietly bleed into a bowl for you once we have the poison, and wait for all this to be over. Not again. Not ever again."

She gives me a long look. "Come, we should rest." She looks over at Sister Courage, still clinging to life.

"No, don't do that. Don't change the subject. I want your word," I say. "That you won't shut me away. I've been on the receiving end of 'greater good' manifestos before and it got me nowhere. Swear on your son that you will not imprison me in Tressalyn."

Her hawkish eyes bore into mine, her face all lines and hard edges in the dim light. The moment stretches, until finally she looks away. "I swear on Silas's life that we won't lock you away." She moves, sitting once again beside her friend, and I curl up with my back to the wall of the barn, facing the fire and the unconscious form of Nia. To my right, deeper in the darkness, I hear Kirin shift. The floor is hard under me, and makes me aware of bones I didn't know I had. It takes a long time for me to drift off, longer still to fight off Lief's face from behind my eyes.

When the cold dawn light wakes us, Sister Courage is dead.

We all stir at the same time, as though called by an alarm. Nia groans and holds her head, and Kirin looms out of the corner he's kept to, his expression wary. It seems Sister Hope has replaced Sister Courage's wimple in the night, and she looks peaceful, her eyes closed, her arms folded over her chest.

Sister Hope stands over the body, her hands clasped so tightly her knuckles have blanched. When she meets my eyes, there's something different there. Something wild, and untethered. But then she blinks, and it's gone, the stern, practical leader of the Sisters returning.

"She is at rest," Sister Hope says. "Once you've broken your fast and readied yourself, we'll leave. Nia, you do the honors." With that she turns and sweeps from the barn.

My mouth feels dry, and there's a nasty taste coating my tongue. I bend and rummage in the sack of food, pulling out one of the remaining apples and taking a bite, savoring the sour juice. The collection of knives I scavenged in Tremayne is in the second sack and I select the two sharpest-looking ones and tuck them into my belt before following Sister Hope outside.

I gasp when I see she's removed her own wimple. Her hair, gray as iron, is coiled around her head, and she turns at the sound of my surprise. She sets the hat down at her feet and I move to stand beside her. She seems smaller without it, and I see the softness to her face, the faint tracery of lines there. She's discarded the vestment she wore, too; now she wears a simple black tunic, one of the cloaks Nia took around her shoulders. I offer her a small smile and she looks levelly at me in return before turning away.

We wait silently in the wintry gray light for Kirin and Nia to join us. We're perhaps a quarter of a mile away when I turn back and see a pillar of smoke, blue against the cloudy sky. The barn is on fire again. I look at Nia and she shrugs. Flames, I think. The Lormerian way to dispose of a body.

We trudge through the barren countryside, every sound and movement causing my heart to thump violently against my ribs. When a pheasant streaks across the path directly in front, wings beating wildly, Nia and I scream, and even Kirin clutches his tunic over his heart. Only Hope remains calm and alert. We walk on, slowly to accommodate Kirin's leg, keeping one eye on the sun as it travels, a white hole glowing weakly in the dismal sky. We stop once to fill the water skins, taking turns to drink the brackish river water, and roll our shoulders, rub our calves. When we reach a wider road—the King's Road, Kirin says to no one in particular—I see tracks where carts have carved deep grooves in the mud, and alongside them hoof- and boot prints, much shallower by comparison.

"These look recent," Kirin says, bending to peer at them.

"Our people had no horses," Sister Hope says, crouching down beside them and pressing her fingers into them.

The back of my neck prickles.

"Perhaps they're from people fleeing Tremayne," Nia says hopefully before she inhales sharply. "Wait. What's that?" She points into the distance and we all look up once more.

Ahead of us, emerging over the horizon, is an indistinct mass, getting larger with each moment that passes, until it finally becomes clear. Men, on horseback. Riding toward us.

Instantly, both Kirin and Sister Hope straighten and draw their weapons, Kirin pulling his sword from the scabbard on his belt and Sister Hope drawing one from inside her cloak. Nia holds a knife ready in each hand, and I unsheathe my sword, gripping the hilt with both hands. Though it's heavy, and I have no idea how to use it, holding it makes me feel better.

"Twylla, go," Sister Hope barks at me. "Nia, go with her. Hide until we're sure it's safe."

"Hide where?" Nia says desperately.

There is nowhere; we're in the middle of a road, in the open countryside. Ahead of us the shapes become clearer. Three of them, two clad in black. And at their helm, a figure in silver.

The Silver Knight.

Lief.

Chapter 4

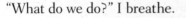

"What do we do?" I breathe.

"*We'll* hold them off," Sister Hope says, looking to Kirin, who nods grimly. "You and Nia, run."

"We'll never make it." I glance around frantically. It's all open fields—no trees or ditches. No cover.

"Twylla." Nia's voice trembles, but her gaze is steady. "We have no choice."

So I run. I hear Nia behind me, then beside me, our legs and arms pumping as we pelt forward. It doesn't take long for my lungs to start burning, for pain to blossom in my sides. Then I hear metal slamming into metal behind me and make the mistake of turning, still running, to look.

Sister Hope has pulled one of the men from his horse, and I watch as her sword plunges into him. Kirin is battling the other man, who is still mounted, his horse rearing and screaming as it tries to avoid Kirin's thrusts.

And Lief is riding us down.

He wears no helmet, but his mouth and nose are covered with a black cloth, his hair tied back from his face. As he gains on us, his green eyes fix on me, blazing with concentration.

I run faster, the sound of hooves beating the ground behind me, getting louder. I glance at Nia and see the terror in her expression, her mouth open in a silent scream.

I turn again, in time to see Lief raise his arm to swing his sword, and I shove Nia out of his path, sending us both sprawling to the ground.

He thunders past, unable to stop the horse in time, and I take the chance to scramble to my feet and run across the fields, screaming at Nia to do the same.

I've gambled on the fact that I'm the bigger prize and he'll leave Nia alone, and I'm right; he turns the horse and comes after me.

But I'll be damned if he thinks he can get me that easily.

I keep running, still clutching my sword. Again the sound of hooves lets me know he's closing in and I turn to see that's he's almost on top of me, a hand outstretched, fingers reaching for me. I swing my sword wildly, missing both him and the horse, and then there's a sharp pain in my neck, and my feet are whipped out from under me, as his fist closes around the hood of my cloak. I drop the sword, my hands scrabbling at my neck, struggling to breathe as I'm dragged after him.

Someone screams and my vision begins to blur. I fumble at the clasp of the cloak, trying to release it. But it won't give, instead it feels as though it's getting tighter, and I realize if I can't undo it, I'm going to die, here, now.

My legs smash uselessly into the ground beneath me as Lief

rides on, either not knowing or not caring that I'm being strangled, and there's nothing, nothing, I can do to stop it, to save myself. Rage at my own helplessness floods me and I feel the final, frantic beats of my heart in every part of my body as darkness starts to close in. I tear at my throat, my chest on fire, my lungs screaming for air. *No. Not like this.*

Then there's a faint click, almost like a sigh, as the clasp finally opens and I'm free, sucking in a huge, gasping breath as I fall. I crash into the ground, rolling to a halt. Bright pain flares across my back but I don't pause, forcing myself, coughing, to my knees, then my feet, ignoring the jolting pain that makes me want to vomit, the red rawness across my throat, fire still in my lungs as I gulp air inside.

A glance over my shoulder shows Lief tossing my cloak to the ground as he slows his horse enough to wheel around, his eyes lit with malice. I turn to run and see Sister Hope riding toward me, her eyes wide, and I slow, looking between her and Lief as they both ride at me.

Sister Hope reaches me first, holding out a hand, and I leap, somehow managing to get my foot into the stirrup, and swing myself over the broad back of the horse, landing roughly behind her. She turns the horse before I've properly found my seat, and I look back again to see Lief perhaps fifteen feet from us. The scarf has fallen and his features are twisted with fury: lips curled, his teeth bared. Before I know it, the knife at my belt is in my hand and I throw it desperately.

His hands fly up too late to protect himself and, amazingly, the dagger hits home, burying itself in his face and sending him reeling to the ground. He lies there, very still.

Sister Hope kicks at the horse, spurring it on, back to where Kirin is helping Nia onto the second one. Both of Lief's men lie dead in the mud.

"Vastel?" Kirin calls as he swings himself up behind Nia.

"Just go," Sister Hope screams.

As we ride, I glance back once more and see Lief staggering upright, hands clutching his head. As though he feels my gaze, he lowers them.

I see red where his face should be.

We get off the road as soon as we can, riding at speed across barren fields and through small woods, until we reach the river Penaluna and begin to follow it south. At first we gallop, desperate to put as many miles between us and Lief as we can, only slowing when it becomes apparent the horses cannot cope. Still: We change direction, going sideways, taking circuitous routes, trying to confuse the tracks we're leaving. It's only after hours have passed, the shadows lengthening on the grass, and we come across a small copse by the river, that Sister Hope nods grimly and draws the reins short, calling to Kirin and Nia that we're going to stop. As soon as I've slid from the horse, sore after months out of the saddle, I take myself down to the riverbank and stare into the gray water, hoping it will clean the image of Lief's bloody face from my mind.

I'm surprised when Kirin comes and sits beside me, and I stay quiet, half lost in my own thoughts, half waiting for him to speak. It's a long time before he finally does.

"How's your neck?" he says.

I raise my hands to the raw skin across my throat. I'm lucky my windpipe wasn't crushed.

"Sore. But my head is still attached to it, so it could be worse." He doesn't smile.

"Are *you* all right?" I ask after a while.

"It's just . . . I grew up with him. I feel as though . . ." He trails off, shaking his head. "Nia told me everything, while we were riding. About you. And him. And Errin. And what he did in Lormere, and in Tremayne." He stares out over the water. "He was like a brother to me. The Lief I knew wouldn't do this. Oh, I know," he says swiftly when I open my mouth to argue, "that people can change. I saw what he did. But I can't make that Lief match up to the one in my head, you know?"

"Yes, I do," I say so quietly I'm not sure he hears me. I know that feeling very well.

We fall silent, but even so, I don't hear Sister Hope come up behind us.

"I'm worried," she says, making us both jump. "Vastel was coming from the direction of the King's Road. And that's the road the Sisters and alchemists would have taken to Tressalyn . . ."

Kirin frowns. "They had no captives with them just now."

Sister Hope's mouth forms a line. "No. But that doesn't mean they didn't find them."

"I'll go and look," he offers.

She hesitates, and I can see she's torn. Then she shakes her head. "No, I don't think splitting up is a good idea. Besides"—she looks up at the sky—"it'll be dark within the hour. I suggest we camp here for the night and rise at first light."

"Camp here?" Nia has joined us, not looking any keener at this prospect than I am.

"It's sheltered, and close to water. It's off the road. It's the best we're going to find."

Nia widens her eyes at me, as though expecting me to protest. I wish I could, but what choice do we have? I shrug.

From the pinched set of her mouth, I suspect Nia has never slept out in the open, and neither have I. On the journey to Scarron, I, and the escort Merek provided me with, took rooms in inns, following a map laid out by him, detailing places to stay, people to ask for, even suggestions of Tregellian food to order for supper, all knowledge he learned on his progress. For a runaway, I was surprisingly well cared for. But I survived last night on the floor in the barn. Perhaps camping won't be as bad as I think.

Predictably, it's worse than I think. When the night starts to fall, it falls fast; we eat the last of the bread, share some water, and by then I can barely make out my companions as we bed down in our cloaks, seeking the softest patch of earth. The barn was warm, and sheltered. There were walls. I'd had no idea about the importance of walls.

I can tell from everyone's breathing—fast, uneven—and the constant tossing and turning that none of us are asleep. But no one speaks. The rushing of the river is too loud to ignore, and every now and then, there are splashes that I know are just fish but that my imagination makes into men coming after us. The winter-bare branches above us stretch like arms, backlit by a sky too full of stars to be reassuring. After a while we start to huddle closer, until we're all lying next to one another, like my brothers,

Maryl, and I did as children. I can feel Nia shaking in front of me, and I don't know if it's because of the bitter temperature, or if she's crying. In contrast, Sister Hope lies still as a stone. But none of us sleep, or speak.

Dawn takes forever to arrive, by which time I'm stiff with cold, my body aches, and I'm silently furious at nothing in particular. I'm not the only one; Nia snaps at Kirin when he finishes the water, though she'd just had some, and Sister Hope barks at them both. I keep quiet and move near the horses, leaning against them, breathing in their comforting smell of hay and warmth. They seem to have weathered the night well.

We're on the move less than an hour after dawn, and it doesn't take us long, using Kirin's compass, to get back onto the King's Road. Until then I'm sleepy, lulled by the gait of the horse, leaning against Sister Hope, but as soon as the wide track comes into view I'm alert, and Sister Hope sits upright, too. We see no other travelers, which we could pretend is because winter is almost here, but I don't think any of us believe that. There is no livestock in the fields around us, and not even the hedge birds are chattering. It feels as though we're at the end of the world.

I feel a tremor run through Sister Hope a second before she kicks back into the underbelly of the horse, driving it into an immediate gallop and forcing me to duck low against her to stay mounted. Behind us I hear Kirin swear, and I tighten my arms around Sister Hope's waist as we fly across the ground. I want to look, want to see what's chasing us. Want to know if it's him. When she draws us to a halt, I'm surprised; I put my hand on the knife at my belt, ready to defend myself.

Then I see them.

As if she were a marionette and her strings had been cut, Sister Hope goes slack in my arms; if it weren't for me holding her, she'd fall from the horse. I take the reins from her fingers as Kirin tells Nia not to look.

I look.

Ahead of us over Sister Hope's shoulder I can see two forms, robed in black, standing against the trees either side of the road. It takes me a moment to see what's wrong with the picture, baffled by Kirin's words. Then, with a sickening rush of under-standing, I do.

There is an expanse of trunk, three or more feet, between the ends of their distinctive robes and the ground. They're not stand-ing against the trees: They're pinned to them.

Kirin swings himself down from his horse, somehow carrying Nia with him. He places her on the ground, where she sinks to her knees, her back to the scene before us. He reaches his arms out for Sister Hope and she drops into them with no effort to hold herself upright. He takes her to Nia and the two cling to each other, and I see Sister Hope's mouth gaping in a silent scream. Nia folds her into her arms and begins to weep noisily.

Without speaking, Kirin and I walk forward.

Either side of the road, Sisters Honor and Wisdom have been nailed to the trees.

Their eyes are closed, their arms above their heads, far above where a man could reach. I can't understand how this is possible, until I remember the golems.

Then Kirin swears again, and I turn and see two more bodies in a ditch beside the road. One male, one female. Neither has the telltale white hair of the alchemists. The civilians Nia mentioned; Terra and Glin, Sister Hope called them.

"There should be others," I say quietly to Kirin. "Five alchemists. The Sisters were taking them to Tressalyn for their safety." I look up at Wisdom and Honor. I remember their stern, cold faces in the Conclave. I look back at Hope and Nia, still on their knees and clutching each other.

"Lief couldn't have done that." I gesture at the pinioned Sisters, keeping my voice low. "Not alone. In fact, I doubt it was the work of men at all."

"Golems," Kirin says, and I nod. What else could it have been?

"He was traveling toward us, though," Kirin continues. "Away from here, back toward Tremayne. Why? Why turn back?"

I cover my mouth with my hand as understanding washes over me. He was on his way back for us—or at least for Sister Hope and Nia. Someone must have given them away.

I can't imagine any Sister giving up secrets, no matter what was done to her. Everything I know about them makes it unlikely. But the alchemists might have. Or the civilians. If they thought it would save their friends . . .

From the way Kirin looks at me, I know he's reached the same conclusion.

"Where are the golems now?" I say finally, turning about and scanning the fields, terrified they'll appear before us.

Kirin lets out a long breath. "The tracks we found yesterday before we saw Lief . . . there were a lot. More than just him and the two men with him. My guess would be a whole bunch of the Sleeping Prince's men—Lief included—started for the south, and at some point they came across the people here and . . ." He pauses, and I look without wanting to at the Sisters. "I reckon they will have carried on afterward, and Lief and the men we killed turned back. Which means Tressalyn is compromised. We won't be safe there."

"No." I have to look away from the bodies. The positions are so unnatural they don't look real.

"Penaluna is close," Kirin is saying. "It's in the mountains. I have family there. They'd hide us, until we can figure out what to do. We could hole up there and . . ."

"And then what?" Something flares inside me like acid, or fire, and I raise my chin, my jaw tightening. "To the best of our knowledge, the Sleeping Prince has taken every alchemist he can find and killed everyone else. He's winning, Kirin."

"Which is why we need to regroup . . ."

"No." My vehemence surprises even me. "I'm done with running away."

"Then where?"

"Lormere," I say. "We have to go to Lormere."

Kirin actually laughs. "Have you taken leave of your senses? Lormere, which he invaded with two golems and won in a night? Lormere that he made completely subservient in under three moons? Twylla, Lormere is the seat of his power."

"Exactly. I'm willing to bet it's to Lormere that he's taken Errin and Silas. And the other alchemists. We need to rescue them if we're to stand a chance of destroying him." I remember what Sister Hope said about hiding in plain sight from Helewys. "Besides, it's the very last place he'd expect me to go."

"We can't just storm the castle, Twylla," Kirin says. "There are four of us. We need to gather forces, seek out friends—"

I cut him off. "So we will."

"How, exactly?"

"Did Nia tell you what I was?" I say, and he shakes his head. "I was Daunen Embodied. I was *hope*. To the people of Lormere, I *am* the living representation of triumph over extreme adversity."

Kirin raises his brows, his expression sceptical.

"Oh, I know"—I shove his shoulder gently when he makes to interrupt me—"I know that it's all made up. I *know*. Lief Vastel taught me that." His eyes widen, but I keep going. "But that doesn't matter. It doesn't matter if it's real or not, so long as people believe. As long as people think that Daunen Embodied coming is a sign. A sign that the war will be won."

He stares at me. "Twylla, this is madness. If he gets word you're alive and plotting against him, he'll come straight after you."

"He'll do that anyway sooner or later, regardless of where I am, or whether I'm hiding or fighting back. So I'm *choosing* to fight back. We'll go to Lormere. By the back roads and the woods. Along the way we'll gather what supporters we can. That's our plan. Come on." I grab Kirin by the wrist and pull him back to Hope and Nia.

"I'm sorry," I say when they look up at us. "I'm so, so sorry. He will pay for this. I swear to you, *I* will make him pay for this. I meant what I said in the barn. The beginning of the end is now."

Nia and Hope look up at me and for a moment, there is nothing in their expressions; it's as though they've been hollowed out. But then Kirin pulls his wrist from my grip and takes my hand for an instant, squeezing it. I look at him and he nods. And when I turn back to Sister Hope and Nia, there is a spark in their eyes, and a question.

"We're going to Lormere," I say.

There is a pause. Then: "Yes," Sister Hope says in a voice made of edges, her hand sliding down to the hilt of her sword. "Yes."

The Tower of Honor

The apothecary is seated at the end of a long table, in a room lined with books. She is playing a game. At the opposite end of the table, the prince works, a map spread across the scarred wooden surface, each corner held down by a miniature golem. As he moves unanimated simulacrum across the map toward an enemy composed of cruder, malformed poppets, one of the golems at the corner seems to raise its arm and scratch its elbow. The prince looks up from his strategizing, staring at the clay being, watching as it finishes attending to its apparent itch, and then returns to pinning the map in place. Everything in the room stills, save the apothecary, who continues with her game, rhythmic thuds emanating from where she sits.

When the golem moves again, seemingly shifting its weight, the prince smashes it into the table, until all that remains is a smear of clay.

He looks over at the apothecary. "It's no good when they start to do as they will."

The apothecary ignores him. She is busy with her game.

She's been playing for as long as he's been planning his battle. The Knife Game, it's called. All it requires her to do is splay her hand on the table and then stab the blade down into the gaps between each of her fingers, over and over. She has become very fast, and very good.

The prince likes the sound that comes when the knife pierces the wood. If the apothecary does it properly, there is a wonderful rhythm to it, a percussive sort of beat, like a heart. He also likes the fear in her eyes as she plays. Her hands are very valuable to her; the idea of losing a finger, or severing a tendon, terrifies her. Of course, if that happened, he could give her some of the Elixir. But she can't be sure he will. He doesn't need her to have hands, after all. That's what makes it so fun for him. He doesn't know what he'd do if she missed, either. He expects sooner or later they'll both find out.

When she speeds up he does, too, moving his players across the map in the war he is always preparing for.

It's an indulgence; he doesn't believe he'll get the war he wants, because his enemies are cowards. They skulked beneath the earth as they plotted against him, and he does not expect an honest, worthy challenge from them. He'd dearly love to meet them in battle, him and his Silver Knight commanding armies of men and golems. Now would be the perfect time for it; he is unconquerable, unmatched. But he does not believe it will come to pass. He believes the end will come all at once, in a rush—one arrow, one mistake. Not his, of course. Hers. The Sin Eating girl's. The heretic's. Almost all of her allies are dead, or under his power. And he's made very sure she'll find no new ones. She is the only threat to him, really. Once she's gone—and it won't take long—it will all be over.

But he is so enjoying planning his war.

He pauses and watches the apothecary as she plays the Knife Game. The knife flashes. She senses his eyes on her and frowns, trying to concentrate. The rhythm slows as she focuses, then speeds up as she masters herself. It annoys him, this confidence, and he reaches toward the pocket he keeps the simulacrum of her in. She looks up at this now-familiar gesture, and in that second the knife slips, and she cries out. The prince smells her blood before he sees it, iron and salt, and he licks his lips involuntarily.

The knife clatters to the table and the apothecary reaches for it, even as she bleeds, unable to disobey the instruction she's been given to play the game, to keep playing. The prince pulls her simulacrum from inside his tunic and unpeels a piece of paper from around its middle.

The apothecary's hand freezes as the command is broken and her body is returned to her.

She looks at the knife, then at the prince, and all at once it seems as though the walls have moved, narrowing, until it feels as though they're pressed together, even as they stand apart.

"Do it." The words are seductive, a whisper from a lover in the dark. "Go on, Errin. Do it."

The apothecary's blood drips onto the table, a dull echo of the earlier sound of the knife.

"There's no one else here." He gestures around the room. "No guards. No servants. Just you and me." He looks at the simulacrum of her and lifts it, tossing it down on the table so it's within her reach. "There. Now I can do nothing."

The apothecary's chest is heaving. Her fingers twitch, and the prince smiles.

Then, slowly, he turns his back on her. He pulls the sheaf of his hair around until it falls over his chest. "Right in the back, Errin. Stab me there, won't you?" he croons, his voice echoing faintly.

She watches him, hesitating. She picks up the knife and stares down at it, the smallest hint of red at the tip from where it cut her.

Suddenly he's beside her, taking the knife from her gently. He licks the spot of blood from the tip and then puts it down, reaching for her hand. He places her injured finger in his mouth and sucks, his gold eyes fixed on her green ones as he does.

His tongue flicks over the wound and then he releases her. When she looks at the cut, the bleeding has stopped.

"I take it you don't want any Elixir," the prince says, and his voice is husky, reminding the apothecary of someone else.

She shakes her head, unable to look away from him.

Then he slaps her, hard, causing her to drop the knife she didn't know she'd reached for once more.

"It's no good when they start to do as they will," the prince says again. "Get out of my sight."

The apothecary turns and runs.

A crash to her left makes her stop, and she sees the knife embedded in the door frame, inches from her head. It quivers, and she feels her own limbs start to tremble. She doesn't look back at the prince as she flees.

Chapter 5

I don't know Tregellan well enough to guide us back to Lormere, so Kirin takes over navigating our course toward Almwyk. I ride with him now, seated in front of him on the dappled horse, my thighs chafing against a saddle made only for one.

At our side, Nia rides with Sister Hope, in their own private bubble of shock and grief. Neither has spoken since we decided to head to Lormere. But every now and then I catch small movements, and turn to see Sister Hope's fingers drifting down to the hilt of her sword as an ugly expression crosses her face. In my mind's eye I see Lief plummet from his horse again, his face bloody from my knife, then I recall the women on the trees, splayed like toys. Each time it makes a thick anger curdle inside me, and I feel my own jaw tighten with the desire to do something violent.

We managed to get the bodies down, Kirin grimly braced against the tree, holding me by the legs as I pulled free the thick iron nails that kept them pinioned, and Sister Hope and Nia waiting beneath to catch them. They were stiff, and cold, but Sister Hope embraced each one and kissed their marbled cheeks. We had no shovels to bury them, so we laid them in the ditch beside Terra and Glin, covering them with fallen leaves and branches, anything to protect them from the animals that were sure to come.

"We need to keep the sun behind us," Kirin says for the third time since we began heading east, and I feel him looking back over his shoulder. I look, too, seeking out that faint glowing disc behind a blanket of clouds. "It will be dusk soon. We'll stop a couple of miles outside Newtown and camp there. Then tomorrow we'll reach Almwyk, and from then on we'll be in the woods."

"We'd be better off traveling at night," Nia says from the other horse. "We're too visible in the day."

"I need the sun to navigate if we're going to Lormere."

"Use the stars."

"I don't know how." Kirin's voice is tight.

"We're safer moving during the day," Sister Hope says, silencing them both. "During the day we can at least see what is approaching us. Or following us. At night we're blind."

An hour or so later, she's proven right. We spy black spots on the horizon that soon become riders on horseback, and I feel Kirin tense, my own stomach clenching with fear. We slow the horses. I pull my knife from my belt.

My palms are damp and slippery as they approach, two figures shrouded in thick cloaks. Impossible to tell whether they're men or women, Tregellian or Lormerian, and the knife feels loose in my hand. I tighten my grip on it, and breathe in and out slowly, ready to lash out if they attack us. But the figures ride on, passing us, keeping their faces covered, and I feel sick as the adrenaline that flooded me has no outlet. When Kirin leans forward and quietly asks if I'm all right, I look down to see the knife trembling, and I tuck it back into my belt.

We camp near a small stream two miles outside Newtown, and after a small argument between Kirin and Sister Hope over who's the most capable, Hope heads alone toward the town on foot to look for supplies, leaving the horses with us. My stomach feels too small, and I pray there's food in my future; I can't remember the last time I went this long without eating. I look around half-heartedly for berries, or roots, but it's almost midwinter and I'm not exactly an expert at foraging or survival. Errin would know, if she was here, I think, and my stomach twists again. *Please let her be all right.* I offer up a silent prayer to whoever, or whatever, might be listening, and move back to where Nia and Kirin are sitting in silence. When Sister Hope returns within an hour, her eyes are wide.

"Newtown is taken," she says, collapsing beside us and rubbing a hand through her hair. "Gates have been put up. They're not much, wooden poles with wire between them, but there are men patrolling them and they wear the sign of the Solaris on armbands. I saw no one else; there's probably a curfew."

"Were there golems?" I ask.

"I didn't see any. But I expect so."

"There's no food, is there?" Nia says.

Sister Hope shakes her head. "I'm sorry."

So we pass another miserable night on the ground, made worse by the icy drizzle that starts an hour after we bed down and persists until I can feel it in my bones. We don't even pretend propriety tonight, snuggling together like fox kits in an earth as the rain blankets us, shivering in unison. As soon as my body finally becomes numb enough to allow a kind of sleep, the sky starts to turn gray and Sister Hope rises, breaking up our nest and prompting us all to rise. It seems none of us are used to going without food, as evidenced by the chorus of angry rumbles that sound when we try to fill up on water from the stream. We check the horses, and then we're on the road and skirting around Newtown before the sun is truly risen.

I'm too exhausted to speak, my clothes are damp and starting to smell, and my stomach growls incessantly; it feels like there's an angry animal trapped in there, gnawing at me. Nia is hunched over and has her arms crossed over her stomach, and Sister Hope's face looks pinched. We need to find food, and soon.

We spy another set of figures on the horizon just after midday, and at once the pall that has fallen over us lifts, as we become alert to a threat, my heart skipping into a now familiar pattern of nervous beats as we once again draw our weapons and wait.

It soon becomes apparent they are on foot, two of them, dressed in brown wool, not armor, and the relief I feel is mirrored on the face of the female of the pair, who cradles a bundle to her chest. We draw our horses to a stop beside them and the bundle in the woman's arms wriggles free, revealing itself not, as I expected, to be a child but a small black-and-white dog. It licks her face and I can't help but smile.

The male addresses Kirin in that thick, singsong Tregellian accent. "If you're heading to Tyrwhitt, I wouldn't bother. Unless you're a supporter of this Sleeping Prince."

"Newtown is the same, and Tremayne." Kirin's voice is gruff. "Both gone."

The other man swears. "Do you know what the situation is in Tressalyn?"

"No. But there were signs on the King's Road that the army marched on south after Tremayne—so . . ."

The man nods grimly and I remember where I've heard the name Tyrwhitt before.

"There was a camp, outside the town, wasn't there?" I say. "For Lormerian refugees. What happened to them?"

"Gone," he says. "They attacked that first. The poor people inside were trapped like rats. There were fences, you see. They tried to get out, to get to safety, but they didn't stand a chance. That's all that saved us, you know. We could hear the screams from Tyrwhitt . . ."

He keeps talking, I see his mouth moving, but I can't hear a word of it. Those poor people. My people. Fenced in a camp, miles from their homes, with nothing but what they could carry, unable to save themselves or their loved ones. It's no way to live. And no way to die.

The rage inside builds again, filling me with fire, and the need to move, to do something. To fight, and avenge, and put things right.

". . . plan was to head to Tressalyn, but now . . ." The man is still speaking and I tune back in, in time to hear him say, "Where do you head for?"

"The woods," Kirin says swiftly. "For now."

The man nods again. "I know some others headed that way."

We all fall silent, and I see the man look over the horses, and something in his face turns sly. With studied nonchalance, he glances over at Kirin and me, then at Sister Hope and Nia, who haven't said a word. Foreboding tightens my chest, and I try to catch Nia's eye, only to see her gaze is fixed on the pack on the man's back, her face mirroring the want in his. The air seems to thicken then.

"We should go," I say, kicking back to prompt the horse into action, and breaking the rising tension that it seems only I noticed, as they all look at me. "Good luck to you both," I say to the man and his wife, raising my arm to reveal the knife at my waist.

"You, too," he says, a faint edge of disappointment in his tone.

I reach for the reins and flick them, prompting the horse into a trot, eager to put some distance between us.

"What's wrong?" Kirin asks when I pull us back to a walk.

"I didn't like the way he was looking at the horses. Or the way Nia was looking at his bag," I say in a quiet voice. "It's not just Aurek's men who are a danger to us." I see his knuckles whiten on the reins. "We need to be careful," I say. "The horses are valuable."

"So are you, apparently," Kirin says. "Listen, maybe we—"

"We've agreed." I cut him off. "We're going to Lormere."

"I was actually going to say, maybe we shouldn't have said we were heading toward the woods. Maybe we should have said the coast. Lief knows who we all are, and how many we are. We'd be easy to track down."

"You're right. And we should avoid people as best we can. No more roadside chats."

Kirin nods in agreement as Sister Hope draws up alongside us.

"Good thinking," she says. There's respect in her tone, almost warmth. It does nothing to fill my empty stomach, but it helps, somehow.

As we arrive on the outskirts of Almwyk the cloud finally breaks and the sun casts a weak but welcome light over us. Kirin guides us through the remains of the Tregellian army's camp—the tents, stores, and stables Kirin told us were here have all vanished. There are a few forgotten weapons buried in the mud, and we salvage what we can: more knives, a mace without a handle, a small sword, a battered shield, a dented helmet. By some absolute miracle, we come across an undamaged ration pack of hardtack and dried meat and fruit, half-submerged outside what Kirin says used to be the captain's tent. We fall on it like animals; even though the biscuit is hard enough to make me worry for my teeth, I can't stop cramming it in my mouth, and neither can the others. I think it might be the best meal I've ever had. We eat until it's all gone, washed down with water from a well in the village. Kirin shows me Errin's old cottage, ransacked, not even a ragged cloak to steal, though I do find a copy of the old Tregellian stories, leather-bound and gilded, beneath an upturned pallet.

I'm about to pack it, to give it back to her, when I'm gifted with another memory: of Lief, on my bed in Lormere, telling me how his mother would read him the stories. Curiosity gets the better of me and I open it, only to see Aurek's face peering out at me. I toss it into the grate as though it's aflame. When I do, the grate shifts, and investigation reveals apothecary equipment hidden beneath the fireplace. Nia exclaims when she sees it, picking it up delicately, and even Sister Hope smiles. We pack it away reverently, and at the last minute I add the book to our bundle, too. Errin can decide if she wants it or not.

There's nothing for it, then, but to enter the West Woods.

Forest of nightmares from my childhood, the place where I believed the spirits of those whose sins weren't Eaten went to languish eternally. Before I traveled to Scarron, I'd only ever seen it from a distance, on calls with my mother. But when I finally had to pass through it, I was pleasantly surprised to find it was green, and warm, and teeming with life. Even now, it's less frigid than the fields beyond the tree line, and much of the greenery is still in place. We dismount and lead the horses through the woods in single file: Kirin, me, then Nia, with Sister Hope bringing up the rear.

The attack comes from all sides. One moment, there are birds calling, then silence, and it's in that silence they appear. Four of them, with scarves over their faces and wicked curved knives in their hands. No livery, no armbands. Not the Sleeping Prince's men. They recognize Kirin at the front and Sister Hope at the back as the main threat, and take them down with ruthless efficiency. A blow to the side of the throat, another to the stomach, and within seconds, both are disarmed and forced to their knees without hope of fighting back. It's so fast that neither Nia nor I have had time to pull out our knives. Nia reaches for my hand and I clasp it, squeezing it tightly.

One of the men, tall and blue-eyed, comes over and stands in front of us.

"Take the horses," I say. "Take whatever you want. Just let us all pass."

"Pass to where?" The voice is muffled through the scarf, but male. And to my surprise, Lormerian.

"I can't tell you. But I promise we're no threat to you."

The man cocks his head, considering. "That cloak looks mighty warm," he says, reaching for it.

But before he even comes close, another figure knocks his hand away. "Don't touch her!" he almost screams.

Then he turns to me and pulls his scarf down, and with a start I recognize him. "Stuan?" I ask, and he gulps, nodding.

"So it is you?" he—Stuan—asks. "I thought it was, but the hair . . ."

"Dyed to get me out of Lormere."

The man whose hand Stuan pushed away pulls his own scarf down, revealing a thin, tanned face.

"Who is she?" he asks.

"It's Lady Twylla," Stuan says. "Daunen Embodied."

My eyes dart to Kirin. Now he'll see why Lormere was the right choice. "It's true," I say, trying to keep my voice even. "I know I look a little different, but I am Twylla Morven, Daunen Embodied, daughter of the Sin Eater of Lormere and former betrothed of Prince Merek."

No one looks impressed, and I realize how unlikely my claim must seem to them. Brown-haired, muddy, and stinking, an old cloak covering a bloodstained dress. No jewels, no red gown, no guards. Not the shining beacon of hope the legends spoke of.

"How's she touching you, then?" the other man asks, gesturing at where Nia still grips my hand. "She was poisonous, Daunen was."

"No, I—" I pause, trying to find a way to explain what the queen did. "I was never poisonous. That was a trick—a lie of the queen's."

"Daunen was the executioner," the man says. "Or you were, if you're her. You killed people. I was there, I worked there, too. We all knew you killed people. I saw the bodies."

"It was a trick," I say again. There is an edge of desperation to my voice, and I tamp it down. "The queen gave them a poison, hidden in their last meals. It was timed to perfection so that it would seem I'd killed them."

There is a pause. Then, "So, you're just a girl now?" Stuan says.

"No. No, I'm not just a girl." Even as I speak, I feel heat rise along my chest and neck, painting my skin red, but I continue. "I've come to lead you against the Sleeping Prince. I plan to fight him, and take back Lormere."

The men look at each other. "Is it just the four of you?"

I feel my cheeks flare again, feel another tremor within as the men look at us. My newly found sense of purpose seems to falter, collapsing, as though not built properly. I glance at Kirin; he's watching me sadly, as though he expected this and wishes he could spare me. Nia and Sister Hope also remain silent, their expressions unreadable. I ponder how Errin would play this—she'd probably have hit someone by now. Then, unbidden, I think of Helewys and how she would weave words and make the most terrible things sound rational. Believable. Possible. "Yes. Though there was only two of us when I defeated one of his golems in Tremayne."

A look of surprise flickers over Stuan's face as he examines me, and I pull myself up straight, attempting to look commanding. It's now or never.

"Look, we need to get back to our camp," Stuan says eventually. "It'll be dark soon. You're . . ." He pauses and looks at his friends, who nod grudgingly. "You're welcome to come if you like. We can talk more about this there."

I feel everyone look at me. "Lead on," I say.

He turns his back on me, and the other men follow. After a moment Nia steps after them, and Sister Hope takes the reins of her horse and joins her. I feel Kirin trying to catch my eye but ignore him this time, fixing my eyes on Sister Hope's back and moving to join her. The biscuit feels leaden in my stomach now, and I wish I hadn't eaten at all.

Chapter 6

They lead us to their camp, nestled deep in the trees, around eight miles from where they found us, and only a few miles from the sea. They talk as we trek through the West Woods, and it turns out all of them are former castle employees; one was a groom of the stable, one a gardener, and the one who attacked Sister Hope was a guard like Stuan, though never one of mine. The men are amiable as we talk, chatting happily to Kirin in particular, asking questions about Tregellan and Aurek's work there. No one talks to me, or looks at me, again. And despite my earlier assurances, they all make sure not to walk too close to me. Nia does, though, walking by my side when the path is wide enough, and helping me over trees when I don't actually need any aid. Every time she does, she shoots a scathing glance at the men.

It takes us almost three hours to reach their camp, where around fifty pairs of eyes all turn, as one, to stare at us.

In their center, presiding over a huge cauldron, is a woman with a classically Lormerian face, strong-featured and suspicious-eyed. "Who's this, then?"

I'm about to speak, to repeat my speech, when Sister Hope steps forward, brushing my arm gently as she passes. "I'm Hope, Hope Kolby. This is Nia, and that's Kirin," she says, introducing the others. "And I believe you know Twylla Morven—though you might remember her better as Daunen Embodied." A gasp rises from the crowd, but Sister Hope—or Hope Kolby now, I suppose—continues talking, drowning out the murmuring. "Nia and Kirin are Tregellian, but I'm from Lormere, like Twylla. Born in Monkham. And we're very glad to see you all."

Everyone stares at me, and I keep my spine straight and my head raised.

"Now," Hope says, her voice firm but kindly, "I'm sure you've heard some things about Twylla, nonsense such as she's poisonous and that she can kill you. But she can't. At least, not with her skin." At that, Hope reaches for me, draping a maternal arm around my shoulders and wrenching another cry from the crowd; one woman even grips the arm of the huge man next to her. Something makes me look at her more closely.

"Lady Shasta?" I ask.

She nods, her head wobbling like an ear of corn on her long neck.

"You got away, then?"

Another nod.

"How?"

Her face contorts for a moment. "We were at our castle in

73

Chargate when word came of the Sleeping Prince's assault. I was sent away but my husband wanted to fight. He lost his life." She lowers her head, and her gargantuan companion does the same. It seems she has found solace for her grief already.

"I'm sorry," I say. Then someone in the crowd cries out.

"She's not dead."

I turn to the figure, a woman, who is pointing at Hope, still embracing me.

"She should be dead. She touched her and she should be dead."

"Of course I'm not," Hope says before I can speak. "Helewys was a liar, and she lied to you all. Including Twylla here. Now, I'm sure you have questions, and I know Twylla will be glad to answer them, and tell you her plans. But we've been traveling for a long time. We'd like to rest. And we'd love some of that food, if there's spare."

The crowd looks at her, and at me, and then at the woman presiding over the cauldron, and I get the impression we're waiting to have a sentence passed on us.

"We're from Monkham," a voice pipes up from the left. "We had the chandlery on Old Lane." The tension breaks, just like that, and the woman by the fire heaps a bowl full of food and holds it out to Hope. Hope steps forward, murmuring, "Be patient. Let them get used to you," as she passes and takes the proffered food, going to sit beside the woman who just spoke and immediately falling into conversation with her. Kirin shrugs and does the same, and soon we're all seated around the fire, eating what I'm told is squirrel stew by the woman who almost throws the bowl at me. Every now and then I'll feel eyes on me, people glancing surreptitiously at me, trying to see the child of the Gods in my face.

No one sits close to me. No one talks to me, asks me where I've been or anything at all. They're happy to talk to Hope, Kirin, and Nia, but I'm ignored.

I see myself through their eyes: Helewys's apparent favorite, the poisoner, the daughter of the Gods. Aloof. Untouchable, inaccessible, and separate in every way. I'd really believed the people would be pleased—excited—to see me, and to plan how to defeat Aurek. I thought they'd be waiting for someone to come and lead them. But instead, they talk tentatively about adding us to a rota of chores, cooking, cleaning, hunting, as if we're going to stay here and build a life in the woods. No talk of fighting back. No talk of revolution. Stay in the place we've been put.

A yawning emptiness blooms inside me; the feeling is familiar, and I recognize it at once. The feeling of hopelessness, weakness, complicity. *Some things are too big to fight,* a voice inside my head—female, Lormerian, powerful—croons. *Just be a good girl.*

"No—you're lying!" Nia's cry jolts me from my thoughts. Her bowl, resting in her lap, clatters to the ground as she stands, her face ashen. The man she was talking to looks momentarily offended, then shrugs, before turning his attention back to the remains of his meal.

Kirin stands and leads Nia away, and it's not long until the group begins to break up, as slowly everyone drifts toward the canvases hung between branches, returning to their makeshift homes.

"What was that?" I lean over to Hope. Her face is shadowed planes in the dim firelight.

"Aurek is selling the alchemists he's taken," she says without preamble. "He's offering them to the nobles and town leaders.

Their very own gold mine to own and use if they swear their loyalty to him. If they use their men and their power for the Sleeping Prince, if they keep their townships in line and squash any revolts—well then, all the gold their alchemists can make is theirs for the keeping—no questions, no taxes. Apparently, two alchemists have already taken their own lives to prevent their enslavement."

"He's *selling* them?"

"Auctioning them, to be precise."

I understand Nia's horror then. "What about Kata?" I ask, and Sister Hope shakes her head.

"We don't know. But we need to get to them soon."

"But they can't all be corrupt?" I say. "Surely there must be some who would turn on him?"

The look Hope gives me is empty. "He's offering them Elixir, too. Once they've 'proven themselves,' whatever that means. Eternal life to those who stand by him now."

Absolute fury consumes me and for a moment I can't move. How dare he offer the use of the alchemists' bodies as payment for them to keep the townspeople in line? Pain in the palms of my hands makes me look down, and I see my hands curled into fists, the nails pressing into the soft skin there. I unclench them, and place them flat on my knees, before taking a deep breath. "What do we do?"

"That's up to you," Hope says. "I can show these people you're not a danger to them, but I can't make them follow you. You'll have to do that. And soon. There's a bounty on your head, Twylla. And this winter is going to be a tough one. You need to make sure you offer them something better than what he's offering."

She's right. Of course she's right. But how?

They give us some blankets, and Stuan helps Kirin fashion a kind of tent for us, a little away from where everyone else is camped, and I assume it's because of me. The fire is extinguished, and the first guard detail takes up their positions, with Kirin volunteering to join them. I curl up behind Nia, rubbing her shoulder gently as I do. I feel her pat my hand back, but she says nothing. Hope lies behind me, and I listen to the snores and whistles from the camp. I need them to follow me, and respect me. But not like Helewys, not through fear. It's not who I am and I don't want to become like her, or even pretend to be. And if I want to stop them from selling me out, I need them loyal to me. I have to make them like me.

So I try. The following day I take my time over my breakfast, watching to see how the camp works, where the power is. It reminds me a bit of being at the castle and trying to decipher the power hierarchy there. The men from yesterday, including Stuan, vanish off into the woods as soon as they've finished eating, and so does another party, three women and a man, armed with bows. They're important, it seems, the hunters, and the defenders of the camp. Two men with Hagan accents chatter as they sit by the fire and sharpen an assortment of swords and knives. The remaining people, including Lady Shasta, begin to gather clothing together to clean, and I seize my chance.

"Let me help you," I say. "I want to be useful while I'm here."

They look at one another, then turn, and I do the same, to find the cook from yesterday watching me. She's the leader. She's the one I have to win over.

"There's enough on washing detail," she says.

"What about helping you with the food, then?" I try for firmness.

"I don't need help, lass."

"I want to do something."

"The chamber pots need emptying," one of the women behind me says, but when I turn I can't tell which one.

I look back at their leader, who shrugs, and I see the challenge in the shift of her shoulders. She thinks I'll say no. She wants me to.

"Fine. Where are they?"

She stares at me and then shrugs again. "Row of trees, back there. They need to be emptied into a hole in the woods. You'll have to dig a new one. Not near the river, not near the camp. Then the pots need to be cleaned and put back."

"I'll do that, then."

Emptying one's own bog pot is unpleasant, but emptying three communal ones used by fifty people is revolting. The smell is awful, but I do it, taking them a half-hour walk from the camp, one by one, carrying them carefully at arm's length, my mind constantly playing me tripping, landing in one, one emptying over me. I dig the bloody hole, and I slop the contents of the pots into it, flinching as they splash. Then I fetch water from the river and rinse them, over and over, until there's no trace of filth in them, and carry them back. By the time I'm finished, the hunters are back and the food is cooking. No one says a word to me, and I accept my bowl of soup in silence and walk to where Nia is, even though I've never been less hungry. If I'd been doing this on the way here, I'd never have complained about the lack of food.

Nia looks pale and worried, but as I sit beside her she wrinkles her nose and shuffles away slightly. "No offense, but you reek."

I'm not offended. She's right. When she moves to the other side of the tent at bedtime, I understand. But I have to keep going. I have to win them over.

I clean the pots again the next day. And the next. And the next. Still no one speaks to me, and I feel as though I've been flung back in time; here I am again, supposedly important but outside of everything. Unwanted. Despised. Nothing has changed. Hope watches me but offers no suggestion. *Let them get used to you.*

The following day I clean the pots so fast that when I get back to the camp, I'm told I can help prepare the food if I wash my hands thoroughly. I think this is progress, until I'm handed the bodies of three rabbits. "They need skinning, and gutting" is my only instruction.

It's been a long time since I've done it, but I remember, and I do it, their innards under my fingernails as I pull their intestines out and throw them into the fire. As soon as they're done, they're whisked away by Ema, the leader and the cook, who doesn't need my help anymore. I wonder if anyone will refuse the meal when they know I've touched the meat, but no one does.

I have no appetite for it, though; I head into the tent where only I am currently sleeping before the sun has even set. Tomorrow I'll get up again and clean their bog pots. I'll do the same the next day.

And likely the day after that. And they still won't like me for it. It's Lormere all over again. I'm wasting time—every second Aurek presses forward puts us all in more danger—but I don't know what else to do. I don't know how to make people like me; I never have. I'm not Errin or Nia, with their quick tempers and fiery hearts. I'm not a skilled actor like Lief. I'm not even like Sister Hope, clever at politicking and knowing exactly what to say. I'm too awkward, too quiet, too serious. I'm not likable.

I am curled into my blankets, breathing through my mouth because of the way I smell, when I sense someone nearby. I roll over and see Hope silhouetted against the moonlight.

"What are you doing?" she asks.

"Sleeping."

She clicks her teeth. "No, Twylla. With this martyrdom of washing chamber pots and skinning rabbits. What are you trying to achieve?"

"I'm doing what you suggested. I'm letting them get used to me, and trying to get them to like me."

"I never told you to make them like you. I told you to make them follow you."

"What's the difference?"

"Leadership," she says. "To lead, you have to be respected. Trusted. No one is going to take orders from someone who empties their chamber pot, and smells as bad as one."

"I don't know how to make them listen to me." I hear the whine in my voice and hate myself for it. "I thought . . . I thought it would be like in the Conclave. I thought they'd listen to me."

"Why?"

The question takes me aback. "I . . . Because you all did. Errin

80

did, in Scarron. And in the Conclave they said they would fight with me."

"We all knew that you were the best option for defeating him. We all knew what you are, and knew what you were capable of. They don't. They only know you as the peasant girl raised up to poisoner, and now you're not even that."

"So what do I do?" Frustration makes me petulant. "Who do I become to get their attention?"

"You have to figure that out. Fast. As you say, we're running out of time. And for the sake of the Gods, take a bath, if you can think of nothing else to do." She tosses something toward me that lands full on my face, and when I pull it away, Hope is gone and I'm clutching a clean gown, russet colored and woolen, and a drying sheet.

I hear a burst of laughter from the camp, and though I know it's not to do with me, it stings somehow.

She's right. No one would follow me as I am. It was so easy to be brave with Errin by my side. If only she was here now.

But she's not, I snap at myself, full of fury. *So stop this. It's not about Errin. Or Merek. Or Maryl. It's about you. For once in your pathetic life, stop living for other people and live for yourself.*

Filled with the need to move, to outrun my anger, I snatch up some of the rough soap and head to the stream, stripping as I near it. I all but fling myself into the icy water, and it flays the breath from my lungs and strips me clean. When I duck my head beneath the surface to wash my hair, my whole body seizes up, and it's as though I'm on fire; but it's a cold, clear fire, full of promise and purpose. A fire to walk through and rise from. I scrub, and scrub, until I can see the red in my hair once more. When I haul myself out of the water, no longer cold, and pull the new dress over my head, I feel reborn. And hungry.

Back at the camp, most people have gone to bed, so I help myself to the dregs in the pot and wolf it down by the smoldering wood. I look up at the sky and see the redness of the sunset above me. Tomorrow will be clear again. Red sky at night, Daunen's delight, as the saying goes.

Daunen, who sang to wake her father so he'd take back the skies from Næht.

And it hits me like a bolt of lightning, what I have to do. What I should have done in the beginning. Of course nothing has changed. I have to *make it* change. That's been my only problem all along. If I want them to see me as their leader, I need to lead them.

The following morning, before dawn, I wake Nia, Hope, and Kirin, shaking their shoulders until they grumble at me. Then I wake the whole camp, bashing the cauldron with a wooden spoon as hard as I can. Within minutes the clearing is full of very angry Lormerians.

"Follow me," I say in my most imperious, most Twylla way. "All of you. Now."

I turn and begin walking as though I expect them to follow. And though it takes a moment, it sounds like most of them do. I hear multiple treads behind me, feet shuffling the leaves, cloaks gliding over fallen branches.

I walk swiftly in the direction that Stuan said the coast was, ever mindful of the lightening of the sky overhead. For the best part of an hour I walk on without looking back, without knowing how many are behind me. At last I break the tree line and look down on the river Aurmere, vast and gray and rushing toward the Tallithi Sea.

I hear my followers shuffle out behind me, muttering darkly, and I look to the right, to where I can see the tips of the East Mountains over the treetops. And as the sun breaks over them, turning the land and the water gold, I start to sing.

My voice is out of practice, and raw, but it's still my voice and I sing into the dawn. I sing "Fair and Far" and "Carac and Cedany" and "The Blue Hind." I sing every song I ever sang at court and I sing the songs I learned growing up at home with my mother. I sing until it feels as though my throat is in ribbons, and the sun rises as dawn breaks over Lormere.

And when there are no more songs, I turn to find every single person from the camp is watching me. Some watchful, some slack-jawed, some with tears on their cheeks. There are hands on hearts, people clutching their loved ones close. Lady Shasta is openly weeping. Ema is nodding her head as though to a silent drumbeat. Whether they're there from belief or curiosity, I don't care. Now they see me. Now they know me. This is my only chance.

"Once, I was death to you," I say. "And much has changed since then. For all of us. We've exchanged tyrant for tyrant. Helewys was a bitch," I spit. "And I hated her as much as you all did. But Aurek—this Sleeping Prince—I hate more. His bloodlust makes Helewys look like an angel. And he will not stop. He doesn't have to; he has monsters and abilities Helewys could only dream of. Unless we stop him, he will take everything, destroy everything, enslave everything. I can stop him." I pause and look at them all, every single one, in the eye, leaving Stuan for last. "I told you I wasn't poisonous, and that is true. But to the Sleeping Prince, I am every inch the executioner you all knew me as. In every fairy tale, there is a kernel of truth, and that is the truth of this one. For him, I am poison. I am his death. And I will deliver."

At the rear of the crowd, Sister Hope beams at me. Without smiling. Without any kind of expression, she is radiating pride, and it fills me up.

"If you wish to live in the woods like pigs, then stay. Languish here until I've saved your kingdom and put it back to rights. But those who aren't cowards, pack up the camp," I say. "I won't hide in the woods anymore. We're making for the East Mountains and we're leaving before dark. There's a refuge there that will hold us all. I want us there within the week, and ready to begin fighting back. It's time the Sleeping Prince learned that the dawn will rise. The dawn will always rise."

I wait for no comment, sweeping through them and back to the camp.

I know they follow me now.

Chapter 7

It takes us less than a day to dismantle the camp and pack our scant belongings. By nightfall, we're three miles deeper into the woods, eating rations Ema the cook spent the day preparing. Night sees us sardined together under a sea of canvas, drowsing until dawn, when we rise and continue.

We keep going like this, slowly, carefully, collecting stragglers and other refugees when we find them, slowly inching our way toward Lormere. On my journey to Scarron it took a whole day for me to travel the woods, but that was on horseback, on the main path. We have to skulk and sneak, sending scouts—Kirin, Stuan, and some others—to check ahead and report back. I have to stay patient, remind myself that we need to be this careful, that this is only the beginning of our journey.

We're around two miles from the edge of the woods when we hear the children. At first I'm not sure if what I'm hearing is real. The acoustics in the woods can be strange; it's not for nothing that

Lormerians think the place is haunted. I turn as I think I hear voices, and I see some of the others frowning, too. It's only when a sharp, high cry cuts away almost as soon as it sounds, and I hold up my hand to stop everyone in their tracks, that I can place the noise. There are grumbles from the back, but I turn sharply, shaking my head to hush them, and they die away. Hope and Kirin move to my side.

"What is it?" Hope asks in an undertone.

"I'm not sure. It sounded like a baby, or a small child. Lost, maybe? Separated from its parents." Hope gives me a worried look and I know my face reflects it.

"I'll go and see," Kirin says.

"What about your leg?"

"It's fine. I'm fine. I'll go easy."

He vanishes into the skeletal trees, and I turn to the others. I murmur in Nia's ear that we have to check something, and tell her to pass it on, and to tell everyone to stay close and quiet. As the message spreads through the ranks, people begin to put their bags and belongings down, sitting on stumps and rotting logs, and pulling food and water from their packs, some moving into the trees to relieve themselves.

Fifteen minutes becomes half an hour, then an hour, according to the movements of the sun overhead, and people begin getting restless. We're close to the edge of the woods, and should, according to Hope's calculations, come out three miles north of Chargate. From there, we need to stay low, and alert, skirting around Monkham and Lake Baha before following the river to the coast, then the coast to the mountains. It's going to be a long and dangerous walk, and the delay now isn't helping settle anyone's nerves.

I'm about to ask Hope to lead everyone onward while I wait for Kirin, when he comes stumbling through the trees, his expression both terrified and furious.

"There are soldiers in the woods," he hisses, not bothering to wait until he's close to tell me.

Everyone explodes into gasps and cries, clutching one another and reaching for weapons.

"Quiet," I hiss at them. "If I could hear them from here, don't you think they might hear us, too?" They fall immediately silent. "Tell us what you saw," I say to Kirin, trying to keep my voice level, and firm.

Kirin reaches for Nia's water skin and she releases it to him without protest. He drinks deeply before rinsing his mouth and spitting on the ground. Only then does he meet my gaze. "They're camped about three miles west of here. There's a clearing in the trees, and what look like Tregellian army tents set up, five of them. They're there. Men. And two golems."

"It's a camp?" I say. "They've set up a camp in the woods. Some kind of base? Outreach post for their march on Tregellan?" I'm thinking aloud.

Kirin shakes his head. "It's not an ordinary camp. You were right—you did hear a child." He swallows. "It's a prison camp, for children."

The group erupts into startled talk, and I'm so taken aback I let the noise go on for longer than I ought before I snap at them. "Silence! Do you want us to be caught?"

I receive a few dark looks, but they go quiet, and I nod at Kirin to continue.

His face is grim as he does. "I saw them, all ages, boys and girls. They brought them out of the tents in groups of ten and sent them into another tent, on the outskirts of the camp. Latrines, I think—they were only in there for a few minutes, then they were taken back to the tents they came from, and the next lot were brought out. They've separated the boys from the girls and they're all guarded by more than a dozen men and the two golems. No other adults. There's a fence around the camp, too, sharpened branches in the ground like pikes."

"How many, do you think?" I ask.

"I counted one hundred and ten."

"Where have they come from?"

"Chargate," Hope says. "That's the closest town to the woods. I'll bet they're the children from Chargate."

"Why have they taken the kids?" Breena, a bowsmith's daughter from near Haga, asks. "What use are they?"

"Control," Hope says instantly. "If he's taken the children, the people will behave themselves. What parent wouldn't do anything to keep their child safe?"

"Gods . . ." I breathe. How clever. How despicable. Pay the nobles to be loyal to him, and take the children from the commoners to keep them subdued. "Do you think he's done it everywhere, to all of the major towns?" I ask, and she nods. "Those poor people."

"We have to do something," Kirin says. "We have to get the kids out. There are only thirteen or so men there. Two golems. We outnumber them. We could take them."

I turn to look at our band of refugees. Yes, technically we have the larger number. And men like Stuan, Ulrin, Hobb, and Tally are trained fighters. A lot of the women can hold their own, too.

But against soldiers and golems in close quarters, and without fire to fight the golems . . . I see him realize this and shake the knowledge away, his need to do something greater than his need to be rational.

"We could do it," he insists. "We'd have the element of surprise."

"Then what?" I ask gently. "Say we do manage it, what do we do with the children?"

"Take them with us."

"Lead a group of children across Lormere into the mountains? And when he found out, their families would be killed . . ."

"We have to do something." Ema repeats Kirin's words and turns to me. The others do the same, waiting for me to speak.

"We will. I promise. But we have to do the right something."

I walk away from the crowd, trusting Hope to keep them quiet as they mob Kirin for more details. I wander into the trees a little way away, trying to clear my thoughts. We do need to do something; those weren't empty words.

But what can we do that doesn't put all of them at risk?

I imagine all those terrified parents. Imagine them all rising up in support of me. The Sleeping Prince is powerful, but if I can rally the people—the Lormerians . . . if they all rose up at the same time. If I can unite them . . .

My head starts to throb, too many thoughts fighting for space. I spot a tree stump and sit down, gently brushing away a spider that's somehow caught on my dress. It clings to my finger, and I watch it scuttling over my hand, turning my palm over, catching it on my other hand when it threatens to go up my sleeve. Eventually, I reach out and encourage it to climb onto a nearby sapling.

And as it climbs, I stare into the distance.

We need to send a signal, something clear enough to give hope but not so incendiary as to cause Aurek to strike out at the Lormerians. Something that draws his attention from the townspeople but doesn't direct it to us. Not completely, at least. He doesn't need to know about us yet.

I can feel the edge of an idea, and I stand, starting to pace.

"Kirin, Nia," I call, and the two come over. I face them, the idea taking shape and solidifying in my mind. And, much to their surprise, I grin.

"How do you feel about leaving a message in Chargate tonight?"

I send Hope on with the others, muttering darkly about foolishness.

"The only thing we can't afford to lose is you," she says accusingly as we part. "Are you out of your mind?"

"We have to do something."

"It doesn't have to be you."

But it does. I have to lead this. I do have to put my life on the line if I'm going to stay their leader and keep them loyal to me. I have to show them I'll fight on the front line with them. That every risk I ask them to take is one I'm willing to take, too. This is the first strike we're going to make, after I promised them I would defeat Aurek.

I saw the horror in their eyes when Kirin told us about the children. And they looked to me to do something. They turned to me. So I have to be at the center of it, and the risk has to be a secondary concern. I have to be a leader and rise up.

I tell Hope as much and she throws her hands in the air.

"If we lose you, we lose our only chance of defeating him."

"And if I lose them"—I point back at the trees hiding my army from my eyes—"then we're all damned. They'll have families affected by this. After all, they must have relatives across the land, nieces, nephews, brothers, and sisters, if not children of their own. What could they get for turning me over to Aurek? What rewards for them and their families? I have to give them a reason to not do that. I have to be bigger, and better. I have to be the only option for them."

"You're gambling it all on a stunt, Twylla. And you might lose."

"I'll definitely lose if I don't gamble at all. And yes, it's a stunt. At its core, it is just a bunch of kids writing on a wall. A wall his men are guarding, surrounding a town he's imprisoned. Violated. We're going to leave a sign that the people inside haven't been forgotten, and not everyone has been defeated. We're writing hope across that wall. A promise that they're not alone. And the people outside the wall—my people—will see their leader risk her own neck to make that promise."

Eventually, Hope backs down—reluctantly, furiously, but she does, and she and the majority of our camp set toward the mountains on the route we've agreed. Nia, Kirin, and Stuan—who we permit to stay once he's proven he can perform a passable Tregellian accent—and I remain in the woods.

The plan is simple: Stuan has put on his armor, and Nia has borrowed a light mail shirt, and the two of them will cause a distraction, making sure their very Tregellian voices are heard echoing out of the woods. This will, hopefully, draw the guards away from a section of the city walls, giving Kirin and me time to daub it with our message. We debated back and forth about what to write, and where, but we've decided.

Tonight will be the Rising Dawn's debut.

The choice to write our message on the outside wall is best; that way no one from within the city can be blamed, so there's no need to punish them by hurting the city's children. It sends the message we want, in a way that carries the lowest risk. We hope. I go over and over it in my head, trying to find a way it might backfire, but am still anxious when I can't find one.

By pure coincidence, one of the Lormerian escapees was a leatherworker, a man called Trey, whose job it was to tan and work skin into saddles. When he fled his home, he brought some of his skins with him, in the hopes of trading them for safety, and his valuable dyes, too, and it's the rich red madder we ask him for. We add beetroot juice from Ema's stores, and flour, to make a thick, viscous red paint that will stain if unnoticed for long enough. We mix our paint in a Tregellian army helmet we took from Almwyk, with sticks we find on the ground, snapping evergreen branches to use as brushes.

We move to the edge of the woods, around a quarter of a mile from Chargate, and set up a kind of camp. We chew on the dried venison we've been left, and stir the paint, adding more beetroot juice when it begins to dry out. And then we just have to wait. We track the sun across the sky, looking at one another more frequently as it starts to lower, the air beginning to cool.

"This is madness," Nia says, poking at the paint. "No one inside will even see it."

"No, but the guards will see it. Someone will have to clean it off. And they'll all talk about it. Word will spread inside the town. That's what we want. We're not sending a message to the outside world but to the people inside the walls, so they know they're not alone. That someone out here is fighting. And we want Aurek to know about it, too. We want him to know that someone, somewhere, is out there."

"If we're caught . . ."

"We won't be. It's easy. All you have to do is talk."

"She's good at that," Kirin adds, and Stuan and I smile before I carry on.

"You'll have armor, and you'll be mostly shielded by the trees. You just need to make enough noise for them to be unsure of how many of you there are. They won't come out of the gates without knowing that." I look at Kirin to confirm this, and he nods. "But they will come looking over the walls, and they will call for reinforcements from nearby."

"And that's when Twylla and I will do our part," Kirin says.

"Exactly. While you have distracted them at the front of the city, we will approach the south wall, paint our message, and go. We'll meet you in the small copse two miles north of the city."

"Are you sure you know where it is?" Nia turns to Stuan.

He sighs. "Yes. For the ninth time, I know where it is. It's two miles north of here, and it's a bunch of trees."

I look up at the sky. "We should get going. We'll see you in the copse after."

Nia frowns. "How long should we wait at the copse?"

I look at Kirin.

"Assume if we're not there by sunrise that we're lost. Follow on after Hope to the mountains," he says.

"But we will be there. And then we'll all go on together." I stand up and collect our makeshift paintbrushes as Kirin carefully lifts the helmet of paint. "Remember, no more than five minutes, then go. Keep moving. Change your voices. Stuan, you have to keep the accent up."

"The Dawn Is Rising!" he says in a near-perfect Tregellian accent. Then he repeats it again in a lower voice; though some of the accent is lost, it's still a close imitation.

"Perfect. Just keep doing that." I look at Kirin and he nods. "Let's go."

I start to feel shaky as we skim down the tree line, my stomach churning with nerves. Within a few minutes we're close enough to the walls that I can see people on the ramparts, made shadows by the torches. I count them: three, four, five figures on the north side, no golems. I can't see the south side from here, but assume it's manned the same way. The west side, where the main gates face out toward the woods, likely has more.

"Ready?" I ask.

Stuan nods, but Nia looks paralyzed, her face stiff, her eyes wide, and I feel sorry for her. She's seen so much the last few days. And strangely, there's something in her fear that makes me feel a little braver. I reach out and grip her shoulders, drawing her away from the boys.

"You don't have to come," I tell her quietly. "If you don't want to. Or if you're frightened."

"I'm not scared," she hisses at me.

"Then you're a bloody idiot, because I'm terrified."

She looks at me and takes a deep, ragged breath.

"Five minutes," I tell her. "That's all it will take. Just remember what I said."

"Keep moving. Change my voice. Stay away from the walls. Run for the copse."

94

"Exactly. Ready?" She nods. "Are you ready?" I ask Stuan and Kirin.

"Let's do this," Stuan says.

"Count to one thousand," Kirin tells Nia.

And then we're off, moving silently through the darkness.

As soon as we break the cover of the trees, I start to sweat, ears straining for the sound of arrows being loosed. We move across open ground, relying on the moonless night and our own stealth to cover us. It's perhaps one thousand feet from the edge of the forest to the west wall, and every single one of those feet feels as though it takes a year to cross. We move relatively slowly; Kirin said quick movements draw the eye more than slow, so we creep, staying low to the ground, even as my body screams at me to run.

Once we reach the wall, I pause to lean against it, my whole body trembling, but Kirin grabs my wrist and shakes his head, urging me to keep moving along the west wall, desperately, terribly aware that thirty feet above, our enemy is keeping a lookout.

We finally turn on to the south wall, and I hear the murmuring of voices. One laughs, and his friend replies. Just two men, on their night shift. There's something about the normalcy of it that makes me shiver. We keep going, walking on and on, skirting the border of the last town between us and Tregellan.

"Will this do?" Kirin says on a breath, and we both pause.

I look back, unable to make out the edge of the city wall.

Every single thing that could go wrong runs through my mind.

Stuan and Nia could get caught. What if the men from the camp come through the woods and find them?

What if one of them gets shot?

What if— But I never finish my thought, because a roar above us shatters the quiet of the night.

"The south wall! Intruders at the gates!" I hear someone call. Then the sound of footsteps on stone.

"Now," Kirin says. He pulls out the paint and hands me the brush.

He holds it while I dip and daub the wall, reaching as high as I can, stretching my arms as wide as I can. I write *The Rising Dawn* in the biggest letters I can manage, Kirin moving with me as I scrawl across the wall. I can feel paint splatters on my face, and on my hands, but I don't stop, moving quickly.

I'm finished in under a minute, and I pause.

"Let's go," Kirin urges.

But something is missing. "Stay there," I hiss at him, and I dip the brush back in the helmet. I paint a line, horizontal, at least eight feet long. I can't see to estimate the middle, but I stop halfway back to Kirin and use my fingers to find the paint, adding a semicircle to the top of the line, able to make it out, my eyes finally used to the dark. Finally, I add more lines, rays emerging from the semicircle.

Not everyone in Lormere can read, but everyone knows what the rising sun looks like. I can see it perfectly—

I shouldn't be able to see it.

Directly overhead, a guard is looking down at us, a torch held over the side of the wall, his face frozen.

Kirin, who has been watching the forest, turns, and I see his mouth fall open. "Run," he hisses.

But something stills me, something in the guard's face. Something desperate, and pleading. I gamble on it.

"The children are safe," I call up as loudly as I dare. "Two miles into the forest."

The man says nothing, still staring. Then: "Swear it."

"I swear."

"Can you keep them safe?" he whispers down, and I nod. "Go!" he hisses, jerking back, and I hear another voice.

Kirin drops the helmet to be found in the morning, and we move as fast as we dare for the woods.

"There! I see movement!"

My blood runs cold at the voice, high above us, and this time I don't need to strain to hear the sound of arrows filling the air almost as soon as he's spoken.

I put on a spurt of speed I didn't know I was capable of and somehow make it back into the woods, the sounds of arrows hitting trees following me in. I turn and find Kirin right behind me, his eyes wide. He grabs my wrist and pulls me in deeper, until the sounds of outrage are distant.

We change direction, turning right and heading north, trying to stay parallel to the tree line. We jog, and run, and stumble, and even when my legs ache and my lungs burn and my sides feel as though I've been stabbed, I keep moving, my breath hoarse and heavy.

Eventually, Kirin changes direction again, and I follow, and we finally leave the woods. Ahead of us is what I hope is the small copse, and I finally begin to relax.

When we get there, Stuan and Nia are seated beneath a tree. The moment they see us they're on their feet, racing toward us.

"You're covered in paint," Nia half sobs, half laughs as she pulls me into a fierce hug. "Not very stealthy."

Beside us Stuan and Kirin clasp forearms, then embrace, too. As they part, Nia releases me and throws herself at Kirin. Stuan looks at me, and hesitates. I find myself grinning, and I raise my eyebrows at him suggestively. To my pleasure he blushes, before reaching out and patting my shoulder gruffly, making me laugh.

"How was it?" Kirin asks.

"Just as you said," Stuan says.

"He was brilliant," Nia replies. "He did so many voices."

Stuan's color deepens. "Did you paint it?"

I nod. "The Rising Dawn. And I did a sun, too. For those who can't read."

"They spotted us running, though," Kirin says. "They'll see it straightaway. But I suppose it's like you said, they'll talk about it."

"They will," I say. "They'll gossip and they'll report it to Aurek. Word will get around. People will start asking questions. So we need to make sure we have answers for them. Get people into the towns. Find out if everyone is as loyal as they claim to be."

"Like the man on the wall."

I think of the guard who turned a blind eye to us.

"Like the man on the wall."

"What?" Nia asks. "What man?"

"Come on," I say. "It's a long walk to the mountains. We'll tell you on the way."

The Tower of Truth

The apothecary lies asleep at the top of a tower, in a bed that could easily fit her four times over. She's propped up like a girl in a story, reclining against silken pillows that still smell faintly, to her mind, of another girl and are moth-eaten in places, but that doesn't disturb the apothecary's rest. Her short hair is fanned out like a halo across them, black in the moonlight. One hand lies on her stomach, the other curled beside her cheek. Her rosebud lips are parted slightly; her eyelids flutter as she dreams.

The prince is in her mind again.

In the dream they're in another tower, one she doesn't know but recognizes immediately from his descriptions: They're in Tallith, standing inside one of the seven towers that orbit the central keep. From beside the window where she stands, she can see the bridges that link the towers to the keep and one another, so the Tallithi royals never have to walk on the ground if they choose not to.

She knows it's a dream because she's heard the reports that say all of the towers are now in ruins; five hundred years of neglect, and the unremarkable savagery of sea air and salt winds have eroded them into stumps, like the teeth of an addict. Yet now she sees them as they were: golden and beautiful.

She knows it's a dream because she is able to keep her back to the prince. She is in control of her body.

He moves to stand behind her, not quite touching her. But close enough that his breath tickles the back of her hair, and she feels the warmth of his body. Close enough that he might as well be touching her, so present is he in that moment. Outside of dreams his skin is cold, lifeless, like the clay he favors for his bodyguards. When he comes to her in her sleep, though, he's always warm. She'd like to keep him from her mind completely, but the vulnerability of sleep is as an open door to him; then he can wander through the hallways of her dreams at will. And though in her waking hours he can write a command and force her body to obey it, in dreams he cannot.

She often wonders whether he prefers the challenge of the dreams. Whether it's more fun for him to have to work to get her to do what he wants.

"Do you like it?" he asks.

The apothecary hears the rustling of cloth as he shifts, leaning forward so his face is next to hers as he speaks again. "I asked you a question, sweetling."

"Don't call me that," she snaps.

She can hear his smile. "My lady speaks," he says, clearly delighted that he goaded her into responding. "Will she grace me with more words from her lovely lips?"

The apothecary presses those lips together, and the prince's grin widens. He turns, speaking directly into the soft pink shell of her ear. "The tower we're standing in is the Tower of Courage. It's where your friend's ancestor stayed, briefly, just before she tried to kill me." He pauses, tilting his head back so his chin brushes against the top of her ear, rubbing gently like a cat. "Over there"—he lowers his head—"is the Tower of Wisdom. That's where your Silas's however-many-greats-grandmother kept her rooms. Mine, as you know, was the Tower of Love."

This time she feels his lips against her skin as they stretch into a grin.

"Which would your tower be? Maybe Wisdom? No . . . No. You're many things, Errin Vastel, but you're not wise. Nor peaceful. Perhaps Truth? You do seem to have a constancy to you. This refusal to be happy with me. Do you think they're out there, Errin? Plotting to come and save you?"

When his fingers grip her chin, she slaps his hand away.

"No," she says. "You don't get to make me move how you want in here." As though she's summoned it in response to her anger, inside the dream she feels a cool breeze behind her, her skin becoming gooseflesh on her arms.

His head tilts, his eyes sly as he assesses her. "I think your friends will come, sweetling. But not for you. They'll come for the philtersmith, because he is a rare and special thing. And the others. The base goldsmiths. But you . . . you're not special at all."

"Then why keep me here?"

The prince laughs. "I said you weren't special. Not that you weren't useful. Silas will bleed himself dry if he believes it will keep you from harm. He tried to take his own life, you know.

Until I reminded him that that would mean consequences for you. And your brother will undertake any task I ask of him as long as he believes me your protector. You're a convenience to me, Errin. Which is odd, considering what a huge inconvenience you've been thus far to everyone else in your life. You've betrayed your father, who you allowed to die. Your mother, who you allowed to go mad. Your brother. Your friends. My kin. I could never have found the Conclave if you hadn't told me you were in Tremayne, with the Sin Eater."

The wind whips behind the apothecary now, icy rain stabbing at her, and she turns to the window.

The prince speaks behind her. "I am the only thing in this world that you have not betrayed." She feels his hand trail down her spine, pressing his thumb against each ridge, punctuating his words with touch. "And it's not for lack of trying, is it? So perhaps I should ask myself, why do I keep you here?"

She wakes up abruptly. Tallith is gone instantly, and she stares into the darkness of her room. Her heart beats sickeningly fast, her whole body seeming to pulse in time with it. She leans forward, drawing up her knees and resting her head on them, wrapping her arms around them.

Then she's moving, standing up, almost tripping over the bed-clothes. She realizes the prince has taken control of her and tries to stop herself, reaching for the bedpost and wrapping her arms around it. But her legs keep driving her forward, with such force she shifts the heavy wooden bedframe an inch before she lets go.

Her legs take her to the windowsill. She climbs up, and onto it, facing the outside.

There was no glass in the windows in her dream, but there is here.

She chokes back a sob as she pushes the window open.

As in her dream, the weather is violent, rain lashes her face like needles, the wind picks up her nightdress and whips it about her thighs. She can't move to hold it down.

"I could make you jump," the prince says softly, from behind her. She didn't hear him come in. "If I wrote it on here"—he holds up a piece of paper—"I could have you throw yourself from the tower. Out here, I very much can make you move."

Dread rises up in the apothecary, her stomach swooping so violently she sways without the prince's instruction. She reaches out to brace herself against the wall.

The prince pulls a pen from inside his tunic and scrawls something on the paper, and the apothecary feels bile rise in her throat, momentarily dizzy.

The prince presses the paper to the simulacrum's body and the apothecary feels herself start to turn.

"No," she whimpers.

She faces the darkness, the might of the wind and rain scouring her face. She cannot see the ground beneath her, cannot see anything.

She hears the scratch of a nib on paper.

Her knees bend.

"Please," she tries to say, but the word won't come.

She jumps.

She lands on her back at the prince's feet, all breath knocked from her; for a moment her lungs cannot fill and she thinks she is going to die. The prince stares down at her; for once his eyes are empty of cunning, for once he seems unamused at his own antics. His voice, when he speaks, is emotionless, fathomless.

"I was willing to make us into a proper family; I was willing to put the time into it. I've sent your brother to fetch your mother, despite needing him elsewhere, in a bid to make you happy. But I don't have time to play with you anymore. Your friends are not the only ones who understand you're replaceable. You're alive only because I permit it, and I am fast running out of patience with you. So tomorrow evening, you will present yourself in the Great Hall an hour after sunset. You will wear something very pretty, and your best smile. And we will dine together, companionably. You will not try to stab me. You will not spit at me or slap me. You will behave with decorum. In short, sweetling, you will make yourself *special* to me, or I will remove you from my game board. I need your brother, and I need the philtersmith. But I don't need you. Bear that in mind."

He turns toward the door, then stops. "The Tower of Attrition," he says. "That's what this will be known as. A place to break the spirits of mares that run wild. Because you will break, Errin. Or you will die."

Once again he leaves her on the floor, too frightened to move, or even cry.

❖ PART TWO ❖
Errin

Chapter 8

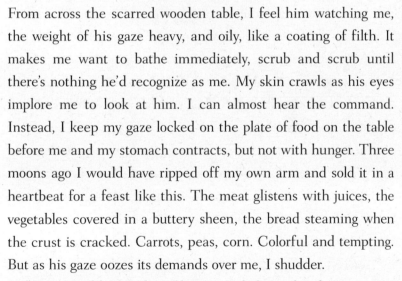

From across the scarred wooden table, I feel him watching me, the weight of his gaze heavy, and oily, like a coating of filth. It makes me want to bathe immediately, scrub and scrub until there's nothing he'd recognize as me. My skin crawls as his eyes implore me to look at him. I can almost hear the command. Instead, I keep my gaze locked on the plate of food on the table before me and my stomach contracts, but not with hunger. Three moons ago I would have ripped off my own arm and sold it in a heartbeat for a feast like this. The meat glistens with juices, the vegetables covered in a buttery sheen, the bread steaming when the crust is cracked. Carrots, peas, corn. Colorful and tempting. But as his gaze oozes its demands over me, I shudder.

"Are you cold, sweetling?" he says. I shake my head. Two moons here has given me a new tolerance for the freezing temperatures, and it's not the cold that makes me shiver as though someone is crossing my grave. "Look at me."

I obey him because if I don't, he'll make me, with his simulacrum. Or he'll kill me. I'm painfully aware that at the doors behind me, two golems stand like the statues they should be, but at a word from him, they'd crush my skull between their gargantuan clay hands. So I lift my head, meeting his golden eyes as steadily as I can. The moment I do, he nods in victory and loses interest in me, returning his attention to his meal.

Now it's my turn to watch him as he picks meat from a thin bone, dropping it onto his plate, his slender fingers grease-slicked and shining in the candlelight. He whistles softly and one of the dogs beneath the table emerges soundlessly, sending a chill through me.

"Sit," Aurek says, and the dog does. He selects a piece of flesh and holds it out to the animal, not flinching even when the mutt's teeth snap shut over the morsel and tear it from his grip. They watch each other, dog and new master, for a moment, before Aurek waves his hand and the dog slinks back beneath the table. I feel my stomach lurch when the coarse fur brushes against my gown.

Aurek holds the bone up, examining it before he sucks it clean. His golden eyes stay fixed on me, emotionless, as he uses it to clean his teeth, tracing his canines with it. He tosses it to the ground after he's done and I hear one of the beasts beneath the table shuffle forward, then the sound of crunching.

"You've not eaten much, Errin," he says. "Is there something wrong with the food?"

"No. It's fine." I poke at my food with a spoon; I lost knife privileges two weeks ago. When I peek back at him, he's looking at me, deadpan.

"If you won't eat, you'll have to be fed."

"I'll eat," I say, pulling the plate toward me. I reach for a leg, chicken, duck, who knows, but I can't make myself pick it up. My hand shakes. I can't. I can't do it.

"Open wide." Aurek grins.

I do it. I put a piece of meat into my dry mouth and chew, and chew, and chew. Aurek watches the whole time as my jaw moves up and down, aching with the repeated motion. Eventually, the food disintegrates into a kind of paste and I force myself to swallow it, feeling it stick somewhere between my throat and my heart.

"There," Aurek says, reaching for his goblet and drinking from it deeply. He sets it down with a satisfied clunk, the grin on his face highlighted by the stain of the wine curving away from his lips. "You eat up like a good girl. You, boy, fetch her some more meat. Nice small pieces; I have no desire to watch her chomping away like a cow at the cud."

A servant emerges from the recesses of the room and does as he's bid, reaching across to take a lump of meat and ripping it into bite-size chunks. His shoulders are rounded, curled in, as though trying not to be noticed, his head bowed so low his chin rests against his chest. My eyes fill with angry, humiliated tears that threaten to spill down my cheeks.

"Give it to her," Aurek instructs him. The servant twitches, and moves to my side with the new plate held in faintly trembling fingers.

Suddenly, my arm jerks out, knocking the plate from his hand. We both watch in horror as the whole lot, food and plate, arcs across the room, the platter hitting the stone floor with a deafening crash, accompanying the snarls from the dogs that bolt from beneath the table. They pause, looking to the Sleeping Prince for permission to eat the fallen food. And the servant and I also turn to Aurek to see what he'll do.

He's laughing silently, his face creased in mirth, his eyes squeezed shut. He takes a huge breath and his laughter becomes loud as he bangs one fist on the table, rattling the goblets and making the candles gutter. I see the simulacrum held loosely in his other hand.

"Your faces . . ." he manages before a new fit overcomes him. "That was beautiful." He wipes his eyes, his shoulders still shaking, as we stare at him. Finally our horror seems to sober him, and an ugly look crosses his face. He sits back in his chair and crosses his arms. "Fine. Just clean it up." The servant begins to bend again to reach for the food. "No. Don't pick it up. Eat it."

I stare at Aurek.

"Have you been struck deaf? Eat it. On your knees, like the animal you are, and eat it."

Without making any protest, the rightful king of Lormere sinks to his knees, then leans forward. On all fours he lowers his face to the ground and begins to eat the fallen meat, the dogs growling viciously as he does, though they make no move toward him. I asked him why they didn't remember him, and he said they likely did. But they only ever obeyed one master, and he was never of their pack.

Aurek beholds him in silence, no trace of enjoyment on his face, but I won't watch. Instead, I look down at my lap and tug a thread from the dress I'm wearing, making a small hole. Merek said he believes it was one of Twylla's; it's too short and too tight on me, the seams straining at my waist and chest. I wonder where she is now, and hope she's safe. I also hope she still wants to fight after she sees the carnage the Sleeping Prince left behind in the catacombs.

He led me through hallways littered with bodies, men, women, and children lying where they were slain. The curtains had been ripped from the doorways, blood was splattered over the stone walls, and I looked away from it as he paraded me through the Conclave. When we'd entered the Great Hall and passed the bodies of one of the Sisters and the Sin Eater, I'd cried out, and the Sleeping Prince had grinned, slipping an arm around me as though we were friends. His triumph was palpable; he exuded pleasure in his victory. I saw Silas briefly, seemingly unconscious, hooded and bound and bundled into a golem-pulled carriage with half a dozen guards. I haven't seen him since we've been here.

That was ten weeks ago, and I still don't know whether Twylla got out. I hope so. And I hope she still wants to fight. Though I have to admit I wouldn't blame her if she turned tail and ran as far and as fast as she could.

When Merek has finished, he lifts his head but remains kneeling.

"Good dog," Aurek says, and the real hounds whimper at him. "Now, why don't—"

We're saved from whatever he may have said next, by a knock. The atmosphere in the room changes immediately, sharpening to a point, and Aurek's voice when he demands the caller enter is like a whip. The servant, dressed in black livery with the Solaris picked out in gold across his chest, can sense it, too, terror plain in his pale face as he bows deeply to Aurek. I look at the scroll in his shaking hand and feel a thrill of hope cut through my fear.

"A message, Your Grace," the man says needlessly, eyes darting to the golems on either side of the door.

Aurek waves at Merek to stand and collect the rolled parchment, and then dismisses the servant, who leaves so quickly it's as if he's vanished into thin air the moment Merek has the paper tube in his hands.

Without Aurek needing to issue the order, Merek takes it to him, closing his eyes and breaking the seal on the message, unfurling it in front of Aurek, who grips his arm roughly and pulls it down so he can read whatever is written on the paper. I see Merek's eyelashes flutter as he parts them, the tiniest fraction, to read the message for himself.

"Leave me," Aurek explodes. "Both of you. Get out!"

I push away from the table, all but fleeing the room, Merek behind me as the golems swing their clubs. There is a crash from inside the Great Hall, the dogs begin to howl, and then I do run, picking up my skirts and putting as much distance as I can between me and the Sleeping Prince. I daren't speak to Merek, and I hear his footsteps move away from mine, pausing to step behind a tapestry that I know conceals a door to the kitchens. I don't look back, or stop.

I hurry through the unlit icy corridors, empty of people, moonlight guiding my way, casting shadows on the floor like prison bars. Once I reach the library, I close the door and lean against it, willing my heart to slow its thrumming in my chest. Minutes pass, until I finally have my breathing back under control, my legs no longer shaking, and I move to the fire I left burning. I'm back just in time; it's beginning to die, and I reach for some of the books I put aside for this very purpose.

The door opens and I wheel around to see Merck standing in the doorway, with a goblet in his hands. He looks at me, then the books in my hand, and finally the fire. Without speaking, he crosses to one of the remaining small tables, puts the wine on it, and grips the chair in front of it.

"Don't—" I begin, but it's too late. He's raised it over his head and brought it smashing to the floor. I throw my hands in front of my face as it shatters, pieces flying everywhere. When I lower them, Merek is already stuffing the wood into the fire, using a leg as a poker.

"I'd rather we burned the furniture than more books," he says pointedly, and despite the cold air I blush.

"Sorry," I say. It's not the first time he's caught me feeding books to the hearth in a bid to stay warm. "You did say these ones would be fine to use."

"If you had no choice, I said. In an emergency." His lips hint at a rueful smile.

I follow his gaze to the shelves, the gaps in them now where we've—I've—taken books and used them as fuel. Ordinarily I'd balk at it, too, but Aurek won't supply any rooms with firewood save those he uses himself. I have a small allowance for the tower room he allocated me, but I've used this moon's up already, and it's too risky to meet Merek there too often anyway. Here it seems reasonable; he always brings something, and if Aurek or anyone else comes, we can say I summoned him to bring me food or wine while I read. To that end, I sit at the table and pull a book about agricultural management toward me, flipping it open. Merek, who has been lighting the few candles in the room from the now crackling fire, turns at the sound.

"What's that?" he asks, and I hold it up so he can see the cover.

He squints to read the title. "Gods, that's old." He moves back to the table with the goblet and looks down at it.

"Are you all right?" I ask softly.

He shakes his head, as if troubled by a fly. "Fine."

"Merek—"

"I don't want to talk about it. Ever. I'd prefer to excise it from all memory. Are you all right?"

"I'm fine. So what did it say?" I ask. "The message."

All traces of awkwardness vanish from his face, replaced with a bright, triumphant expression. "They struck again. The Rising Dawn. Last night. Here, in Lortune itself." He pauses for effect, and I stare at him, openmouthed. "They daubed *The Rising Dawn* and drew the half sun on the door of the sheriff's house. And then they released a dozen live rats via a window. The sheriff was woken up by his wife's shrieking." He almost smiles. "The letter begged forgiveness, said a patrol had passed every ten minutes and that they neither saw nor heard anything until the screaming started. There was no sign of how they got in; no one left their posts, no one saw anything."

"About time they showed up here," I say. "I was beginning to think they'd forgotten about Lortune."

Merek makes an amused sound. "It makes me wonder, though . . ." He frowns, and walks to the window, his back to me as he trails a finger down the shutters, tracing the grain of the wood. "How do they work?"

"What do you mean?"

"Think about it, Errin. In the last two moons, there have been Rising Dawn messages left across the land, beginning in Chargate,

114

then Haga, Monkham, and now, finally, here." He turns to me, his eyes bright in the firelight, a spot of color high on each cheek. "Same words. Same sigil. Eight weeks after the first message was left in Chargate, after working their way across the country, they attack—for want of a better word—here and, as you say, finally. They *finally* strike in the heart of his power. Now, there's no way the townspeople themselves could be behind the attack; Aurek is doing everything he can to keep the Dawn's activities quiet, no one is allowed to speak of it—we've all been warned to hold our tongues or lose them. And no one, save Aurek's most trusted men, is allowed to travel between towns. So either Aurek's own men are organizing or aiding a rebellion—which is unlikely—or the Rising Dawn is somehow infiltrating the towns. And if that's the case, what if they're rooting cells inside them, one by one. Not getting in and then out, but just getting in, waiting for the right moment to rise up—"

"Merek . . ."

"They're gathering support." Merek walks back to the table and picks up the goblet, raising it to his lips. "They're spreading their message. They're preparing people to fight back. That's why it took them so long to get here. This is it."

"You're jumping to conclusions, Mer." I put my book down and cross my arms. "The townspeople would be the first to hand the rebels in if they were here—their children are being held hostage. There's no way they'd tolerate strangers in their midst. He's counting on it; that's where his power is. And there's nothing to suggest the Rising Dawn is doing anything anywhere other than just passing through, leaving messages to keep hope alive. I'm not criticizing them!" I say when his expression darkens. "If anything, I'm glad they're being smart about it. Anything more might make him retaliate against innocents."

He frowns, taking another sip of the wine. "Maybe."

"Definitely. And I know you don't want that."

"Of course I don't," he snaps. "They're my people, Errin. They're the reason I stayed."

I let out a long sigh. "Give me some of that?" I ask, and he brings it to me. I drink, and pass it back to him, mixed feelings battling for dominance. On the one hand, I need the bright burst of joy when Rising Dawn messages are reported, because it means someone—hopefully, Twylla—is out there fighting back. It means Merek and I aren't alone.

But at the same time, there's terror every time the Rising Dawn does anything, because of the children. Ever since I learned he had golems sweep the towns in the dead of night, instructed to take the children from their beds, I've been torn between secretly cheering the rebels on and being frightened their assaults will make him lash out in an even harsher way.

The people have been promised the children will be kept safe, and returned, when Aurek believes the people can be trusted. But if they do anything rash, or rebellious . . . He left the threat unspoken, because he didn't need to say it aloud. If anyone tries anything against him, the children will suffer. And Aurek doesn't know the meaning of mercy—he even had nursing babies ripped from their mother's arms.

The thing that frightens me the most is that I can't help but wonder if I gave him the idea, when he saw how much I would do to save Lief and Mama. The power of *family first*.

"Say you're right," I begin. "Say they are somehow here in Lortune. What do we do?"

"We find them, and we join them." He says it so quickly I know he's been waiting to. Eventually, we always come back to this point.

"I can't leave," I remind him. "You know I can't. Not while Silas is here and not while Aurek has that . . . thing to control me."

"He's going to kill you if you stay, you know that."

"Not if I behave myself."

Merek raises an eyebrow.

"Shut up," I tell him. "I'm trying, at least."

"We're back to square one, then," Merek says, handing the last of the wine to me. "Waiting. For something." His mouth is set in a hard line.

"For Silas." I try to comfort him. "Sooner or later, Aurek will slip up, we'll find out where Silas is, and then we can all run." The second I allow myself to think of him, it's like I've been punched in the stomach. I wrap my arms around myself, battening down the waves of panic that roll through me. "Perhaps we could tie me up, to stop me from doing anything under *his* control? I'm sure between the two of you, we could manage."

"If we could find another alchemist . . ."

"Don't even think of it," I spit, and Merek falls silent.

He runs a hand through his hair. "I promised the people safety. The day they crowned me I swore to the land I'd bring them peace and prosperity and freedom. I promised progress. Every day that passes is a day I fail them further. I need to do *something*."

"Go, then." I fail to keep my voice even. "Go and find her. She needs you."

"And leave you here?"

"Yes. I don't want to be the reason you believe you're failing your people. Go."

He takes a deep breath and holds his hand out for the goblet.

"It's empty," I say.

He tuts softly and then sighs, running a hand over his head again. "For the best. Listen, I'm sorry, Errin. I shouldn't take it out on you. I'm just . . . I should be the one coordinating a rebellion. I should be leading this. It's my responsibility. I'm angry with myself, not you."

"It's fine. But you should go." I try to smile. "If there's a revolution happening, then you need to be a part of it."

"Do you really think Twylla would forgive me if I left you behind?" He takes a deep breath and stretches. "If I go, then you're coming with me. *When* I go, you're coming with me. You and Silas."

I smile. "Agreed."

Merek sighs. "I suppose I'd better go. Some of us have to be up at dawn to start scrubbing chamber pots."

"The thrilling life of the undercover king," I say. "Will I see you tomorrow?"

"If it's safe. I'll come in the afternoon."

He reaches out and grips my shoulder, gently squeezing it, then picks up the goblet and leaves. I close my book with a thump, sending dust blooming into the air, coughing as I stand. I'm about to slip it back onto the shelf, when I change my mind and toss it onto the fuel pile instead. Merek said it was outdated.

I thumb through some of the other titles, hoping this might be the time I see the book on alchemy that I missed all the other times. Merek's mother apparently collected everything she could on it, and yet I've found nothing in here. Either they were stored somewhere else or Aurek removed them long ago. I pull out one book on botany and flick through it, but I drop it when the door to the library flies open and Merek stands there, his eyes wide.

Aurek's coming for me, I think. *I've pushed him too far somehow. This is it.*

But I'm wrong.

"Lief's returned," he gasps.

Chapter 9

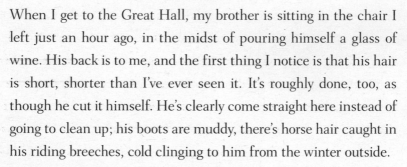

When I get to the Great Hall, my brother is sitting in the chair I left just an hour ago, in the midst of pouring himself a glass of wine. His back is to me, and the first thing I notice is that his hair is short, shorter than I've ever seen it. It's roughly done, too, as though he cut it himself. He's clearly come straight here instead of going to clean up; his boots are muddy, there's horse hair caught in his riding breeches, cold clinging to him from the winter outside.

He turns slightly at the sound of my knock against the already open door, and I see his profile, as familiar to me as my own face. Then he looks back to Aurek, who is watching me with an amused expression.

"Errin," he says. "This is a surprise. Usually, I have to summon you. Longing for my company, were you? Missing me terribly?"

"I . . ." I look at Lief's back, resolutely turned from me.

"Or did you somehow sense your brother had returned? He's barely sat down and yet here you are. I was a twin, so I know about the sibling bond. The mysterious power of it." He smiles silkily. "That must be it. Because otherwise, the only conclusion I can reach is that you were spying." The smile drops, leaving his face blank of expression.

I shake my head rapidly. "I was in the library. A servant saw him arrive and came to tell me."

Aurek gives me a long look, and then a slow, silky smile curves his lips. "Fine. I suppose you may join us. Aren't we all family here, after all? Come, sit down. Share in the news."

Throughout this, Lief stays silent and unmoving. The only other chair is on the other side of the table, opposite him, and I feel Aurek watching me, his mouth a smiling trap as I walk around the table.

When I look over at my brother and I see his face, I understand why Aurek is smiling like he's waiting for the punch line.

Lief wears a patch over his right eye.

I gasp. "What happened?" I forget Aurek, forget that I hate my brother. There is a purple scar snaking from beneath the patch like lightning, bisecting his cheek down almost level with his lip. It's healed badly, pulling the skin tight, so the right side of his face looks on the verge of a sneer. His other eye looks brighter beside it, but not wholly human. He looks . . . feral.

"Ah-ah." Aurek holds a hand up. "We'll get to that. Let's get the business out of the way first, shall we?"

"It's done, Your Grace," Lief says, his wound giving him a faint lisp, dragging his words into a hiss. He pulls something from his pocket, a bundle in green velvet, and stands, taking it to Aurek, before returning to his seat. I can't stop staring at him, and his skin flushes, as though he can feel my gaze.

121

Aurek opens the package Lief gave him and smiles, placing it on the table so I can see it. I crane my neck and peer inside. I know what it is instantly, even though I've never seen it in real life before, only ever seen its mark once or twice.

Nestled in the cloth is a wooden handle, polished conker red and smooth, with a large, thick gold disc at its end. I know that on that disc, etched into the metal, is a vast and multi-branched tree, its roots spreading just as far beneath the ground as its canopy does into the sky.

The Seal of Tregellan: made from the melted crowns of our former royals and forged the morning of their execution to represent the new republic of Tregellan. Now come full circle back to a king's rule. Every law, edict, bill, and mandate passed in the last one hundred years wore this seal, to declare the democratic decision of the Council. My own Apothecary Pledge was stamped with it and sent back to Master Pendie. My License to Practice would have been sealed with it, too, and hung where I worked so all could see I was Council approved, the seal legitimizing me.

I realize as I've been staring at it that my brother and Aurek have continued talking.

". . . Tressalyn is yours now; the rest of Tregellan will fall in line soon after. The terms were more than acceptable to the majority of the Council, and those few who opposed were . . . removed from office," Lief tells him.

"And you have the alchemists?" Aurek says.

"All five. Retrieved and awaiting your pleasure, Your Grace. Their escorts have been dispatched. Two of the Sisters."

"And the Sin Eater girl?"

I hold my breath, hoping—praying—he knows nothing.

"Conflicting reports indicate she's in both Penaluna and Scarron, Your Grace." He taps his fingers on the table. "If I were to guess, though . . . I'd say she fled to Scarron. She's a creature of habit, and cowardice. She'll go where she feels safe, where she believes she has sanctuary. Here, she hid in her temple when things didn't go her way. Out there, it was Scarron she fled to once she left here. She'll cling to what she knows."

Aurek nods. "So you have people on their way there, yes?"

Lief pauses. "No, Your Grace. I took the liberty of instructing a company to head to Penaluna, and to make their presence known en route."

"Why?" Aurek stares at him.

"Because if rumor reaches her, as I'm sure it will, that she's being sought there, it'll be easier for me to approach Scarron and capture her. I plan to leave within the next few days, with your permission. If she's there, I'll be back with her a fortnight tonight. My word on it."

Aurek laughs, throwing his head back. "Granted, of course. Excellent. Really, really excellent work. You expect her to be alone?"

Lief nods. "As good as. The price on her head is enough to tempt all but the saintliest into handing her in. And she's not exactly accomplished at endearing herself to people."

Aurek purses his lips. "Hmmm. Yet she has support. You've heard of this group—that call themselves the Rising Dawn?"

I don't move a muscle, but something in my face must give me away, because Aurek looks to me. "Something you'd like to add, Errin?" he asks. I remain silent.

"I have," Lief says, when Aurek turns his attention back to him. "My men in Chargate and Monkham both wrote seeking instructions as soon as the first incidents occurred. I gave orders to increase the patrols and to capture, not kill, anyone they found committing offenses."

"*Not* kill?"

"I can't extract information from the dead, Your Grace."

Aurek smiles again, clearly thrilled with him. Lief the strategist. He sounds even less like my brother than he did in the bone temple.

"There was an incident here last night," Aurek tells him. "The Rising Dawn, daubed across the sheriff's home. Their symbol on the walls. And rats. Live ones. Released into the sheriff's home."

I see the corner of Lief's good eye twitch. "Here? In Lortune?"

"Here. I need to know who did it, and how. I worry"—Aurek pauses, frowning—"I worry that perhaps your control over my men isn't as absolute as we believe. If she is in Scarron, it means there are people here acting as her agents, people with power and access to gates, walls, and so on . . ."

Lief reaches for his wine. "Your Grace, I can assure you—"

"I don't need your assurances, Lief," Aurek says. "I need to know who in your ranks is a supporter of the Sin Eater bitch and I need their heads on my gates. I don't hold you responsible for it. Yet. Don't fail me, my brother."

"Yes, Your Grace," my brother says, bowing his head.

I relax somewhat. If Aurek thinks that the dissenters are his own men, he's unlikely to hurt the children; his supporters are the only ones whose families have been left intact.

"Good. You've done well, my friend. Now, let's talk about this scar. Will you have some Elixir for it? I could have some brought to you in a matter of moments." Aurek shoots me a sly glance and my stomach gives a now familiar twist as my thoughts turn straight to Silas. I don't make a sound, though. I don't move a muscle.

"I'd prefer to keep it, actually. As a reminder not to underestimate the slipperiness of women."

"Ahhh, so a *woman* bested you in a fight."

Lief smiles with the left side of his face. "A Sister, Your Grace. To be precise, two Sisters. On the King's Road, while collecting your alchemists. They're ugly, but they fight well."

"I take it they're fighting on some other plane now?"

"What's left of them, Your Grace." Lief smiles, and I scowl at him.

"I'm glad Father never lived to see this," I say quietly, the words slipping from my mouth before I can pull them back. I don't risk looking at Aurek, keeping my focus on my brother. But he doesn't offer me the same courtesy; instead, he throws me the briefest of glances, then sips his wine, and the snub is like a slap.

"Ah." Aurek claps his hands, the sound startling me. "That reminds me, did you find your mother?"

"What?" I stare at Lief, reeling once more, though this time I don't care what Aurek thinks or does. Not in that moment. "Lief?" He raises his glass again, ignoring me, and I lunge out of my chair and reach across the table, smacking it from his hand. "You have Mama? You brought her *here*?"

I cannot believe he brought her to this place—to be trapped as I am. With *him*. Aurek howls with laughter, slapping the table again, and Lief turns with slow, exaggerated motions to watch the goblet as it spins on the floor. Lief shrugs, then looks at Aurek, still avoiding my eye, and gestures to the bottle on the table.

"By all means," Aurek says, and Lief reaches for the bottle, drinking from that instead. "Do you see what I've had to put up with in your absence?"

"I apologize for my sister, Your Grace."

"Don't you dare," I snarl at him. "Don't you dare speak for me when you won't even look at me. Where is she?"

Lief puts the bottle down. "Might I go and refresh myself, Your Grace?" he asks, ignoring me.

"Of course. See your mother settled, do what you need to, and I'll see you in my presence chamber. We have much to discuss. And, seemingly, to celebrate."

"Lief." My voice climbs into a shout. "Look at me."

Lief stands and bows. "Your Grace is kind." He wheels around and leaves, as though I'm not even in the room.

"Lief!" I call. He closes the door behind him, not with a slam but with slow deliberateness, and I stare after him, my heart thudding in my chest.

"Would you like to see your mother, Errin?" Aurek says softly.

I turn to him, every inch costing me. "You know I would."

"Then just ask, sweetling. That's all it'll take. Just ask."

It's a trap. It must be. I stay silent.

"No? You don't want to see her? You can't bring yourself to say 'please' to me?"

I can't take the chance that he might, for once, be telling the truth.

"Please," I hear myself say. "Please, can I see my mother . . . ? Your Grace?" I add.

He rises and walks the length of the table, coming to stand in front of me. "So you can be nice when you want to be." He lifts a pale hand and strokes my hair, and I wait for his fingers to tighten, clenching my teeth together, braced for the yank I'm sure is coming. But it doesn't. He cups my cheek and looks into my eyes. "Keep it up, and we'll see. But you have to learn to behave, sweetling. I'll have no unbroken mares in my stable. Ask me again tomorrow. Ask me as nicely." He leans in and presses a kiss against my forehead, and even though it makes my stomach lurch with disgust, I hold myself still.

He pulls away, clicking his fingers to summon the dogs, and leaves me alone in the Great Hall. The Seal of Tregellan is still on the table, and I walk to it, picking it up. It's lighter than I expected. I close my eyes.

I lie in bed, but sleep won't come. I've jammed a chair under the door; I have done this every night since I thought he was going to make me jump from the window. Not that I expect it to stop him from entering if he chooses, but it will at least give me warning. Though he hasn't come into my dreams at all since then.

I roll over onto my stomach. I wonder where Lief is now—if he sleeps, or if he sits with Aurek still, laughing together. The thought makes me furious and I flip onto my back, hitting the pillow with my fist. I'm furious that he brought Mama here. Aurek told me he'd gone to fetch her, but I didn't believe him. I'd thought she would be safe enough in Tressalyn, safer than anywhere else. And now she's here. With me, and Silas. Trapped.

I don't know how Silas is. I only know he still lives because Aurek is radiant these days, his beauty and vitality obscene compared to the castle and people around him.

I move onto my side and bunch the covers up and around my ears, watching the shadows move around the room as the night passes. When the dawn comes I'm still awake, eyes staring at nothing. I sit up when someone tries to enter the room, a muffled voice swearing. Merek. Finally. I stumble out of bed and pull the chair away, flinging the door open.

And look into the face of my brother.

He pauses in the doorway, a tray of food in his hand. He's dressed head to toe in black, his scar just as shocking in the morning light as it was last night. As I take him in, see the lines on his forehead, the stubble on his jaw, he examines me in return, his one eye assessing me before it flits around the room, moving from the bed, to the bureau, then the window, and I see the tic in his jaw as he looks around him.

"I expect it's different in here from when you last saw it," I say, and his green eye flashes as it comes to rest on me once more. Merek told me what Twylla had not. The truth of what my brother did to her, and to him.

"And you wonder why you're having a hard time here," Lief says quietly.

For a moment I consider telling him what Aurek has done to me while he's been away doing his dirty work. I think about telling him that his precious king keeps a doll in his pocket, made of clay mixed with my hair and my blood, and he uses it to make me eat, make me dance, make me do whatever he wants. That I've woken up and found myself standing on one leg at the top of the stairs, teetering precariously, or underneath my bed with my face pressed into the dust, and I know that it means that somewhere in the castle Aurek is sleepless and amusing himself by toying with me.

That sometimes he has me climb into his lap and sit there while he strokes my hair and tells me about the old days in Tallith.

The seven towers of Tallith castle and the walkways between them, his life with his sister and his father. That sometimes he sounds so wistful and lonely that I forget for an instant that he's a monster, lulled by his soft voice and his hands in my hair. Until he turns my face to his and I see him, and I recall exactly what he is, and the look in my eyes reminds him that he might control my body, but he can't control my mind. Then he throws me to the ground and leaves me there for hours, unable to move until he wills it. I could tell him about the times the rightful king of Lormere has had to carry me to my rooms and clean me as I once cleaned our mother because Aurek's neglect, or malice, has meant I've soiled myself.

But I don't, because I'm too frightened that he already knows and that he doesn't care. When Aurek first made the doll of me, I was filled with the wild hope that Lief's actions and behavior were because he was being controlled, too. I thought maybe he hadn't betrayed me, or Tregellan. I wondered if he was a puppet, too. But he's not. He chooses this.

He carries the tray to the bureau and places it on top before he walks to the window and pulls open the shutters.

"Leave them, it's freezing in here."

"It smells stale in here," he says mildly. "It needs airing. I'll ask for your fuel ration to be increased. You might as well have mine while I'm not here."

"Ration? It's being rationed? Is that what he told you?"

"Errin, it is being rationed. Until things are stabilized, there will be some shortages."

I shake my head at him. "He has meat on the table every night. And fresh vegetables."

Lief sighs and rubs the bridge of his nose. "How are you?" he says, his voice still maddeningly soft.

"Are you joking?" I say.

He opens his mouth, but then appears to bite back whatever it was he'd been about to say. "You'll be pleased to know Lirys is alive. And Carys, too. They've been moved to Tressalyn and accommodated there. As my personal guests."

I stare at him, and he stares back, and I get the impression he's waiting for me to thank him. When I remain silent, blinking dumbly, he nods at the tray.

"It's bread and butter, porridge, and an egg."

"Doesn't it bother you?" I say finally.

"Does what bother me?" he replies, an edge creeping into his tone.

"This. All of this. For starters, me being here. In rags. You know whose dress this was, don't you?" He remains silent. "I'm your sister," I say. "What happened to *family first*?"

At that he whips around, his face cold. "Where do you think I've just come from, Errin?"

"I *know* where you've just come from. From murdering our countrymen on *his* orders."

"I came from seeing to our mother. Our mother, who I brought here from an asylum," he says.

"Are you really blaming me for that? You left us, remember? You left us for three moons. If anyone is to blame for her state, it's you." He doesn't reply, and the silence between us thickens, congeals like fat. "How . . . how is she?" I ask when it becomes too much, and he flinches but says nothing, and I become aware of each heartbeat becoming a hard, dread-filled thing in my chest. "Lief?"

He half turns so his face is caught in profile against the wintry light. "I don't know. She doesn't eat. Or sleep. She just stares. She can't . . . She won't take care of herself. At all." Then he turns to face me. "Is this what she was like, why she was in that place? Because she's mad?"

"She's not mad." I step forward. "*He* does it to her."

"Does what?"

"Ask him. Ask him about the simulacrum. Ask him what he did with them, to her. To me. He made dolls of us. He came into my dreams at night and he made her attack me, every full moon. He called it his 'little joke.' For three moons he did it. He's doing it still. He must be. Can't you see; he's a monster. You're working for a monster."

"I can't—" Lief says, and strides across the room, back to the door.

I step toward him, hands raised, and he grabs my wrists, wrenching a cry from me at the flash of pain his grip brings. He releases me straightaway, his face ashen.

"Forgive me," he says, reaching for me, but I step back.

"Listen to me," I hiss at him. "He spent three moons whispering in her mind. She was already grieving Papa, and then you vanished, seemingly into thin air. And while you murdered your way across Lormere on his orders, he was in her head, making her act like a beast."

Lief shakes his head, and I curl my lip back to show him my chipped tooth. "She did this while he was controlling her. She attacked me and pulled me to the floor. Our mama, Lief. Does that sound like her to you? Ask Silas. He'll tell you. He was there. While you were gone, he was there and he saw it all."

He looks down at the floor, and there's a moment when I think I might finally have reached him. But then he raises his head, his eye fixed on the door behind me. "I'll come and escort you to dinner later," he says quietly. "Try to wear something that fits you tonight."

"This is all I have!" I fly to the wardrobe and throw the door open. "Her summer clothes. That's all I have."

"You could have asked for something warmer," Lief says. "I'll have something sent up." With that he turns and leaves.

I hear his footsteps on the stairs, slow, unhurried, and I shout after him. "Why don't you care?"

When the door slams, I throw myself down onto the bed and scream into the musty pillow until my throat is raw and I'm trembling from the cold, or the horror, I don't know which. I roll onto my back and stare up at the ceiling, unable to stop shaking. I pull the covers back over me but I can't get warm.

He has me and Mama, and Silas and Lief. Silas he will bleed dry for the Elixir. He will kill me when he has wearied of me. And Lief, too, most likely, if only he knew it.

And I realize then that none of us will make it out of this alive. Not me, not Silas, and not Mama.

Chapter 10

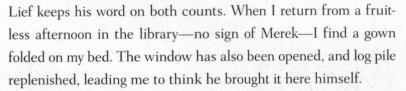

Lief keeps his word on both counts. When I return from a fruit-less afternoon in the library—no sign of Merek—I find a gown folded on my bed. The window has also been opened, and log pile replenished, leading me to think he brought it here himself.

The dress is creased, and smells musty, and has obviously been salvaged from a storage chest. When I hang it to air, there are black mildew spots on the lace collar and cuffs, and a layer of dust puffs out, causing me to recoil. But it's longer than any of Twylla's dresses, and the thick blue velvet promises a little more warmth, too. When I try it on, it's too big, but still an improvement. And, hopefully, the smell will keep Aurek away from me.

Lief says nothing about it when he comes to collect me. He's in black again, and in the shadowy corridors his face looks harsh, the eye patch adding to the impression. He moves with purpose, the loss of one eye seemingly not causing him any problems.

"Whose dress was it?" I ask when it becomes clear he isn't going to speak. "Was it the queen's?"

For a moment he is silent. Then, "I don't know."

"Where did you find it?"

"In a chest."

"How's Mama?"

"Resting. It was a long journey."

"When can I see her?" When he doesn't reply, I ask again. "Lief, I want to see her. When?"

"When His Grace permits it."

He's saved from my response as we round the corner to the Great Hall and the doors swing open, manned by the golems Aurek keeps close to him as a personal guard.

Lief drops into a bow as soon as he crosses the threshold, and after a moment I do the same, reluctantly bending at the knee toward Aurek. But when I raise my head, he's not looking at me, or at Lief. Instead he's bent over papers, ignoring the food at the table.

Lief hesitates, until Aurek murmurs at us, "Sit," and like obedient children we all but tiptoe to the table, Lief at Aurek's right, and me two places away from him.

Still, Aurek does not look up; instead, he pushes a piece of paper toward Lief, who begins to read it. I crane my neck to read it, too, but Lief shoots a scowl at me and moves his arm to block it from my view, continuing to read.

He looks up sharply. "Have there been more incidents like this, Your Grace?"

Aurek nods his head, silver hair trailing on the table, his eyes still on the paper he's engrossed by. "Chargate. The soldiers put it down. Four of them lost their lives in the process."

"Is there . . . Do you know why?" Lief asks.

"It's of no real consequence," Aurek says, rustling through the sheaf. "It's always been a problem; eventually, they become harder to manage, the longer they exist. Mostly, it means we need to rely on soldiers more, outside of the castle, or anywhere I am not."

"I'll see to it. And have the men replaced."

Aurek nods, and then looks up. His eyes narrow as they land on me; apparently he's only just realizing I'm there, too.

"What are you doing here?"

"I . . . I came for supper."

"Did I summon you?" he asks, but it's not meant as a question, not really.

"I brought her, Your Grace." Lief surprises me by speaking up. "Forgive me."

"Seek my permission next time," Aurek says coldly. "I'll feel more inclined to indulge your love for your sister when she manages to find hers for me."

"Yes, Your Grace."

"Leave," Aurek tells me. "We'll have food sent to you."

As soon as he's stopped speaking, the golems on the doors pull them open, ponderously stretching out their arms in tandem. I push back from the table and stand, dropping the briefest of curtsies before I flee the room, shivering as I pass them, my head full of thoughts. What were they talking about? Put what down? What's always been a problem? Not the Rising, surely? But what else could it be?

135

I need to speak to Merek, but another servant eventually brings my supper to me, and I can't risk arousing suspicion by asking for him. Tomorrow, I tell myself. I'll find him tomorrow.

It's hours later and I'm just getting warm enough to drift off to sleep when the door opens, swinging back on its hinges and smashing into the wall, as Aurek flies across the room at me.

I barely have time to sit up, to cry out, before he's gripped my wrist in one hand and cut my left palm, releasing my wrist to take the simulacrum from his pocket. When I move away he points the knife at me, a silent warning, and I still at once. He keeps his eyes fixed on mine as he presses the doll against the cut.

"Hold it," he demands, curling my fingers over it to keep it in place. He slices the tip of his own thumb and we both watch as a bead of blood, red as mine, wells up. Then he takes the simulacrum from me, smearing his blood into the clay, mingling with mine. As we both watch, our blood is absorbed, the surface of the poppet is clean, as if it never happened.

Then he leaves without a word, closing the door behind him. I stagger out of bed and tear a strip of fabric from one of Twylla's dresses, using it to bind my hand, breathing slowly in an attempt to calm my racing heart. I stare down at my hand, watching the blood seep through the fabric, winding another strip over it. I hate when he does this.

Then a new thought occurs to me: Why does he do it?

Why does he have to come and take more blood? I trace a finger over the bandage and try to recall all the times he's cut me, pressing the clay to the wounds. Often. Usually after I've done something particularly vexing to him. I'd just thought he was being cruel, reminding me I was under his power. But what if there's more to it . . .

I remember once, in the early days here, in the war room, one of his miniature golems began to move without his command. He crushed it, telling me, "It's no good when they start to do as they will." I hadn't thought about it before, but it means that after a while, they do things he hasn't instructed them to.

Was he talking about his golems tonight? In Chargate, and the other place. Have those he sent out into Lormere started to act of their own accord? I play his and Lief's conversation over and over, and the more I think about it, the surer I become. The longer they exist, the more his golems will start to behave independently, especially if he's not there to keep giving them commands. I'd stake my life on it.

And that must mean that if he doesn't keep adding fresh blood to the simulacrum of me, sooner or later he won't be able to use it to control me, either.

I lie back against the pillow, acutely aware that I won't get any sleep tonight, my mind a hive of thoughts.

I receive a note from Aurek the next morning, before I've dressed, informing me that I won't be required at dinner tonight, nor the night following. That's exactly what it says: "Won't be required," as though I'm the scheduled entertainment that has been postponed. I suppose for Aurek I am. It's cursory, that single line, and it tells me he's preoccupied, too busy to bait me.

Still, I demand that the servant who brought the note wait, and I write back, as politely as I can, asking if I might see my mother. Three hours slip by while I wait for a reply, and the walls close in, inch by inch, until I can't stand it. So I grab my cloak and leave my rooms, intent on tracking down Merek. But at the bottom of the stairs, a surprise: two men, waiting outside the tower door, clearly acting as guards.

We all stare; clearly, none of us expected to see one another.

"Am I a prisoner?" I ask.

The guards exchange a glance. "No," one ventures after a moment, though he doesn't sound sure.

"Then what are you doing here?"

"Captain Vastel asked us to make sure you were attended," the same guard replies.

"Did he?"

They both nod.

"What are your orders?"

"We're to accompany you around the castle, and keep you from harm."

I glare at the men, but there's no humor in their words. Fools.

"Has Captain Vastel mentioned anywhere that might be . . . particularly unsafe?" I ask.

"We've been asked to keep you from the north tower—that is, the Tower of Victory—and the Tower of Valor. You're permitted everywhere else, so long as we're with you."

The Tower of Victory—the former north tower, which Merek told me was originally used for the Telling and funerals—is where Aurek keeps his chambers. The south tower—the Tower of Valor—was where the Lormerian royal family lived. Though I can't be sure, I'd be willing to bet it's where Lief's quarters are, and where my mother is, too.

"Why am I not permitted to go to the Tower of Valor?" I test them. "What if I need to see my brother?"

The second guard, silent until now, finally speaks in a firm tone. "If you need to see him, you'd better ask us to send word to him."

So not both fools, then. This one knows it's not my safety anyone is worried about. "Of course. May I ask your names, if you are to accompany me everywhere?"

The men silently confer again, and then the chattier one shrugs. "I'm Crayne," he says. "This is Thurn."

"Well, Crayne and Thurn," I say. "I need to go to the library."

I don't speak again, turning away and sweeping down the corridor as best I can. My breath is visible, white in the chilly air. I'm wearing another dress of Twylla's, green this time, heavy cotton. It's less tight than the red one, and marginally thicker, but still exposes my ankles to the bitter air, and makes me wary of breathing too deeply. As I round the corner to the library, something falls to the ground, just missing me; I look down and see ice. There are icicles hanging from the unlit candelabras. I glance at both men to see if they are shocked, but their faces are carefully blank, and when I look closer I see the fur lining their cloaks. When we arrive at the library I step inside, and to my horror, Thurn steps inside with me, jamming his foot into the door as I try to close it.

"I'd like to be alone," I say.

"Captain's orders are that outside of your tower, one of us is to keep you in sight at all times."

"But I'm perfectly safe in here." I throw the door wide and gesture at the empty room.

Thurn says nothing, stepping past me and taking up a position by the door. When I scowl at him he reaches out and pulls it shut, raising his eyebrows at me.

I turn my back on him and walk to the shelves, shaking with rage. I keep my back to him and thumb through the books, as if looking for a specific one. I need to tell Merek what I learned last night at dinner, and what Lief said this morning, but he won't be able to linger here with a guard listening in. Especially one who seems less dim than usual. Merek is confident that no one here knows who he truly is, sure his altered appearance, and the fact he was only back in the castle for a moon before Aurek came, means he's unfamiliar to everyone here. But I was able to recognize him, and I'd rather he didn't risk it with anyone else. Especially now that Lief is here. Merek has to stay away from Lief.

I pull a volume from the shelves and take it to the table, leaving it there on the pretense of looking for something else, trying to think. I need to see Merek. With my lovely new guard, it seems the only place I'll be alone is in my rooms, but will they insist on accompanying a servant in? I need a reason for him to stay longer than it would take for him to deliver or fetch a tray. I pull another book down and add it to the first. I keep doing this, pretending to choose books that I need, all the time racking my brains for a way to get Merek to return to my rooms and keep him there for at least five or ten minutes. Enough time to tell him my suspicions about the golems, and the simulacrum; that's all I need.

Thurn coughs pointedly, and I shoot him a sharp glance, which he returns levelly. So I add another book to my stack and drag a stool over to the shelves in the corner, standing on it and looking at the dusty spines of the books there. One catches my eye and I pull it out. The cover feels familiar against my fingers, and yet strange at the same time. It's less tattered and stained than the book I knew, as would befit being kept in a royal library.

The Sleeping Prince, and Other Stories.

It might have something useful in it. There's supposedly a kernel of truth in every fairy tale.

I place it on the top of the pile and lift it, staggering over to the amused-looking Thurn. "Here." I shove them into his chest hard, forcing him to react instinctively and grab them. "Bring these to my room." I pull the door open and stride out, biting back a grin that feels like a stranger to my face.

Back in my tower, I sit at the bureau and wait, flicking through one of the books without seeing the words. I pace, and I pick up a new book and attempt to read it, but I can't concentrate. I can't stop fidgeting, either. Merek said Twylla would spend whole days up here, leaving only to pray in her temple, and I have no idea how she managed it. What did she do up here; how did she keep from going mad? No wonder she was so quick to fall for Lief; he must have been the first exciting thing that had happened to her in years.

I build a fire and sit in front of it, waiting. Sooner or later, someone will come with food, and I just have to hope that it's Merek this time. Hopefully, in the brief moments he can be here without making the guards suspicious, I'll be able to tell him what I know.

But when Merek does come, with a tray of food and a goblet of maybe water, maybe wine, he shakes his head ever so slightly as he enters, giving me a split-second warning before Thurn appears in the doorway behind him. I look at him, my heart sinking, and then to Merek.

"Thank you," I say. I reach out to take the tray, but he doesn't pass it to me, instead lifting the bowl and the goblet from it and placing them on the bureau beside the pile of books. If I wasn't watching, I would have missed the tiny piece of paper that fell from his sleeve into the bowl. He places the spoon atop it, and bows.

"I'll return in an hour for the tray, madam."

"No bother. We can bring it down," Thurn says. He walks over to us and lifts the goblet, sniffing it. "Very nice," he says, peering at it as he puts it back down.

A cold sense of dread starts to build as he examines the tray, and when he reaches for the spoon the note is hidden beneath, I speak. "Then you can fetch my milk posset when you do. And tell the kitchen I want lavender in it. I'm not sleeping well. A hot pan for the bed would be nice, too."

He releases his grip on the spoon as he sneers. "Of course, my lady. Whatever you say, my lady." He turns to Merek. "Did you get all that? Milk and a pan. Bring them."

Merek nods and leaves me, and I sit down at the bureau and lift the goblet. Thurn is still watching me, and I feel a stab of anger toward him. I stare at him. "Did you want something else?"

He smirks. "Let us know when you're finished," he says, and makes to leave.

The moment his back is turned, I scoop the note out and hide it beneath the lip of the bowl, so when he pauses in the doorway and looks back, I'm lowering the spoon and chewing on my tongue. I sit and eat, pretending to read until I can hear him walking away.

I make enough noise with the spoon against the metal bowl to reassure anyone listening, and use my left hand to unfurl the gravy-soaked note. The ink has started to bleed, and there are only a few words written on it. *I'll be back. Play along.*

Play along with what? And when?

I finish the food for want of something to do, and then, despite the early hour, I pull one of Twylla's thin robes over my dress and take the book of fairy tales to the bed. When I hear footsteps on the stairs, I arrange my face into a scowl, expecting one or both of the guards. I'm half-right; it's Thurn, and Merek is with him, a hot pan in one hand and a mug in the other. He walks around the bed, holding the mug out to me.

"Your posset, miss. There's no lavender, I'm afraid."

"Of course not," I say. "That would have been too much to ask for."

He ignores me. "And your hot pan," he says. Then he drops the cup, gasps loudly, and swings the pan high over his head.

As Thurn shouts and springs toward him, and I scream, Merek smashes the pan onto the floor by the bed. It springs open, the hot coals inside flying out, scattering across the room.

"Rat!" Merek bellows, pointing to the pan.

And sure enough, beneath the pan is the body of a rat.

There is a moment of silence when we all are still, Merek pointing at the rat, Thurn looking furious as Crayne storms into the room and looks at us all, trying to understand what's happened. I can smell the coals burning the rushes, and I look at Merek. He winks. I don't know what is meant by the wink, but in a fit of improvisation, I execute a perfect faint.

*　　*　　*

143

They arrange me carefully on the bed and I lie very still while they argue about what to do. Merek goes around the room, extinguishing the coals—I hear the hiss as they burn out—all the while insisting that someone go to Aurek, to warn him that the Rising Dawn may have infiltrated the castle. Crayne agrees with him, but Thurn points out that it's just one rat, and that it is an old castle.

"I've been working here for two years, and I've never seen a rat inside the castle before," Merek insists. "The stables, I'll grant you. But the smell of the dogs normally keeps them out of here."

"It's winter—they're bound to come inside," Thurn says. "And it's not like the dogs come up here."

"True," Crayne says, with no indication of who he's agreeing with. Thurn gives him a filthy look.

"With all due respect, I believe His Grace would want to know about this," Merek says. "I'm sure you heard about the incident in Lortune town . . . At the sheriff's home . . ."

Thurn looks uncomfortable for the first time.

"Look, I'll go to him if you're frightened," Merek says. "You stay here with the lady and make sure she's all right—ladies are often, erm . . . ill after they've fainted—and I'll go and tell him I saw a rat, and I killed it. I'll make it clear to him it was my action, and my decision to tell him. You won't be blamed. I'll tell him you wanted no part of it."

I don't need my eyes to be open to know Thurn will be wearing an ugly expression at Merek's words.

"You will not." I hear the dark edge in his voice. There is silence for a moment, then: "I'll go to His Grace *with* the vermin and tell him it was killed in here." I notice he makes no mention of saying who did the killing. "Crayne, stay on that door. She doesn't leave. No matter if the room fills with rats. And you"—I assume he means Merek, and have to fight to keep my eyes closed—"you'd better clean this up and keep an eye on her." There is a pause, and then he says, "Problem?"

"No," Merek says in a voice just the right side of sullen. Clever, clever Merek.

I hear Thurn leave, and wonder how Merek plans to get rid of Crayne.

But he doesn't need to.

"I'll wait outside," Crayne says. "I'm not much of one for illness."

On cue I sit up and begin to retch loudly, leaning over the bed until I've heard the door swing shut.

"That was disgusting. Talk fast," Merek says.

"That was brilliant," I say in a low voice. "Where did the rat come from?"

"I found it in the stable earlier, already dead. I hid it in my breeches; I was terrified it would fall out halfway up the stairs. I had to walk on the side of my foot."

"Brilliant," I repeat. "Listen, Lief thinks Twylla is in Scarron; he's heading there himself to find her."

Merek shakes his head. "He's wrong. She couldn't coordinate the Rising from there."

"On that, Aurek is suspicious it might be some of his own men, turned traitor. Helping her."

"Is he?"

I nod. "He believes it's the only way they could be so coordinated. Merek, she *might* be in Scarron. It's possible. She's known there; the people would protect her, I'm sure. It would make

145

sense for her to go there." I take a breath. "But there's something else. Aurek was preoccupied at dinner—and he mentioned an incident—two in fact—one in Chargate, and one somewhere else. People died, and said he'd have to *put something down*." Merek looks puzzled. "I think he means the golems. That they started to act without his commands. He's mentioned something along those lines before, but I didn't pay attention then. But I think the golems in Chargate went rogue and had to be stopped. I think the longer they exist, the more independent they become. Eventually, he can't control them, so he has to destroy them."

Merek stares into the distance, frowning. "It would explain a lot. Why he hasn't made an entire army of them. Why he's recruiting men instead . . ." He turns his focus on me. "Wait. Is it possible the simulacrum works the same way?"

I lean forward. "I'm sure of it. He came racing in here last night, not long after he got the news, to get more blood. I think he needs to keep it fresh to maintain control over me."

"This is perfect, don't you see? It means you can leave. We can go and find the Rising."

"If he's just replenished it, it'll be at its strongest. I'd need to wait until it starts to wear off at least before I run, and even then—"

"How long will that take?" he interrupts me.

"I don't know."

"Errin, we can't afford to wait. I won't let anything bad happen, I promise. I won't let you put us at risk."

"You weren't there, in Tremayne," I say. "It was my fault. I underestimated him, and he used it against me, and hundreds of people I knew died because of it. Besides"—I finish what I was trying to say—"I can't leave Silas."

"Don't you think he'd want you to stay—"

"And my mother is here. Lief brought her back with him. I think she's in the Tower of Valor."

Merek swears.

But before he can say any more, we hear voices, male, echoing up the tower stairs.

Merek steps away from the bed as the guards return, and to my absolute horror, my brother is with them.

Merek instantly lowers his head, bending into a low bow, shrinking away as though he truly is the servant he's pretending to be. Lief doesn't even look at him, fixing his one eye on me.

"Have you ever seen a rat in here before?" he asks.

"No." I keep my voice quiet, trying to sound weak.

Lief peers around the room, his eyes raking everything, and my heart stops when his eyes seem to linger on Merek, still bent over in submission. Lief walks to the bureau and opens the drawers.

"What are you doing?"

"Checking for droppings," he says, rifling through some old papers. I see pictures of flowers on the pages before he closes the drawer. He looks at everything: the drapes, under the bed, in the closet, watched silently by me, the guards.

Finally, he turns back to me.

"You fainted?"

"Briefly. A moment, nothing more."

"Because you saw a rat?"

"It was a shock."

"I'm sure it was. I believe it's common for a lady to experience a fainting fit after seeing one."

Merek becomes utterly still.

"I hope you feel better now," Lief continues. Then he turns to Merek. "Clean the mess up."

Merek nods his still-bowed head, and Lief frowns. But he says nothing else, sweeping from the room, the guards following him like dogs.

I look at Merek and find him staring after Lief, his lips parted.

"What's wrong?" I mouth.

"We're so stupid," he says in a low, flat voice.

"What?"

"Where did you grow up?"

My heart begins to race as realization washes over me: I grew up with my brother on a farm.

There are a lot of rats on farms.

Merek says nothing, instead bending down and gathering together the now cold coals scattered across the floor.

"That was too close," I say as he tosses them into the fireplace. "If he'd paid any attention to you . . ."

He remains silent, still bent, seemingly examining his blackened hands.

"You have to go. Now."

He looks up at me, his eyes wretched. "I know."

Chapter 11

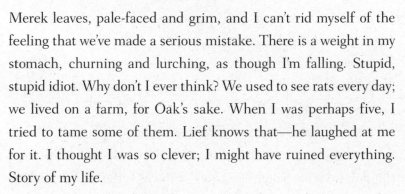

Merek leaves, pale-faced and grim, and I can't rid myself of the feeling that we've made a serious mistake. There is a weight in my stomach, churning and lurching, as though I'm falling. Stupid, stupid idiot. Why don't I ever think? We used to see rats every day; we lived on a farm, for Oak's sake. When I was perhaps five, I tried to tame some of them. Lief knows that—he laughed at me for it. I thought I was so clever; I might have ruined everything. Story of my life.

I try to sleep, but the pitching sensation keeps jolting me awake. Every sound is footsteps coming to arrest me, or Aurek coming to force me to jump from the window. I fret for Merek, imagining him being dragged from wherever he sleeps and interrogated, beaten, tortured. Killed. Dying as a servant in the castle his family built centuries ago. I put the chair under the door, but it doesn't help. I knot myself up, inside and out, tangling my legs in the sheets, sweating despite the cold. What will Lief do?

I must have fallen asleep, because I'm woken by pounding at the door, and shouting. I open my eyes and sit up in the same moment, blinking through the haze in the room. My mouth is suddenly as dry as a bone. This is it.

"Open the bloody door!" one of the guards—maybe Thurn—screams. "Open the door, you silly cow, unless you want to burn to death."

I realize then that the haze in the room isn't from sleep but from smoke, but even then, I don't put it together, looking to my own fireplace in confusion, expecting to see it ablaze, or the candles guttering. I even glance at the floor to see if the rushes are alight, if maybe Merek missed an ember of coal and it's caught. But no . . . that was hours ago—

The door slams against its hinges as someone on the other side tries to force it open, and I fly out of bed, pulling the chair away, standing back as the door swings open and the two guards fall into the room. Behind them, smoke begins to pour in, filling the space, and I look at the guards.

"Move," Thurn says, and I do, racing barefoot down the steps in the dark, gripping the rope rail and moving so fast it takes the skin from my palm. The boots of the men thunder behind me and they burst into the corridor seconds after I do, almost trampling me.

"Fire!" The cries come from everywhere; the smoke is thicker down here, choking, and a new kind of panic bursts in my chest. Thurn grabs my arm roughly and starts to run, dragging me with him. The stones are hard and cold and I try, impossibly, to hold my breath. My eyes sting, and from nowhere I remember the fire I started at Chanse Unwin's house. We fly through a door and I almost fall when the ground becomes a stair, saved only by the guard's grip on my arm. I gasp as cool night air, still smoke-flavored, fills my lungs, and I begin to immediately shiver. Thurn continues to pull me to where a crowd stands, servants and guards, and as we round the walls, I see the source of the fire: the north tower, the Tower of Victory—the tower Aurek claimed for his own.

Flames burst from the windows, lighting up the scene, as smoke mushrooms into the sky, black against the indigo night. Noises echo off the stone walls, glass smashing, the sounds of wood screaming as it tightens and warps in the heat. At the base of the tower, shadows are moving like ants, rushing toward it, throwing buckets of water that mostly go nowhere near the fire; the little water that does reach high enough evaporates into steam immediately.

A cloak is flung around my shoulders, fur-lined and smelling of sweat and wine. I look around to thank whoever gave it to me and see I'm surrounded by a few dozen people, the remains of the staff at the castle, all of them watching the tower silently. I scan each of their faces. I only know Thurn beside me; Crayne has vanished. And I can't see Aurek, or my brother, my mother, or Merek in the crowd.

Merek. Was this his doing—a distraction for his escape?

I turn to the guard. "What happened?"

He doesn't reply, staring at the castle, and I turn back, too. The blaze is traveling; I see it glow in new windows now, spreading from the tower along the corridors.

"All hands to aid!" someone booms in the distance, and a few of the people assembled glance at one another. But no one makes to move, turning back to watch the flames licking the sky.

"All hands!" The owner of the voice looms into view, a burly, huge red-eyed man, black soot smeared across his cheeks, a gold band on his arm. "You." He points into the crowd. "And you. All you men. Get to the chain at the well and help them." The men he's pointed at pause, and then begin to walk away, but they make no effort to hurry. "You two." The man gestures to my guard. "What are you waiting for? Get to it."

"The captain of the guard ordered us to stay with his sister," Thurn says.

"The captain of the guard just gave orders that every able man needs to work on putting out the fire," the man barks. "No exceptions."

"I'll wait for his word on that."

"Oh, will you, now? What's your name?" the man barks.

When Thurn remains silent, I speak up. "He's called Thurn," I say, crying out as Thurn squeezes my arm.

"Well, Master Thurn. You get to the chain and help stop the castle burning to the ground or I'll tell the king you refused to help. I'll tell him you preferred to stay with the women and watch as his home went up in flames. Let's see what he thinks of that."

The air between the men becomes taut with anger, and finally, Thurn lets go of my arm. "You'll pay for that, you little bitch," he hisses in my ear as he passes me. "Crayne," he bellows at his colleague, calling him to heel. Then: "Stay right there," he spits at me. "Woman," he calls to a hooded figure facing the fire. "Watch her."

152

The woman shrugs her agreement. As soon as Thurn and Crayne have jogged out of sight, she turns her back on me. I peer around, searching the crowd for Merek.

Then I see something else. Not Merek. Something even better, and my legs turn to water as I understand what I'm looking at.

A halo of white, seemingly bobbing along, until it vanishes around a corner.

Silas.

Silas Kolby, clad head to toe in black, being led away from the castle by a figure similarly clothed. For a wild moment I think it's Merek with him, and I'm elated, my body poised to run after them. Then I turn to the left to see a parade of people, also in black robes, being led in the opposite direction by a larger escort, each one with their hands behind their backs. All of the alchemists, then, that Aurek has kidnapped, being moved from the castle.

Of course. Aurek must think this is an attack by the Rising Dawn, directly on him. He'll want to be sure they can't rescue the alchemists.

I don't hesitate; I wait only until the group of alchemists has vanished into the pitch black, cast a brief glance at the woman who was supposed to keep an eye on me, and stumble after Silas. I keep my treads as light as possible, following the figures to the stables, watching as they enter one of them. I creep over and edge around the side of the one they're inside, and wait, listening intently. There is no sound, though; neither Silas nor his jailer speaks. I only hear the distant shouts from the castle. I'm about to move, when I hear the squeak of hinges and I freeze, holding my breath at the sound of a barrel sliding into a lock. Then footsteps, fast, as though jogging, becoming fainter as they move farther away.

By the time I've summoned enough courage to move back to the front, I can't see anyone, only the glowing outline of the tower where the flames illuminate it.

I take a deep breath and pull back the bolt on the stable door before creeping inside.

I find Silas in the third stall along, bound to a hook on the wall. Whoever brought Silas here has left a torch in a bracket, and the kindness of not leaving him in the dark surprises me. The hood has fallen, or been shaken from his head; his hair has grown so it sticks out around him like a dandelion. His back is to me; even from behind I can see he's gloved, and he turns sharply as I gasp. Above the gag between his teeth, his eyes widen.

For one beat of my heart I can't move, can't believe he's here, that he's standing up, that he's still strong enough to have hate in his eyes, hate that vanishes when he sees me.

Then I'm on him, throwing my arms and legs around him. He staggers, and we both fall back into a pile of sweetly rotting hay.

"Sorry, Silas, I'm sorry." I clamber off him and pull the gag from his mouth.

He laughs and then groans. "Untie me?"

His voice paralyzes me for a moment, as husky and secretive as ever. I'd imagined it, over and over, but my rememberings were so much less than the actual sound of him speaking. I reach down and tug the knots at his wrist until the rope falls away, and the moment his arms are free, they're around me and I'm pulled against his slim body. My own arms snake up around his neck and

I press into him. He kisses the top of my head, again and again, showering my hair with kisses.

"I didn't know if you were really here," he says, his covered fingers moving to my face, stroking it, as I do the same to him, brushing his hair back when it falls in his eyes. "I asked every day if you were here, and they wouldn't say. I didn't want you to be here."

"It doesn't matter now. Can you run? Are you hurt?"

He shakes his head but doesn't meet my eye. I sit back, take his hands, and pull off the gloves.

It's both worse and better than I could have hoped for. Aurek had made me believe the Nigredo was so advanced that Silas was all but bed-bound, but in reality it's still just his hands. Every finger is black now, both thumbs, and the palms and backs of his hands, too. I push the cuffs of his tunic back and see that it's spread along his arm, coming to a stop a few inches below the inside crease of his elbow, a mimic of the gloves he wore to hide it. I bend and kiss the skin where dark meets light, on both arms, and look up to find him watching me, his head tilted, and my heart stutters.

"I thought it would be worse," I say, swallowing the catch in my throat.

He shakes his head, taking my hands in his. The cursed skin feels cool against mine, calming me. "He can't afford to go too far, can he? He needs me healthy. What about you? How are you?"

"Just fine. Aurek doesn't bother with me," I lie. "Come on, you're leaving now."

"Then let's— Wait. *I'm leaving?* What about you?"

I shake my head. "I can't. My mother is here. Lief brought her."

"Lief wouldn't let anything happen to her, would he?"

"I'm scared Aurek will take out his anger on her."

"Why would he? You just said he doesn't bother . . ." He stops, looking at me. "So that was a lie, then? He's very *bothered*, I take it?"

"Silas, we don't have time for this . . ."

"I'll go with you. I won't without you. It's that simple. Last time I let you out of my sight, you got yourself captured."

"You got captured, too," I protest.

"The time before, you got your spine broken," he continues. "I've learned my lesson, Errin Vastel. As if—*as if*—I'd go and leave you here." He pulls away and crosses his arms. "Choose. *We* go." He emphasizes the togetherness of the statement. "Or *we* stay."

I gape at him, at his lovely, uncompromising face. Lief wouldn't let anything happen to Mama. Whatever else he is, he's not that far gone. "Fine. We go."

He reaches for my hand, hauling me up with him.

I'm not even all that surprised when the door gives a telltale squeak, then slams against the wall of the stable, driving us apart.

Aurek stands in the doorway, his teeth bared, murder in his eyes.

"Oh, you've done it now, sweetling."

Chapter 12

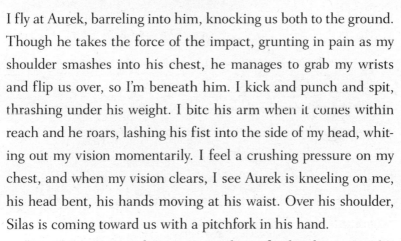

I fly at Aurek, barreling into him, knocking us both to the ground. Though he takes the force of the impact, grunting in pain as my shoulder smashes into his chest, he manages to grab my wrists and flip us over, so I'm beneath him. I kick and punch and spit, thrashing under his weight. I bite his arm when it comes within reach and he roars, lashing his fist into the side of my head, whiting out my vision momentarily. I feel a crushing pressure on my chest, and when my vision clears, I see Aurek is kneeling on me, his head bent, his hands moving at his waist. Over his shoulder, Silas is coming toward us with a pitchfork in his hand.

"Run!" I scream at him as I smash my forehead into Aurek's lowered head, feeling his teeth scrape my skin. "Go."

Then there is something cold at my throat and Silas freezes, releasing the pitchfork the moment before Aurek says, "Drop it, nephew."

It clangs loudly in the wooden building and I feel wetness dripping down my neck. Then the pain comes, sharp and hot. The knife Aurek holds cuts into me, and when I swallow, the motion drives it a little deeper.

"Get on your hands and knees," Aurek says, moving off me, keeping the knife pressed firmly against my throat.

Silas obeys immediately, his eyes on mine the whole time.

"Please don't hurt her."

Aurek hauls me up, moving behind me, keeping the knife against my pulse as the blood slides behind the collar of my nightdress. "I'm going to kill her," he says, his voice barely above a whisper, his mouth brushing my hair. "So rid yourself of any illusions you have that your cooperation might save her. It won't. All it will determine is how fast she dies."

Ice-white terror roots me to the spot, my skin crawling as wave after wave of horror, at his words, at his touch, rolls over me.

"Please," Silas says.

Aurek laughs, and licks my ear. "No."

There is noise behind us—footsteps, multiple pairs, men with swords and torches of their own. They come to a stop just out of the line of my vision, but I see their shadows, long across the floor. "Bind my nephew and take him somewhere secure. Actually secure this time." Aurek turns. "Where is Lief?"

"I don't know, Your Grace," a male voice replies.

"Really?" Aurek moves, swinging me around after him like a doll. I catch the briefest glimpse of Silas being bound by three men, his arms pulled behind his back. But his eyes are on me.

"So," Aurek continues. "Someone sets my castle on fire, and my most trusted lieutenant brings my philtersmith to hide in this most secure of locations, the stables, where he's conveniently found by his sister. I smell a rat, Errin, and it's not the one from your room. That was part of the plan, I take it? Make me paranoid?"

"I don't know what you're—"

He jabs me in the side of the head with the handle of the knife before I can finish and Silas bellows, trying to tear himself from where two guards are now restraining him.

"Do you know what I think?" Aurek says as the guards drag Silas past me, out of the barn. I watch him for as long as I can, and then Aurek's fingers are digging into my jaw, forcing me to look at him. "I think the Rising Dawn is *you*. And whatever ragtag bunch of miscreants here you've convinced to help you. Quite possibly your brother, too, because you'd need someone on the outside. But I will find out. I told you, back in the heretics' bone temple, that the only way to stop an infestation is to scotch the nest."

He says nothing else, spinning me around and clasping my hands behind me. "Get me rope," he spits at one of his men, and within moments my hands are bound so tightly my fingers tingle.

Then his hand is in my hair and he walks, pulling me along. My scalp burns as he strides back to the castle and I stumble behind him to where the crowd still stands, now watching a second tower ablaze.

Aurek throws me on the ground before him with such force that I bite my own lip and blood floods my mouth. "Gather everyone here," he orders his men. "My golems will deal with the blaze."

They don't hesitate, rushing off toward the fire. Aurek pulls a simulacrum from his pocket, and at first I think it's the one of me, until he scratches a command directly onto the clay. He looks up, waiting, and appears satisfied when four golems loom out of the darkness. The crowd draws in, nervously. Aurek pulls some paper from his ever-present sheaf and writes on it, tearing it into four. The golems lurch forward and he presses a piece into each of their palms. At once their movements become purposeful, and they fan out, forming a loose circle around us all.

The guards he sent away return with smoke-stained men in tow, most of them coughing, all of them red-eyed and panting. They join the crowd, some heading toward friends, others eyeing Aurek and the golems warily. The scent of danger mingles with the smoke.

"No one leaves. The golems are instructed to kill anyone who tries."

Shocked murmurs pass through the crowd, and people shift, either stepping closer to or away from their neighbors. The guards begin to protest.

"Even you," Aurek says in a voice that makes it clear he means it. "We have a problem." He raises his voice to boom over the rush and roar of the fire. "And the problem is trust. I trusted you. All of you. But it seems I was wrong to trust her." He jabs at me with his foot. "I believe she has betrayed me, and to that end I need information. I want everyone who has served her in any way over the past ten weeks to step forward. If you have cleaned her clothes, made her meals, step forward. If you've guarded her, come forward. I wish to learn how deeply the vein of her treachery runs, and for that I shall require your aid. And honesty." When no one moves, Aurek sighs. "You'll find having my home set ablaze sours my mood somewhat. I implore you not to make me ask a second time."

Thurn and Crayne exchange a brief glance before Crayne steps forward, Thurn a split second after him. I scowl at them, spitting blood onto the ground. Thurn smiles with a hungry expression.

More people step forward, no one that I recognize: a few men, two women around my mother's age, a boy who looks around nine or ten at the most. Merek's face is absent from the line that forms before Aurek, and I feel a glint of satisfaction that he did manage to get away.

Until he's pushed forward by someone behind him. "He takes her meals up," the woman responsible for his exposure crows, and my heart plummets. He doesn't look at me, all of his attention on Aurek as he steps in between one of the women and the little boy.

"Have any of you aided the girl in passing messages outside of the castle?"

They all shake their heads. Thurn says, "No," loudly.

"Has she ever asked you to?"

Again, Thurn is the only one to answer verbally; the rest deny his question in silence.

Aurek tilts his head as he considers them. Then he looks at me.

"Errin, have you ever asked, forced, bribed, or threatened any of these poor simple peasantfolk into supporting your cause?"

"You know I haven't," I say thickly, through swelling lips.

He shrugs. Then his hand lashes out, the knife still in it, across Thurn's throat.

A line forms, red, then it gapes, and blood spills from it freely. Thurn looks at Aurek, his mouth a perfect O of surprise. Then he falls, his life spewing out of him and into the dead grass.

"I'll ask you again." Aurek grins at me. "Who helped you? Him?" He points the knife at Crayne.

"Your Grace?" Crayne says, and it's the last thing he does as the knife flashes again. Crayne gurgles as he dies, his hands clawing at his throat as if he can push the blood back inside and hold the wound closed. He takes a long time to die, and Aurek watches him impassively.

The woman who stood beside Crayne begins to cry. "Tell him it wasn't me," she says to me. "Please. Tell him."

"It wasn't her," I say, unable to bear it. "It wasn't any of these people."

"But it was someone?" Aurek glares at me, pointing the knife. "Someone here is the Rising Dawn?"

"Yes," I lie. "Yes. I am the Rising Dawn; it's me. It's all me. And I did have help, but not from them. From no one here tonight."

"Tell me who. Name names."

"I—I never learned their names," I plead. "It was too dangerous."

Aurek shrugs. "I don't believe you." He plunges the knife into the chest of the woman, who immediately crumples to the ground. "I'm going to kill them all anyway."

"No!" I scream, my throat raw as he pulls the knife from the body of the woman and advances on Merek.

There is movement behind me.

"Lief," Aurek says, his voice pleasant. "How good of you to join us. And just where have you been?"

"I went to retrieve . . . something," he says, frowning. "But it was gone." He looks at me, and for a moment I think I see relief in his gaze. But then it disappears, as his attention snaps back to Aurek.

"Really?" Aurek says. "See, I find it odd that a fire started in that particular tower—*my* tower—mere hours after a rat was found in Errin's rooms."

Lief's gaze moves from Aurek to me, then back to his master. "I don't follow, Your Grace."

"I sincerely hope that's not true." Aurek twists the words.

Lief swallows visibly. "I only meant I don't understand the connection, Your Grace."

Aurek blinks. "You know that the Rising Dawn had rats released into the home of the Sheriff of Lortune, do you not? I've been puzzling over just how the Rising are managing to strike in such varied locations. I put it to you, did I not, that I believed it might be an inside job? That some of my people were, in fact, behind it all?"

Lief is deadly still, watching Aurek as one would watch a viper.

"I think your beloved sister here might be the Rising Dawn," Aurek says, his voice soft now. "Or at least the local faction. And I think someone in my castle is helping her. I fear you might be that person."

Lief's eyebrows rise and the night seems to pause.

"I am sorry to hear that, Your Grace" is all he says.

It's Aurek's turn to frown. "Is that it? I say I suspect you of treason and you say you're *sorry to hear it*?"

Lief bows. "You are the king. I cannot argue with Your Grace. It is not my place."

Aurek's eyes narrow, and he tilts his head. "That's your defense?"

Lief looks up at him, and when he speaks his voice is soft. "You know I've betrayed people I've claimed to care about in the past. It wouldn't be unreasonable for you to assume it was in my nature. That it *is* my nature."

I risk a glance at Merek, who has his head lowered to keep his face in shadow. When I look back at Aurek, he's staring at Lief with obvious bewilderment.

"Do you love your sister more than your king?" he asks.

"I love my sister. And my mother. But you have my loyalty."

Aurek watches him a moment longer and then takes a step back and waves his hand in my direction, gesturing at the crowd.

He's letting Lief continue the interrogation. A new well of loathing for my brother bubbles up inside me as he turns to me, his expression smooth and calm.

"Did you start the fire, Errin?"

"No. I was in my rooms. They"—I jerk my head toward the corpses of Thurn and Crayne—"were guarding the door. Not that you can ask them to corroborate it."

"Did you *ask* someone to start the fire?"

"No. The first I knew of it was when they dragged me out in my nightgown."

Lief peers at me. "The rat in your room. Did you plant it?"

"No."

His eye narrows. "You're lying." Aurek looks from him to me, head cocked as he watches us. "She knows something about the rat. Who was in the room when you saw this rat? Your guards? The dead ones? And who was the other man, the servant who was with you when I came to you?"

"I don't know—he wasn't there when I saw the rat," I say quickly, my heart pounding so hard that I fear my ribs will crack.

The look on Lief's face is the one I've seen my whole life. When I ate the last of the honey cakes and said I didn't. When I broke one of the wooden cows he so cherished. When I borrowed his bow and left it in the woods. The flat, angry stare of an older brother.

To my surprise, the silence that blossoms between us is broken by Aurek drawling, "In the interest of honesty, which possibly only I am actually capable of, this guard here"—he nudges Thurn with his toe—"said that he was the one who saw it, and that he was the one who bludgeoned it with the heating pan."

I can't breathe, can't believe that Thurn's arrogance might save Merek.

"Also, in the pursuit of the truth, I have to confess I don't follow your chain of thought," Aurek says to Lief, with more than a hint of mockery.

"I believe you're right, in that the Rising is an organization, for want of a better word, which has some presence here," Lief says, bowing slightly. "I just want to know if my sister is really part of it before you punish her."

Lief looks from me to the line of servants remaining. All of them are round-shouldered, their eyes on the ground, trying to make themselves as small as possible, as though that might save them from Aurek's wrath. His eyes roam over all of them, resting very briefly on the women, and the child. But when he comes to Merek, he pauses, and another frown crosses his face.

I watch his expression slacken, his eye glancing to the side as though remembering something. Then he smiles, a slow, humorless smile, and the bottom falls out of my world.

"You were the servant, weren't you?" he says to Merek. "You brought the drink?"

Merek looks up, eyes full of defiance.

He knows, and I know, that Lief has recognized him.

"Or were you? Perhaps I'm mistaken. Perhaps you missed the theatrics," Lief says softly, and Merek's eyes widen.

Lief turns to Aurek. "I don't know about the rat, Your Grace. I can swear to you, though, on the lives of my mother and myself—and for what it's worth at this point, my sister—that I am not part of the Rising. Though I can't vouch for Errin's innocence."

Now it's Aurek's turn to look surprised. "And if I killed her?"

"My mother might miss her," Lief says simply. Then he looks around, and his expression moves from carefully blank to confused. He spins in a circle, apparently forgetting Aurek, Merek, me, and the Rising.

"What is it?" Aurek stares out into the darkness.

"Forgive me, I . . . Where's my mother?"

"What?"

"I went to the Tower of Valor, but she was already gone, yet I don't see her . . ."

Aurek scowls. "So that's why you weren't where I'd ordered you to be."

Lief and I stare at him. "Please, Your Grace?" he asks.

"I had her moved to the Tower of Victory after the incident with the rat. I thought she'd be better protected there, should the Rising come."

Lief looks down at me as though I might have the answer. I can't tell if he's acting or not. I can't read him at all. He turns to look at the Tower of Victory, fire licking out of every window, the

166

rooms between them red and bright. "No," he says in a small voice that I've never heard before, and then he runs, pelting toward the castle.

And as I realize why, I follow him.

The golems swing out at him as he breaks past them; one begins to lumber after him, but then it freezes in place, turning slowly back to the crowd as I pass it, and in the back of my mind I know Aurek must have commanded it not to hurt us.

I race after my brother and watch him disappear into a doorway thick with smoke. As I approach it to go after him, he stumbles out, his arm over his face, coughing violently. "Too hot," he chokes, grabbing my arm, forgetting everything that happened just moments before. We cling to each other as we run around the tower, looking for another way in.

The door is on fire, smoke billowing out into the sky, and Lief turns, pulling me back toward the door we first ran to. But now flames are licking at that, too, and I have to grip Lief with both hands and dig my heels into the ground to stop him from going in again.

"You'll die," I cry as he peels my fingers from him.

"Mother is in there," he spits, pushing me away.

Then a figure passes us, tall, gray, and lumbering, heading straight into the flames. I watch, openmouthed, as it walks through them, seemingly impervious to the heat. I turn to Lief, to see Aurek has also joined us. He doesn't look at either of us, gazing into the flames; the light reflecting in his eyes makes them look alight, too.

And despite everything, the three of us stand together and watch, eyes trained on the doorway for any sign of movement.

When I glance at my brother, I see he's crying from his single eye, an endless tear running down his face, and my stomach twists.

The golem emerges with something black and red and smoking in its arms, and Lief lets out a howl and sinks to his knees.

The golem's hide looks paler, cracks spread across it, and as it reaches us, it crumbles into dust, fired like a pot in the heat of the blaze. The thing in its arms falls to the ground.

I turn to Aurek, without knowing why, to find him looking back at me with pitiless gold eyes.

"I never knew my mother," he says.

Chapter 13

He doesn't say anything else, but walks away, leaving my brother rocking on his knees, and me staring after him, completely numb. I look back at the thing on the ground—my mother, I tell myself—and I can't feel anything. It doesn't look like a person. It doesn't look like anything.

"I'm so sorry," Lief sobs, clawing at the ground. "Mama, I'm sorry." He hasn't called her Mama since he was eight. I remember when he first called her Mother at dinner. "Pass the butter, Mother," he said, and she was so surprised she dropped her spoon and splashed the table with her soup.

My mother is dead. She's dead. She will never splash soup again. I will never see her smiling again. She will never braid my hair in a crown over my head for me again. I will never taste her bread, nor her butter. She will never place a cool hand to my forehead when I'm ill.

"This is your fault," someone says, and Lief looks up at me. "This is your fault," the voice repeats, and I'm dimly aware I know that voice, that it's my voice. My words. "You brought her here."

"No. I just wanted her to be safe," Lief chokes out.

"With him? You thought she'd be safe with him?"

"Someone out there might have used her to get at me." Lief claws at the ground. "I didn't know. I didn't think—"

"You never do!" I scream at him. "It's always what *you* need, what *you* want, what *you* think is best. And now she's dead. You've been killing her for months and you've finally managed it."

I hear footsteps behind us and, expecting to see Aurek or some guards to haul me off somewhere, I spin around with my fists raised. Merek has come to a stop, his hands over his mouth, as he looks down at Mama. "I'm sorry," he says. "Oh Gods, I'm so sorry. I never meant—"

"Was it you, then?" I ask, the words coming from my mouth as though divorced from me. "You started it?"

He nods, his face a mask of misery.

"I thought it must have been."

"I didn't know . . ." But when he says it, and falls immediately silent, it doesn't burn me up as it did when Lief said it. "I thought she was in the south tower. I didn't know he'd moved her to the north. He was in the Great Hall, with him—" He jerks his head toward Lief. "I thought it was empty. It was just supposed to be a distraction," he says softly. Then he takes my hands. "I'm sorry. Errin, I'm so, so sorry. I didn't know. You have to believe me."

"I don't blame you," I hear myself say. "I blame him." I turn to my brother.

"Errin, please," Lief says.

"You brought her here." Though I speak quietly, the words echo off the stone, surrounding us. "You drove her mad. You murdered her."

Lief covers his face with his hands and bends double, pressing into the grass.

"As far as I'm concerned, my whole family is dead," I say to his bent form. "Papa died in Tremayne, and you and Mama died the day you left for this place. You're dead to me, Lief. Do you hear me? I have no family now."

The thing moans.

"She's alive," Merek shouts, instantly bent by her side. Lief moves to her, too, reaching for her hand. Another gurgling moan escapes her, and I stare at her, unable to understand how she can be alive. The little of her that isn't blackened and charred is red and shiny, and along one arm it's bubbled and weeping. Her hair has been burned away completely, eyelashes, eyebrows, all gone. Her gown has melted into her skin.

Dead, she was terrible, but alive . . . she's a nightmare.

"The Elixir." Merek looks up at me. "She might recover with the Elixir."

Lief shakes his head, his other hand over his mouth.

"It cured your sister's broken spine," Merek snaps. "Surely it's worth a try?"

He doesn't look up, doesn't say anything. Doesn't move.

"I'll go and ask," I hear myself say, my voice sounding very far away. "I'll beg."

Lief's head snaps up. "He won't do it for you. He's more likely to let her die to hurt you," he says. Then he swallows. "He might do it for me. Go. I'll ask him. You escape while I'm gone."

Merek stares over my mother at him, and Lief stares right back. "Why would he do it for you?"

"I'm all he has," Lief says in a small voice, and it's as though someone has pushed ice into my stomach.

"You were all we had, too," I say, and he closes his eye, another tear falling from it.

"Go," he repeats.

"Errin?" Merek says tentatively.

I open my mouth to say I can't, now more than ever. I can't leave her and not know whether Aurek gave her the Elixir or not. Before I can speak, there is a strange creaking, then a crack. All three of us look toward it, in time to see the Tower of Victory crumble, dust and debris flooding out. Merek throws me to the ground and covers me with his body as it rolls over us. I hold my breath and press my face into the ground.

When the rumbling stops, Merek pulls me up. He's covered in soot and dust, utterly unrecognizable.

"Go," Lief says in a broken-glass voice as he struggles to his feet. "Both of you. I'll deal with the simulacrum. I'll do what it takes to heal Ma— Mother, and you know Silas will be safe, so long as he can make the Elixir. But you'll be dead before dawn if you stay."

So he knew all along what Aurek was doing to me, and he did nothing. I can't move.

"Errin." Merek speaks softly. "Please."

I look up at him and blink.

"Let me do this," Lief says.

I nod at Merek and, from the corner of my eye, see Lief sag with relief.

"You fix this," I say to him, feeling no pleasure when he flinches. "You owe me. You owe her. You were raised better than this."

He hangs his head and I turn away, unable to stand the sight of him anymore.

"Where can we get out?" Merek asks him.

"The North Gate. And take this." I look back as Lief pulls a piece of paper out from inside his tunic. When I just stare at it, unmoving, he holds it out to Merek, who takes it. "Take care of my sister, Your Highness," he says with a small bow.

"What is it?" Merek holds the paper up.

"Read it," Lief says, sounding more like his old self. "Go, if you're going. I have work to do."

"Wait. One last thing. Why didn't you tell him who I was?" Merek asks.

Lief takes a deep breath and dusts down his uniform. "I owed you." He wipes his face on his sleeve and lifts the patch momentarily, giving me a glimpse of pink emptiness behind it. He doesn't look at either of us again, but vanishes into the night after Aurek.

"Come on," Merek says, holding out his hand for mine.

I look down at Mama. She hasn't made a noise for a while, but I can't think of that. Not now.

I take Merek's hand.

Merek seems to know where to go, and I run beside him, arms propelling me forward, surging into the darkness, bare feet slapping the ground so fast it sends shock waves along my legs. It feels good to move, and I power forward, as if I can outrun what just happened. I have to trust Lief. I have to trust that he'll do what he can to save Mama.

We reach the North Gate in a matter of moments, and Lief told the truth; it's barred and bolted, but there are no men guarding it. We skid to a halt in the frozen mud, and I help Merek lift the thick piece of wood from its braces across the gate, fear and urgency lending us strength, and tug back the iron bolts that were buried deep in the stone. Without speaking, we both turn and take one final look back at the castle, burning wildly, before Merek takes my hand again and pulls me out of the castle grounds.

We race along the side of the wall, the shouts from the castle getting quieter, until we reach a narrow lane that seems to lead down into the town. From there I hear the distant rumble of voices, and I drag Merek back from it, but he shakes his head. "We need to go through the town to an ally of mine. We need cloaks, food, and water. You need clothes. And boots. We won't survive if we don't get supplies."

"We'll be caught if we go into the town." My voice sounds hoarse, the smoke and the screaming shredding my throat. "There's a curfew."

Merek shakes his head. "Aurek gave orders for everyone in Lortune to be roused to help put the fire out. Look." Merek points down the lane, and after only a moment I see a man and a woman, wrapped up warm, racing past, heading in the direction of the castle. Then another man runs past, followed by a second, and a third. I can see the muted colors of their cloaks; dawn is coming. "It'll be chaos. As long as we don't linger, and we stay out of the soldiers' way, this is perfect."

I'm aware that it's dangerous, stupid even. It could be one of my ideas, it's so reckless. But he's right; I'm wearing a nightdress, for one thing. So I take his hand for a third time and allow him to lead me down into Lortune town.

It is just as chaotic as he believed it would be, a wall of noise rising up as soon as we pass the buffer of the buildings. People are dashing left and right, calling out to one another, and it becomes almost immediately clear that very few of them are heading to aid their king. Instead, they dart from one building to another, whispering news to one another, passing one another small bottles, bundles of clothing, taking advantage of the commotion to act as freely as they've been able to in a long time, avoiding the guards who try to herd them toward the castle.

Merek pulls me through, yanking me down an alley to a squat building at the end. The windows are dark, but he pounds the door anyway.

"Open up." He hammers with his fist. "Open—"

The door flies open, almost taking me with it, and a woman, tiny, wizened and crumpled like a raisin, stands there, brandishing a stick with a sharp metal tip on it.

"I'll die before I help that Tallithi bastard, so there's no point asking me to haul water," she hisses at Merek. "I'd sooner throw myself into the fire."

"I don't want you to help him. I want you to help me."

She looks between the two of us. "Help you with what?"

"Getting us out of here, finding Daunen Embodied, and getting my throne back."

The baldness of his confession shocks some of the heaviness from me.

The woman leans forward, looming out of the darkness to peer at him. Then, to my surprise, she chuckles.

"I knew it wasn't your head up there," she says, grinning wickedly, exposing a mouth with far more gum than teeth. "I knew it. That boy had laughter lines by his eyes. I can count on one hand how many times I've heard you laugh."

She holds up her hands to demonstrate, and I feel another jolt of shock as I register the missing fingers, two on her left, one on her right. She cackles again at the look on my face, and then reaches for us both, grabbing one of us in each hand and pulling us inside her home, closing the door firmly behind us. For someone who can't be less than eighty, she's incredibly strong. And fast.

It's warm in her cottage, stifling even, and I look around to see the windows covered in thick fabric, to hide the light and keep the heat in.

"Margot Cottar." Merek introduces the woman to me when she turns from bolting the door. "This is Errin Vastel." She spins around to glare at me, and he carries on quickly, "Yes, she's the Silver Knight's sister. But definitely not on his side."

"I hate him," I growl.

Margot looks me up and down, and nods, as though Merek's vouching for me and my words are enough. "So what do you need? I assume that's why you're here."

"She needs clothes, whatever you have that would be fit for running and riding, and boots. We need cloaks, water. Food."

"Where do you head?"

"Scarron," I say, as Merek says, "We don't know."

Margot looks between us. "I'll get your things while you decide." She bustles off through a small door into another room, leaving us alone.

Outside, I hear people passing the cottage, but their voices are muted. The room is small, possibly smaller than the front room of the Almwyk cottage, though it's cleaner and better cared for than that place ever was. A small, well-worn table is pressed against a wall, two equally weathered chairs beneath it. There's a rocking chair by the fire, a thickly woven blanket matching the rag rug on the floor. There are little touches, too, a small vase on the mantelpiece, empty at the moment, a toy soldier, its paint chipped almost entirely away. A basket full of yarn at the side of the chair.

"I think she's in Scarron." I look at Merek, who is examining the room, too. "Lief told Aurek the same. It would make sense. She has a house there; it's isolated, difficult to reach at this time of year, and the people there love her. I saw them. They'll protect her."

Merek shakes his head, dismissing the idea. "She can't be organizing the Rising Dawn from there."

"If it's even her behind it," I remind him. "We can't be sure."

"I know it's her," Merek says. "Don't ask me how, I just do."

I sigh. "Then where do we go?"

"I don't know. She's probably hiding somewhere. As you say, remote and secure."

I think frantically. "Silas said his mother lived with a group of women near the East Mountains. Wait, you don't think . . ."

Merek's face goes slack, his mouth opening. "How did I not . . ." He trails off, shaking his head. "Of course."

"What?" I demand.

"There *was* an order of women based there. Very secluded. Very private. I wrote to them to ask if they'd take my mother once Twylla and I were married."

"You what?"

He shrugs. "They refused. What?" he says when I continue to gawp at him.

"You planned to ship her off to a bunch of nuns in the mountains once you were married? Like unwanted clothing. Like something you owned." Something loud falls to the floor in the room Margot went into. We both look toward the doorway, then back at each other.

"You didn't know my mother," he says quietly.

"Even so. That's a terrible thing to think you can do."

Merek takes a deep breath. "My mother killed my stepfather. Possibly my father. In fact, she killed a lot of people. Shipping her off, as you put it, would have been a kindness. A less merciful king would have had her executed on numerous counts of murder."

We both fall silent, listening to Margot rummaging loudly, muttering to herself at the same time.

"How do you know her?" I lower my voice. I don't bother asking if we can trust her; we wouldn't be here otherwise.

"She's the great-aunt of one of my personal guards . . . and friends," he adds. "She raised him and his brother and sister when their parents died." He pauses. "The sister was Dimia."

"Oh." I don't know what else to say for a moment. "And the others?"

"My mother had Asher, the eldest boy, executed while I was away on my progress. His brother, Taul, was with me at the time. I don't know where he is now—he rode for Tallith the day I deposed my mother, to recover his sister's body. He never came back."

"I hope he's miles away." We both turn to see Margot Cottar in the doorway, her small arms loaded with provisions. "I hope he got in a boat and sailed over the Tallithi Sea to somewhere warm and wonderful and full of naked young women or men eager to please him."

Merek smiles wryly.

"See what I mean." Margot smiles a toothless grin in my direction. "More likely to get blood from a stone than a laugh from him. Here." She brandishes the pile at Merek, who goes to collect it.

"You ought to show me more respect," he says, passing me a thick woolen overtunic, leather breeches, a white shirt, and a pair of battered boots. "I'm the king."

"You've been usurped," Margot says bluntly, tossing underwear at me and grabbing Merek's arm, pulling him around so I have some privacy to change. I quickly pull the underwear on under the night-dress, and then shuck it off, slipping the undershirt and tunic over my head and tugging the breeches on. "I'll show you respect when you kill that monster and get your crown back," Margot continues.

"Liar," Merek says smoothly. "You've never shown me a day's respect in my life."

"I had five brothers, three husbands, brought up eight sons of my own, and then two great-nephews. I learned the hard way that if you give a boy respect before he's done anything to earn it, he'll walk all over you. Pretty prince or not. If you put the Sleeping Prince in his grave, I'll kneel to you and kiss your feet. Then you'll have earned it."

She turns back to me and winks as I haul the boots onto my feet. "Thank you," I say. "These are wonderful."

"They were Asher's, when he was around your age. Not the boots. They were my Mia's. Never seemed right to get rid of them. They're good boots. Glad they'll come in useful."

I nod solemnly. "I'll take care of them."

Her mouth quirks as though to make one of her snappy remarks, when the deep, booming ring of a bell sounds in the distance.

Merek and I exchange a panicked glance. "He knows," I mutter.

"It could be another call to aid at the castle," he says, but his expression makes it clear he doesn't believe it, either.

"We have to go." I turn back to Margot. "Thank you, for everything."

"There's no need," she says firmly. She holds out a bag to me. "I've packed bread, water, a bit of cheese, a bit of ham, and some—"

I hit her in the face before she has time to finish.

She flies back, crashing into the little table. I lunge around wildly, hands clawed and reaching.

"Merek, stop me," I beg, my body moving entirely against my will. I knock a vase from the mantel, kick a chair and cry out in pain, but still I move, lashing out, kicking and wheeling and hitting. "Merek, please!" I scream as my fingers snarl in Margot's shawl.

She twists away but stumbles and falls, leaving me with the garment in my hands. Merek drops the bag and rushes at me, but I manage to hit him on the side of the neck, causing him to stumble.

"What are you doing, girl?" Margot screeches at me, scrambling away.

"I'm sorry, I'm sorry," I repeat, trying desperately to wrench myself away from them both.

Somewhere out there, Aurek has commanded my simulacrum to attack, so attack I do, lurching toward her as she cowers in a corner.

"You said she could be trusted!" Margot cries at Merek, still gasping on the floor.

My hand knocks against the sharpened stick she held when she opened the door, and then grips it tightly as my arm swings it high over my head.

"Run," I whisper.

As she shrinks to the ground, looking every inch the elderly woman she is, I feel arms around me, binding mine to my sides. I thrash my head back, but Merek dodges, tightening his grip.

"You have to stop me," I say. "Please, Merek." I kick back, striking his shin and loosening his hold for a moment. Then his arm is around my neck, the inside of his elbow pressed against my throat, and my thrashing becomes wilder as he squeezes, denying me air.

"Sorry," he says.

I look up at him as blackness clouds my vision, still struggling. Then I'm gone.

When I come to, everything is still black, and a faint pressure across my nose, the sensation of rough fabric on my skin, tells me I've been blindfolded, though I'm sure Aurek can't use the simulacrum to see through my eyes. My neck feels tender, and my wrists chafe against the rope binding them behind my back. My legs, too, are bound at the ankle. In the distance the bell is still ringing, a deep ominous sound that I can feel echoed in my heartbeat.

"Hello?" I say to the room.

There is a noise overhead, a creaking sound, then footsteps on stairs.

"Hello," Merek says from somewhere to my left.

"Is she all right?"

There is a small silence. "Yes. Frightened. But also angry. Not at you," he adds quickly. "At the Sleeping Prince. For controlling you in that way."

I hear a second set of steps on the stairs, slower than Merek's, and I wait until they shuffle into the room.

"I'm so sorry," I say immediately. "I never meant to hurt you."

Neither of them says a word, and behind the blindfold my eyes dart back and forth.

Then short, cold fingers touch my face, the gaps between some of them too wide.

"Why is she blindfolded?" Margot asks.

"Because . . ." Merek begins, then stops. "I don't know. I didn't know if he could see through her eyes, and would see where we were. I don't really understand how it works."

"I don't think he can see through my eyes," I say, and immediately the blindfold is pulled away. "I don't know for sure. But I don't think he can. The golems can't see, but they use some other sense to attack, and I think it must be the same with me. And he can't control my mind, either. He can only make my body do things. He writes the command down on a piece of paper and then wraps it around the simulacrum."

"But how is that connected to you?"

"Blood. He feeds my blood to the doll, and adds a drop of his to activate it."

Margot nods, and looks over at Merek.

"Blood degrades," she says. "It's a natural substance; it'll break down. Without a fresh supply, he won't be able to control your body anymore. But for the time being, he can control you at will."

"He can get into her dreams, too," Merek says.

"Could he get into your dreams and control your body at the same time?"

I hesitate. "Once, I was dreaming, and he was talking to me in the dream, and then I was awake, but I was standing on the windowsill. Not in my bed . . ." I shiver, remembering. "We were both awake by then—I don't think he can do both at the same time."

"Well. You need to decide what you're going to do," Margot says. "It's not practical for you to be bound all the time. What about when you're on the move? What about when you have to clean yourself? What if you're attacked?"

"I *told* you this," I say to Merek, anger at myself making my words sharp. "I told you the risk of my leaving. I knew Aurek would do something like this. I could have killed you," I say to Margot, shame coloring my cheeks.

"It'd take more than a slip of a girl to kill me," she says over her shoulder, but even I notice she sounds less full of bravado than she did earlier. Before, she was all jokes and waspish words. Now, though, she's unsure. Because of me.

"Maybe I should go back," I say to Merek. "Give myself up."

He gives a long sigh. "That would be a very stupid thing to do," he says bluntly. "Firstly, you'd be dead before sunrise. The fact we both got away tonight is a miracle; we won't get another chance. Secondly, as Margot said, blood decays. The spell, or whatever it is he's holding you under, will fade. And besides, Lief said he'd try to destroy it."

This time, Margot and I sniff identical sounds of dislike and distrust. Then I remember the piece of paper Lief handed to Merek.

"What was on the parchment? The one Lief gave you."

His eyebrows rise as he remembers and leans back to pull it from his pocket. He unfolds it, frowns, and then holds it out to me.

It takes me less than a second to understand it's the recipe for the Opus Magnum. In my brother's spidery handwriting.

It's all there, everything I remember from the table in the Conclave. Sal Salis, a pinch of marigold, morning glory, a vial of angel water, spagyric tonic, three bay leaves, the root of a mandrake, convolvulus, yew bark, ears of wheat. Asulfer. Quicksilver. The times at which the flowers and leaves need to be picked, the way they need to be stored until used. Even a recommendation for the kind of wood to use to create the fire. The process for every part written down, possibly for the first time in living history—in any history.

The key to defeating the Sleeping Prince.

Merek stares at me over the paper. "How?" he asks.

I shake my head, still struck mute by it. It's exactly what I need to deconstruct it. With it, I can reverse every single detail. Beside me, Merek is beaming, really truly beaming, causing Margot to stare at him. I can see her lips moving as she talks, and he parries the remarks with his own, the danger that I am forgotten in light of this new miracle Merek said we wouldn't get.

"Give that to me." Margot snatches the recipe from me, returning to her back room. I look at Merek in alarm, but he shakes his head, trusting her. When she returns, she hands him the paper, and I see something glistening on the surface. Merek pulls a face as he takes it and folds it delicately, replacing it in his pocket.

Where did Lief get it? Not Silas; Silas would have told me. A twinge of guilt makes me wonder where Silas is now, and I offer up a wish that he's all right, that he won't be punished for this. Then my thoughts turn to Lief, and I wonder if he's survived his treachery. And what motivated it. I understood why he allowed Twylla to escape—because of what they had shared. And I understood why he kept Merek's identity secret—Lief never liked to be in anyone's debt. But handing us the key to the Sleeping Prince's destruction? Getting the recipe must have taken work, and skill.

It doesn't make sense.

Whose side is Lief on?

Before I can give it any real thought, I become dimly aware that the bell outside is ringing faster, becoming frantic, as though the ringer isn't pausing between hauling on the rope, pulling it down again almost as soon as it's tolled. Margot crosses to the window, moving the covering aside a fraction and peering out.

Then she spins away from the window. "You need to go," she says. "They're searching the houses."

Chapter 14

Merek moves almost before Margot has finished speaking. He tugs the knots at my legs until the rope unspools.

"What are you—?"

"You're going to need to run. So we'll have to risk leaving your feet free, for a while."

He moves behind me and unties my wrists, too, but keeps a tight grip on them. With an apologetic twist of his mouth, he binds them again, in front of me, though he leaves a foot of loose rope between them, so I have some movement.

"What if he commands her to return to him?" Margot asks.

Merek hesitates.

"Tie more rope around this." I hold up my hands and nod at the bindings. "Like a leash. Then you can pull me back if you have to."

Margot opens the tiny back door and peers out, and Merek quickly knots a new length of rope to the one at my wrists, then hauls the sacks onto his back. He holds my lead in his hands and we wait for Margot to give us the all clear.

"Now," she barks, and we go, bolting from her house like racing dogs from their posts.

We don't even say thank you or good-bye as we leave; there's no time. We run full pelt to the back wall. With Merek's help, I get up and over the wall, landing in someone else's small yard, and we keep moving that way, him linking his fingers together so I can stand in the cradle of his hands and haul myself over fence after fence, avoiding the main thoroughfare. At the end of the row, we climb over a last wall, and then we're back on the streets. The sound of the bell drowns everything else out, I can't hear voices, or footsteps, or even my own boots against the muddy lanes.

Merek keeps the rope leash between us short, so I know which passage to turn down not long after he decides it. We see no one, not even the twitching of a window slat or a shadow on a wall.

We stop behind a tavern that has cobwebbed windows, an air of neglect surrounding it. We both lean against the damp wall to catch our breath, my lungs burning as I suck down the icy air.

"There's a trade gate the other side of the pub," Merek gasps between breaths. "I don't know if it's manned."

"Won't it be locked?"

"Only one way to find out."

"Wait here," Merek says, and before I can protest, he's dropped the rope and vanished around the corner. Fear spikes as soon as he's out of sight—what if I'm possessed in this very moment?—but then Merek is back, picking up the rope again and giving me a grim sort-of smile.

"Unmanned, and the lock looks intact. I'll need your help."

"You shouldn't have done that," I hiss.

Merek says nothing, jerking his head to indicate we need to leave.

The bell sounds farther away now, deadened by the buildings between us and the castle.

"Lift on three," Merek says, bracing his hands under the thick wooden plank lodged inside iron braces.

I place my own, bound hands under it.

"One. Two—"

The bell pauses for a split second, and in it I hear the whisper of metal sliding against leather. I whirl, and come face-to-face with a pair of soldiers, the triple gold stars on their tabards glowing faintly.

"Merek." I barely have time to warn him before they're on us, knives in hand like assassins.

I raise my bound arms in the nick of time, the knife of the man nearest me biting into them, fraying the outer edge of the rope. I kick out immediately, making contact with his knee.

He grunts at the impact, and staggers, grabbing outward instinctively to stay upright. But I'm not ready for it, and he pulls me off balance, so we both tumble down.

I roll as I land, which saves me from being winded, but my body still judders as the ground meets my side, and he recovers first, crawling over to me. His hands scrabble for my shoulders, trying to pin me, spittle flying from his mouth as he roars a battle cry. I raise my knee between his legs, and miss. He reaches for the rope attached to the binding on my wrists and begins to pull it, but as he shifts to pull it from between us, I force my shoulder up, catching his chin and making his teeth smash together with a terrible crack. Then I knee him again, and this time I get him, his eyes glazing as the pain consumes him. Another knee to the stomach to get him off me, and then I push myself up, panting heavily. As he bends double, cradling himself, I slip my bound arms over my head and pull back, pressing the rope into his throat, trying to knock him out, as Merek did me.

I chance a look over at Merek as the guard fights against me, his struggles becoming weaker. Merek is removing a dagger from the other man's side, wiping it clean on his tunic before putting it in his belt.

He looks over at me and nods grimly, and at the same time I realize the man I've been fighting has stopped moving. When I unhook my hands from his throat, he falls, rolling slightly and staring up at the sky with bloodshot eyes.

It takes me a second to understand that I killed him.

"Come on," Merek urges me, but I can't move.

I killed someone.

"Errin," Merek barks.

I don't take my eyes from the dead man. He has a little scuff on his chin, and I can see some of it is silvery white. He's perhaps my father's age.

Behind me, Merek grunts loudly, and there is a splintering, breaking sound, followed almost immediately by an almighty crash.

I turn slowly, moving as if I'm suspended in honey, to see the gate is now open. Then Merek's arms are under my shoulders and he's hauling me up.

Once I'm upright, he moves to look at my face.

"Are you hurt?"

I shake my head.

"Then let's go."

He grabs my wrists and pulls, and I totter after him, twisting to look once more at the body. I killed someone. It should have been harder.

Merek pulls me out into the wild darkness of Lormere, dragging me off the road and into the fields that surround the capital city. In the gray light of winter dawn, the trees look like skeletons.

We cross one field, then another, then another, jogging for a while, then walking, turning back to watch the red light around Lormere castle grow fainter and fainter until, after almost two hours, even the faintest glow can't be seen. I wonder what Aurek will do if the whole castle burns to the ground. Where will he go? Who will pay for last night?

Did he allow Mama the Elixir?

A mist thickens the air, coming from nowhere, and I stay close to Merek, but I'm so focused on keeping my eyes on him instead of where I'm going that his warning, "Mind the brook!" comes too late. My foot cracks the thin layer of ice atop it, sending a wave of freezing water into my boot and shocking me out of my thoughts with a small "Oh!" of surprise.

Merek sighs heavily and pulls me from the small stream as I mutter curses under my breath. He leads me over to a stately, thick tree, and urges me to sit. I sink down on to the ground, nestling myself between two forked roots and leaning back.

Silently, he drops the bags to the ground and lowers himself before me. He pulls the boot off, holding it up to tip out the droplets of water that have remained.

He reaches for one of the bags, rummaging inside it, pulling various fabric objects from it. When he's satisfied, he reaches for my leg again, peeling off the now sodden sock.

The intimacy of it shocks me, and I try to draw my foot away. "What are you doing?"

He gives me a dark look. "On my progress, we got stuck in Tallith. There was a terrible storm, and our shelter got soaked. Everything got soaked. Clothes, sleeping rolls, food. We had to manage. But it wasn't good. And it got a lot worse as the days passed. You know, there's a certain type of fungus that grows in the damp recesses of feet."

"Oyster foot," I say automatically. It's named for men who stand all day in seawater, gathering oysters from their underwater beds, and don't let their feet dry off before they put their boots on.

"Then you know of it? And how uncomfortable, and smelly, it can be."

"Did you get it?" I ask.

A smile ghosts the left corner of his mouth. "No. I was a proper prince about it and insisted that my boots and socks be dried out before I put them back on. Some of the others scoffed, and wore their damp boots with pride. I took the ribbing with surprising good grace." He starts to pat my foot dry with one of the cloaks while I pretend it's not awkward to have a prince dry your feet for you.

"Because you knew what would happen to them?"

He nods. "I spent four years reading everything I could about life in the field. Every army document, every herbalist's manual. If there were commendations for boys who learned how to survive in the wild, I would have earned them all."

"What did they do, when it happened?"

He gifts me with one of his rare, hard-won smiles. "They asked me how to fix it. And I took some lavender, vinegar, and some wild garlic, and I made a paste that cleared it up within a fortnight."

I feel my own lips curve, because it's exactly the right thing to do, and I would never have expected it of him, even after I've seen firsthand how resourceful and clever he is. But then I remember the dead guard and I lower my head.

Apparently satisfied I'm no longer at immediate risk from oyster foot, Merek eases a new, dry sock onto my foot, then stuffs the boot with another piece of cloth and puts it aside.

He reaches into the second bag and pulls out a water skin, and some of the bread and ham. He offers them to me, and I take what I want before passing them back, watching as he rips the bread apart and places the ham inside.

"I've never killed anyone before, either," he says quietly, when he's finished chewing. "Well, not directly. Not with my own hands."

I look up. "Not with your own hands?"

He shakes his head. "I'm responsible for my mother's death, indirectly. Had I not imprisoned her, he wouldn't have found her."

I've never asked Merek about his mother. I assumed she'd died when Aurek came, but I've never probed into the details. I stay silent, waiting.

"From what I heard, she tried to pretend she was a commoner to get free, once he'd announced he killed me. But some of the prisoners he took told him the truth. So she tried to offer him alliance, which was what she wanted all along. Apparently, he laughed in her face. He didn't even kill her himself. I wasn't there." He pauses, pulling the cloth free from the boot and seeking out another one, stuffing it inside. "But the guards in the guardroom talk a lot. And someone has to fetch and carry for them. They said . . ." Again he stops talking, and I lean forward, reaching for his still hands with my bound ones. He nods gratefully. "They said he had a golem snap her neck. That when she said she deserved to be killed by him, monarch to monarch, he laughed at her. And kept laughing."

"Merek," I say quietly.

"So she's one. Then I suppose you could lay at my feet the deaths of every Lormerian who died when he invaded. Soldiers, staff, citizens. The boy who died in my place, too. Everyone in Tregellan, when he wasn't stopped. And your mother." He looks up. "If Aurek won't give her the Elixir, then I'll have killed her, too."

"Don't," I say sharply. I can't think about it. I can't afford to be angry with him. In the distance, I hear the faintest sound of dogs barking, the haze distorting the sound. "Just don't, please."

After a moment, he speaks. "Let me ask you something, then. Did you mean to kill the man who attacked you?"

I shake my head. "I was trying to knock him out."

"Whereas I was definitely trying to kill the guard I fought with." He looks down at the knife tucked into his belt. "And I'd do it again. I suspect I'll have to, before this is over. I feel a little stupid, though."

"Why?"

He waits for a long moment. Then: "Death always seemed so easy," he says finally, speaking out into the night. "I would read stories full of brave warriors and assassins and how they would deliver speedy deaths, and then walk away. They'd go to the taverns and drink with their friends, or go home to their lovers.

They never said anything about how they felt afterward. They took a life, and that was that. So easy. So . . . *normal*. And yet I don't think I'm ever going to forget how it felt to kill that man. It's one thing to cause a death, but another to deliver it. With hardly any pressure, or thought, I managed it. And I felt every inch of the knife sliding into him. I think I always will." He looks down at his hands. "They don't tell you that part."

The dog barks again, louder now, and all the hairs on the back of my neck stand up.

"Merek," I say. "He wouldn't send the dogs after us, would he?"

Merek looks at me, his face blank. Then he rips the cloth from my boot and throws the boot at me. As I scramble to put it back on, he gathers up the discarded fabric and shoves it in the bag. He lifts it, flinging it as far away as he can, trying to distract them, buying us a few extra seconds. Hopefully. He shoulders the second bag as a chorus of barks and howls rends the night apart as the dogs catch the freshness of our scent.

"We have to get to water," Merek says, reaching for the rope at my wrists and slicing it through with the knife. He sees my horrified expression. "You'll need all the momentum you can get. Besides, I'd rather you killed me than the dogs."

Then once again, we're running.

Every single second I'm waiting for my body to betray me, for the command to come that will stop me in my tracks. Even as we fly through the fog, pain burning in my sides as I gasp for breath, I imagine the slow stop, the turn, the hounds leaping toward me, jaws open, stinking breath in my face.

A little ahead of me, Merek is running for all he's worth, cutting through the meadow like a blade, arms swinging back and forth with precision as he moves. I wish it was dark, wish we still had the cover of night. I feel too exposed out here in the open. Every now and then, Merek glances back, eyes on me, then over my shoulder, before he turns back in the direction we're heading.

Though he said we need to get to water, he didn't say if there was any near, and I keep the refrain *please-please-please* in my mind. We leave the meadow and find ourselves in a small copse, where we have to take care, as roots hide in the shadows to trip us up.

At one point I gasp that maybe we should climb the trees, but Merek snaps "No" at me without even turning around. So we keep running, out of the woodland, into more farmland, the muscles in my legs screaming from weeks of disuse, my lungs and chest burning, sharp pain in my side. The dogs still bark behind us, getting ever louder as they get ever closer.

"There!" Merek screams, and it seems that whatever he's spotted is enough, because he pelts toward it, widening the gap between us. I do the same, a cry wrenching itself from my lips as I force my poor body to pick up speed.

Then my ankle gives, and I stumble. I feel the layers of skin rubbing away on my palms as my hands fly out to protect me. My knees take the brunt of the fall as I slide forward on the momentum of my running, scraped raw beneath the breeches, and I close my mouth and eyes against the mud and stone that fly into my face.

The dogs are even louder.

I look behind me and for the first time I can see the dogs, cutting through the dark, shadows low to the ground as they race toward me.

Then Merek is there, hauling me up, an arm around my

waist, and I try to move but my ankle hurts, my knees hurt, my hands sting.

"Just go," I tell him.

Instead, he swings me up and into his arms, grunting under my weight.

Over his shoulder I can make out the patterns in the dogs' fur now, striped and brindled, their teeth gleaming as they yip and call to each other, running us down. I turn to the front and I see something shining, silver—water—glittering ahead of us. We're going to make it.

Something slams into us from behind, and I fly out of Merek's arms, landing a few feet from the water's edge. Merek is on his front, one of the dogs on his back, savaging the supplies pack there, food flying out, but the dog ignores it, intent on the man beneath.

Merek looks up and his eyes are terrified.

This beast is not of their pack.

I stagger to my feet and my hands reach for a rock behind me.

I throw the first one at the beast with all my might, and miss. But the next one hits its flank with a wet popping sound, and the dog snarls and looks up at me. It bares its teeth and a low, primal rumble echoes from it.

Even as my legs turn to jelly, I fire a third stone, missing at first as the dog dodges, but its motion moves it into the path of the fourth, the rock hitting it square in the face. It whimpers in apparent surprise, then leaps off Merek and heads straight for me.

I take a deep breath and throw myself backward into the water, the dog's face inches from mine as I crash through the frigid surface and all the air is pushed from my lungs. The world becomes black around me, and for a moment I don't know which way is up or down. The water is cold, thick, and pressing; my palms and knees sting where the skin is raw and bleeding still. I spin, trying to stay calm and get my bearings, but bubbles cloud my vision and I start to sink. I'm too heavy. The cloak, the boots. They have to go.

I feel the urge to breathe start to pull at me and panic sets in, my heart racing.

Think! I tell myself.

I tug off my boots, dropping them down into the murky water. Then I hold myself still, ignoring my lungs' frantic demand for air, and open my eyes, looking for the cloak. When I make out the edge of it floating above me, I push in that direction, and finally break the surface. The moment I do, I unhook it from around my throat and watch as it floats away.

As I gasp for air, I peer around until I see Merek, fifteen feet away from where I've surfaced downstream and I strike out to get back to him, fighting the current, the water feeling dangerously warmer as I get used to it. As I get closer I see Merek crawling toward the river, the dog dead with his knife sticking out of its temple. There is a moment of relief, and I call out to him.

Then two more dogs move silently out of the mist.

"Merek!" I scream, but with a snarl they both leap forward, one landing on his back and the other clamping its jaws on to his leg.

His scream is high-pitched, inhuman. He's still trying to move toward the water, his elbows scraping the riverbank, even as the dog on his back grips his cloak between its teeth and begins to shake its head.

Merek moves with it, shrieking like a trapped hare, and I can't bear it. I swim toward him, but the current keeps buffeting me away, urging me back downstream, and he looks up, meeting my eyes, and I see him give up. I see the moment he decides to stop fighting, and it fills me with rage.

I push forward, horror and fury propelling me to the bank, where I spot more stones and rocks. I dig the fingers of my left hand into the bank as an anchor, and using the water as leverage, I surge upward and grab a rock with my right, driving the rock straight into the jaw of the dog on Merek's back. It releases Merek's cloak and snarls in my face, but I smack it again, watching as blood sprays into the air from its nose.

The second dog releases Merek's leg and lunges at me, trying to aid its brother, but the first dog snarls and snaps at it. In response, the second dog launches itself at its den mate, knocking it from Merek's back.

That's all I need to grab Merek and pull him into the water with me.

As the two beasts roll and scrap on the bank, and as more join them, instantly throwing themselves into the fray while their human masters are so far behind, I tuck my arm under Merek's neck and allow the current to take us away.

Please, I beg the night. *Don't let him take control now.*

Chapter 15

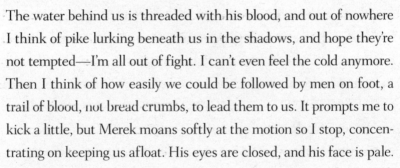

The water behind us is threaded with his blood, and out of nowhere I think of pike lurking beneath us in the shadows, and hope they're not tempted—I'm all out of fight. I can't even feel the cold anymore. Then I think of how easily we could be followed by men on foot, a trail of blood, not bread crumbs, to lead them to us. It prompts me to kick a little, but Merek moans softly at the motion so I stop, concentrating on keeping us afloat. His eyes are closed, and his face is pale.

"Merek?"

His eyes flutter open. "Sorry. I'm all right." He rolls away from me, onto his front, his head immediately going under. Before I can reach for him, he surfaces again, gasping and grabbing for my hand, keeping us together. "I'm all right. Just . . . We need to get out."

I nod, treading water. We both look around.

"Where's safe?" I ask. I don't think we're far enough away to get out on the side we were on but have no idea what might await on the opposite bank.

He shakes his head. "Nowhere. Lake Baha has to be the closest place. We haven't passed it. This flows into it, as well as on to the estuary."

His voice sounds weak, and in the water I squeeze his fingers. He squeezes back.

"What's at the lake?"

"More water. It's a saltwater lake. Lake Baha. There are—were, I don't know anymore—salt farms there. Shelter."

"Maybe we'd be better off staying in the water for a bit. It's not that cold anymore."

"That's why we need to get out," he says. "It's far too cold for us. If we can't feel it, we're in trouble." He starts to kick, one hand still holding mine, and I do the same.

"There aren't any waterfalls on this stretch, are there?" I gasp.

"No," he calls back. Then: "Branch. Ahead. Get ready." I twist in the water to see it, low and hanging over the river. "We'll have to let go of each other."

"All right."

"Ready? One . . . Two . . ."

On three he lets go of my hand and pushes up, out of the water, and I do the same. I manage to hook my elbow over the branch, leaving my lower body in the water.

The chill morning air hits me so hard it's a physical blow.

"Gods . . ." Merek groans, and I don't know if it's his leg or the temperature that pains him.

He begins to inch along the branch, hand over hand, and I do the same, heading for the bank opposite the one from which we entered the water. He scrambles up the bank, dragging his injured leg though the mud and making me wince.

"We have to get to this Lake Baha," I tell him when I collapse beside him, my clothes bleeding river water into the ground beneath me. I immediately start to shiver, my teeth juddering together as the cold air slices away the false warmth of the water.

He nods, rolling onto his back. I do the same and raise my hands to my face. At first they won't move, too heavy, too stiff, as though I left all my strength in the water. There's a moment when I almost stop trying. A voice in the back of my head tells me to rest, to close my eyes. I want to obey it. Instead, I force myself to sit up, inch by inch, whimpering as water from my hair sluices down my back.

We have nothing, I realize then, hopelessness filling me. We've lost our cloaks, our food. I have no boots, and when I look over at Merek, I see the only one he has is the shredded remains of the one on his left leg. We've lost everything. Including—

"Oak's sake. The recipe," I start, the words turning to a cough.

Merek sits up, too, slowly, as I did, patting down his pockets clumsily like a drunk. He pulls out the piece of parchment, tearing it a little, and I gasp.

"Did it survive?" I ask, even though I know it can't have.

To my astonishment, Merek sniffs it, then grins, holding it up to me.

Aside from the tear he just made, it's perfect.

He offers it to me and I take it. It leaves a residue on my hands, one I know, and I raise them to my nose.

"Pig fat," I say, and Merek nods.

"Clever Margot." He tucks it back into his pocket, and moves onto his knees and then his feet. He winces as he puts his left leg down, and a muscle twitches in his jaw. "We need to find

201

sh-shelter . . . and warmth . . . soon. We're s-soaked, and it's mid-winter . . . and it'll start getting dark in a few hours. We have to be inside by then." The words are decisive, but his voice isn't, slurring and halting, and a spasm of worry fans out across my chest. We're both in a lot of danger, and we're both pretending otherwise.

I haul myself upward, leaden limbed, trying to sound stronger than I feel. "Just watch me. I'm not to be trusted, remember. If I do anything, you have to knock me out."

He almost smiles. "Promise. C'mon."

We've barely gone a few feet before it becomes apparent his injured leg won't take his weight, and I worry we might not make it up into the mountains to the convent, even if we do find shelter and get warm first. But I keep my thoughts to myself, concentrating on the next part of the journey, telling myself if we can get some rest he might improve. It's all I can do.

I put an arm around him and allow him to lean on me as we move slowly downriver, one ear cocked for the sound of yips and howls coming toward us. After a while I stop shaking, and feel that Merek has, too, and I point out to him that it must mean we're warming up, even as I hear the lie in the words.

He doesn't reply, leaning on me heavily, and when I look at him, his eyes are closed and his lips are blue. The stab of fear that should follow is faint, like a ghost of pain, and I know that should worry me, too, but I can't feel anything, numb inside and out. My head droops, and I see my feet and focus on them, one in front of the other. Bare feet. No boots. One, then the other. Just concentrate.

We stay by the bank, moving inch by inch, Merek gray-faced with effort, or cold, and me desperate to rest, to sit down. To sleep. I don't do any of this, somehow moving forward, keeping him upright. I think wildly that I should thank Aurek for forcing me to eat; if I were any weaker, I don't think I'd have made it this far. My clothes don't dry but stick to my skin, heavy and damp, seeming to weigh more by the moment, so that every step is a battle.

"I need to take some clothes off," I say. "We'll go faster."

"No," he growls through gritted teeth.

"They're too heavy."

"You'll die. And so will I. Just keep moving."

"Merek—"

"I said move."

I don't have it in me to snap back, as if there's a glass wall between his words and me. Instead, I keep moving. After what feels like decades, we see the vast expanse of Lake Baha in the distance, and tiny blocks scattered around it that I hope are houses.

I look up at Merek to see he's walking with his eyes closed again. It spurs me on, and I move faster, pulling him with me. We're so close.

We reach the first house and I lower him to the ground and pound the door with my fist. The only thing I can think is that we have to get inside. It doesn't matter who's inside. We have to get inside this house. When no one answers, I slam into it with my shoulder, only to cry out when it doesn't budge.

"I'm going to have to break in," I say, looking at Merek. His eyes are closed. "Merek," I shout, and he nods faintly, lolling to the side. There's a burst of panic in my belly that drives me around the house, until I see a horn window—just like the ones in

Almwyk—and push it inward, shattering the slats. I poke as many of the shards away as I can, and then haul myself inside.

It's a few degrees warmer, until the wind rushes through the hole I've made, and I pull the woolen curtains over it, tutting when they wave about like flags.

I lurch through the house and unbolt the door. He sits where I left him, and when I touch his shoulder, his eyes are glazed, as though newly woken.

"Come on," I say. I hold my hand out to him, and he takes it, his skin clammy to the touch. I haul him up and guide him inside, taking him straight through to a bedroom, a carved four-poster bed in the center. "Get those wet clothes off and get under the blankets," I say. "All of your clothes. I'm going to see what I can find."

I leave him, hoping he obeys me—and that he's alive when I return—and begin to search the house, shedding my own clothes as I go. I move past a wide, blackened range that takes up one whole wall, copper pots still hung on hooks around the edges. There's a small pantry in a recess, and I see bottles and jars there, which lifts my spirits. There's a bureau, elegantly carved, and a dresser still full of crockery and tableware. In the center of the room is a table with four chairs around it, also carved with flowers and lions and serpents tangling together; and in front of the range is a second, low table between two ornate rocking chairs. There are no rushes on the floor, but no rugs, either, and my bare feet make no sound on the floor. The whole house reeks of love and pride and care; the curtains at the window are red gingham, almost unbearably bright and lovely after everything that's happened.

The final room yields a small, screened indoor privy and a washroom, complete with a large chest, and a huge tin cauldron they must have used for bathing. The idea of sinking into a hot bath makes me shiver with longing.

When I open the chest I almost start to weep at the sight of the thick, plush towels piled inside, and I pull them all out, wrapping one around my hair, another around my body, and making a cloak of a third. I can barely feel the fabric against my skin, which is bone white and mottled with blue veins. The urge to lie down engulfs me again, and I slap my cheeks before taking the rest of the towels through to the bedroom.

Merek lies on the bed, one of the blankets pulled over him, his clothes on the floor. His eyes are closed and there's a terrible moment when I can't tell if he's breathing. I drop the towels on his stomach, relieved when he looks at me. "Dry yourself, and get under the covers. I'll be back in a moment," I say. I pick up his clothes and collect mine, too, taking them back to the bathroom and draping them over the sides of the cauldron. I don't hold out much hope for them drying without a fire, but what choice is there?

Back in the parlor, I raid the chest, and find nothing useful. But in the drawer in the dresser, I find a small saltcellar and a bottle of something labeled *Dawn Water*, which smells like plain old water to me when I uncork it, so I take it, relieved I won't have to go back outside. In the pantry, I find my much-longed-for willow bark, already made into a paste, catch the astringent tang of lemonbalm in it when I smell it. I pick through the rest of the basic apothecary kit and feel myself smile.

If the owners of the cottage came back now, I'd kiss them. There's no food, or water, but I don't care. This is everything I need.

Merek has copied me when I go back to him, one of the towels around his shoulders like a cloak, another wrapped around him, tucked under his armpits. He sits up, the blankets pulled back to expose the bites in his leg.

The wounds are deep but haven't reached bone, and are surprisingly clean; I'd expected more tearing. The blood has clotted well and I'm pleased with the way it looks. I sit at his feet and tear up one of the smaller towels, dipping it in the Dawn Water and beginning to wash the wound. Merek swears violently and tries to jerk his leg away, making the wound begin to bleed again, and I scowl at him.

"It hurts," he says needlessly.

"It's Dawn Water."

"Really?" He sounds lively for the first time since we fled from the dogs.

"What is that?"

"Holy water. Supposedly blessed by Daunen."

"Twylla blessed this?"

"No, I doubt it. It's most likely just river water, bottled and sold to believers."

I continue to clean, until all of the river muck and mud from the way here is gone. I wash my hands with the Dawn Water, then dip my fingers in the balm and work it gently into Merek's wounds. I cover the whole thing with another torn-up towel, tying it off.

"There," I say. "You can chew on some of the willow bark if you're in pain."

Merek says nothing, leaning forward and taking the rags, the balm, and the water from between my knees.

"What are you—"

He takes my hands and begins to clean them, doing exactly as I did to him, gently dabbing and patting, then smearing the balm into them. Then he binds them with bandages, too.

"You need to tie me up," I say. "We're lucky nothing has happened yet."

"I expect Lief came through on his promise."

I say nothing, leaning down instead to put the ointment and the water on the floor. Merek catches my wrist.

"I don't understand him," he says, his eyes on mine. "He has killed for Aurek. Taken land for him. But he's helping us."

I shrug helplessly. "I don't know. I don't know what to believe." He saved Twylla, but damned me. He knew what Aurek was doing—to the children, to the towns, even to me—but did nothing, even bringing Mama to the castle. But he gave us the recipe, protected Merek, and helped us escape.

I can feel Merek watching me, and I meet his gaze. "I can't figure it out. But until we know for certain, I'm too much of a risk, free." I hold out the last strip of towel to him.

Merek sighs, and silently binds my wrists with it, and then lies back, nestling into the pillows. "Let's go to bed." He colors instantly the moment the words have left his mouth. "I mean, we'll be warmer next to each other, not . . ."

"I know what you meant. And you're right. Without a fire, body heat is our best bet."

He pushes the blankets aside and I climb in, lying on my back next to him. I close my eyes, but all of the tiredness I felt has inexplicably vanished. The bed is hard, and the blankets smell of other people. Then I feel his hand, his fingers twining through mine. My eyes fly open and I turn to him.

"Thank you," he says. "You saved my life."

"You saved mine."

"You tended my wounds."

"You tended mine."

He squeezes gently. "When all this is over, I'm going to make you a bloody duchess."

"Can't I be the Royal Apothecary?"

He chews his lip as he considers. "Only if you let me help."

"Done. But in my kitchen, I wear the crown. Remember that."

He almost-smiles. "Naturally." He squeezes my fingers one more time and releases me, rolling onto his side, his back to me. His towel cloak shifts and I see his skin, bare compared to the tattoos along Silas's spine.

Then I roll away, too, transitioning from conscious to asleep in the space of a heartbeat.

I can tell he has a fever the moment I wake up; he's far too warm, and it's a nasty kind of warm, the white burn of flame as opposed to the caress of the summer sun. I sit up and look at him, still asleep, his breathing shallow, high spots of red on pallid cheeks, and I think, *Not again.*

I rip the blankets away and descend on his leg, ignoring his stirrings as I pull at the bandages.

The wounds are clean, smelling faintly of lemonbalm, and not inflamed. *Not inflamed.*

He has a chill. Not the lockjaw. Just a chill.

"What are you doing?" he asks. "Gods, I feel terrible."

"You have a chill," I say. "From being in the river, I expect."

"So why— Oh." He nods at me. "The wound's all right, then?"

"Clean. Healthy as it can be."

He sighs in relief, then looks around.

Daylight is streaming in through the small window, golden through the horn-covered window, and again it reminds me of Almwyk. From nowhere I feel a pang of nostalgia for the filthy, frightening place. It was a different kind of frightening there, though. As long as you played by the rules and kept your head down, you'd be all right.

I cannot believe I'm reminiscing about Almwyk.

"How long did we sleep?" he asks.

The moment he says it, I realize my throat is parched, a dull throb in my head from dehydration, and my stomach gives an angry growl. I look out the window at the shadows on the ground.

"I'm guessing close to a whole day. Perhaps even more."

"A whole *day*? How?"

I shrug. "I don't know. I suppose we needed it." My bladder announces then that it, too, has needs, and I swing out of bed, struggling with my bound hands to keep my towel in place. "I'll be back."

My clothes aren't fully dry, the hems and seams still damp, but they will have to do, and I pull them on, stiff and reeking, after I'm finished, cursing my limited movement the whole time.

When I return, he leaves, taking coltish steps, and returns fully dressed, too, smelling just as horrendous as I do.

"I can't believe I'm saying this, but I need water," Merek says. "And boots."

We both look down at our bare feet. "Maybe some of the other houses have supplies."

With no other option, he nods his agreement, and we cautiously leave our small sanctuary. We scan the surroundings, relieved to see no other signs of life, save a tern aloft on a draft on the far side of the lake.

"Perhaps they think we've drowned," I say.

Merek doesn't look convinced. "I don't think he'd believe that without a body."

We find a water barrel behind one of the houses, and though the water tastes stale, we spend half an hour taking gulps of it— slowly, so we don't make ourselves sick. In one house we find a pair of boots with the sole half flapping off like a tongue. They're too big for Merek, never mind for me, but he stuffs rags into the toes and pulls them on anyway. I find a pair of suede slippers in another, and take those; thin as they are, they're still some protection from the ground. We find a dented tin jug with a lid that we fill with water to take with us, and then return to the house we slept in to get more towels—fashioning the largest into cloaks—and the small medicinal kit.

"To the mountains, then?" Merek asks.

"How do we get to the mountains?"

"It's a day and a half walking, at least, to get to the base of them. We'll have to head toward the coast and follow it along into the mountains. It's either that or double back and go behind Lormere castle."

My heart sinks. "I suppose the advantage is Aurek will assume we've gone to Scarron to join Twylla."

"Let's hope so." He looks into the distance, as if he can see the mountains. "Let's go."

❖ PART THREE ❖
Twylla

Chapter 16

I go from sleeping to waking in an instant, holding myself still in the pitch black of the room, my right hand inching silently beneath the pillow to the knife I keep there. My fingers curl around the handle, and I hold my breath, listening. But the only thing I can hear is Nia snoring softly on the other side of the room; whatever woke me was probably in my own head.

As my heartbeat returns to normal, the last vestiges of sleep fade away, leaving me annoyingly wide awake. So I reach for my robe and throw it around my shoulders before feeling my way carefully across the floor, heading toward the door. At the last moment, I trip over something and stumble, crying out, and the snoring stops abruptly. I bend down to rub my toe and listen to the sound of flint being struck. A second later, candlelight flares and Nia is glowering at me.

"What time is it?" she asks, her voice fogged with sleep.

"Still early, I think."

"Then why are you up?" she grumbles, putting the candle on her nightstand before burrowing back into her pile of blankets.

I look down to see what I tripped on, scowling at her clothes and boots piled in the middle of the floor. I shoot a filthy look at the covered lump on her bed, wondering how on earth her poor wife copes. I've never known anyone so messy in my life, and I had two brothers. Biting my tongue, I cross the room to the bowl and ewer, splashing my face with water a fraction above freezing. I pour fresh water into a tumbler and drink it, before turning back to my roommate.

"Do you need the candle?" I ask.

"No," she says into her pillow.

I roll my eyes, crossing the small room and picking it up, leaving Nia to her sleep.

As I walk down the corridor, heading toward the Sisters' former parlor—now the room I've commandeered as our strategy room—I hear a voice, a man's, rumbling and fast. Curious, I push the door open and find Hope spreading a map over the large table, pinning the corners down with half-empty glasses and whatever else comes to hand. Her gray hair is coiled around her head, and I can see the thin edge of her nightgown beneath her robe. The room blazes with light, every candle lit, the fire high in the grate, illuminating the hooded man who stands before it with his hands spread, and for a moment it looks as though he commands the flames. He pushes back his hood, revealing the dark skin and hair of Kirin Doglass. He turns at the sound of the door closing behind me.

"You're back!" I say, rushing over and adding my own candle to a curling corner before hugging him.

"Only just." His arms close around me and we embrace. He smells of horses, and sweat, still cold from being outside. "Lortune was completely locked down. Our spy couldn't pass on the message until a few hours ago. I was about to come and wake you." When I look up at him his eyes are bright, almost manic.

"What is it?" I ask, immediately alert. "What's happened?"

"The fire we saw was Lormere castle," Hope says.

"The castle?" I turn to her, then back to Kirin, who manages to look both grave and excited as he nods.

We were all up until late, watching the red glow down in the valley, far below where the Sisters of Næht housed their order. We'd known the fire was in Lortune when I sent Kirin to find out what was happening, but I'd thought it was businesses, or homes. Not Lormere castle itself.

"Was anyone hurt? Any word of Errin?" I ask. "Silas?"

"Silas is fine. He's precious to Aurek, remember."

"And Errin? Is she all right? Do you know how the fire began? Was it deliberate? Tell us!" I demand.

"I'm sure he will, once you give him a chance to speak," Hope says drily.

I bite back a retort and nod, as Kirin grins, his cheeks dimpling.

"I don't know for sure how it started, but I do know there was an incident. With Errin. She found Silas during the blaze and they tried to escape." When he pauses I lean against the table, needing the support. "Aurek caught her, dragged her before the crowd and accused her of starting the fire, and being the leader of the Rising Dawn."

"No," I breathe. "Errin started it?"

215

"I don't know, and she denied it, obviously. So Aurek started killing anyone who'd served her, naming them as accomplices. Then he turned on Lief, saying he thought Lief was acting as a double agent."

"*What?*" Hope moves around the table to join us. "He rounded on Vastel?"

Kirin nods. "Lief managed to convince Aurek his loyalty lay with him, but said that he wouldn't vouch for Errin and—"

"Typical," I spit, my heart thudding in my chest.

"There's more," Kirin says. Something in his tone has Hope and me exchanging an anxious glance before looking back at him as he continues.

"Lief realized his mother wasn't in the crowd—he'd assumed someone else had moved her to safety. What he didn't know was Aurek had taken her to a different tower—the one that went up in flames first. And she was in there still. Lief, Errin, and Aurek all ran to the tower, but the next thing people saw was Aurek mad with fury, crying out that Errin had escaped, and one of the servants with her."

"And?" Hope demands. "What then? Where's Errin? Where's my son?"

"Silas is still at the castle, imprisoned again. Errin is on the run, possibly with this servant." He pauses. "Aurek sent men with dogs after her."

"Dogs?" I ask, a shiver running down my spine. "The queen's dogs?" I remember them all too clearly.

Kirin nods, his mouth a thin line, and the taste of bile fills my mouth. *Please, please let her have gotten away.*

"Gods," Hope shudders, giving voice to my thoughts. "I hope she made it. I take it her mother didn't survive."

"Silas made the Elixir for Mrs. Vastel—Aurek granted Lief that. She is saved."

"Of course he did," I scoff. "Aren't they best friends—brothers—in all this?"

Kirin says nothing.

"What?" I look at him. "Am I wrong?"

"Aurek blamed Lief for Errin's escape. He . . . punished him."

"How?"

"Thirty lashes. He delivered them himself. Our spy watched the whole thing. He was taken to Lortune town square, tied to a pole, and Aurek whipped him unconscious in front of the crowd."

Hope raises a hand to her face, and I stare wildly into the fire.

I see the image in my mind, Lief's back, smooth and lithe, bared to the winter air. I see the sleek smile of the Sleeping Prince as he raises his hand and announces to the crowd that Lief deserves this. I see them, wanting the violence but fearing it at the same time, both lust and loathing. I see the whip curling through the air, slicing into Lief's skin. Him slumping forward, his back in tatters.

Kirin speaks again, softly. "Apparently, he left Lief tied there until he woke. He waited for Lief to say thank you before he'd allow him to be untied."

I dash three steps across the room and throw up into the bucket we keep ready to douse the fire.

There's a cool hand on my forehead, and Kirin kneels beside me, his eyes drawn down in concern.

"Do you want water?" he asks quietly, and I nod.

He's back within a moment, a tumbler in his hand, and I sip at the contents, letting the cold liquid soothe me.

"I assume he's been given the Elixir," Hope says from somewhere behind Kirin, a bright edge to her voice.

"He refused it." Kirin looks at me as he speaks. "Apparently, he said he'd rather bear the marks of his folly and learn from them. As with his eye."

His eye. Every time I think about his eye, guilt floods me, even as I know it shouldn't. I did that to him. To all intents and purposes, I cut out one of his green eyes. And just as I don't understand why he refused the Elixir then, I don't understand why he's done so now. Where did this streak of masochism come from?

Kirin watches me, and I summon a smile. "All right. So I take it the hunt for Errin was unsuccessful?"

"Of the five hounds unleashed, only one returned. But not with her."

"Then she's out there, somewhere. We need to contact every ally across Lormere and tell them to watch out for her. If they see her, or hear news of her, they are to get her to safety and let us know immediately so we can bring her here."

"I'll go back out now." He turns to leave at once.

"Wait," I say. "You said Lief was taken back to the castle? So it's still intact? Is Aurek still there?"

Kirin nods. "But the fire was bad. The north and east towers were destroyed, in the end. That entire half of the castle is ruined."

My tower still stands, then.

"Apparently, Aurek has it under lockdown," Kirin continues. "He's ruling from the south tower now, using the queen's old rooms. Barely anyone is allowed in or out."

"He's scared," Hope says, raising her brows at me. "He knows what it means if Errin finds you."

"Having her would only be the first step. We'd still need an alchemist to tell us how to make the Opus Magnum."

"For all he knows, we already have an alchemist," Hope says. "We have to consider that Errin's escape might provoke him into doing something more."

She's right. And that is exactly what we've been trying to avoid these past few moons. We can't afford to do anything that would make him lash out. We need the Rising to give him something tangible to focus on, as well as to rally the people to us. But we're balancing on a knife edge. Giving hope to the people while not frightening him too much.

"We can't risk pushing him into acting, not yet," I say. "Nor retaliating by harming the children he has prisoner. We need to send word to the Rising cells to drop any action for the time being. Put it on hold until we have Errin, and the recipe. Hold off on everything." I take a breath. "And to that end, contact the watches at the child camps," I tell Kirin. "Send word to Gareld, Serge, Tarvy—all of them. If it looks as though he plans to harm the children at any of the camps, I want enough people ready to get them out."

He nods, his face hard. If we have to strike to get the children out, we'll expose ourselves and our network, and lose the fraction of an advantage we have. It's a risk. But none of us would sacrifice the children for our cause.

"Spread the word," I continue. "Tell everyone to be ready, just in case. Things could move very quickly and I need us all to be prepared for it."

"I'll send messengers now."

"Thank you. Then make sure you eat. And rest. And . . . bathe."

Kirin raises an eyebrow. "Are you saying I smell?"

"Like a horse." I summon a smile despite my dark thoughts—an old skill I developed for Helewys, and deploy often as a general. He returns it easily. "I'll join you all for dinner."

He sweeps out of the room and I turn to Hope.

"Are you all right?" she asks.

I walk past her, heading to the table and peering down at the map, as if I might see a miniature Errin on there. Hope comes to my side.

"We have to find her," I say.

"And we shall. Now, answer my question. Are you all right?"

"I don't know," I admit. "I don't know."

"Would a fight help?"

I look over at her. "Oh Gods, yes."

I leave a note for Nia, telling her we're in the yard and to come straight to us, then I head to the armory—once a storeroom—to suit up. Hope is already there—her armor is missing from its stand and I can hear her footwork on the flagstones in the courtyard beyond, and the occasional sound of metal on metal as she strikes the pole at the center. I quickly braid my hair and tuck it into my tunic, before donning my own leather armor.

It's red, made out of old saddles, and it fits me like a glove.

I strap on the leg braces, buckling them around my calves and thighs. The tunic next, fastening it at the sides, twisting to make sure it's loose enough to move in. Then finally my arm braces and my helmet. We tried, when I first began training, to have me in metal armor, but a lifetime of sitting around being solemn meant I simply didn't have the strength to wear it for long, let alone fight in it. Even lightweight children's armor was too much, and that was after two moons of training, running, climbing, and lifting barrels of flour as makeshift weights. So Trey, the leatherworker who helped us make our red paint, took a knife to a whole host of old saddles we liberated from the Sheriff of Haga's stables, and fashioned me a series of body plates from the thick crimson leather.

Red like the rising dawn.

Once they're on, I kick out my legs, swing my body, raise my arms, and when I'm happy I lift down my sword belt from its hook and draw the blade, checking it over.

Hope tells me it was Silas's, the sword he used to practice with. When she offered it to me, telling me her son used it as a child, I thought she was insulting me. Until she explained about weight and balance.

"No point having a large weapon if you don't know how to use it," she said, grinning, and I got the joke a little after everyone else started laughing. But I got the point, too. I couldn't lift a sword like the ones Merek and Lief had fought with. But this, three feet long, thin as parchment, and with a sturdy but light hilt . . . this I can lift, even more easily than the one I took from the Conclave. It's *my* sword now. Hope said I should name it, but I think it's like a living thing; you can't name it: It already has a name. I just need to wait for it to tell me.

Satisfied, I sheathe it and fasten the belt around my waist. I step out into the courtyard, and as though she senses me, Hope turns. Her gray hair is hidden under a helmet—metal, like her armor. Hope has decades of fighting experience behind her, decades of training with sword and staff and bow. But as she told me, even the most seasoned fighter can be unlucky.

"Speed, and stamina," she told me the first time she allowed me to pick up a sword. "You're too small and too weak to be able to fight aggressively. So learn to defend yourself. Attacking takes more energy than defending. Tire them out, then quickly end it. Nothing fancy. No showing off. Wear them down, then strike."

"Sin Eater," she says now, bowing to hide the curve of her lips.

"Don't call me that."

"Stop me, then."

In that moment I could hug her, for giving me this distraction, for trying to rile me up. It's kindness.

But I don't hug her; instead, I lunge at her, eager for first contact.

The metal we hold rings like a bell, sparks flying, as she raises her sword to defend my blow. She twists her wrists to drive my sword down, and I dart back before she can thrust at me. Such is her skill that she fights with a blunted weapon when we practice; I'd be dead ten times over by now otherwise.

She spins out of the thrust and crosses the sword over her body, beckoning me with her chin.

"Come on, princess. At least try."

But I don't, beginning to circle her, foot crossing foot, and she does the same. My leather armor creaks faintly, and I don't take my eyes off her.

She feints at my left, and I swing out to block the attack, only for her to come at my right. I whip my body out of the way, the tip of her sword catching my breastplate, and she laughs. I strike out and it's her turn to dodge as my sword glances off her sword arm's vambrace, the metal ringing like a bell.

"Ouch," she says deliberately. "That wasn't very ladylike."

"You talk too much, old woman," I say.

"You've asked for it," she counters. And then she moves.

She is a whirling, flashing, unstoppable force, a black blur of controlled fury as her sword comes for me from every conceivable angle. Even if I had the skill to attack, there's simply no time; it's all I can do to block her movements and she's driving me backward, ever closer to the wall.

Then she stumbles on a stone; it's a fluke, an utter chance, but it's exactly what she trained me to hold out for, and I use it.

I wallop her vambrace again, making her gasp, and in the moment she takes to regain control of her wrist, I am on her, and now she is the one trying desperately to deflect my strikes; she is the one whose sword is swinging like a crazed pendulum as she repels attack after attack after attack.

I sense that victory is near, can feel that she's becoming desperate, and a fire lights inside me. I pull my arm back to put as much power as I can into my swing to disarm her.

And she plunges her blunt blade into my chest, defeating me as decisively as if she'd truly struck me.

I stop fighting at once and let my sword fall to my side, allowing exhaustion to take over. Panting, I lower myself to the ground, a luxury of the way my armor fits. Poor Hope has to remain standing, leaning against the metal pole as she labors for breath, too. She glances over at me and grins.

"Better?"

"You know I hate when you call me Sin Eater and princess."

"And you know I hate it when it's not a challenge," she says, smiling again. "You fought really well. But you need to learn to fight like that without being provoked into it."

"Aurek is the chattering type." I take a deep breath, in and out. "He'll definitely want to taunt me."

"Assuming you survive long enough to fight him."

Her words are cold water over me, reminding me that what we're doing is serious, and deadly. I feel my face fall, and I push up off the ground.

"Twylla," she says as I turn to go back inside. "You really did fight well. You've come a long, long way."

We smile at each other again, and I start to unbuckle the straps on my arms. A wash, I think, is in order. Then breakfast. Then plotting.

I've barely taken a step when Stuan comes flying into the courtyard, eyes wild.

"Come on," he chokes, pressing his hand into his side. "Come on."

Fear floods me and I redo the buckle with trembling fingers, picking up my sword and following him. Hope is beside me, as grim-faced as I am.

We run down the corridor, and I try to control my heart; whatever it is, we will deal with it.

The front doors to the convent are wide open, against my explicit instructions, and I charge through them, eyes scanning the area. They light at once on a group of people approaching; mine, I recognize, and another man and woman. The man is limping, the woman helping him walk. More refugees.

No.

She looks up and stops dead, this woman, and I see her mouth open wide.

And then we're running toward each other; she's abandoned her companion so fast that he almost falls.

The distance between us closes rapidly, and then my arms are around her and I stagger back as she throws herself against me.

"Oh, Errin. Thank the Gods, thank the Gods," I breathe into her hair.

Her stinking, revolting hair.

I thrust her away from me and look at her, something filthy wrapped around her wrists, smeared with unidentified muck. "Did you camp in a pigsty?"

She grins. "We may have hidden in one."

At that, I look over at the man she's with, and it's as though my skin is far too small for my body.

"I burned down the castle." His head is shaved, his face pale. His bones are too prominent, and his eyes look as though they belong in the face of a much older man. But his voice . . . that's still the same. And how he never smiles all the way. "So I hope you weren't planning to move back in."

"I thought you were dead," I say.

"Try not to be too disappointed," Merek says, and then— then—he smiles, and it's as though the sun has come out.

A sob escapes my throat and I step toward him.

Merek, rightful king of Lormere and the man I almost married, faints.

Chapter 17

Errin can't stop smiling as she tends to Merek. As soon as he came around, she had him peeling off his shirt and rolling his trouser leg up so she could inspect, clean, and dress his wounds. She keeps pausing in between every action to smile; she cleans around the puncture wounds carefully with strips of gauze and rose-scented water, then grins widely, wrinkling her nose. She rubs a salve into the bites, then beams over at me. Merek keeps shaking his head in amusement; it lights up his face, taking some of the haunted, hollow look from his expression.

I can't believe he is alive. I can't take my eyes off him.

My fingers itch with the urge to push Errin away and tend to him myself. Never mind that I wouldn't know what to do. I want to touch him, to feel his skin under my fingertips. Then I might be able to believe this. Instead, I fuss with the gauze, tearing much more of it than Errin could possibly need, just watching. Merek. Alive. Here.

Stuan and Ulrin, another former castle guard, carried an unconscious Merek ceremoniously through to the men's dormitory and gave him a room to himself, which I think is supposed to be a mark of respect for his status. It seems Merek will be afforded every courtesy, including privacy—something none of the rest of us have.

I can hear, beyond the curtained doorway, that the corridor is crowded with people who just want to be near him, look at him when the curtain flutters aside as Errin moves between the table where her remedies lie, and her patient. The true king of Lormere, alive, and miraculously returned to them. After moons of living under Aurek's nose, spying on him and aiding Errin, he burned down his own home and fled in the night to join the rebellion. There will be songs composed about Merek Belmis—Gods, I might even write one myself.

I lean against the wall, still in my leathers, watching Merek as he and Errin chatter back and forth about the treatments she's chosen.

"Why not the lavender and ginger?" he asks.

"Because cloves also have pain-relieving properties. And garlic is more powerful."

"It's also smelly."

"We slept in a pigsty two nights ago. You can't get any smellier; it's impossible."

"You can't talk to me like that anymore. I'm important here."

"Don't make me decide this wound needs a salt bath."

"You wouldn't dare."

She gives him a look that is pure Lief: eyebrow raised, smirk, and he rolls his eyes as my heart aches.

The way they talk, the ease of it, it makes me happy, sad, and more than a little jealous, all at the same time. I've never been that easy with anyone, not even Lief. Even now, trading insults and blows with Hope, it doesn't have the same balance to it; we're more mentor and mentee than equals. I want this. I want to be like this. As if he can sense my thoughts, Merek turns to me.

"Can't you do something about her impudence?"

For a moment I can't speak, as if I'm not all the way there. "I wouldn't dream of it," I say finally, and instantly feel stupid. Why couldn't I think of something witty? But Errin grins at me again, and begins to bind Merek's leg with fresh bandages.

"There." She ties a knot in the top of the bandage. "All done." The moment she's spoken, her face falls, as if she's given herself permission to be tired. She sways gently, fatigue heavy on her face.

"What about you?" Merek speaks sharply, noticing her sudden weariness, and leans forward to take her hands, inspecting them. The familiarity of it makes my stomach jolt.

"I'm fine. Just tired. I fell over," Errin explains to me. "We both got pretty bashed up." She pulls her hands away from Merek. "But I really would like a bath. As I said, pigsty." Her stomach rumbles tellingly. "I could eat, too," she adds.

I need to find out everything that happened in Lormere. I need to know what they know of Aurek's movements and plans. The urge to actually do something, after moons of planning and training, itches inside me, fire in my veins.

I need them to tell me everything. Everything about every moment since I last saw them both.

But I can wait one more night.

I paste a smile on my lips, one that becomes real when she smiles back at me. "Turn left, go through the courtyard, and the women's quarters are in front of you. The bathhouse is at the far end."

"Will there be . . . Can I get hot water from somewhere? I've been dreaming about a bath." Her smile is rueful.

I grin. "Go to the bathhouse and you'll see."

She gives me a confused look, then shrugs. "I'll find you after."

"I might actually join you there; I'm a little sweaty from fighting."

"Excellent. I'll ask for enough water for two."

She pats Merek on the foot as she leaves, the corridor instantly coming alive as she exits. I see half a dozen eager faces before the curtain falls back into place, and hear as many offers to "escort the lady wherever she'd like to go."

I turn to Merek to smile, to find him watching me, brown eyes sweeping over me. He colors when I meet his gaze, and I find myself blushing, too, without knowing why. Cursed auburn hair. Cursed treacherous complexion.

"Fighting?" he says, tactfully ignoring both of our red faces.

"I'm learning the sword. I was practicing when you arrived."

"That explains it." He nods to the armor. "It's good work."

"I have good people. And I'm doing well. Although I don't think I'm ever going to become a master swordswoman," I add, the words stilted, hollow-sounding to my ears. I feel awkward now that Errin isn't here to balance us, despite the need to talk to him. Not that I was the life of the party when she was here.

"It wouldn't actually surprise me if you did." He looks me up and down again, his eyes lingering on every part of me, drinking in the breeches, the leather plates, the tunic beneath them. "You look good."

I return his scrutiny, the bruises patterned across his chest, his ribs countable beneath them. "I wish I could say the same about you."

"It's been an interesting few moons."

There's an invitation there, to ask about what he's seen, what he's done. And I want to know. I pause, torn between staying with him and going to find Errin. But a timely cough from beyond the curtain reminds me half of the commune is out there, straining for every word. As if aware of it, he shrugs. "Perhaps now isn't the time, though."

"No. I'm sure Errin would advocate rest. Unless you'd like to look around? I could ask Kirin to show you where everything is."

For a moment I think he looks disappointed. "No. Rest, I think. I have one question, though. *Are* you the Rising Dawn? Is that you?"

I nod, and his lips quirk in that familiar way.

"So everyone here is part of it?"

"Every last one of us. You can meet them all as soon as you're ready. Ema, our cook, has been looking for a reason to roast a goose for weeks, so I'll tell her to have at it. We'll throw a feast to celebrate."

He raises his brows. "No need on my account. After the last few moons, bread I don't have to pick the mold off of would be a feast."

"I'll make sure someone stays close in case you need anything," I say, making my way to the doorway. I throw the curtain back, staring at the crowd, all of whom become incredibly and immediately interested in the walls.

"Don't you lot have anything better to do?" I ask, shaking my head as they mumble excuses. "Go on. Away with you. You, Hobb, I know have at least a dozen swords that need sharpening." The blond guard hangs his head and disappears immediately, followed by others who clearly don't wish to be named and shamed in front of their king. But others loiter still, so I put my hands on my hips and address them. "That applies to you all. Breena, I heard you complaining this morning that you had arrows to fletch. As for you, Ulrin—"

"I just want to say hello to His Majesty. I was on his progress with him," the giant, bear-like man says in a voice pitched like thunder. "Hello, Your Majesty," he calls.

"Hello, Ulrin. I'm looking forward to catching up with you later," Merek replies.

I let the curtain fall into place. "Now, His Majesty needs to rest. Please. Back to work."

They nod their agreement and finally disperse, Ulrin's massive form dwarfing Breena's reedy one. The mutter of excited voices carries down the hall, though. Their sovereign has returned from the dead—as handsome and courageous as ever.

I stalk away from them, saving my sigh until I'm far enough away. I have no explanation for it, but I feel unsettled, and uneasy. I need a bath.

I stop by the kitchens, incurring Ema's wrath when I help myself to a couple of apples and some cubes of cheese. When I reach the changing room for the women's bathhouse, I shed my clothes and my armor, hanging the panels carefully, less mindful of my everyday wear. I unpick my braid and let my hair fall loose, covering me as I walk into the bathhouse.

I scan the room, looking for a brown head peeping over the top of one of the baths. There are six baths down here, carved from red-veined marble, arranged like the points of a star. Each one is twice my height in length, and not much less in width and depth. And each one is filled with naturally hot water that bubbles up from the hot springs beneath the ground. The room is full of steam, and the smell of sulfur, which I'm long since used to. I peer through it, unable to see my friend.

"Errin?" I call.

"I'm not leaving here." Errin's voice echoes faintly off the low ceiling. There is a splash, and then I see her head emerge. She must have been lying down in the water. "Hot water. All the time. I cannot believe Silas grew up with this. I cannot believe he didn't tell me." She falls quiet.

I make my way over to the bath on her left and place the food on the rim. "Is he all right?" I ask as I step into the water, a delicious shiver racing up my spine.

For a long time she doesn't reply. Then: "Yes. No." I hear the sound of a slap against the water, and when I look over, she's hidden from me again. "Even if he's all right now, he won't be for long." Her voice sounds far away. "Twylla, we have to get him out."

"We will. I promise. I promise," I repeat, then I, too, slide down and allow my hair to fan out around me.

Again she is silent for a while. "This is nice, though, this bathing. Relaxing. It's hard to be terrified like this."

"I know." I speak to the ceiling. "Growing up we had a tin bath that we'd fill with well water, in front of the fire. Once a moon. At the castle it wasn't much better, being at the top of the tower. You know, the queen used to wax lyrical about the water in the mere, and I hate to admit it, but she had a point. It's heavenly."

I roll onto my front and lean on the side of the bath, water dripping to the floor. Across from me, Errin does the same.

"Hello," I say, smiling. "Apple?"

"Please." I toss one to her and she catches it neatly, so I follow it with some of the cheese. There is a loud crunch as she bites into the fruit and then moans. "I missed you," she says through her mouthful.

"Are you talking to me or the apple?"

"The apple." She pops a cube of cheese in her mouth. "And also the cheese."

"I missed you, too." I smile. "Are you all right?"

She doesn't reply immediately, polishing off her food. I toss her the second one. "Yes. And no. There's so much . . . *so much* I need to tell you. I . . . I don't know where to begin."

"It's the same for me. I wish . . . Gods, Errin, I wish you'd been with me," I say in a rush.

She smiles. "You have your army."

"I do."

"*How* do you have an army? And the Rising Dawn—that's you? Wait. Start at the beginning. Tell me everything."

So I tell her.

I tell her of the flight from the Conclave, and meeting Kirin, which makes her beam at me across the bathhouse. "His fiancée is alive!" she cries. "She's in Tressalyn. Oh, he'll be so happy."

But then I have to tell her about Lief, and the Sisters.

"*You* did that?" She stares at me, steam rising from her hair, her eyes wide, green, shaped like his. "But he said the Sisters did it. Two of them. He never said. He never even said he'd seen you."

"Perhaps he was ashamed after being bested by me."

"Perhaps . . ." She doesn't sound convinced. "I can't figure him out, Twylla."

"What's to figure out?" I say, harsher than I mean to.

"I don't . . . He's done some horrific things, but at the same time he's—"

"He's chosen his side." I cut her off.

She hesitates as though she'd say more, but instead shrugs. "What happened next?"

I tell her of our journey, and what happened in the woods—all of it, my grand announcement to the camp and how unimpressed everyone was, the chamber pots. Finally realizing what to do and how to win them over. The way the sun rose that morning, the rays reaching out to me like the hands of old friends.

And how we came here, to the House of the Sisters, in the East Mountains of Lormere. How we gathered up more people as we traveled, afraid and angry. How we—Hope, Kirin, Nia, and I—founded the Rising Dawn as a way of sending a message to the captive Lormerians, and to distract Aurek from searching for me.

"So they're in every town?"

"Every one. We have a network over the whole of Lormere, and we have chains of spies stationed and hiding across the country. We pass messages along that chain. A fair few of our contacts are his own guards."

She crows. "He was afraid of that. How did you manage it?"

I beam. "Pure dumb luck. On our first attack, I was caught by a guard. He should have turned me over—but he told me to run. I should have known that loyalty born out of fear might not be loyalty at all. So once we were established here, I had one of my men, Gareld, seek out that same guard. He came over to us there and then, and told us which of the others felt the same. And then they told us of others they knew, and so on. They almost all have children, children he's taken."

Errin sighs. I tell her that we know every camp he's holding them in, from the children of Chargate in the West Woods, to the children of Lortune, who are being kept not three miles from where we are now in a cave system in the mountains. And I tell her we've managed to find spies and followers in the villages that Aurek thinks he has under control. She's impressed.

"It wasn't actually that hard," I say. "He's hurt so many—there were people itching to strike back, in whatever way they could. They just needed to know they weren't alone. A lot of his guards only knelt to him to save their families. So we send messages through them, small things to do, coordinated across Lormere. Nothing that would really rile Aurek, nothing that would force him to retaliate, because in truth we're not fit for all-out war. We don't have enough people to take on his army, and even those we do have aren't fighters. But"—I lean forward eagerly—"we can do more now you're here. We could start work on piecing together the Opus Magnum recipe. I know it will be hard work, but there are thousands of books here—perhaps one of them—"

"I have the recipe," she says.

Her words ring around the room.

"For the Opus Magnum," she continues. "Or rather, Merek has it."

"You *have* it? How?" I breathe.

"I don't think you want to know," she says, looking down. It doesn't matter, I tell myself. The recipe is the important thing. Assuming it truly is the recipe.

"It's real," she says, as though she's heard my thoughts. "It's the real thing. I remember."

My skin prickles with excitement. This is it. We have the recipe. And Errin. And me. We have what we need to defeat Aurek. We can end this now.

It's more than I could ever have hoped for.

"How long do you need to make it?" I'm trying not to get too carried away, but in my head I'm frantically calculating—I'll need a day or two to get everyone together—to send word out to the Rising across Lormere and to reach out to those in Tregellan who have promised to support us when the time comes. But then . . .

"It's going to take a while to make it."

"Well, of course. How long are we talking? A week?"

Errin's face falls and she shakes her head. "I still have to deconstruct it, and then we need the ingredients. It's going to be difficult, getting some of them. The herbs and plants are fairly commonplace, though mandrake is restricted. But it's not impossible to find, and this area is known for it. The asulfer is here, in the mountains, as evidenced by the water." I hear her splash her hand against that selfsame water. "But the only place I know to get the Sal Salis is the Conclave, and Merek thinks we'll have to go to Tallith to get the quicksilver."

"Tallith?" I stare at her. "But that will take at least a moon—six weeks realistically, maybe even eight if the weather worsens."

"I know." She meets my gaze, her expression apologetic.

Two moons . . . "And there's no store here? No mine?"

"I can ask . . ." She doesn't sound hopeful. "Perhaps the Sisters left some behind when they moved to the Conclave . . ."

"Two moons," I say softly.

"I'm sorry," she says.

"No," I say, trying to hide my obvious disappointment. "You have nothing to be sorry for. Nothing. This is fine—more than fine."

I decide I'm done then, and I stand, letting the water sluice down my back, my hair a sheet. I leave wet footprints on the tiled floor behind me as I fetch towels, binding my hair in one and wrapping the other around me.

"Do you have to go?" Errin asks, and I turn to see her watching me, her eyes wide.

I feel a rush of pity for her. In the warmth of the bath she looks like a flushed child. And then I remember what Kirin told me about her mother. "I don't know if anyone else told you yet, but your mother is healed. Aurek gave her the Elixir. She's going to be fine."

I don't tell her what Lief endured after it, and the joy that fills Errin's tired face makes it worth it, until her expression falls again. "Thank the Oak, of course," she breathes. "But Silas . . ."

"Silas would have happily done it for your mother. He would have chosen to, you know that. Now, I'd better tell Nia we've got another roommate, so she needs to pick her clothes up."

Errin's face lights up again, and I can't help grinning back at her.

"She snores, too—" I pause as I hear footsteps, many of them, echoing, heading toward us. "What now?" I breathe.

Stuan, Kirin, Ulrin, and Hobb burst through the curtain into the baths, making Errin shriek and duck down under the water.

"What is the meaning of this?" I shout at them as they skid to a halt, looking from me in my towels, to Errin's shocked eyes over the top of the bath, and back to me.

"It's—it's her." Ulrin points at Errin. "She's a danger to you. His Majesty told us the Sleeping Prince can control her, make her do things—attack you, and us—"

"I thought I told you to leave His Majesty alone?"

Just then, Merek limps into the room. "I said it's unlikely but possible," he counters, as all the men drop into loose bows that prompt him to narrow his eyes. "I said he had the ability, but we suspected the threat had been nullified. I wish I'd kept my mouth shut."

I turn to Errin, who now looks sheepish, chewing her lip. "It's true."

I sigh. "All of you out." I point to the doorway behind them.

"But, my lady . . ."

"This is the women's bathhouse and therefore you have no place in it. Go. I can take care of myself, as well you all know."

There is a moment when I think they might argue, but eventually they shuffle out. I look at Merek, who is faintly pink around the cheeks. "You too, please."

He nods at once, then speaks to Errin. "I didn't mean for this to happen. I'm sorry." Then he gives me a last glance and leaves us, dropping the curtain firmly in place behind him. I pull the towel from my head and walk back to my bath, dropping the second one to the floor as I climb back into the water.

"It's not completely bad news," she says. "It's to do with simulacrums. And golems."

"Tell me," I demand, reclining in the warmth.

So she does.

Chapter 18

Errin's wrists are loosely bound for the feast, and Stuan insists on sitting on her other side, directing Kirin to mine. There is a great pantomime over whether she should be allowed a knife and spoon, but a dark look from me sees her being handed them nervously. In her place I'd probably belt one of them with the spoon and blame Aurek, but Errin is apparently cleverer than me, for she meekly eats her goose, her movements slow and deliberate. I don't like to see her wrists bound, don't like the idea she's escaped only to be imprisoned again. But she takes it with good humor, and I can't be offended if *she* isn't.

After our time in the bathhouse, Errin and I had spent the remainder of the afternoon copying out the recipe for the Magnum Opus, numerous times, giving copies to Kirin, Nia, Hope, and me, and letting Errin and Merek have one, too. Other copies have been hidden around the commune, just in case.

As predicted, Merek is surrounded by people from the moment he arrives, all trying to sit beside him. Lady Shasta—or Ymilla, as she insists we all call her now—makes a beeline for him, squashing herself in beside him and instantly laughing, though Merek can't have had time to say anything funny. Ulrin, who she has previously been sitting with, glares at her, picking at his meal moodily. I offer him a smile and he glares at me, so instead, I turn back to Kirin, who is filling Nia in on what she missed this morning.

When I look back at Merek, Ymilla's hand is resting on his arm as she talks, and he's pushing his food around his plate, nodding halfheartedly. When I'm finally able to catch his eye, he holds my gaze deliberately, before standing, taking his goblet with him, and moving to the doorway, walking stiffly on his bandaged leg. Ymilla looks from him to me, and drops her knife with a loud clang, and the rest of his band look dejected at his leaving, their end of the table immediately quieting.

Merek gestures with his chin for me to follow him, and I nod to say I'll follow, but then Hope asks me a question and draws me into a discussion about the Rising.

I sense, rather than see, him moving back into the doorway, can feel him watching me as we talk. I shoot him a quick glance to let him know I know he's there, but stay seated, answering questions. When the conversation finally changes course and I feel I can leave, I look up in time to catch him turning away, slipping out of the room. I wish the others a good night and go after him.

Merek is seated a little way along the corridor, on a wooden bench, sipping his drink. He looks up at the sound of my footsteps

240

and pats the bench beside him. I take a seat, my knee bumping his as I do, and turn to meet his gaze before I look him over.

His hair is beginning to grow back; there's half an inch of fuzz shadowing his head now, no sign of the curls that will follow if he lets it grow. There is a shadow on his jawline, too, and around his lips. There was a roundness to his cheeks before, but now his face is all angles, sharp cheekbone, stern brow. He still looks like his mother, but I can see his father in his face now, too. He looks like a man. He looks like a king.

"Quite the group you've assembled here," he says.

"Aren't they something."

"I never thought I'd see the day Lady Shasta would follow your orders."

"I'll have you know Ymilla has become a dear friend," I reply.

"Really?" He turns his head to look at me, his expression wry.

"No. She still dislikes me, but you know her—she likes to be close to the power."

He chuckles, a brief, unguarded laugh, before falling silent.

"How are you?" I ask, and immediately regret it. It's too big a question. And too small, too, considering our history.

As if he thinks the same, he sighs slowly. "Alive."

I wait for him to ask me the same question, but he doesn't, his eyes still roving over me, finally resting on my hands clasped in my lap. "You've changed," he says eventually, his voice soft.

I follow his gaze and look down. My hands are rough, reddened, calloused from training with the sword and the bow, from washing my clothes in icy well water, from climbing stone walls. I pull my sleeves down and he leans across, pushing the fabric back. He looks at my hands, turning them over in his own, and I watch him. He traces a healing pink scar—I forget what caused it—along the back of one, before twining his fingers between mine, watching me as he does.

"I mean you," he says. "Not the way you look. Or the way you speak. You've picked up some Tregellian inflections, though, you know."

"A lot has happened," I say, well aware of how bland I sound. How quickly it seems I've forgotten everything that has happened since I left Lormere. Everything I've seen and done is lost in the face of his being here. My prince. My king. My once-future.

He raises his brows. "I know. The castle was rife with rumors of your escapades. How you destroyed a golem singlehandedly. How you slipped past the guards to climb the city walls at Chargate and daubed them with 'The Rising Dawn.' How you loosed live rats in the sheriff's home in Lortune. How you broke into the castle and filled Aurek's bed with vials, all labeled 'poison,' just to show him that you could get to him anytime."

I smile. "You shouldn't believe everything you hear. You know full well I didn't go to Lormere castle. You were there."

Then he smiles, and my heart catches. His eyes glitter, and lines that make him look so much older fan out from the corners, his face crinkling. They're new. "And the others?"

I wait a heartbeat. "All true. Though I didn't personally put the rats in his house, and I never climbed the wall at Chargate. But I was the one who painted the south wall. It was our first attack."

"What was it like?"

"I shook so hard I'm surprised the rattling of my teeth didn't give us away. But I had to do it. I had to show the people I was trying to lead, that I meant what I'd said."

"I'd say it worked. How many of you are there?"

"There were four of us, in the beginning. Me, Hope, Kirin, and Nia. We found the others in the West Woods, and persuaded them to follow me, and picked up some stragglers on our way here; more escaped and joined us when they could. We number around one hundred now, here, with more on their various watches across Lormere, some in Tregellan trying to find us aid there, and also stationed hiding in pairs to help us carry messages faster. There's more in the towns, so perhaps five hundred of us in total."

"Five hundred?" he says, and I hear his disappointment.

"Merek, this was never going to be a war won on a battlefield. He can make soldiers from clay, who need no food, no shelter, just his instruction."

"Actually, the golems aren't infallible," he begins, but I stop him.

"I know. Errin told me. But we're still outnumbered and have too few resources to engage him right now. So our goal is to sow havoc across the land, and force him to dilute his army until it's thin enough for us to get through, directly to him, and end the fight then. I don't believe he has any true allies, certainly none who'd defend him if they saw he was losing." Except one, I think. Except Lief. Who stayed even after Aurek beat him senseless.

From the way Merek is looking at me, I know he's thinking of Lief, too. "He helped us escape, you know," he says finally.

"Then it must have served him somehow."

"He gave us the recipe."

I'm shocked, but I try not to show it. "It makes no difference. It changes nothing."

"Errin said you'd say that."

"Then she was right." We lapse into silence, he sipping at whatever is in his goblet—wine, I assume.

"Errin also says you think it'll be two moons before we're ready to attack."

I nod. "It seems like a long time to wait, but it won't be, not with all we have to do. We have the list of ingredients we need for the Opus Magnum. It's a blessing you escaped, in every way. What we have to decide now is who is going to fetch the ingredients we need—who we can afford, and trust, to send. There's no point all of us going after them on some kind of mad quest; it'll take too long, and it's vital both Errin and I stay safe until we have the poison made. You, too."

Merek nods. "It's a good amount of time to prepare properly. And the children he's holding? Do you have a plan for them, too?"

"They'll be liberated as part of our opening gambit. Coordinated uprisings across Lormere, and the children at the camps freed and taken to safety. When he sends out reinforcements to fight in the towns, we'll strike at the heart of his stronghold."

"What if he *doesn't* send out reinforcements? What if he goes to ground?"

"Then we free the towns and amass an army of people large enough to go and lay siege to him. Either way, we have a plan."

We both fall silent, both lost in our thoughts. And mine turn to Lormere. To Lief. To him helping them.

"Did . . . Lief really give you the recipe?"

Merek nods. "He did." He stops and frowns, then looks at me, reaching for my hands. "This is hard for me to say. I wish . . . I wish I weren't the kind of man who had to say it. But . . . I think he regrets what he's done. I think he'd help us, join us even, if we could get a message to him."

"No," I say.

"He said something to me. He said, 'Perhaps you missed the theatrics.' It made me think of the trial, you remember? *Theatrics.* It's not even that he said it, but the way . . ."

The hairs on my arms stand up, but I ignore them. "I remember. But I can't believe he meant anything by it."

Merek takes a breath. "Because of what he did to you?"

I look at him. "Because he can't be trusted. Because time and time again, he's betrayed the people he's claimed to love. Me. His sister. His mother. You weren't there in the bone temple. He didn't care what he'd done to Errin. He regrets nothing. He might feel sorry for himself right now, but he'll already be planning a way out. He'll land on his feet. That's what he does. And believe me, Merek, these aren't just the words of a bitter ex-lover. These are the words of someone who has thrice had run-ins with him, and only come out of them well by luck or his whims. I trust Hope. I trust Kirin. I trust Nia. And Stuan, Ulrin, Ema, Breena. I trust you and Errin most of all. But I do not and will not trust him. I can't afford to. He's made his bed, he can lie in it. Alone."

Merek nods.

"So you're right," I say. "I have changed. I'm not a fool anymore."

"I never thought you were." Merek releases my hands gently. "And that's still not what I meant by it." He stops, and I wait for him to continue, but when he speaks it's to say, "I think I'll get some sleep. It's been in short supply recently."

I feel strangely as though I've been dismissed, as if I've disappointed him somehow. "Good night."

He unfolds his long body and pushes himself to his feet, then reaches down to me. I take his hand, allowing him to pull me up. We stand, a handspan between our chests, and I look at him.

"I'm very glad you're alive," he says. Then he takes a breath before biting his lip and frowning again, this time at something over my shoulder.

I turn to see Errin and Kirin in the doorway, others behind them. The feast is over. I look back at Merek to find his expression is closed.

"Good night," he says, walking away from me, and I watch him go, his limp more exaggerated now. He must be tired, I think.

Errin comes to me, followed by Kirin. "Everything all right?"

"All well. We were just catching each other up on a few things."

"My lady." Stuan appears behind us. "I've spoken to some of the boys, and we'd be happy to stand guard outside your chamber tonight. Or inside."

"I bet you would," Errin says under her breath, and I have to twist my mouth to stop myself from laughing.

"That's kind, but I'm sure we'll be fine."

I don't wait for his reply but loop my arm through Errin's, mostly to upset Stuan, and guide her to our room.

Nia has moved her things from the floor but, instead of putting them away, has left them in a pile on her bed. Someone has brought a pallet in and placed it in the middle of the room, leaving soft ropes woven from chamois on top. I brush them aside and help Errin down onto it.

I am about to tuck her in when she stops me.

"You have to tie my feet. And tighten the bonds on my hands. I promised them you would." Her mouth, the only part of her face I can see, is a grim, determined line.

Silently, I bind her feet with the chamois rope, then tighten the knots at her hands—firmly, knowing if I don't she'll complain. When I'm done, she lies back and looks up at me.

"I killed someone," she says.

I blink, momentarily stunned. "Oh."

"A guard," she continues, as though we were in the midst of talking about it. "One of Aurek's men. While we were escaping. I didn't mean to, but I did. I strangled him."

I exhale slowly before I reply. "Well, it sounds like if you hadn't killed him, he'd have either killed you or taken you back to Aurek. You had no choice."

"That's what Merek said."

"Merek is very clever."

"I just . . . I wanted you to know." She pauses. "Does it . . . Does it ever go away?"

"What?"

"The feeling."

And she doesn't need to explain, because I *do* know. Even though I never actually killed anyone, I still have the guilt, like a scarf, like a noose, hanging around my neck. The feeling that I took something that wasn't mine, that I have something because I denied someone else. No matter that I didn't truly take a life; I watched people die believing I'd killed them. People died because of me.

"Yes," I lie. "Eventually you make peace with it. You won't forget it, but it won't haunt you."

247

Her sigh is soft. "Thank you." She rolls onto her side. "Good night, Twylla," she says, and I cover her with a blanket.

"Good night, Errin," I say softly. I listen as she drifts off to sleep, am still awake when Nia comes in a little later and climbs into bed without moving her things. Soon the room is filled with their soft, sleeping sounds, little huffs and snorts, and it should be a comfort. But I can't settle. It's a long, long time before I drift into an uneasy sleep.

The following morning, I rise early to take Merek and Errin on a tour of the commune. We're the only ones in the refectory, though Ema, and Breena, on rotation as her assistant that day, have been up baking for two hours already, as evidenced by the fresh rolls still steaming in baskets along the wooden tables.

Errin and I sit in sleepy, companionable silence, tearing hunks of bread apart and blowing on our fingers when the steam lightly scalds them, before dunking the pieces into golden-yolked eggs and gobbling them down. Errin's hands are still bound, loosely, but that's not stopping her from devouring her breakfast.

"Where does all this food come from?" she asks, wiping her bread in a smear of yolk that escaped the shell.

"The Sisters' stores. There are cellars beneath the compound that have enough food to feed a small army. Literally, as it turns out. Flour, grain, oats, hams, sides of venison. There are chickens, goats, and sheep, all around half a mile away, in a pasture owned by the Sisters. They were set up to be self-sufficient, so they didn't have to rely on outsiders for anything."

"Like the Conclave."

"Exactly." I hesitate before asking, "What was it like at the castle?"

"Foodwise?" she asks, and I nod. "For me, all right. He made sure I was fed. I dined with him whenever he told me to, and he certainly didn't ration his own table. There was meat, and wine. Silas looked well, too, in terms of food, at least. He wasn't starved."

"And for the others?" I mean Merek, and she knows it.

"Not so good. We never spoke about it, but . . ."

"The results speak for themselves," Merek says, entering the refectory on bare feet. He looks a little better than he did yesterday—the purple stains beneath his eyes have faded—but he is so thin, almost gaunt, the too-sharp planes of his face advertising how mistreated he's been. He's dressed in a pale blue tunic—the material looks soft, well washed—and brown breeches that are faded at the knee. Like the pink homespun gown Errin wears—the twin of my green one—his clothes will have been scavenged from those left behind by the alchemists and their families when they fled. Simple, homely, well-made garments, designed to last. I've never seen him in anything so normal-looking. And from the way he shoots swift, curious glances at me, I assume he's thinking along the same lines. I smile to myself and concentrate on my breakfast for a while.

When I next look up, at Merek tearing into bread as though he hasn't seen real food for weeks, and Errin, oblivious to the hint of yolk at the corner of her mouth, it strikes me how very young we are, and how unfair all of this is. Why are we the ones doing this? Why didn't the Council of Tregellan fight back? Why didn't the

Lormerian lords and ladies muster armies from their tenants? Why has it fallen to us to fight Aurek?

Merek points out the yolk on Errin's face, and instead of blushing and wiping it away, as I would, she leans over and dips her finger in his egg, wiping yolk on his face, too. His mouth falls open, aghast, and Errin crows with laughter. He shakes his head at her, and I see him trying desperately not to laugh, too. My heart catches, as though on a thorn, and I sigh without meaning to.

Merek looks over at me. "Are you all right?"

"Yes. Of course," I say. Again I search for the right thing to say, the words that will be the key to allow me to join in, that will unlock an easy, joyful place for me in their friendship. Again my heart aches, because I want to be part of this so, so badly, and I'm not, and I don't think I ever can be. Neither of them are like this with me. Of course they like each other more than they like me. Who wouldn't?

I'm jealous, I realize. Not of them, but of him. Of the way he's walked back in so easily and slotted in, when I always feel like I'm the wrong shape or size. This is how it will be for him once we've defeated Aurek. He'll stride victoriously back to the throne, while I hover in the doorway, not knowing whether to stay or go. Waiting for scraps from the table.

And I can bear it no longer. "I have to go," I say. "I'm sure Kirin will be happy to show you around. I'll have him sent to you."

"Twylla?" Errin says. Her face is concerned, and I hate myself then, for doing that to her.

I take a deep breath and force myself to smile. "I just remembered I had some business to see to before the council this afternoon. I'm sorry. Stupid of me to forget."

Errin looks at Merek, who turns to me. "Of course. Can we help at all?"

I shake my head. "You still need to heal. I'll see you at lunch."

I don't give them time to reply, almost running from the room. My eyes sting; I can feel my chest and face reddening, becoming blotchy, and I try to decide where to go until this has passed.

"Twylla?" Hope steps out of the corridor to the women's quarters as I rush past.

"I'm fine," I say, but my voice cracks.

"Like hell you are," I hear her mutter, then the sound of her wooden shoes on the flagstones behind me.

"Please leave me," I sob, unable to keep the tears locked down.

She grabs my arm gently and pulls me to a stop, and I twist away, not wanting her to see me like this. She spent so long thinking I was weak, I don't want her to think I am again.

"Come with me," she says, leading me back to the courtyard, then down a short passageway and into the gardens. I go without hesitating, too tired to fight.

At this time of year the earth is bare and frosted, ice glittering over the soil. Hope told me when we came that the potatoes and beets we're now eating were harvested from here, and that come spring, they'll begin to grow again, but you'd never believe there was life waiting down there, to look at it.

She leads me down paths between squares of earth, all slumbering until the weather turns, until we come to the small orchard. It's as bare as the gardens are; the branches look forlorn and naked without their leaves.

Beneath a large apple tree is a bench, and I think she means for us to sit on it, despite the fact I have no cloak, but we walk past, approaching a stone archway around a wooden door, and then she reaches into her pocket and pulls out a small key chain that jingles softly when the iron keys on it dance together. She opens the gate, which tellingly doesn't squeak, and then beckons me through into another small garden. And at the far end of it is a tiny cottage, like something out of a fairy tale.

It's wooden, with ivy climbing up the sides, the green vibrant compared to the muted winter palette around me. It is a little lopsided, the chimney squat, the door too wide. It's incredibly charming. She walks down the path toward it, and I follow, realizing with sudden certainty that she's brought me to her own cottage, where she lived, once, before she became a Sister. Where she raised Silas.

I follow her to the door, which she unlocks, and then we enter. As I'd suspected, the air isn't stale, and even though there is little furniture, just a chair and a small table, it has the feeling of someplace used. And loved. The floors are swept free of dust; the wooden chair gleams.

"It's my secret," Hope says. "But a secret is always better shared," she adds pointedly.

She busies herself at the small hearth, kindling a fire, and then reaches back into the recess of the wall, pulling out a pot and two tin mugs and hanging the kettle over the smoldering wood.

"I'll make some tea" is all the explanation she gives.

When the metal kettle begins to whistle, she wraps her cloak around her hands and pulls the kettle down, adding the tea leaves to it and swirling it around. As she moves, practiced and sure, my awkwardness begins to creep back in and I wrap my arms around my knees. When she's deemed the tea done, she pours it into the two mugs and sits in her chair.

"Tell me," she commands.

"I'm not weak," I say.

"I know that." She rolls her eyes. "Tell me something I don't know."

"I feel . . ." I pause, then turn slightly, so I'm talking to the leaded window rather than her. "I don't know. I feel strange. I feel uncertain. Off."

"Since when?"

"Yesterday."

"When Errin and Merek arrived, or before?"

"It's . . . hard. Seeing them together."

"Together?" Her voice sharpens.

"Not romantically. Errin loves Silas, I know that." Hope says nothing. "But the two of them being here . . . Merek was part of my world before, and she's part of the new world I know. A world I built. And I don't . . ." I trail off. "All I wanted was to rescue Errin and Silas, and defeat Aurek. I hadn't thought about what would happen next. And I know that's stupid, because if we win, there will be an after, and someone will have to be in charge of it all."

She nods. "Merek is the deposed former king, from the only ruling family Lormere has ever known. Now that he has returned, he can take his rightful place and rule. As someone has to."

"Yes."

"And you want it to be you instead?"

"No!" I say without thinking. But then I pause. Do I want it to be me? "No," I say again slowly, testing the words for truth on my tongue. "I don't want to rule Lormere, not really. But I don't want to lose what I've built here, and it feels . . . shaky to me at the moment."

"Because Merek is here?"

I nod. "He's . . . What I was when he knew me is so different from who I am now. I don't know how to reconcile the two." I smile sourly. "The helpless princess, and the leader."

"Why do you have to?"

I shrug. I don't know. I reach for my tea, and at the same time feel hands in my hair. I turn, and Hope holds out a small twig.

"I think you got a little too close to the trees," she says, and I turn back, allowing her to pluck the rest out.

"What if . . ." I say, relaxing as her fingers comb through my hair. "What if Merek being here will change things, change the way the people see me? What if they stop listening to me? What if they look to him as their leader now? Or Errin? Because let's face it, Hope, I'm not exactly popular. I'm not charismatic. I don't have anything witty or clever to say. I'm good at giving orders to people. But now a real leader is here—"

"*You* are a real leader," Hope says sharply, pulling a little too hard on my hair. "Who rallied them in the woods? Who made them follow her here? Who organized soldiers, scouts, and rebels? Who set a watch on the children? Who cleaned with them, trained with them, and promised them a better life? That was you, Twylla Morven. And yes, you had help and support. But so does every leader."

"He's their king."

"So what? We already know kings come and go." She pauses. "I don't think this is about Merek, not truly. Is it?"

"I just feel . . . When will I be sure?"

"Sure of what?"

"Of me. Of who I am. Of what I'm here for. When will I know?"

Hope laughs. "Never. You never will. No matter what happens. You will always have those moments of doubt and you will always make mistakes."

I turn around to look at her.

"And it will only get worse. As you age. As there's more to lose. Lovers, friends, children. You think I'm always sure of my path?"

"Are you telling me you're not?"

"I was *sure* you would be as intractable and officious as your mother, Gods keep her in peace. I was *sure* Errin was in league with her brother. I was *sure* coming to Lormere was a terrible idea. I was *sure* the Rising Dawn would get us all killed."

"It still might."

She chuckles. "It might. But that doesn't mean I was right to assume it."

"You always seem so sure."

"And that, my girl, is the secret. Quake all you must on the inside. But on the outside, you must be stone. And you never know; with enough practice, it might become the truth."

She cups my face for a moment and then reaches for her tea.

"Two last things: Firstly, I doubt Merek wants to take this from you. And secondly, even if he did, I think the people would follow you over him anyway."

I scoff.

"You said it yourself; you built this world and you gave it to them when they had nothing else. That kind of currency goes a long way, Twylla. Deeper than you know. I'm sure they're all glad

Merek's alive—he's an asset to us—but I don't for one second think they'd welcome him as their leader. Because he hasn't earned it. You have."

Her words make my eyes burn. "I hope you're always around to remind me when I'm being a fool," I say.

To my immense surprise, she leans forward and kisses my forehead. "You are your own worst enemy, Twylla Morven. Now, that's enough," she says, seeming surprised at herself. "You have a council of war to open."

"Thank you. For this. And for showing me this place."

"I know you won't tell anyone about it. After all, you're not exactly popular." She smirks, and I smile. "You're you. And that is quite good enough."

I help her bank the fire, and rinse the mugs in a water barrel at the rear of the cottage, before we make our way back. I let her go on ahead of me, pausing in the gardens to think. I keep expecting this to get easier. But maybe what I need to do is acknowledge that it won't. That there will always be something to battle, small or large. And that's all right. I just have to keep fighting.

"My lady?" Stuan appears. "We wondered where you were."

"I'm here," I say. "After lunch, could you gather Hope, Kirin, Errin, Nia, and His Majesty and have them come to the council room?" He nods and bows, and I make a snap decision. "And I'll need you there, too. But no one else is to know."

He looks surprised, and pleased, puffing out his chest. "Yes, my lady. As you wish."

Chapter 19

Though I trust every single soul at the commune, there is a lot riding on us taking Aurek by surprise. Our resources are too finite to engage him in direct battle until we absolutely have to.

There are a lot of *ifs* our plan relies on: If Aurek doesn't know that Lief gave Errin the recipe; if he doesn't know that Errin has found me; if he doesn't know that I'm in the mountains behind his ruined castle. All these *ifs* that I'm hoping will buy us the time we need to collect the ingredients, assemble the deconstructed Opus Magnum, and place our people where they need to be.

"I need to put together three scouting parties," I tell the crowd in my room. Stuan stands in the doorway; if someone approaches he'll let us know. Merek, Nia, and Errin sit on Nia's bed, with Kirin and Hope on mine, as I lean against the small wardrobe. "One to go to Tregellan, to the Conclave for Sal Salis; one to Tallith to the quicksilver mine; and one to go a little deeper in the mountains to collect the asulfer."

Stuan half turns and frowns at the unfamiliar names, and I meet his eye. He looks back, unwavering, and nods, before scanning the corridor once more. Hope, Nia, Kirin, and I all agreed that it would be best to protect the secrets of the alchemists as much as we can. Our people know that rescuing the alchemists is a priority, but we've never clarified why, allowing them to assume it was because the gold would be useful to us. No one has mentioned Silas's abilities, or our hopes for the Opus Magnum. That it's the only weapon we have against Aurek.

"We don't have time for the same group to go to all of the locations. It has to be three teams, simultaneously. And it has to be people who know what they're looking for, and where to go."

I see the flat look on Nia's face as she understands what I mean. "Nia, I need you to return to the Conclave for the Sal Salis. I'm sorry. I really am. But no one knows it like you do. Kirin, I want you to go with her."

Nia closes her eyes and I feel terrible, because I know what I'm asking. I know what she's going to have to face going back there. I was there when we left, and her grief then was unbearable. Three months down the line, she'll face horrors.

"I'll go in," Kirin says. "You just come with me, tell me what to do, and I'll do it."

Nia looks at him gratefully. "All right. I can do that."

"Thank you, both of you. Merek," I continue, "if your leg allows for it, I need you to go to Tallith."

"Is that wise?" Errin asks. "Sorry," she adds when I glare at her. "I know you won't have just plucked the idea out of thin air. I'm just not sure his leg is up to it. Or that someone in his position should be out there, unprotected."

I look at Merek, his face expressionless as he watches me.

"He's the only one of us who's ever been there," I say. "Stuan, I want you to go with him."

"No, my lady," Stuan protests. "I think Miss Errin is right. This isn't wise. His Majesty shouldn't go, and I think my place is here."

"Well, if you can think of anyone else who knows Tallith, please, I'm all ears," I snap.

"Ulrin," Stuan says quietly, not meeting my eyes. "He must have gone if he was on the progress with His Majesty. My lady, I don't wish to contradict you, but I can't leave you unprotected." Hope clears her throat and Stuan colors. "Not that you would be unprotected. But still, I'd do better here, and you can send Ulrin in my place. He's trustworthy."

"I'll go with Ulrin," Hope says.

"No," I say immediately. "I need you here."

"But you don't need me?" Merek speaks for the first time.

"What?" My voice rises in my confusion. "What do you mean?"

"You don't need me. You're happy to send me off to Tallith, so you don't need me here."

"Merek, until two days ago, I thought you were dead," I say. "Besides, it's not about who I need here. I'm asking the people who are best for the job to go."

"So if I wasn't here, who would you send?"

That silences me.

"I'll go," Hope says again. "I know what quicksilver looks like, and I know there was a mine not two miles outside of Tallith city; it was in one of the old books. This Ulrin can come with me as my guide. Then you don't need to trust him. I'll tell him it's to do with the Sisters. That's all he needs to know. And if we go by boat, down the river, instead of through Tregellan, Gods willing, we'll save some time and avoid too much attention."

"Can you sail?"

"I can," Nia says. "My brothers live on the estuary; they taught me. If I show Hope the ropes, we can all travel down the Aurmere together, and Kirin and I can get out at Tremayne. They can sail on to Tallith, and back, and we'll return on foot. It'll make things faster."

Merek sits back against the wall, and Hope looks at me, waiting. I don't want to do this; I don't want her to go away from me. It's not that I don't need Merek, but I need Hope more. Surely she must understand that, especially after earlier? I frown at her, trying to convey this, and she looks back at me levelly.

"Very well." I cave in. "You'll all go by boat, as Nia says. Stuan, you and I will be going to get the asulfer, then."

"I can come with you to do that," Merek offers.

"No, thank you," I say, feeling a stab of victory as he reddens. "Errin, obviously you'll be here, working on deconstructing the Opus Magnum. Will the rest of you be ready to leave at first light?" I receive four nods in return, none of them enthusiastic. I don't blame them; I don't want any of these people away from me, facing the dangers they're inevitably going to. But I don't trust anyone else enough with these secrets. "Stuan and I will also go tomorrow, after early training. We'll say we're gathering herbs for Errin. We should be back by sundown, all going well. Agreed?"

This time they all nod.

"We'll keep the date of our attack as two moons from now. Enough time for you to go and come back, for Errin to make the potion, and for everyone here to be as well prepared as they can be."

Stuan is the only one of us who looks remotely happy with the outcome of the meeting.

Four hours after my secret war council ends, we call everyone in the commune to the refectory for the public version of events. Momentous, because not since we first arrived here and assembled the Rising Dawn have I insisted that everyone present attend one of the war councils. I even send word to some of the watchmen, risking a reduced watch to ensure as many people as possible hear me tonight.

Elderly Dilys and Bron from Monkham; Breena, who hates politics and shuns everything in favor of working with her hands; and even Ymilla are all here for the first time since we arrived. They file into the room in rigid silence—the same room where they gather around communal tables, passing bread and tureens of soup to one another, joshing and bickering—yet you wouldn't know it from their stern faces. Only Ymilla, who I'd expected to be angry on hearing that Ulrin would be leaving in the morning, seems unperturbed by the summons, beaming at Merek as he passes her. He nods back at her, a puzzled expression on his face, meeting my eyes as he approaches me. I'm still angry with him, though, so I refuse to acknowledge it.

Soon the walls around the room are lined with people who haven't been seen since we first set up camp here. I stand at the front of the room, with Kirin, Nia, Stuan, Hope, Merek, and Errin. I wait until they've stopped fidgeting and fallen silent, their eyes on me. Then I begin the speech I've spent the afternoon working on.

"Thank you all for coming," I say. "These past few moons have been difficult and dangerous for us all. There is not a person gathered in this room who has not risked themselves in one way or another for this cause. Every one of you has stayed loyal to the Rising Dawn—to me—and when this is over, I'll see to it you are repaid."

Beside me, Merek nods, confirming my words. And I realize too late, when I see the looks exchanged, the smiles, the frown on Ymilla's face, what message it might send, that the two of us seem united in this, that I feel I can make a promise this large. And after the way I followed him out last night, and sat with him in the dark, I've clearly reignited their memories of what we once were to each other.

I briefly lose my thread, but then I remember what Hope said. Stone without. Quake within.

"Certain things have fallen into place that have greatly furthered our cause," I continue, pausing until the low murmurs that follow this announcement die away. "Things will move forward quickly from now. Tomorrow our spies will go out and pass the word on to our allies in the towns to begin preparing for battle. We estimate in two moons' time we will be ready to strike at the Sleeping Prince in the heart of his domain." Gasps echo through the room, and I raise my voice over them. "From tomorrow, we begin preparing for that. Those of you who have been training in sword and bow, we will train twice daily from here on in." I pause to take a breath. "Eight weeks from today, the Rising Dawn in every town will be instructed to hide the weak and the old, and to set fire to the homes of the lords and sheriffs. They will be asked to fight their captors and overthrow them."

I see one of the men, Linion, who left his widowed sister and her sons in Lortune when he ran for his life, prepare to speak, and I raise my voice to prevent the interruption. I know what he's going to ask anyway; he's never forgiven himself for leaving them behind.

"Shortly before the rising, a team will be sent to rescue the children from the mountains and bring them here. The other children will also be liberated, in the first wave of action. Once our allies have begun to liberate the other camps, the townspeople will get the signal to rise against their captors, and then we here will go down into Lortune and engage with the Sleeping Prince. Thanks to the damage from fire at the castle, he won't be able to hole up in there and wait us out. His only practical option will be to send out troops to deal with the risings. And as soon as his forces are dispersed, we strike."

The room erupts into cheers, people clapping and stamping their feet, and I feel my skin flush with pleasure, until Ymilla calls:

"And then we can restore King Merek to the throne!"

She beams over at Merek, who bows his head graciously as my skin heats with something closer to anger than joy. I feel a vicious stab of satisfaction when the cheers for this are less enthusiastic, and look back at the crowd.

"So let's enjoy our supper tonight. At dawn tomorrow, our work begins."

With that, I sweep from the room.

It was my idea to leave them alone tonight. Ema has been instructed to open extra barrels of wine, not too many but enough to give everyone who wants it a treat. She's also roasted one of the goats, cooking it in some concoction of spices that smells heavenly. Tonight they can feast and enjoy themselves, because as of tomorrow, we are on the countdown to invasion. This will be the last time for a while that they can be frivolous. For some of them, it might be the last-ever time they are.

So I leave them to it, planning to go to the kitchens and eat there, then have a bath and an early night to make up for the wretched sleep I had last night.

But it seems Merek has other thoughts.

"Twylla," he calls, following after me.

For a moment I keep walking, but then I stop and turn. "Yes."

"Can we talk?"

"Do you not want to join in the feasting?"

"You're not."

"I'm not going to be their king. You should be in there, showing them how much what they're doing—what they're sacrificing—for your kingdom means to you."

"Have I done something to wrong you?"

"No, of course not."

Merek sighs, a long, impatient breath. "Why did you want to send me away?"

"I wasn't sending you away. I told you: You know Tallith. And you can defend yourself. It made you the most practical choice."

"And that's the only reason?"

"What other reason could there be?"

He steps closer, his eyes glinting in the torchlight.

"Well?" I ask.

264

"You tell me."

"I don't have time for this." I turn, but he steps in front of me.

"Twylla—"

"Everything all right, my lady?" Stuan's voice travels down the corridor. I turn to see him, a shadowy figure hovering under one of the arches.

"We're fine," Merek calls.

"My lady?"

Merek looks away from me, to Stuan, and frowns, and I feel a surge of gratitude toward my former guard. Who would have thought it?

"It's fine, Stuan. Thank you. Go back to the feast."

I hear him walk away, his tread slow, reluctant.

When I look back at Merek, he's watching me, but his eyes are narrowed, as if I've confused him. "Are we still friends?" he asks finally. "I mean, if we ever were really friends."

"I'm your friend."

"And you would tell me the truth?"

"Merek, I have no reason to lie to you."

He sighs as he apparently thinks over my words.

"Good night," I say, turning back to my room.

"Wait. Let's have a drink," he says suddenly.

I'm not sure I've heard him properly. "What?"

"You and me. Let's have a drink. To hell with it, let's get drunk."

"Why would we do that?"

"Because we never have—well, you never have, have you?" I open my mouth to protest, but he continues to speak, his expression intense, reminding me of the day in the Hall of Glass, when he kissed me. "Because we're young. Because we may be dead in two moons' time, so we should live now. Have one night where you give in to yourself."

"I did that once before, if you recall," I snap without meaning to. "It nearly lost me my head. But of course, if you want, I'll 'give in to myself.' We might even end up in bed together; would that please you?"

He turns instantly scarlet and looks away. I don't know where the words come from. And as I look at him, floundering in shock, all of the anger I felt toward him vanishes.

"Sorry," I say. "Gods, Merek, I'm so sorry. That was uncalled for."

He looks back at me, mortified, and shakes his head. "No. No, my behavior was at fault there. I don't know what . . . Please forgive me."

I nod. "Of course. Of course I do."

As soon as I've spoken, he makes to leave, and I call after him. "I . . . I would like to share a drink with you. If you still want to."

He nods warily.

"I'll get some wine and meet you in your room." His color deepens, his skin almost crimson as he nods. Then he turns in a rush toward the men's quarters, leaving me staring after him, feeling odd.

He's composed when I enter, sitting stiffly on his bed with his legs crossed at the ankle. I smile to reassure him, and pour us both a cup of wine. He takes it, muttering a thank-you, and immediately brings it to his lips.

I sit on the floor, a safe distance away, and sip at my own wine.

"So," I say, when it becomes painfully obvious he isn't going to speak. "That was perhaps a little cruel."

"No, no, it was deserved. I did say you'd changed. The old Twylla would never . . ." he says, burying his face in his glass again. When he surfaces, his expression is serious. "I don't like Errin," he says. "Not in that way. I like her, very much. But not romantically."

I blink for a moment, stunned, unsure why he's telling me this. "All right . . ." I say slowly.

"I didn't know if that's why you wanted me to go away. Why you were being so . . . impatient with me."

"You thought I was jealous of Errin?"

"No! Gods, no. I know where you stand, as far I'm concerned. I thought it might be because you were trying to protect Silas, in which case I wanted you to know I have no intentions of causing anyone any upset. I have no plans to come between another pair of lovers," he adds quietly.

"You didn't come between Lief and me," I say sharply. "We both knew I was betrothed to you. You only acted within the realms of what you believed to be true."

"As did you."

I sip my wine, shaking my head.

"I don't blame you." Merek's voice is still soft, and I meet his gaze. "I never have. You were used. By us all. Even me."

I return the glass to my lips, buying myself some time. "It's all very much in the past now," I say finally. "And if I'm honest, I'd rather deal with your mother one thousand times over than what lies ahead."

He raises his cup to toast me.

"Besides," I add, "if you'd seen them together, you'd know Silas doesn't need my nor anyone else's help in holding Errin's heart."

Merek snorts softly. "What's he like?"

I think of the golden-eyed man who cradled Errin in his arms, fighting back tears and putting his own life on the line for hers. I think of his cool determination making the Elixir, and the way he stood by her side in front of his mother, in front of all of his people. I think of the way he threw himself at Lief to defend her. "He's wonderful. He's a good man."

"I hope to meet him one day." He finishes his glass and leans forward, reaching for the bottle to top it up. Uncharacteristically I down mine, too, and hold the glass out. He hesitates, grinning, then fills the cup.

"You don't have to prove anything to me," he says. "I was being an ass."

"I'll have you know, in Scarron I had a glass or two quite often, while I was reading at night."

"You learned to read?"

"I did."

"I was going to teach you," he says, not meeting my gaze. "If we . . . After . . . I never understood why Mother didn't want you to learn. What kind of queen can't read?"

"She never meant for me to be queen. I was only ever supposed to buy her time. And as for preventing me reading, it was a way of keeping me weak, and vulnerable. As were most of her actions. And I don't want to talk about her anymore. Not tonight."

He nods his agreement. "Were you happy in Scarron?"

"Yes. I think so. It's a strange place, so far from everything. But it's what I needed. How were your three days as king?"

"Nightmarish. I was almost glad Aurek came." His face falls as soon as the words leave his mouth. "I don't mean that."

"I know."

"Are you really going to put me back on the throne if we win?" he asks, his eyes burning into mine.

"Who else?" I say, my tone harsher than I mean it to be. "Unless you think a council like in Tregellan is a good idea?"

He shakes his head immediately. "What's to be done about them?" he asks. "I mean, to all intents and purposes they've washed their hands of the whole situation in return for gold."

"Bureaucrats," I say, and just like that, we're back on safe ground. "No point in getting their hands dirty if they don't need to. Lormere never had any real value to them, except for what they could sell us."

"They must know that eventually he'll come for them," Merek says. "Lormere has very limited resources, and Tregellan has a lot. Sooner or later he'll have enough golems, and enough gold, to do to them what he's done here."

"I expect they're hoping someone will stop him before then."

"Us, you mean. While they do nothing to further that cause." He scowls. "And after? Say we win; what do I do with them if I take the crown? They'll want their alchemists back."

"They won't go," I say with certainty. "And we know Tregellan doesn't have an army."

"So . . ."

I start speaking, just letting the words come as the ideas form, all of my knowledge of Tregellan and Lormere, everything I've seen and read and learned over the past four years of living in both countries pouring out of me. "So you offer them sanctuary here. Offer what Tregellan gave them—a home, the choice to practice, or not, as they choose. But with freedom. Tregellan kept them underground, ostensibly because of Helewys. But no one in Lormere would be hunting them anymore. So they could live freely here. And without the alchemists paying the Council of Tregellan to keep them hidden, the Tregellian treasury will soon run low. We're their only viable trade partner, unless they heavily expand their shipping fleet, which they can't without more gold. So they'd have to sign a treaty with us, or risk bankrupting themselves, and we could make the terms very favorable. You could have your apothecaries and your sciences. Schools. Universities. You could make it very appealing for the finest minds to come here. And you'd have to ensure the people hold the current Council to account—the citizens of Tremayne, Newtown, and Tyrwhitt will certainly want to see some justice for what they've endured. They won't be happy that the Council submitted to him. Help them install a new council. Sign a new treaty that allows both countries to benefit. Start afresh."

I exhale, taking a large swig of wine and emptying the cup again, slightly stunned by my own apparent knowledge. When Merek doesn't speak, I see him staring at me, his lips parted.

"What?"

"My mother's biggest mistake was underestimating you."

"Well, I didn't exactly give her much to go on." I think of my conversation with Hope earlier. "I can't really blame her for thinking me a little fool."

"I never did," he says. His eyes are clear and focused. Without his hair, you can see the planes of his face, fine and strong. His mouth looks wider.

"I know," I whisper.

I hold his gaze, and the walls of the room start to feel smaller, the

270

temperature somehow rising. Sweat prickles along my shoulders, my throat dry. I glance at the wine bottle and see we've finished it. My cheeks feel hot and Merek Belmis is still looking at me. It feels as if he's looking through me. As my eyes move back to meet his, his tongue moistens his upper lip, and I find myself hypnotized by the motion, and then I mimic it, and his breath catches; I hear it.

Would it be so wrong if something were to happen?

I reel away from the thought as if it was a physical thing. "I'll get more wine," I say, breaking the spell.

"No. We have training in the morning. Hope asked me to work with you. We should probably get some sleep."

It takes me a moment to understand he's rejecting me, too. And to my surprise, it hurts.

"Of course," I say in a too-bright voice, hauling myself to my feet and staggering in the process.

He reaches out a hand and steadies me, and heat rises again in my skin.

"I'll see you in the morning, then." I turn to leave, only for his hand to curve around my hip, urging me to turn.

"Twylla."

There is a familiar twist in my stomach, but not one that's ever come from Merek saying my name before. When I look at him, his pupils are wide in the dim light, his dark eyes fixed on mine.

"If you were less drunk—"

"I'm not—" I begin, but he continues talking.

"All right. If you hadn't had *anything* to drink, and if I was a lot surer about what I think just happened, I would cheerfully pull you into my bed right now. I've wanted to for a long time, you know that."

I swallow.

"You said once that if you came to me, it would be because you chose me. And right now I don't think it's a choice you can make." He pauses, and then grins wickedly, in a way I've never seen him smile before. It's so startling that I look down. "However, if you ever come to me sober, because you've decided you do want me, I will make it worth your while."

I look back up at him to see his eyes blazing. His fingers tighten momentarily on my hip before releasing me.

"Because I still want you. And only you."

I flee from the room before I do something we both might regret.

Chapter 20

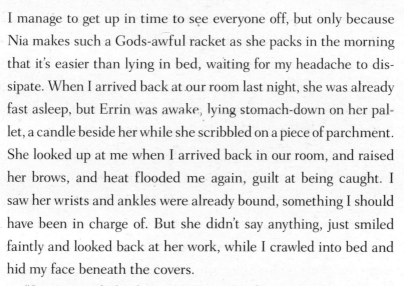

I manage to get up in time to see everyone off, but only because Nia makes such a Gods-awful racket as she packs in the morning that it's easier than lying in bed, waiting for my headache to dissipate. When I arrived back at our room last night, she was already fast asleep, but Errin was awake, lying stomach-down on her pallet, a candle beside her while she scribbled on a piece of parchment. She looked up at me when I arrived back in our room, and raised her brows, and heat flooded me again, guilt at being caught. I saw her wrists and ankles were already bound, something I should have been in charge of. But she didn't say anything, just smiled faintly and looked back at her work, while I crawled into bed and hid my face beneath the covers.

"So, you and the king. Missing the feast. Together. We all noticed. Ymilla was distraught." Nia's voice is rich with questions as she hastily stuffs her things in a bag, barely looking at them.

"We had plans to make. We're about to go to war."

"Is that what they call it in Lormere?"

"Nia," Errin warns, sitting up and rubbing her eyes one by one with her bound hands.

Nia says nothing, suppressing a smirk as she finishes packing. I throw Errin a thankful glance and she gives me a nod of solidarity.

When I arrive at the refectory with Errin, Merek is already seated. I feel my skin start to heat, and mutter at Errin that I'll see her later, as I turn to sit with Stuan, Hobb, and some of the other men instead.

The moment I sit, they all stand and bow, and across the room I see Merek's mouth twitch.

"Gentlemen," I say to the guards, imploring them to sit. "No need to be formal. I just wanted to thank you all for your hard work."

Stuan and Hobb sit up tall and nod. And as I tear into my bread, I see Errin and Nia have joined Merek, along with Ymilla.

I look at Ymilla, younger than Helewys, older than I. Older than Merek, too, but what does that matter? She smiles at him from beneath her eyelashes and I wonder if he'd consider her. She knows court life, loves it, even. Of all of us here, I think she's the one who misses it most of all. She'd be a good wife to him.

I stab at my bacon and glower at Hobb and Stuan when they exchange questioning glances. Forcing a piece into my mouth, I chew furiously. Why am I wasting time thinking about who Merek might marry when I have plenty to actually occupy me? Like a war.

I keep my head down for the rest of the meal, listening idly to the chatter of the guards, until they fall silent, looking beyond me. When I turn to see what caught their attention, I find Merek is standing behind me.

"Are you ready to practice?" he says.

I look up at him. "Are you able, with your injury?"

"Yes."

"I'll see you out there."

He turns sharply away, leaving me watching after him. I can tell he's trying to disguise his limp. Stupid boy.

I say a discreet good-bye to Kirin, Nia, Hope, and Ulrin—who has been sworn to absolute secrecy about where he's going—making no more fuss than I would if they really were going on a spying mission. Kirin promises that he and Nia will be back within a week, that they won't tarry at all, and that they'll be careful, and Hope says she expects to not be much behind them. Despite that, they take rations enough for two weeks, causing Ema to eye us suspiciously.

When I step into the courtyard, Merek is waiting, leaning against the wall and seemingly staring at his reflection in his sword.

"You look fine," I call.

His lips quirk. "If we're exchanging compliments before blows, so do you. Sleep well?"

"Like a log," I lie. "You."

"Not so well. Disturbing dreams. Images in my head that were hard to ignore."

I blink. "Pity. Perhaps you should go and rest. After all, you're still recovering from serious wounds."

"We're at war. Twylla. No time to rest." His smile is politic, not a smile at all.

"You're right. We're all very busy. Can we begin?"

He snorts, a kind of laugh, and bows. "As my lady so desires."

I bow by return and then we begin to circle each other. After a moment, it becomes clear he's waiting for me to strike, so I feign a blow. As soon as he moves to block it, I swing back and catch him on the thigh with the flat of the sword, delivering a sharp slap that makes him yelp.

"Really?" he says, the creases at the corners of his eyes blossoming. He swings his sword in an arrogant figure eight and then lunges at me. And the very moment I move to defend the blow, he taps my backside with his sword.

I glare at him. "If you're not going to take this seriously."

"You started it."

I roll my eyes. I make a few thrusts, and he parries, but lightly. At first I think he's taking care with his leg, and I try not to make him work too hard, fearful of hurting him further. But then I realize he's not holding back because of himself, but because of me. He won't fight me.

I work a little harder, moving faster, thrusting at him more often, and still he barely moves to block me, still he doesn't fight back. It reminds me of when Lief and he fought, and how Lief played with him, made him think they might be equals, and it makes me furious at the stupid games we all keep playing with one another.

So I attack.

I go against everything Hope ever taught me, slashing and hacking and moving so fast his sword is a blur as he blocks every strike. And I strike, and strike, and strike, because out of nowhere I'm full of rage and I don't know why. I just need to keep hitting, and Merek keeps taking it; never once does he attempt to disarm me.

"Fight back," I spit at him. "I don't want your charity. Fight back."

As I whirl my sword, I catch Stuan, Ymilla, Ema, Errin, and Hobb standing watching us. So many faces I know. Watching him doing so little as I give it everything I have, and the weight of the humiliation is crushing. I falter for a moment, lowering my sword. I look over at Merek and see he, too, looks upset, his mouth tight, his eyes darting between me and the crowd. When he finally attacks, I feel nothing but relief.

"How's your arm?" Merek asks as I glower at him. Back in our rooms, Errin is patching me up. Merek looks wretched.

"Fine." Errin finishes applying some kind of green paste to the shallow cut on my forearm.

"Your turn," she says to Merek, and I stand, maneuvering past him as he sits down and presents his cheek to Errin.

My eyes meet hers as she applies the same paste to the graze there.

I didn't mean to cut him. But I'm sure I see recrimination in Errin's eyes as she attends to Merek.

Without saying a word, I leave them, moving swiftly down the corridor to the women's wardrobe, to prepare to go into the mountains. I pull out pale brown colors that will blend into the mountain at winter. High above us the peaks are white year-round, reigned by snow and ice. But the water of Lor Mere, the namesake pool of the land, is perpetually warm, the ground heated by the hot springs beneath it, and that's where we'll find the yellow asulfer rocks we need for the Opus Magnum. I change into the tunic and breeches, pulling out a belt and cloak to match and putting my boots back on. My hair is wound against my head, and I dull it using a powder Hope showed me how to make from walnut and rhubarb, muting the red to a light muddy brown. I throw a thick brown cloak around my shoulders and then head off to meet Stuan.

But when I approach the doors, it's Merek who waits for me.

"Where's Stuan?"

"Guarding Errin. He doesn't feel comfortable leaving her here without you or Hope, under the circumstances. So I offered to take his place."

I scowl at him. He's dressed similarly to me, muted colors, loose-fitting clothes. There's a small messenger's bag over his shoulder.

"I know where the mere is," he says. "I've been often. So I won't be useless to you."

"What about your leg?"

"It's fine."

"We'll have to climb."

"I said it's fine."

I'm not going to win here. "Let's go, then. I'd like to be back by nightfall."

It's not the first time I've left the compound under the watch of someone else, but it is the first time I've left it without Hope, Nia, or Kirin being there. I trust Errin and Stuan—in fact, I trust everyone. They're not fools; they're not going to run wild without my being there. But I feel guilty, as though I've left them undefended. Merek, to his credit, lets me brood on it as we walk the mountain paths, through the high meadow where the cows still graze, thanks to fortunate mountain currents, and along the goat-made tracks, occasionally coming across some of the strange-eyed, pretty beasts perched on rocks.

We pause at noon, the sun a pale gold blur above us, and Merek shares the water and food from his bag. Then we walk on, and an hour later we come to the mere.

Ever since I arrived at the castle, the queen talked of her mere. It's supposedly the pool Lormere was named for. Lormere—the Lord's Mere. Named after Dæg, and the golden rocks embedded in the earth around it.

No one told me it would stink.

The air is heavy with sulfur, thick and choking, a thousand times worse than in the baths, and I glare at Merek with streaming eyes.

"This was the fertility lake?" I gasp, burying my chin inside my cloak and taking a deep breath.

He nods, his own face covered so only his eyes peek over the top.

I shake my head, moving closer to the water. It's warm here, and soon I have to choose between coming to terms with the smell or boiling alive in my cloak. I shed the cloak and leave it over a rock as I explore the mere, breathing through my mouth. There is the one large pool—clearly the bathing one—but small ones around it, like moons or courtiers, and these are much more active, alive, bubbling and belching and rushing, and surrounded by sticks bearing torn red flags. When I pull my gloves off and dip my fingers in one, the heat is almost too much; I have to snatch them back out and blow on them.

And when one of the pools shoots high into the sky in a roar of water, I scream and fall back onto the ground.

As the jet evaporates into the air and a cavern appears momentarily beneath where the water erupted from, I hear Merek laughing.

It stings and I scramble back to my feet, brushing golden dust from my clothes. "Thank you for the warning. Hilarious to laugh at the peasant girl who knows nothing. Pity your mother couldn't have seen it." His face falls instantly, but I don't allow myself to feel bad for it. "We're here to do a job, if you've had your fun, Your Majesty."

He grabs my arm as I spin away and tugs me back around to look at him. "Forgive me," he says instantly, no excuses, no explanations. Just remorse and the offer of a genuine apology. I'd forgotten that about him. "I should have told you what would happen." He pauses, and I shrug an acceptance. "Please." He pulls a little, asking me to go with him. And I allow it, letting him lead me to a few feet from where the water emerged. He stands behind me as I cross my arms, and leans down to speak softly to me. "Look," he says. "It's like the ground is breathing. You'll know when it's going to go, because it looks like it's taking one final deep breath. Watch. In, and out. In, and out, getting deeper each time."

I watch the water, and see that he's right. The cavity beneath the pool is like a mouth, sucking in, pushing out, and the water ebbs and swells with it.

"It won't be long." Merek's mouth is level with my ear, his breath stroking across the shell of it. I can smell the herbal paste Errin smeared over his cut, but before I can let my mind wander that way, the water explodes into the air.

I gasp and step back into Merek. His hands grip my hips reflexively, holding me, and we watch the water surge upward before it falls, tapering into mist and then vanishing.

"Let's get these rocks and go home." His voice is a rumble against my back, and I nod.

He releases me, and we begin to gather the stones, prying them out of the mud and adding them to his bag. We take a lot, giving Errin plenty to choose from. We work in silence, though every now and then I feel his eyes on me, and when I think it's safe I steal glances at him, watching his long fingers turn over the stones, watching him chew his lip as he decides what to take and what to discard.

I pluck out one final chunk of yellow rock, all but inured to the smell of the water now. I toss it over to Merek and then sit back, wiping at my face. My hand comes away damp and grimy, sweat and steam and the powder mingling together, and I wipe my hand on my breeches.

"Do you think we have enough?"

"I'd say so."

Merek stands, and stretches, and slings the bag over his shoulder. "Come on," he says. He walks over, offering me a hand, and I grab it. He pulls me up, and I make the mistake of looking into his eyes. They're hungry, dark, and his lips are parted.

And I know with sudden conviction I'm going to kiss Merek Belmis.

He grabs my wrists and becomes motionless. "Listen," he breathes before I have a chance to be embarrassed.

I do, trying to hear beyond my own thundering heart.

Then I hear what he somehow miraculously heard: voices, and footsteps. Distant, but still too close for comfort.

We move fast, ducking behind an outcrop of rock as I scramble to pull my cloak out of view. Minutes pass, and the voices get louder. Lormerian, male, and gruff. I can't make out more than the occasional word. The tone isn't urgent; it sounds like they're grumbling. As it begins to quiet down, Merek turns to me.

"What else is near here?" he says quietly. "The children's camp?"

I shake my head. "That's a mile east of here, roughly, over the next pass." I point to our right at the small ridge there. "There is a route directly there from the ground that's much easier to climb."

Merek looks after the men. "Maybe there's some reason for them to use this path instead? Avalanche on the usual route? Landslide?"

"It's possible." I hesitate.

"Let's follow them. Just to be sure of where they're going. Anyone in the mountains is a bad sign."

I nod and throw my cloak over my shoulders, he takes the bag of asulfer, and we track the men, climbing a little higher than them, and keeping our distance. There are four of them, wearing black tabards with the Solaris on them. Two carry large sacks, which, despite bulging heavily, don't appear to trouble them too much. A third carries a thick canvas roll, which seemingly is heavier, for he walks slower and shifts the weight from one arm to the other, until the fourth man takes it from him. Merek and I don't speak at all as we follow their path across the mountain, occasionally falling behind when we have to move farther up, or down, in order to keep following them. It soon becomes apparent that Merek's hunch was right and that, for some reason, the men are using the path to the mere to reach the children's camp.

As we get closer, Merek tugs my cloak and gestures for me to stop. "Where exactly are the children being kept?"

"There's a cave system," I whisper. "Three large caverns, and a few smaller ones, though we don't know how far back they go. The smallest children are in one, and the men there have assigned the older girls to care for them. Come on—let's get a bit closer and I'll introduce you to our men on watch."

I move on, scrambling higher, until I find a narrow path almost completely hidden by rocks. There are three men sitting at the end of the path and all of them turn sharply, bows and pikes in hand as they hear us, relaxing only when they recognize me.

"My lady," the men say, low voices in tandem, as we get closer.

"Tally, Rutya, Serge," I greet in return. Serge's eyes widen when he sees Merek, and he tries to bow.

"Your Highness. Forgive me, I mean Your Majesty. Hobb said you were alive . . ." he begins, and attempts to bow again, as the other men also move to show their respect without giving themselves away.

"Be at ease," Merek says, and Serge sits back down, though he stares at Merek as though seeing a ghost.

"We saw these men approaching from a different route," I say, pointing at them beside the smallest of the caves. I move up, beckoning Merek forward so he can see them.

Carved naturally out of the sheer gray rock face, the caverns gape like the mouths of giants, three in a row, though separated by huge walls of stone. Outside each of the largest caves, six men stand guard armed with bows, knives—one even has a large many-tailed whip that makes me feel sick to look at—and pace up and down, talking to each other.

The newcomers approach the cave, and the guards hail them, relaxed, clearly recognizing their visitors.

"I wish we could hear what they were saying," Merek murmurs, and I nod.

"Does this happen often?" I ask Tally. "Visitors, I mean?"

"This is the third time."

"The third? When was the first?"

"A week ago," Rutya chimes in. "Four men came, and went into the caves—like that, look—" He nods to where the men we've followed are entering the middle cave.

"What's in those sacks? Food?" Merek says.

"No, sire. The food delivery comes once a fortnight. The first lot were empty-handed."

"Who's kept in there?" Merek says, looking back at the cave.

"The boys. Aged five and over."

We all watch the mouth of the cave, and my skin prickles with apprehension. "Did they go into the same cave last time?"

"Yes, my lady," Serge confirms.

"And we don't know what's in the sacks?"

"No, my lady."

"Why was this not reported?"

"We did report it, my lady. We sent a message back to Hobb, who said to keep watch and to come immediately if anything changed. It hasn't. They just go in with bags, and come out later without them. And we've seen the children, when they're brought out to use the pits. They're not being harmed. In fact, they looked well, healthier than before, and some of them were wearing better clothes."

"Why only the boys, though?" I say, more to myself than with the need for a response.

But Merek replies, "We need to find out." He turns to me, his expression serious, and I nod.

We stay there, crouched behind the rocks as the sun moves

across the sky above us. When the men eventually leave, they carry nothing, and we all press ourselves more firmly into the rocks, until the indistinct sounds of their chatter have long faded.

"My lady, I don't wish to give you orders, but it's getting late and the mountains get cold at night," Serge says gently, and Rutya and Tally nod.

"He's right," Merek says, and I swivel around to look at him with raised brows. "We should go, if we're going." Even as he says it, he shifts his weight from one leg to the other.

I turn back to the men. "I'm going to double the team here. I've got an odd feeling about this, and if anything happens, I want there to be enough of you to fight, as well as have someone come and warn us. And I want to know the moment anything else unusual happens down there. Something is up, I'm sure of it."

"Yes, my lady," Serge says.

"Expect the new men to arrive tomorrow. Is there anything else you need in the meantime?"

"No, my lady."

"You're sure?"

He nods, and his fellows join in.

We bid them farewell and scuttle down the track, keeping low. There is a bite to the air as the sun sets, and I start to move a little faster; we don't have lanterns, not that we could use them up here, and it's a cloudy night. When we reach the mere, a fog hangs over the small valley, and Merek reaches out, grabbing my hand and pulling me to a stop.

"What are you doing?"

He doesn't say anything, waiting, staring into the mist until he finally seems satisfied. "Sorry," he says. "I had to be sure."

"Did you hear something?"

He shakes his head, and won't be drawn further. When we move off, his limp is more pronounced, and without saying a word, I pull on the strap of the bag and hold my hand out. When he swings it over his head without protest and hands it to me, I realize just how much pain he must be in.

We arrive back at the commune after dark, and the last part of the journey is slow going, partly because of his leg and partially because of our caution. Merek hasn't spoken since we left the mere, and I am poised at every step to break his fall if his leg gives way. We hail the first set of guards, then the second, as we arrive back at the commune.

"Thank the Gods we're back," I say as I push the doors open. When he doesn't reply, I look at him, and see his face is strained, his lips drawn into a line. "Merek?"

"I'm all right." He speaks through his teeth.

"I can see that." Without asking permission, I put my arm around his waist. "You need Errin."

And as if I've summoned her, she appears, Stuan chasing closely behind her, hand on the hilt of his sword. Errin's wrists are still bound, and her cheeks are flushed, her eyes bright; her hair, though tied back, is falling loose around her face.

"There you are," she says. "Do you have my asulfer?"

I hold the bag up.

"Good." She smiles, a satisfied little smile. "Because I've done it. I've deconstructed the Opus Magnum. I know how to make the poison. So, as soon as we have the rest of the ingredients, I can make the Opus Mortem."

Chapter 21

"You've what?" Merek and I chorus. His surprise makes him stagger, and I have to brace to support him. His hand moves to mine at his waist, and I thread my fingers through his without thinking.

"I've done it. I've been working on it all day. All last night, too. I couldn't stop. It's actually very simple, because the asulfer and the quicksilver cancel each other out. You just reverse the quantities and—"

She finally pauses and looks at Merek, who is almost gray. "You're an idiot. Why didn't you tell me to shut up? Come on. Help him." She turns and commands Stuan, who does so immediately. Merek releases my fingers and moves his arm around my neck, doing the same to Stuan on his other side.

Between us, we get Merek to his room, Errin at our side, cataloguing his symptoms with her eyes. His brow is damp by the time we get there, and it glistens in the light of the candles I place on his bedside cabinet so Errin can see what she's doing.

"I need my hands," she says to Stuan, and he looks at me for permission before he loosens the knots. Errin rubs her wrists faintly, red marks across them, before reaching for Merek.

She places her hand on his forehead and sighs. "No fever," she says, as much to herself as to us. Then she moves down the bed, rolling his trousers up in a brisk, businesslike manner. His ankle is clearly swollen, the skin shiny, and she looks up at him darkly. "Did I not say to rest?"

He shrugs, and I see her mouth become small as she unwinds the bandages and examines the wound.

"It's not infected. You must have the luck of your Gods."

"Or it's my exceptional breeding," he says. For a moment we all pause, looking among one another, until he gives a tired laugh. "Forgive me. I expect that's only funny if you're Lormerian. And me." When we continue to look bewildered, he sighs. "Because my parents were . . . Never mind."

Errin ignores him and turns to me as I shake my head. "Can you go to our room and get my kit?"

I hurry down the corridor, through the courtyard to our room and back again, finding a burst of energy I didn't know I had. Stuan has taken up a position by the door, watching Errin intently.

Errin takes the kit from me and begins to pull out bottles and jars, placing them on the bed. And despite the pain he must be in, Merek tries to sit up. Errin shoots him a filthy look.

"You need to rest."

"No chance," he says. "This is nothing short of a miracle, and I want to know how you did it."

Errin beams, pulling a jar toward her. "It's really simple. In apothecary, everything has an equal and an opposite. And you can use something called the Petrucius Table to work out what those equals and opposites are. Every element, every plant. Everything. For the equal, like cures like. And for the opposite, it's about achieving balance. You find similar qualities and you match those. In this case, the quicksilver and the asulfer are the opposites, so they're the match. You see?"

Merek hums in agreement, and I just stare at Errin.

Errin rolls her eyes to the side as she thinks. "All right. For example, if you're poisoned, the best chance of a cure is something that negates the original poison, yes? So you need the equal of it, but the equal opposite, to cancel it out. The Petrucius Table helps you choose the path, based on the best match. Therefore, to deconstruct something, you have to find the opposite of each component. And in apothecary, and apparently alchemy, you build the opposite into the original potion."

This does not sound at all simple to me, and I look at Merek, only to find he's nodding at Errin as though he understands completely. Stuan looks as confused as I do, and I feel very warmly toward him in that moment.

Errin shoots me a small smile, as though she can sense my discomfort, before she continues. "So all I had to do was fit the ingredients into the Petrucius Table and slide them around until I'd achieved balance."

"And that was easy?" I say.

"Some parts were easy. Obviously, quicksilver and asulfer opposed each other, as they're the only mineral elements. So I just need to reverse the quantities in the Opus Magnum of each."

"What about the plants?" Merek asks, his eyes eager now. "Because marigold and morning glory have the same properties, theoretically, and the quantities are similar. Obviously, mandrake is the balance to one, but which?"

"Marigold," Errin says instantly.

"How can you be sure?"

"Because yew is the natural opposite of morning glory," Errin scoffs.

"Explain," Merek says, but before Errin can begin, I stand up.

"I'm sorry. This is fascinating, but I need to eat," I say, "and bathe."

Errin nods, but Merek looks tired again, sinking back against the pillow.

"I'll have something sent to you," I say to him. "Errin, you're a wonder."

"My pleasure," she says. "Now all we need is for the others to return, and the remaining ingredients, and we can do this. We can kill him."

"With the . . . Opus Mortem," I say, and she nods. "Where did you find the name?"

She grins impishly. "I made it up. It made sense."

"Silas will be so proud of you," I say.

The spark goes out of her eyes then. "Yes . . ." she says quietly. "I hope he gets to see it."

I look at Merek, pleading with him to do something.

"Can you take me through it?" he asks. "I'd love to see how it all works."

She nods absently, then again, a little firmer the second time.

"Yes. But let's get this seen to first." She looks at me. "Do you have any injuries you need me to look at?"

"No. I'm fine. Just bone tired. I'm going to get some rest."

I pause in the doorway and watch as she opens the jar and begins to rub salve into his wounds. When he meets my eyes, my stomach swoops, and I nod good-bye, leaving them to it. I mean to go to the kitchens to eat, and I mean to bathe. But instead I head straight for my room, where I collapse face-first on the bed and fall asleep without even taking my boots off.

When I wake, the room is empty, though someone has pulled off my boots and thrown a blanket over me, all without waking me. I roll onto my back, feeling heavy and thick, throwing my hands above my head.

Then it all comes back: the men visiting the caves, Errin's success with the Opus Mortem. I sit up and groan. I ache, and I feel hollow. And I smell a little ripe.

I have the bath I wanted last night, and bind my hair up. As I make my way to the refectory to see if anything has survived from breakfast, I hear the clash of metal upon metal and, ignoring my now furious stomach, divert to the main courtyard, where I secret myself behind a pillar and watch the occupants of the commune fight one another.

Merek is seated in one of the corners, Hobb with him, conversing, in between calling tips to fighters. Row after row of people brandish swords at one another, some with more success than others. I step out into the courtyard, skirting around, observing them as I make my way to Merek. Hobb sees my approach and waits for me.

He speaks immediately. "Forgive me for not telling you about the activity at the caves. I was waiting to discover more before I reported."

"It's fine. Have you learned anything else?"

"Nothing useful in that regard. Though we have word that Aurek appears to have gone into hiding. Since the fire, he's holed himself up in his tower, won't see anyone, won't do anything. My man says he's heard Aurek goes to the kitchen to watch his meals being prepared, and then forces at least three people to taste them before he'll eat. No one is allowed in his tower; he has golems on the door, and everywhere he does go."

"What about Lief—the Silver Knight?"

"The Silver Knight and six others rode for Scarron."

For Scarron. They still think I'm there.

"If that's all, my lady," Hobb says. I nod, and he steps back into the field, shouting encouragement at the fighters.

"How are they doing?" I ask Merek quietly.

"For people who have never fought before, they're doing well."

"Not well enough, though?" I read the implication in his voice.

"Not against soldiers Lief has trained," Merek admits.

"Perhaps we should split them," I say. "Those who are good enough to fight men hand-to-hand keep training with the sword, and those lacking could be taught to fight golems."

"Who would teach— Ah." He smiles. "Of course. The resident golem slayer."

"It's not that hard. Stay out of their way, and use fire."

Merek's eyes light up. "Yes . . . At the castle, the golem that went into the fire disintegrated when it came out."

292

"It dries them out, like the clay they are. Makes them easy to shatter. And it exposes the commands inside them. Once the command is destroyed, it founders."

"Like the simulacrum. They're nothing without the alchemy powering them."

My thoughts turn to Errin, and I know Merek's have done the same when he says, "It seems as though Lief kept his promise. He must have destroyed it."

"Perhaps" is the only reply he gets. First time for everything, I suppose.

"What about those who aren't good enough for either sort of combat?" Merek nods at where poor Breena looks in more danger of stabbing herself than an enemy.

"We play to their strengths. Breena is a gifted archer, and she's been teaching the others. So let's allow them to focus on the discipline they favor. I wonder . . . if Errin could make us something we could dip arrows into, some compound . . ."

"They'd have to be very good archers to make that safe for us," Merek says.

"They would be. Where is Errin, by the way?"

"She's set up a laboratory, down the corridor." He points toward the south wing of the commune. "I'm going to help her once I've finished here."

"Make sure you get some rest, too."

"Wait." His fingers curl around my wrist as I move to leave. "I'd like to talk to you."

"Not now," I say. "I have to see Errin. And you have work to do here."

"I'll find you."

I nod, and he releases me, though I can still feel the warmth of his skin on mine, and his eyes on me, all the way back into the commune.

Errin has indeed set up a laboratory, using a hodgepodge of glassware, stoneware, and clearly whatever she has been able to steal out of the kitchen. She's somehow—and I suspect from the way Stuan glowers at her, tapping the rope from her wrists against his leg, that he was involved—dragged one of the giant wooden tables from the refectory down here, and is using it as a bench. At one end of the bench is a collection of jars and bottles, with herbs, plants, powders, and liquids inside. In the center is a makeshift fire pit. And at the end, pens and reams of paper, already covered in scribbles. I wander over to look and see what I expect is the famous Petrucius Table, drawn on thick parchment, held in place by an assortment of empty vials and a knife.

"Now it begins," Errin says, looking gleeful, clapping her hands together.

"What are you going to do?"

"Gather everything I have, split it down into the quantities I need, and prepare it if it needs it. And I have to brew my own spagyric tonic."

"Of course. Spagyric tonic. What would we do without it?"

Errin gives me a wry look. "The one I need for this is rosewater, essentially. But not cosmetic rosewater. Just the essence of the rose in the tonic."

I hold up my hands. "Tell me how to be of actual help."

She grins; even my ignorance is amusing now that she's in her element. "Well, until everyone else is back, there's not much to be done as far as the making of the Opus Mortem goes." She walks to the crowd of jars at the opposite end of the table and holds one up. It contains a twisted, warped root that looks eerily human. "We have mandrake, thank the Holly. It's a horror to harvest. Oh, I need yew bark. I don't suppose you know of a handy yew tree nearby?"

"There could be hundreds out there for all I know. Identifying trees is not my main talent."

"Some poisoner you are." Errin grins.

"I know what yew looks like," Stuan says, startling me. I'd forgotten he was there. "It makes good bows."

Errin and I turn to him. "See. I don't need to know trees, I have Breena," I say. "I'll ask her to go. She's a bowsmith's daughter. A bowsmith herself now."

"She'll know it," Stuan says.

"Wait," Errin interrupts. "Is she making bows for you here?"

I understand. "Oh Gods, I am an idiot." I shake my head at myself. "We'll see if Breena has yew here."

Errin takes a deep breath. "Then this is it. This is really it."

I look back at her, and then at Stuan. "This is it."

I leave Errin with Stuan, who is spending less time flinching at her every movement now. Poor Stuan, who seems destined to spend his life guarding one potentially dangerous girl or another. I walk back through the commune, feeling restless. In the courtyard a new set of people is training, and I nod to them as I pass. The air smells thick with baking bread, yeast, and rosemary and that *warmth* that bread always emits. I call into the kitchen and find Ema working with Trey, the pair of them kneading violently. I go to the larder and snag myself an apple, still crisp, and the bite I take as I enter the gardens is tart, and perfect.

I sit down in the gardens, on the ground, the wool of my dress shielding me from the cold ground. I try to visualize what it will be like here when the spring comes. Then I wonder if I'll see it—if I'll see spring at all. The past few days have felt like a whirlwind; after moons of slow planning and seeding, it seems that now the time is coming for the harvest.

I'm not surprised when I hear someone enter the garden, and know without turning that it's Merek.

"Am I intruding?"

"No."

He comes to sit with me, lowering himself gingerly, stretching his injured leg out. I finish my apple and dig a small hole, burying the core in the earth. I can feel him watching me again, the weight of his gaze familiar, like a favorite cloak put away for summer and taken out again in time for the winter celebrations. Warm. Safe.

"What's happening, with us?" he asks finally.

"I don't know," I reply immediately. I knew the question was coming, I knew it as soon as he told me he needed to talk to me.

"But something is. It's not just . . . It's not just me again, is it?"

"No," I admit. "It's not just you."

"I was worried . . . After last time, I can't . . . I'm not very good at reading you, as you know." He shrugs ruefully. "I don't really trust my own thoughts in that respect anymore. I've only been here a few days, and there's so much happening, and just because things haven't changed for me . . ." He trails off. "I don't know what I'm trying to say. I got it so very wrong last time."

"You're not the only one."

"That's another thing. I know you said your feelings toward . . . him have nothing to do with what happened, but . . ."

"It's none of your business," I say gently.

"I know. I suppose at least I know that it's not all in my head this time. I'm not making something happen that you don't want."

"I don't know entirely *what* I want." I'm honest with him—I have to be. "I don't understand what's changed for me, or what it might mean. Or if I even want it to mean anything. Yes, something has changed." I look into his dark eyes. "But I can't think about it at the moment. I have to think about the war, and Aurek, and defeating him."

"Of course." He smiles at me, a soft, real smile, before reaching for my hand and raising it to his lips. "Thank you."

"For what?"

"For telling me the truth. Now I'm going to go and get some of that rest I keep hearing so much about. I'll see you later."

I watch him go, taking a deep breath. Then I turn back to the barren garden and once again sink my fingers into the earth.

Every morning, I wake up in the hope that today is the day Nia and Kirin, and Hope and Ulrin, will return. At first I know it's a foolish wish, because not nearly enough time has passed for them to get to their destinations, harvest what they need, and return. But being a fool has never stopped me before, so every time I hear hurried footsteps, I can't help thinking that it's someone come to tell me they're home.

In the meantime, I double not only the men on the caves but send people across Lormere to every camp to reinforce those already there. Serge and Tally send word that men keep coming and going every three days, but they have no idea why, and they don't believe the children are being harmed. I tell them to keep watching, to report back anything they see, no matter how small. Not knowing what—if anything—it means is a constant tick in my mind. I know I'm missing something.

Errin and Merek work on getting everything ready for the Opus Mortem, as far as they can, with Stuan still watching over Errin, though a lot less vigorously than before. When Merek unbinds her hands fully so she can work unhindered, he barely raises an eyebrow. I think we've all stopped worrying that she's anyone's puppet now.

Hobb reports that Aurek is still hidden behind what remains of the castle walls, seemingly waiting for Lief to return.

Breena has yew bark to spare, and Errin sets Merek to drying it gently over the fire before calcifying part of it and adding it to the stores. Errin also makes her spagyric tonic, and Merek marvels at the difference between it and the cosmetic version—which she also makes so he can compare them—while I stare at them both blankly because I can neither see nor smell the difference they both assure me is obvious. Errin teaches Merek how to make the Opus Magnum while they have some of the ingredients to hand, and the two of them begin working on remedies and salves for war injuries—just as Errin once promised me, she becomes my apothecary. She makes something she calls firewater, a thick green liquid that gives off an astonishing burst of heat when lit, so powerful I feel it on my face from across the room. When I'm not training with Hobb, or taking my turn in the kitchens, I find myself heading to the laboratory, at peace when I sit and watch them work, even if I don't understand it.

A heavy, expectant weight starts to fall over all of us as time drags on and nothing moves forward, making us restless. Days become weeks, the deadline for our strike approaches, and yet we're in stasis. We could not be more ready. Breena has used every scrap of wood, feather, and gut string she's got to make us bows and arrows. Our swords and knives are so sharp they whistle through the air during training sessions. Errin and Merek can go no further with their work without the quicksilver and the Sal Salis, and they could open their own shop with all the lotions, salves, and potions they've been making instead.

Only Hobb is pleased, because every day we have to wait is a day his fighters become a little stronger, and a little better. A little more likely to survive a battle. But when we're not training, the waiting is like an itch they cannot reach; petty disputes and fights break out daily, and it gets harder to resolve them as everyone stews.

And the longer this nothingness goes on, the tighter my own fears grip me. Hope and Ulrin would have reached Tallith in less than three days on the river, and it shouldn't have been much more coming back, even traveling against the current. So where are they?

The dreams began the night they left, and the longer they're away, the worse my night terrors become. Every night I see them dead, Kirin and Nia caught and killed. Traveling on foot through Tregellan, following a road that was dangerous before the Council offered their loyalty to Aurek. In my dreams I see mercenaries smashing their heads in as they sleep. I see turncoat soldiers hanging them before baying crowds. I see the Sisters pinned to the trees on the King's Road, and at night they wear my friends' faces, and there is no one to help me get them down. My throat is hoarse in the morning from screaming, and Errin looks more and more worn from spending her days making potions and her nights dragging me from endless nightmares that keep us both awake.

After two weeks of this, Merek moves quietly, without fuss, into our room, taking Nia's bed, and Errin moves to his. Then it's Merek's calming hand on my forehead when I wake, it's Merek's arms I shake and sob in, Merek who tells me I was asleep, it was just a dream, chanting it over and over, stroking my hair, until I calm myself. He holds me until I fall back into a dreamless sleep, my face pressed into his chest, breathing in the smell of him. When I wake, he's already up and gone, back to the lab.

We never speak of it; it becomes something that happens, something to be endured and then ignored. If it exhausts him, he never shows it. The rest of the commune can tell something is wrong—Errin and Merek are not the only ones woken by me—and they know it's to do with my missing friends, but they don't know what the stakes are, how much hinges on their return. I begin to regret that we didn't all go together. Keeping all these secrets, and being kept in the dark, adds layer upon layer of strain, until my skin feels as though it's made of paper, and I worry I'm moments away from flying apart.

Finally, four weeks after they left, a night comes when I'm sitting in the armory, putting off going to bed even though it's long past time, halfheartedly polishing an already gleaming sword, when I hear the footsteps I've been waiting for. I throw down my cloth and sheathe the blade, turning expectantly.

Hope stands there, her clothes dusty, purple shadows under her eyes, her skin gray with fatigue.

She crosses the room in three paces and thrusts a pouch into my hands; the stones inside click together as I take it. "Don't let it touch your skin. It's toxic."

Then she throws her arms around me.

I hold her so tightly that she grunts, pushing me away. "I'm all right," she says. "Bloody boat foundered near Monkham. We had to trek back from there. We ran out of rations a day early."

"Come," I say. "Let's get you some food."

"I don't want food," she says gruffly, unhooking her belt and hanging it on the wall. "I want wine. And my bed. Ulrin snores like a bear. Ymilla is welcome to him. Where are the others?"

"Errin is in the laboratory she set up. I expect everyone else is sleeping."

Her eyes narrow. "Nia and Kirin?"

"You've beaten them back."

She frowns, and her expression makes my stomach feel as though I've swallowed rocks. Every dark vision from my nightmares flashes before my eyes. I wasn't worrying for nothing. I am right to be afraid.

"I'm sure they're fine," Hope says.

But she knows the words are hollow. I should have gone in their place. What happened to the girl who wrote on the walls of Chargate city? Why did I send Nia when I knew she didn't want to go?

"Wine," Hope says again firmly. "Then we'll decide what to do."

She links her arm through mine, and we step out of the armory, only to come smack straight into Nia as she flies around the corner, sending both Hope and me staggering backward.

"Nia! You're back!" I gasp, but one look at her pale, tearstained face stops me in my tracks. "What's happened—?"

Kirin appears behind her, and his face is as grim as hers. "He's training the children to fight," he says without preamble. "He's had his men training them—we saw them, at the camp in Chargate." His eyes meet mine. "He's going to make them fight."

Chapter 22

"Slow down," Hope says, all traces of tiredness vanishing as her spine straightens and she crosses her arms in front of her. "Tell us what you saw. From the beginning."

"There were roadblocks everywhere; that's what kept us away so long. Almwyk was a fortress; we had to make a detour south to get into the woods, and the path took us close to the Chargate camp, so we decided to check on it, and Gareld and the men there." Kirin keeps his tone level, reporting like the soldier he once was. "Gareld told us men had been in and out for days, bringing bags of what they assumed were supplies, and that the latest pair had just left."

I suck in a deep breath. This is exactly what Merek and I saw at the caves.

"We were suspicious," Kirin continues. "So when these men came just after lunchtime, we waited until they'd made their delivery, and then we followed them."

"You *what*?" Hope says angrily, but I wave her into silence.

"We trailed them back out of the woods, getting as close as we could. We didn't hear much, but we heard them talking about which boys' skills were coming on, and which ones they thought were likely to cause problems. One of the men said he would write to the captain that night to let him know the boys would be ready enough to fight soon."

"They fight with sticks wrapped in cloth," Nia says. "Just sticks, padded, so there's little sound. Gareld and the others are too far away to hear it. One of the men complained of being hit, and said how much it hurt, even with the padding. They were laughing about it. They said the boy who did it—Ellis—was coming along nicely. They think he'll be ready for a blade soon. Him and some others. They talked about getting ready to move them."

"Move them where?"

"They didn't say."

"What about the girls?" I ask.

"Aurek wouldn't think to teach girls to fight," Hope says. "He wouldn't think them capable."

"He's going to have a terrible shock in the near future, then, isn't he?" I say. "We need to wake everyone."

Hope looks at me. "What do you plan to do?"

"We need to get the children out of the camps. All of them. As soon as we can."

Hope shakes her head. "Twylla, you yourself said it—we need to be coordinated for this to work. We don't have the resources for anything but one strike. If we do this—"

"We can't leave the children there," I say. "Not now. We have to get them to safety. So this *is* our one strike."

"Twylla . . ."

"If the people find out their children are being prepared for some sort of battle, they'll riot." I'm shouting now, my voice echoing back at me. "They'll riot and be killed, and we'll be sold out before the sun sets tomorrow and on a gallows by sundown. We need those children out now, and we need to strike immediately after. We have all we need so that Errin can finish the Opus Mortem." I look at Nia for confirmation that she and Kirin were successful, and she nods. "We send word via the scouts that we're liberating the camps tomorrow night," I continue. "And then—we fight."

"Twylla?" Errin appears, with Stuan shadowing her. Her face lights up when she sees Hope, Nia, and Kirin, but she stops dead a split second later, sensing the dark mood. "Don't you have it?"

"They have it," I say before anyone can speak. "But the plan has changed. We have information that Aurek has been training the children to fight. He's had men teaching them combat. We're going to be fighting an army of children."

"We have to get them out," Errin says immediately, and I could hug her.

"We will," I say. "Wake everyone. Now."

Hope and Kirin look at each other. "Wait," Hope says. "Let's get more information. Then we can decide what to do . . ."

"I've already decided," I snap. "I am not leaving children there to be trained as soldiers and used as weapons. This is it. Whether we like it or not."

Hope's lips thin. "Where's Merek?" she says. "He needs to hear this, too."

I give a short nod. "He's probably in my room," I say, turning crimson when Hope, Nia, and Kirin all stare at me.

"I'll go," Kirin says, darting off down the corridor.

The rest of the commune has heard the commotion, and people are emerging, their anger at being woken turning to relief, then confusion.

"What's the matter?" Ema asks, rubbing her eyes.

"Anyone still asleep, rouse them," I say.

"Twylla . . ." Hope warns me for a third time.

I turn to her and lower my voice. "If you were them, and you discovered we kept this from you—even for one night—would you forgive us? Some of those children are their children."

Finally, she nods her agreement.

"We need everyone in the refectory," I say. "Now. It's urgent."

"What's happening?" Ymilla asks, looking between all of us. "Are we under attack?"

"No. But we need to begin our offensive sooner than planned."

"When?"

"Tomorrow night," I say. "The first wave of the attacks will begin tomorrow night."

I can feel Nia, Hope—everyone—staring at me as though I've lost my mind. For a whole minute, there is perfect silence as everyone waits for me to . . . what? Laugh, as if I was joking? Tell them I've changed my mind? Finally they understand I mean it. I see the way the realization ripples through the crowd like water; faces become stony, or slacken, color heightens, or leaches away. They look at one another, hands reaching out for other hands, to grip arms, shoulders, around waists.

"I will explain everything to you. But for now, please wake everyone who isn't up, get dressed, and go to the refectory." When they begin to move back into their rooms, I seek out Trey. "Go to the lookout guards on the posts and summon them here," I tell him.

"All of them?" he asks.

"All of them."

He nods and vanishes immediately.

Then I turn to Nia. "You have the salt?"

She nods and shrugs a bag from her shoulder. When I look at Errin, she reaches for it.

"Go and finish the Opus Mortem," I tell her. "I'll come to you as soon as I'm finished."

Errin swallows, her jaw set firmly as she turns in the direction of her laboratory. Hope puts an arm around Nia and gives me a resolute smile before leading her toward the refectory.

Merek doesn't even look at them as he passes, his eyes fixed on me, Kirin behind him. "What is it?"

"Aurek is training the children to fight. That's what those men were doing at the caves—bringing weapons. Teaching the boys how to use them."

Merek looks thoughtful. "Are you sure?"

"We overheard men talking about their training," Kirin says.

"No, I believe that. I just mean . . . why *children*? He has men, and he has his golems. He doesn't need the children to fight. At the moment he'd already outnumber us on a battlefield. Numbers aren't his problem."

"They would be if everyone rose up against him," Kirin says.

"But we don't *have* everyone. We need the townspeople for that, and they can't and won't fight so long as their children—so long as their children . . ." Merek stops, and in that silence I understand what Aurek has done.

"That's why," I say. "That's what he wants the children for. A shield—a human shield. If he has child soldiers on his walls, the townspeople won't attack them. They won't stand with us when we fight. We won't be able to fight."

"Surely the children wouldn't fight their kin, though?" Kirin says, shaking his head.

"We don't know what these children are being told," I murmur. "Whether they're being told to fight or their families will die, whether they're being told to fight because their families are fighting, too. Whether they've been told their families don't love them anymore, and that only Aurek does."

At that, Merek moves to my side, but I can't look at him. I know he, like me, is thinking of his mother and her manipulations. But I don't have time to think of the past now.

"We have to get them out," I continue. "We always planned to get the children out before we attacked. That hasn't changed. It's just become more urgent, in light of this new development."

One by one, they all nod. I look up at Merek.

"Errin's gone to make the Opus Mortem," I say to him. "She'd appreciate your help."

He nods, his expression troubled as he leaves us.

"Every three days these men come?" I ask Kirin, and he nods. "And you left the woods how long ago?"

"It took us two days to get back."

So they would be due at the camp again tomorrow. I make some rapid calculations and come to a decision. "Come on."

"What are we doing?" Kirin asks.

"We're going to the strategy room," I say. "You need to know what's going to happen next because I'm putting you in charge of overseeing it. Then I need to put my armor on."

Chapter 23

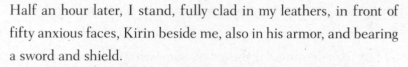

Half an hour later, I stand, fully clad in my leathers, in front of fifty anxious faces, Kirin beside me, also in his armor, and bearing a sword and shield.

"Aurek is training the children to fight," I say without preamble, and immediately the room explodes into panic. Kirin smashes his sword against his shield until they fall mostly silent, and I can continue. "As soon as I'm finished here, small teams of fighters will leave to go to the camps, tell the watchers our information, and reinforce their numbers. At midnight tomorrow, the camps will be liberated. All of the captors are to be slain; no mercy is to be shown. The children at the caves will be brought here; in Monkham, moved south into the small woods there. Those at Chargate will be taken deeper into the woods, to where our old camp was, and at Haga, the woods near the south mountains. There they will remain until word is sent that we are victorious."

I take a breath and carry on. "Once the camps are all clear, the uprisings will begin drawing Aurek's army away from his castle. And once the fighting has begun, we will go down into Lortune, where we will battle our way to the castle and engage with the Sleeping Prince."

"But you said we had two moons." Ymilla speaks up from where she's nestled in beside Ulrin once more. "It's barely been one."

"I know. But we can't allow the children to remain in the camps if this is what's happening. Not least because if the townspeople hear their children are being used like this, there is a very real possibility they'll turn on their captors before we're ready—before we're coordinated across Lormere. And if that happens, we will lose our only window to attack him. It has to be simultaneous—every town at the same time—and we have to be in control of it. So it will be tomorrow."

Silence rings around the room, a devastating contrast to the cheers and celebrations of the last time we came together. After moons of waiting, of stewing, the moment is upon us, and I can taste the fear in the room, bitter and gritty, like the pith of an orange. It tastes how feasts with Helewys used to.

"If you don't want to fight, I understand," I say, speaking without planning to, as Kirin turns to me sharply. "I can't ask you to die for me. So if you want to leave, and hide, I won't stop you." I look around, noticing how many of them won't meet my eye, and my heart sinks, because this is all the force I have. But I'm not Helewys, and I'm not Aurek. I want them to choose.

"Kirin will give you the rest of your instructions." I look at him and he nods. "And, Hobb, you have the best idea of who is skilled where. Work together to make sure our teams are as strong as they can be, and send the scouts and additional warriors out tonight. Everyone else should go back to bed for now. Get some sleep if you can."

I don't say anything else, leaving them there, the stillness of the room following me. I had expected them all to start shouting once I left, but no one speaks.

I head to the armory first and strip off the armor, only put on for effect, and then make my way to the laboratory.

A greenish, bitter herbal odor snakes through the air in the corridor as I approach, making me wrinkle my nose. I knock on the door, then push it open.

In here the smell is nauseating, but Merek and Errin don't seem to notice it. They're both working separately at different ends of the bench, both with duplicate tools before them: a fire pit, vials, bottles, flasks, jars of powders, bottles of clear and blue-tinged liquids. Both have rigged up some arcane system with pipes and bottles and other things I don't know the name of.

Merek looks up as I enter, and his expression stops my heart. He's not smiling, but the look on his face is fierce with joy. He gives me a small smile but then returns to his work, absorbed back into it immediately, and I realize it's the first time something has ever pulled his eyes from mine like this.

I walk over to Errin and see that she's preparing the asulfer and the quicksilver. I missed this part in the Conclave.

"Almost ready," she says. "I just need to wait for the mandrake reduction to finish."

My mouth turns down at the corners. "What's Merek doing?"

"Making the Opus Magnum."

"Why?"

"For the casualties. It was Merek's idea. We're prepping it in secret, and then if Silas wants to use it afterward to help people, that's up to him. I don't agree, but as Merek said, it should be his decision."

I nod. It's a clever idea; I should have thought of it. "Can I help you at all?"

"If you want." She moves along the bench to peer into the pot atop her small fire, wrinkling her nose and pulling a grotesque expression. "I think we're there. How much do you remember from last time?"

I look down the bench at Merek, who's sprinkling yellow flower petals into a ceramic bowl with deep concentration before adding six drops of what I recognize as their spagyric tonic.

"I remember that part," I say.

"This time you can see it all, as we're working backward. We're going to start with the quicksilver and the asulfer. Silas set them alight and collected the smoke, but we need to boil them and collect the steam."

"All right," I say, already confused.

Errin, though, seems to know exactly what she's doing, and she takes two stone dishes already full of glowing-hot stones and uses tongs to push them into two small cauldrons full of water. The red quicksilver goes into one, and the yellow asulfer the second. She fits them with lids that have tubes coming out of the top, traveling down into flasks."

"I designed them myself," she says proudly when I stare at them. "The steam will collect, and become liquid, and drip into the flasks."

"They're wonderful," I say, and she laughs.

"Thank you," she says. "In the meantime, the mandrake reduction is ready, if you could crush the calcified yew bark into a powder?" She nods toward a pestle and mortar and I take it, lifting the heavy pestle and beginning to grind.

We work like that, the three of us, for the next hour. Merek finishes his Opus Magnum first, not needing to wait for anything to distill, so he comes to help, taking over from me when the pestle makes my arms ache. Errin watches closely as a thin layer of red-and-yellow water collects on the bottom of her flasks.

"All right," she says. "I'm ready."

A strange hum seems to fill the room, barely audible but somehow loud despite it, settling over us like a mantle. Even Stuan, until now motionless by the door, seems to feel it and stands up straighter.

"Start praying to your Gods," Errin says. Then she moves.

She pulls a white bowl to her and simultaneously adds the red-and-yellow solution. The white bowl is placed over the fire pit, and then she reaches for the other ingredients. The mandrake, the wheat, the flowers, the tonic, the angel water. All added with precise, exact movements. When I glance at Merek, I see him watching hungrily, his expression sharp, and I feel a rush of pleasure that he's able to see this, to do this thing he always wanted to. I reach out and take his hand, and he squeezes my fingers without ever looking away from the alchemy.

Finally, Errin unwraps a piece of paper, revealing the crystals inside it. Sal Salis. Salt of salt.

She looks up at us, and I hold my breath as she sprinkles it into the mixture.

I don't quite know what I expect to happen, but nothing does.

Merek lets out a long, shaky laugh that implies he was waiting for something to happen, too.

"The Opus Magnum doesn't change until the blood is added," Errin says.

"Of course," I say, rolling up my sleeve. "Do you need me to sit down?"

Errin hesitates. "There's something I have to tell you. Something no one outside of the alchemists knows."

Merek, still gripping my hand, steps closer to me.

"What?" he asks.

Errin looks between us.

"Tell us," I say.

"To begin, you have to know that the power of alchemy lies almost entirely in the blood of the alchemist," Errin says, and I nod, because I already know this; it's what my mother said. Errin fixes her attention on Merek. "The blood is the active ingredient. The Elixir only becomes the Elixir when Silas's blood is added. Until then, it's just the Opus Magnum, a base potion. And so is the Opus Mortem. It's poisonous, yes. It would kill any mortal man. But the thing that makes it dangerous to Aurek now is Twylla's blood. Do you understand?"

"I think so," Merek says.

"Good. What is the acknowledged purpose of alchemy, in the books?"

"To transmute base metals to other substances," he says. "It's turning lead and iron into gold, using the Opus Magnum."

"And if the active ingredient in the Opus Magnum is blood . . ."

"There's iron in human blood."

Errin nods. "Yes. And every time an alchemist performs their alchemy, every time they mix their blood with the Opus Magnum, it changes it. And it changes a part of them." She pauses. "They're all cursed. The aurumsmith's curse is called Citrinitas, and it turns part of them to gold. Real gold. They have no idea which part until they do the alchemy. Every time, it could be a fingertip, a toenail . . . something internal . . ."

Then I understand. And I keep understanding, implications battering me like waves. "Oh Gods." My stomach rolls violently. "Wait—Silas?"

"The philtersmith's curse is called Nigredo. It seems to cause death of the flesh. As he heals, it hurts him. It's in his hands, so far. It'll likely be his feet if he carries on. He can still use them, but not well. It'll get worse, the more he does."

"And you think if Twylla adds her blood to the Opus Mortem, she might develop this curse?" Merek speaks my thoughts aloud, and I look at Errin.

"Not those curses. She's not a philtersmith or an aurumsmith."

"Then what am I?"

"I don't know. I don't think there's a word for it yet."

"When were you going to tell us?" Merek's voice is clipped and precise, a contrast to how I feel.

"There didn't seem any point until we had the ingredients."

Merek is gripping my hand so tightly now that I'm in pain, and I pull away. He looks momentarily hurt, then glares at Errin again, as though that, too, is her fault.

"Merek," I say gently, and he turns back to me. "I have to do it anyway. You understand that, don't you?"

"But we don't know what might happen. You might . . ." He swallows. "Tell her," he demands of Errin. "Tell her it can wait until she's had time to consider this and make a proper choice about it."

Errin looks at me helplessly. "If you really want to . . ."

"Of course I don't." I do, a little. I also understand that I can't, not really. But it means the world to me that they would give me a choice. That Merek wants me to have time to make a choice. I look up at him. "I'm choosing this." I say the words aloud. "Knowing what it might mean. And it's not Errin's fault. Stop shouting at her."

"I know." He looks so wretched that I reach up and take his face in my hands.

"I'll be all right."

He leans down so his forehead rests against mine, bringing his own hands up and resting them atop my own. "Promise me."

"I promise."

"And if you're not?"

"Then, hopefully, you'll be too distraught to be angry that I lied."

He sighs, amused despite himself. "I'm staying with you."

I close my eyes for the briefest moment, then pull away from him, turning to Errin. "All right."

She holds out a small knife to me. While Merek and I talked, she continued working, pouring the potion into seven vials. "One drop of blood in each," she says. "You need to prick your finger, wait until a drop of blood wells up. Then I'll press the vial to it and we'll let them mingle."

I nod. Seven vials—seven attempts at murdering him.

"Is that many really necessary?" Merek asks, and I shush him.

"Ready?" Errin asks.

Suddenly I'm back in the Telling Room, waiting for Rulf to take my blood. How odd that it's come to this. How strange that here I am, giving up my blood to make a poison. How similar, and different, all at once.

Dreamily, I take the knife and make the first cut.

I suck my breath through my teeth; I'd forgotten how much it hurt. We all watch, waiting for the blood to well up from the tiny slit. It blooms deep red, and then, the instant before it can run, Errin presses the first vial onto it and tips it up, so the blood mixes with the Opus Mortem against the cut. The poison turns a brilliant white, and Merek, who has been staring at me so hard I'm surprised I'm not bruised, gasps, and covers his face with his hands.

"What is it?" I ask, ice filling my veins. "What's happened to me?"

Errin looks up at me. "Your hair."

"Is it still there?" I reach for my hair and pull it around. "Oh."

A thick section has turned white, like Silas's, like Aurek's. It's shocking against the red. But it could have been so much worse.

"Is that it?"

Errin nods, and Merek lowers his hands, breathing out slowly. "That's it," he says. "Forgive me. I was so . . . Thank the Gods." He turns away and runs his hands over his head.

"Are you in any pain?" Errin asks.

"No. Except for the cut." I look up at Merek's back and smile.

"All right." Errin takes a deep breath. "Next one."

I make another cut, and another, and another. Merek returns to my side and places his hand on my shoulder as we work. I make seven cuts, cutting almost every finger on both of my hands. Every time I mix my blood with the poison, Merek's fingers tighten on my shoulder as assumedly another chunk of my hair turns white. I wish there was a mirror so I could see it happening. I don't move, though, watching Errin as she concentrates on mixing the Opus Mortem with my blood, until we're finished and all of the vials have been blooded.

"I survived," I say when Errin has corked the last bottle. She looks at me, a smile already at her lips. I watch as it slides from her face like water on a pane of glass. I watch, in slow motion, as the vial she was holding slips from her hands. I even move to catch it.

"Your eyes," she gasps, not even looking at the poison as the vial smashes against the floor and it leaks everywhere.

Merek is in front of me within a heartbeat, and then he recoils, too.

"What's wrong with my eyes?" My voice is too loud, too shrill.

Stuan steps forward, and then flinches as he sees me.

"What's wrong with my eyes?" I repeat. I can still see just as well as ever.

Stuan keeps coming, unsheathing his sword.

Merek moves in front of me as if to defend me, but Stuan holds up a hand, offering me the hilt with the other. "Look." He holds out the shining metal.

I push Merek aside and reach for the blade, taking it gently and holding it up to my face.

It's not only my hair that's changed color. My eyes, once green, are now completely white.

Chapter 24

All three of them are staring at me, their expressions a mix of repulsed, fascinated, and shocked.

"Stop looking at me," I demand, and they do, all of them turning away. I raise the sword again and examine my eyes. The irises have vanished, and I have to admit the effect is disturbing. With entirely white eyes set in my pale, freckled face, and the colorless cloud of my hair framing it, I look monstrous. I look dead.

"Wonderful. What are the others going to think when they see this?" I say. "They're already terrified. How will it look when I emerge with white hair and eyes?"

"Can't we play up the Daunen angle?" Errin says, as Stuan once again gazes at me with open disgust. I meet his eyes, and he immediately looks away. "Can't we imply it's something to do with that? Some sign of favor?"

I look at Merek, who, to his credit, doesn't flinch. "It's possible . . ." he says.

"But?"

He takes a breath. "I always swore I would do things differently from my mother. I'm not going to push the Gods on people. If the people want to believe, that's their choice; but for me, implying we'll be victorious because of a living Goddess is counterproductive. I want the people to choose for themselves where their faith lies."

I smile at him, and he holds my gaze. Warmth blossoms in my stomach.

Errin clears her throat pointedly. "Well, let's discuss this again in the morning. Everyone should be in bed now anyway. It's late. Or rather, early," she says, dousing her fires and tidying the ingredients away. Merek turns to help her, and I look at my reflection again.

"I think it's best to keep covered, for now," I say. "There will be too many questions, and everyone is already on edge."

"Your helmet," Merek says as he passes a flask to Errin. "We'll have some mesh put over the eye slits."

I nod. "That'll work. We'll have to keep me away from the children, too."

"It'll be a nice surprise for Aurek." Errin turns, grinning. "When you descend on him, white-eyed and gnashing your teeth."

I narrow my newly pearlescent eyes at her.

"That's exactly the look you should go with," she adds cheerily.

"Well, as long as it has some use."

They finish their tidying swiftly, efficiently, and Errin places the Opus Mortem in a small wooden box, which she cradles in her arms before looking at me expectantly.

"I suppose we'd better get some sleep, then," I say.

There's an awkward pause, when no one knows quite what to do, or where they ought to go. Errin breaks the moment.

"Come on, Stuan, time to tie me up for bed."

He splutters furiously, and Errin tips me a wink as she sashays out of the room, him trailing behind her like a puppy.

"Come on," Merek says to me, holding out a hand. It feels natural and unnatural all at once to take it.

We walk slowly down the corridor of the women's quarters, not speaking. We see no one, hearing the sounds of slumber from behind the other curtains. When we reach my—our—room, he holds the curtain aside and I enter, remembering at the last minute that Nia is back, and expecting to see her there. But the room is empty, and a hollow weight fills my stomach. We're alone.

Merek follows me, and I feel oddly present, more in my skin than I've been aware of before. Usually, he works so late in the lab that I'm asleep when he comes to the room, and I see him only when I wrench myself from my nightmares. When I hear the curtain rustle again, I think he's left me, and turn, panicked, only to see him reenter with a candle, lit from the torch in the corridor.

He places it on the table by his bed and looks at me. And in the bright glow of the flame, his eyes are hungry.

"If you'd rather I left, I understand," he says.

I shake my head, my mouth too dry to speak.

"So you don't mind if I sleep here?"

I shake my head again.

"Twylla . . ."

"I don't mind if you stay," I manage to say, in a voice that sounds aeons older than I am. Then: "I want you to stay."

321

A shudder runs through him, but he stays still, watching me.

"Unless you want to go?" It dawns on me that he might be asking for permission to leave. That he only meant to walk me here and then leave. "You can if you want."

"That's not what I want." His voice is low, intimate. A bedroom voice.

When I hold out my hand, he comes to me, taking it, pressing it to his chest, then his cheek. Gently, I move it away and reach for the bottom of his tunic, pulling it over his head. He raises his arms to help me, and I drop the garment to the ground. Then his breeches; I loosen the belt and the ties until they slip down his narrow hips, pooling at his feet, and he steps out of them.

It's his turn, then, to pull my tunic off, to unlace my breeches. We uncover each other with gentle haste, fingertips brushing lightly over skin, but never lingering, never seeking. When he drops my undershirt to the floor, we look at each other, naked, our skin gleaming faintly in the dim candlelight.

He takes my face in his hands and presses one kiss against my lips, holding it there, the skin of his chest a whisper against mine. Then he takes my hand and leads me to my bed. He climbs under the covers and I follow, molding myself around him as he lies back, my head on his shoulder, one of his arms under my back, the other over my waist. I rest a hand on his chest, feel his heart beating beneath it, tangle my legs between his. Without speaking, we lie down together and curl around each other like kittens. I can feel that he wants me, and I want him, too, the ache low in my belly, my heart thrumming like a harp string. But neither of us does anything more. The hand on my shoulder rises to stroke my hair, and he turns his head, kiss after kiss landing softly against my brow.

I turn and kiss the hollow where his neck and his shoulder meet, breathing him in.

Then, for the first time in four weeks, I fall asleep and stay peacefully asleep, in the arms of the king of Lormere.

When I wake I'm alone, and I sit up so rapidly that I make myself dizzy.

Merek is fully dressed, and seated on Nia's—his—bed, a cup in hand, steam spiraling out of the top. He looks over at me and blinks, momentarily startled by my eyes, but then his gaze moves lower, and the way he smiles sends a shock wave of feeling down my spine.

"Good morning," I say.

"Good afternoon."

"Is it? Oh Gods . . ." I pull the sheet up over my chest and swing my legs off the bed.

"It's fine, Twylla. Everything is under control. Hope, Nia, and Kirin have been up since a little after dawn, and they've arranged everything according to your instructions. The scouts and support have been sent out to their stations. Kirin has a list of people who are going tonight, and it's a sizable group."

I blink at him, a sharp pulse of irritation crackling through me. "I should have been there."

"A good leader delegates." He puts his cup down and walks over to me, the bed dipping as he sits, tumbling me into him. "And you did. And it worked. Congratulations."

I tamp down the annoyance and raise a small smile. "So who is going tonight?" I ask.

He runs his thumb along my collarbone, goose bumps rising along my arms. "Kirin, Hobb, Breena, Ema, Ulrin . . ." He reels off a list of names. "Stuan, and me." He kisses my shoulder.

"Stuan isn't staying here with Errin?"

"No." He pauses. "You are."

"What?" I shift away from him.

"Listen, I told Hope about your eyes—don't look at me like that, I had to warn her because—"

"You went to her while I slept, to discuss me?"

"Twylla—"

"Shut up, Merek," I snap at him, and he flinches. "Are you telling me after everything that happened between us before, you went and arranged things without me? Again? You climbed out of my bed to go behind my back and make a plan with my army?"

"Twylla, please . . ."

"Get out!" I shout at him. "Go."

His eyes widen but I don't care. With the sheet still wrapped around me I stumble from the bed and search for my clothes, my fury mounting when I see them folded, placed on the bureau.

"Why are you still here?" I round on him as I reach for my undershirt. "I told you to leave."

And he does.

The underarm of my tunic tears in my haste to yank it over my head, and I rip it off and throw it into the corner of the room, reaching for another, almost tearing that one, too. As soon as I've pulled my boots on, I fly from the room like a storm, blazing down the corridor, looking for Hope, and Nia, and Kirin. Those traitors.

324

My footsteps thunder through the stone passageways, warning anyone in my path to move as I head for where I know they'll be, ensconced together, plotting without me. So they think they don't need me now? That I've played my part? I throw open the doors to the strategy room and find them all in there, the whole group going to liberate the camp tonight. Even Errin sits with them, and they all turn as one to stare at me as I stand in the doorway, seething.

"If you think—" is as far as I get before they all start bellowing.

"Her eyes! Her eyes!" I can hear Breena moaning.

"Her hair!"

"What's happened to her?"

"She's like him!"

"Silence!" Hope's voice rings through the room.

They immediately obey and Hope looks at me.

"Merek told you, about tonight?" she asks.

He flinches when I meet his eyes. "He extended me that courtesy," I spit.

Hope looks between us, her expression thoughtful, then around the room at the others, and I follow her gaze. Everyone save Errin and Stuan is staring at me, mouths turned down at the corners, hands balled into fists, unable to conceal their revulsion. Their fear.

"You see now one of the reasons why it's not a good idea for you to be involved in the liberation of the children," she says quietly.

And I do. Nothing could have demonstrated it more.

"I could wear a helmet," I say. But I know it's too late.

"What the bloody hell happened to you?" Ulrin asks.

"We had an accident in the laboratory last night," Merek says. "We were making some healing potions and she was splashed."

"And that turned her hair and eyes white, did it?" Ema asks. "Changed the color of them? Give over, Your Majesty. We weren't born yesterday."

"You're right, it wasn't an accident in the laboratory," I say, anger spiking again when she looks back at me and winces. I tamp it down; it's not her fault. "I can't tell you what happened, because it's not really my story to tell. But if you truly don't want me to come with you tonight, I won't."

"It's not us, lass, it's the children." Ulrin speaks for them all. "If they see you . . . If this brainwashing thing is true, it's going to be hard enough to convince them we're on their side. I don't imagine a white-eyed woman is going to convince them we're not the bad guys here. How long is this . . . *accident* going to last?"

"I don't know. I believe it's permanent."

They start to mutter again, and Stuan shifts his weight menacingly. I feel a rush of affection for him.

"It'll put the fear of the Gods into the Sleeping Prince, though," Hobb says finally, echoing what Errin said last night. "If you go at him the way you flew at us in here, he'll hand you the crown and fall on his own sword."

A few of them smile, Ulrin laughs, and I know it's over. That's it. I'm not going tonight. I'll wait here, like an anxious princess waiting for her prince to come home. Like before.

I want to bolt from the room before I lash out and hurt someone. I want to go into the garden and bury my hands in the ground. I want to go and hide in Hope's cottage and cry until I'm wrung out.

I want to pluck Merek Belmis's stupid brown eyes out of his head so he can't gaze at me with that sorrowful, pleading expression.

But I do none of those things.

"Tell me the plan." I leave Stuan and take my place at the head of the table, making sure to meet everyone's eyes with my white ones, not looking away when they flinch. "Talk me through the whole thing. I want to know every detail of what you're going to do."

The relief is palpable as everyone draws together around the table and Kirin begins to speak.

Merek remains by the door, but he can take himself through it and walk into the ocean for all I care right now.

With half of our people now moving stealthily across the country to be in place for the final battle, I decide to move everyone remaining to the women's quarters, freeing up the men's for the children. The rooms will be crammed tight, but they'll be better here with us than in the mountains. As everyone leaves to move their belongings, I return to my table and look over the map once more.

"Where shall I sleep?" Merek appears at my side, his voice low.

"You can sleep where you like. I honestly don't care," I reply, not bothering to keep the volume down.

I can feel him watching me, and I fix my attention on the West Woods, clamping my teeth together to stop myself saying any more.

"I'm sorry," he says before he moves away, leaving the space where he was, cold.

I look up to watch him leave, and catch Errin's eye. When she raises her eyebrows, my own pull into a scowl and I look back at my map, forcing myself to focus on routes we've planned.

We come back together, all of us, later in the evening, and without planning to, we head as one into the kitchens and put supper together, chopping vegetables, passing spices, cutting bread. We behave as a family, and when it's time to eat, I sit with Errin and Stuan, wedging myself between them and refusing to acknowledge that Merek is there at all. I make him the black sheep of us, and soon everyone is turning a little away from him, understanding that he's lost my favor. Hope's words in the cottage come back to me, about how they would choose me, but I take no pleasure from them now.

I know I'm being childish and that we have much bigger issues to contend with, but I can't put out the fire inside me. Of everyone, I trusted him, and Errin, the most. Of everyone, I thought he knew me, understood me. And in the end he did exactly what Lief did, what the queen did, what my mother did. He made a decision on my behalf.

He robbed me of the chance to be there at the start of my own plan. He issued orders to my people, sent out the parties without even bothering to check with me. He assumed control. At this moment, I can't forgive him for it. I don't know if I'll ever be able to.

Once the supper is over, once the last of the gravy has been mopped from the bowls, they all leave to go and put on their armor, the large room emptying quickly. Merek lingers, attempting to catch my eye, but I plant myself in the midst of them all, laughing and jostling with them. I move amongst them, helping tie buckles, passing padding and gauntlets when I'm asked. I hug them, pat shoulders, even kiss Stuan's cheek. In the corner, Merek puts on his armor alone; like everyone else's, it's mismatched and cobbled together from scraps of armor, and whatever else we could find. But on him it looks saddest of all; whether that's because he's the king and should be clad better, or because he's on the outside of this, I don't know.

Finally they're ready. Everyone falls silent at the same moment, looking amongst one another.

"Good luck," I say. There's nothing else to say. "Come back safely. All of you."

Stuan, Kirin, and Hobb all bow, and the others nod. All of the camaraderie has gone, replaced with focus, and fear. The faces of the people before me look both younger and older all at once—when Nia smiles at me from inside her already dented helmet, I can see her as a girl, and how she'll look as an old woman. They turn to leave, and Errin and I follow them, right to the doors.

As they start to disappear into the night, I call Merek back without ever fully planning to do it.

"Merek. Wait."

He stops, and turns, looking at me cautiously. Errin melts back into the commune, leaving us alone. I walk toward him, and he toward me. We meet in the middle. For a long moment I look at him, unable to find the words I need, half tempted to slap him and then send him on his way.

"I'm still furious with you," I begin.

"I know, and—"

"Will you let me finish?" I say, and he nods, hanging his head. "I'm still furious with you. You left me out of my own plan. You should have woken me so I could be included. So I could be the one who gave the order to go. I worked so hard for their trust, Merek. You have no idea." At that he raises his head, questions in his gaze, but I don't allow him to ask them. "I know you're the rightful king of Lormere, but here and now, this is mine. My kingdom. My people. Weeks of preparation and training and risk went into making this plan. And you took control of it, from me, without a second thought."

He nods, but keeps his eyes on mine. "I am so very sorry, Twylla. I would give anything to earn your favor again. To right this wrong."

"I'm glad you feel that way," I say. "And to that end, I insist you come back in one piece, so I can make the next few days an absolute misery for you because of it. Do I make myself clear?"

He looks momentarily confused, and then smiles. A real, true smile.

"You've got a lot of making up to do, Merek Belmis," I say. "So I'll see you back here by morning. All right?"

"As you command, my lady." He sweeps into a bow and smiles again before jogging after the others, who've very sensibly not waited for him.

I watch until the gleam of his armor fades, and then close the doors.

There is no one in the refectory; Bron and Dilys, and assumedly Ymilla, too, have gone to bed. I make my way down the women's corridor, heading to my room. Errin isn't there when I enter, and I'm too restless to sleep, so I leave and walk back to the kitchen, fetching some wine and two goblets. I take them to the laboratory, sure that's where I'll find Errin, and as I get closer, I can hear her muttering to herself. Despite everything, I start to smile.

But my smile dies when something in the room breaks, and she cries out. "No, please. No."

Panicked by the terror in her tone, I pick up my pace and run into the room.

Errin stands alone, with the box of Opus Mortem in front of her. In one hand she clutches a vial, and as I watch, she drops it to the floor and stamps on it, where the shards and liquid join others there. She looks over at me, tears streaming down her face, even as she reaches for another vial.

"What are you doing?"

She stares at me and lifts a second vial, holding it up so the liquid glows white in the light.

"Is something wrong with them?"

She drops it to the floor and crushes it beneath her heel.

"Errin? Errin, stop it!"

I rush at her and she snatches a third vial, screaming, "Help me!" even as she throws it at me. I duck and it hits the door frame to my right and explodes.

"We were wrong," she whimpers. "We were wrong to not keep me tied up."

The simulacrum.

I drop the wine and the goblets, running to her, prying the box from her hands. But still she reaches for them, and I shove the box into her outstretched fingers and keep the last two vials close to my chest as I back away, horrified.

"You have to knock me out." She stumbles toward me, glass

crunching beneath her feet. "Please. Hit me, do something. I won't stop. I can't."

I keep backing away until I hear footsteps approaching from the outer doors.

"Twylla?"

"Ymilla, thank the Gods! Listen, I need you to—"

"She's here," Ymilla says, and her voice is triumphant. "Down here."

Errin understands what's going on before I do.

"Run," she tells me as she lurches toward me, trapping me in the corridor between her and Ymilla. "Push me aside and run."

When I glance back at Ymilla, Lief is standing beside her, dressed in black, a patch over his right eye, half a dozen men beside him.

"You bastard," Errin screams at him. "I trusted you. And you— you bitch, you treacherous, scheming bitch. You'll pay for this."

"Yes, she will." Lief turns and waves a hand at one of his men.

Before Ymilla can turn, the man has planted a dagger in her chest.

"Don't bother feeling sorry for her," Lief says. "She's been reporting to King Aurek for weeks. She wrote to him and told him Merek was alive, and here with you. She offered to be his spy, if she could have her title and home back. Sadly for her, King Aurek has no use for the two-faced."

"And yet he trusts you," I say.

Lief's expression darkens. "Very witty. Very clever. Pity you didn't see through her."

"I'm a terrible judge of character," I say.

I look at the woman on the floor, her life pumping out of her, her mouth gasping like that of a fish.

"Sorry." I turn to Errin. Then I shove her aside and run. I hear footsteps behind me, multiple pairs, as I bolt back down the corridor, through the courtyard and toward the armory.

Inside, I pull my sword down from its hook and spin around, in time to see Lief entering the room.

He raises his eyebrows.

"Are you going to fight me?" he asks.

In reply I pull the sword from its sheath and hold it out.

"Twylla . . ." he says.

I don't wait for him to draw his sword.

I swing at him and he twists aside, the blade missing him by less than an inch.

"Twylla . . ." he tries again, but I bring my arm around on his blind side, slashing at his forearm. I don't get through the leather gauntlet there, but I make contact, and it's enough to cause him to pivot away and draw his own weapon.

For a third time I swipe at him, and he deflects the blow easily, the flat of his sword smashing into mine and sending shock waves down the blade, jarring my forearm.

I hear footsteps again, and then two of his men are in the doorway. They look between us and one of them smirks, firing my rage. I feel my lips curl back in fury.

Lief glances briefly over his shoulder, and as he does, I try once more.

This time his sword crashes into mine with such force that I lose the blade; it flies from my hand and skids across the floor.

In the second it takes me to begin moving toward my sword, my only hope, Lief has hold of my arm, pulling me around to face him. He pries the vials from where I still grip them in my left hand. He drops them to the floor, crushing them under his boot.

"No," I say, bending as if to scrape the remnants together.

He pulls me upright. "It's over, Twylla."

"Merek . . ." I whisper.

"Will find more than he bargained for at the caves."

I look down at the shards there, everything we'd worked toward, gone. My people out there, walking into a trap. Then I look up, into his eye, and he looks back at me without flinching.

"So we've both gone for a new look." He waves his hand in front of his eyes. "You're still beautiful, though. We can't say the same about me anymore."

"Go to hell," I whisper.

Behind him his men watch us closely.

Lief leans in. "What makes you think we're not already there?" he asks.

He kisses my cheek lightly, the cord of his patch scratching my face as he pulls away.

I raise my hand and slap him, hard; the crack rings through the room, and I hear his men suck in their breath.

The last thing I see is his hand rising, followed by a sharp pain at my temple. Then nothing.

Chapter 25

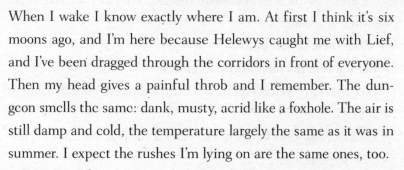

When I wake I know exactly where I am. At first I think it's six moons ago, and I'm here because Helewys caught me with Lief, and I've been dragged through the corridors in front of everyone. Then my head gives a painful throb and I remember. The dungeon smells the same: dank, musty, acrid like a foxhole. The air is still damp and cold, the temperature largely the same as it was in summer. I expect the rushes I'm lying on are the same ones, too.

I sit up and try to get my bearings, and as I move I hear a growl in the dark.

"Oh, piss off," I hiss at the beast.

A low chuckle curls out of the shadows, and then I hear the sound of a flint being struck.

In the sparks before the flame takes, I see flashes of white, and two gold discs gleaming like the eyes of an animal between the bars of the cell door. Then, as the candle lights up, the face of Aurek, the Sleeping Prince, is revealed.

He has been sitting, it seems, in front of the cell in the pitch black, waiting for me to wake, though I have no idea how long I've been unconscious. Beside him is one of Helewys's dogs, and he rests a long-fingered hand on top of the beast's head.

"Hello, Twylla," he says, and his voice is as beautiful and alluring as I remembered. "I've been looking forward to meeting you."

"You must be Aurek."

"I am." He holds the candle up and looks at me. "You've been asleep for a very long time. I was concerned that Lief had hit you too hard. The temple area." He raises a hand to his own head and taps the side, his silvery hair rippling under the motion. "It's tricky," he continues. "You have to be careful." He leans forward, peering at me, his head cocked like a bird's. "I didn't know your eyes were white. Lief never said. I like them. It's like someone scooped out the eyeballs and replaced them with pearls." He pauses, as though waiting for me to thank him for the compliment. When it becomes apparent that isn't going to happen, he continues. "Perhaps that's what I'll do with your skull, once all your flesh has finally decayed away. Pearls in your eye sockets. Rubies spilling from your mouth."

I keep my face as still as stone.

"I'm going to make a crown out of your ribs," he continues. "A sceptre from your thigh bone."

"I'm not overly concerned with what you do with my skeleton. It's not as though I'll be using it if I'm dead."

He laughs again, the sound merry and bubbling, and it echoes around the dungeon. "Everyone led me to believe you'd be a meek, quiet little thing."

"I was, once."

He looks at me, and I look right back, exploring him as his gaze roves over me. From behind the panel in the bone temple, I could see so little, but now I see the resemblance to Silas, an uncanny one, in fact. If Silas grew his hair, or if Aurek cut his, they could pass for brothers. He's handsome, as is Silas, but more polished, more arranged, somehow. Like Merek used to, he has that sheen of entitlement over him, like a gloss.

"No, I don't think Lief would like it," he murmurs finally, and I meet his eyes once more.

"What?"

"If I took you to my bed."

"You'll need me to be a corpse for that, too, I'm afraid," I say coldly.

"I meant as my bride, fool," he says. "You have power in your veins. As do I. I'd like to see what kind of children we'd make. My others were only ever aurumsmiths, you see. I can make gold, but I can also give life. With you, I wonder . . . I make life; your blood, if it's like your ancestors', defeats the Elixir. So perhaps our children could raise the dead," he muses, and I work to suppress a shiver. "We'd make little necromancers. We could conquer everything then. They'd have silver eyes . . . ." He smiles. "Imagine it."

I push down the horror of his words. "Is that why you're here? To make me an offer of a truce? Marry me and this will all be over?"

"Lief said once you were going to be queen. I can make you queen now. Queen forever, with the Elixir. If we breed the philtersmith, we never need worry about running out."

I stare at him, unable to hide my disgust, and he seems genuinely surprised by it.

337

"Is it truly so repellent to you? I'm offering you a chance to live."

"Oh, I'm utterly repelled. But . . ." I pause. "In other ways your words are very welcome."

He narrows those golden eyes at me. "How so?"

"In my experience, victors don't offer bargains," I say. "They don't need to. Which tells me something didn't go as you'd hoped."

His face is as expressionless as a statue's for a moment. "An odd thing to say, when you're sitting here in a cell."

"Who don't you have in a cell? That's what I'm wondering."

"I think I would have preferred the old Twylla better," Aurek says. He rises to his feet in one swift motion. "Last chance. Join me?"

"They got away, didn't they?" I stretch my lips into a smile that has nothing to do with amusement. "The rest of the commune. They defeated your men."

"I'm going to have your heart canned and eat it with caviar and quails' eggs," Aurek hisses through the bars, now demonic as his face scrunches up with rage. "I'm going to gorge on it."

I force myself to laugh, loudly, looking at him as I do. For a moment I think he'll open the door and kill me now, but he turns, furious, the dog at his heels. He takes the candle with him, leaving me laughing in the dark.

My next visitor comes later; I'm not sure how much time has passed. But I've been expecting him. When I see the light glowing on the wall, I sit up, and watch as Lief approaches me.

The dramatic irony of the situation isn't lost on me. Here I am again in the dungeon; here is another man looking at me with

338

disappointment in his eyes. Eye, in Lief's case. Again I'm struck by how everything has come full circle, how all roads have led me back to Lormere castle, back to poison, back to betrayal.

"Where's Merek?" I ask, because with Lief I don't need to pretend. With Lief I never have, and that's the most heartbreaking thing of all.

"We don't know," he says, because he doesn't have to pretend with me, either. Not anymore. "He and the people he was with were ambushed, you knew that. Some fell. Most did not. But we will find them."

"Who fell?"

"I couldn't say." His face darkens. "Merek got away. And the Sister."

"Nia and Kirin?"

"I didn't see their bodies."

"What of the children?"

His face tightens. "I'm not one of your so-called Rising, Twylla. I don't report to you."

"No. You report to the Sleeping Prince."

"Yes." He nods. "I do."

"So they won, then? The Rising Dawn? They liberated them? You might as well tell me; your *king* insinuated as much. He offered me the chance to join him. Be his bride. Bear his children. That would make me your queen, would it not?"

No expression crosses Lief's face.

"I think he hoped I would say yes, bring the Rising to heel. They must have caused quite an uproar."

"There is no Rising anymore. It's over. Those who escaped will be found. And even if a tiny fraction of outliers thought to imitate your rebels, it will make no difference in the long term, Twylla. Once you're dead, and once Merek is really dead, there will be nothing to rally around. It'll be over."

I hang my head in a show of denial, because I don't want him to see that I hear what he's not saying, at the words between his threats. The rebellion has happened anyway. Somehow, one of the towns, maybe all, have risen up. That's what he means by "rally around." The Rising rose. Perhaps is still Rising.

"Will you at least tell me where Errin is?" I will my voice to sound strained.

It works, because he replies. "Confined to a cell. Nowhere near here. She's awaiting trial, too, but His Grace has already promised her leniency, as a favor to me for bringing you to him."

"She'll never forgive you."

"She never would have anyway. But she's my little sister. I care more about her living than her forgiveness."

"Why are you here?" I look up at him again.

"I brought you your supper. And a gown to wear tomorrow. Unless you want everyone's last image of you to be as you are now." He puts the candle down, far enough away that I can't reach through the bars for it, and walks to a pile on the floor. He returns, pushing a bundle of red cloth through the bars, followed by a tin carafe of water, and a sack, which I assume contains food. I look at the heap of things, then back at him.

"Tomorrow?"

He nods. I suppose it makes sense. Killing me will strike a blow to the rebels. The longer I'm alive, the longer they can hope . . .

"I'm your executioner," he says.

I'm not sure I've heard him properly.

"I'm the best option," he says when I continue to stare at him. "I'll be fast, at least."

"You're going to kill me?"

"I'm going to execute you," he corrects.

"Is there a difference?"

His lips twist as he almost smiles. "No. You know there isn't. You remember."

I don't remind him that I never actually executed anyone. For the first time since I woke up down here, fear starts to trickle through me. I look at him, his scarred face, the patch over his eye. His hair, shorter now. I barely recognize him.

"How will you do it?"

"Sword."

I nod, as though that's acceptable to me, when inside I'm shaking.

"What would happen if I told Aurek you spared me in the bone temple?" I ask. "What would he do?"

"I expect he'd be angry at first. But given that you're here now, the result is the same. Nothing will change that. And the delay has meant we now have the added bonus of identifying a great many troublemakers who might have gone unchecked had you been captured then. Things have ended well for us."

"You're the kind of person who always lands on your feet, Lief."

He slams his fist against the bars. "Do I?"

I don't know why, of all the things I've said to him tonight, that sentence is the one that makes him angry, but it does, and I'm taken aback, because until now, he's been calm and controlled.

Emotionless, even. But this is the Lief who screamed at me on the stairs of my tower and kissed me, who begged me to forgive him. This Lief's eye blazes like the aurora.

I take a deep breath. "It looks that way to me."

"Did it ever occur to you that this is all your fault?" His voice is low, guttural, the words coming fast. "That if you'd just . . ." He turns to look over his shoulder, and when he next speaks, his voice is barely above a whisper. "I wouldn't have met him had I been with you. None of this might have happened this way if you'd listened to me. This is your own doing."

"And had you not conspired to ruin me, we might have been living in Tremayne now, with your mother and Errin," I say. "You did this. To all of us."

His face falls, loss carved across it for the briefest moment. Then he turns and walks away, no final retort, no last word. He leaves the candle, though I doubt he meant to. And then I'm alone again. With no hope of getting out of this mess.

The dress Lief brought is the one I was wearing the day he first kissed me, and I know he did it deliberately, one last slap to the face. I imagine him searching through the wardrobe until he found it, choosing it with this in mind. I wonder if Aurek told him he'd be the one to kill me, or whether he asked for the opportunity. I crush the dress in my hands.

I consider not wearing it to spite him, but he's right, I don't want the last image the Lormerians have of me to be in a torn, filthy tunic and old breeches. Perhaps I can still do some good, still be a symbol to them. So I put on the dress, surprised to find it's tight on my arms and shoulders, where I've built muscle learning to fight. I comb my fingers through my hair, and use some of the water and my old undershirt to clean my face as much as I can. I shiver as the water runs down beneath the bodice; the dress is too thin for the weather, designed for days under the sun, and he didn't bring me a cloak. Still, it's not as though I'm at risk of dying of a chill, is it?

Sometime after I've dressed, and finished the last of the water Lief brought, four men materialize from around the corner. They enter the cell as though I'm a wild animal, staring at my eyes, poking at me with swords, trying to make me turn around. I'm flattered that they think me such a threat, so I make it worth their while, refusing to cooperate until one of them slaps me and, as I reel from the blow, takes advantage to pull my arms behind my back and tie my wrists.

Once I'm finally restrained, I'm bundled out of the dungeons and up the stairs. As we climb, I smell old smoke, and when we step out into a bright winter morning, I turn back to see the ruin of Lormere castle, two of the towers still standing, but half of the keep and the other two towers have been destroyed. Most of the stone is blackened, and the sight makes me sad, despite everything. My jailers pull me away, pushing me into a cage on wheels, drawn by a donkey, no room to sit and barely enough to stand. As the cart begins to move, I fall, smashing into the bars and biting my tongue. The men laugh and I spit blood at them. After that I stand, gripping the bars, looking out as we make our way to the main gates.

No one lines the route into the town square. I saw executions here before I came to the castle, and back then, there would be crowds. People would come from all over Lormere for the biggest ones. But today there is no one, just me in my cart, and the guards, and I wonder if Aurek banned them from attending. There seems little point executing me publicly if no one will see it. I look up at the houses and shops as we pass, expecting to see people peering out, if not in the streets, but there's no one. It's like a ghost town.

Wind like knives rushes through the town square, sending the triple-starred pennants Aurek has had mounted fluttering loudly, snapping against each other. My eyes are drawn to him instantly, sitting alone in a box, four golems outside it. He makes a pretense of lounging in his chair, surveying his nails, dressed entirely in gold, his hair pulled back into a low ponytail beneath his crown. Merek's crown. I look around and see more golems, and count them: fifteen. Fifteen golems that I can see.

He's frightened, I realize. Still.

Then I look around the rest of the square.

Here are the people who were missing from the route, hundreds of them. It seems he's had his soldiers drag every single man and woman of Lortune into the square. People are pressed shoulder to shoulder, surrounding a dais, at its center a block of thick wood. The wood is already stained dark, and I shudder.

Not one of the people assembled looks as though they want to be there; every single face is grim, flint-eyed, their mouths set in lines, but they stand dutifully and stare at the block. So Lortune was not one of the places that rose up. I feel a moment's terror then, that I'm wrong and that nowhere rose up. What if the Rising really is over? What if this is where it all ends?

No, I tell myself. *Something* happened; Lief almost said as much. And Aurek is frightened. I know he is. He wouldn't have made his offer if he was winning.

When the cage door is opened, I step serenely forward,

imagining my skeleton is made of iron, locking down my fear. In my whole life I have never been as afraid as I am now, never felt a maelstrom inside me as violent as the urge telling me to run, to at least try. I won't give him the satisfaction. When one of the men grabs my arm roughly, a low hiss runs through the crowd. Until then, they were utterly silent, no jeering, no shouting or calling me names. They said nothing. Now the small sound, the small rebellion, gives me courage.

The crowd parts as I begin to walk toward the platform, and I find myself meeting their eyes, smiling gently left and right to them. They murmur "my lady" as I pass, bowing their heads to me. None of them seem frightened of my white eyes. None of them seem to care at all. Instead, they offer me smiles, and bows, their affection radiating from them.

And I know Aurek will have every single one of them slaughtered for it when this is over.

When I reach the top of the stairs, I turn to face them, and another hiss, low and guttural, threatening, begins to rise from the crowd.

Lief has arrived. Dressed all in black, his face blank of all expression.

His sword—Merek's sword—in his hands.

He doesn't look at me. He climbs the stairs to the dais slowly, heavily, as though he's the one sentenced to die, and I realize this must have been where Aurek whipped him. That it's possible some of the old bloodstains I'm standing on came from his back.

All at once the fear that evaporated as I smiled at the people fills me.

I'm going to die.

Now. At the hands of the first man I ever loved.

It's not fair.

I look at him, bewildered, and see something like regret flicker in his eye.

"Make her kneel," Aurek calls.

Lief looks at me as though he expects me to do it, but I shake my head. He reaches for me and pushes at my shoulder. I resist him, but he keeps pushing.

"You need to kneel," he says. "You don't want to be standing for this. Please."

The finality in his voice—the kindness—has me sinking to my knees as though I'm melting.

"Twylla Morven, Sin Eater of Lormere," Aurek calls in his rich, velvet voice. "You have been brought here to die for your crimes against the House of Tallith, both historic and present. Your blood is a disease; your existence is an abomination. And for that, you shall die, and your body will be desecrated like that of a beast." He pauses, casting a filthy look at me before he stands, stepping forward and leaning on the edge of his box, staring at the crowd.

"Behold her, your scarecrow queen. Look upon this puppet mirage of safety. Nothing but a parody of leadership, nothing but straw stuffed in old clothes. And that's what stood, hoping to frighten the crows away." He pauses. "It ends, today." Aurek's voice rings across the square. "Give me your fealty, give me your respect, and I will see you rewarded. I was heir to the greatest kingdom this world has ever known, and I can give that to you—*will* give that to you. Wealth, prosperity can all be yours. A better land, free from superstition. Free from foolishness. No more weakness. And we will move forward together."

He looks out at them and then nods to Lief.

Lief pushes my head down onto the block, and I let him. Gently, he turns it to the side, so I'm facing away from Aurek, and I think that's a kindness, too, that he won't let the last thing I see be Aurek's golden eyes.

Scarecrow queen. Nothing but a dupe, alone in a field, hoping to keep the crows at bay.

"You should close your eyes," Lief says.

"No." Dupe I might be, but I'm not a coward anymore. I want to see the world as I leave it.

He sighs, then frowns. He bends down and pulls at the ties on my wrists, tightening them. Then he straightens.

It hurts to force my eyes so far to the side, but I do, watching Lief draw his sword and raise it above his head. His eyes follow the blade and he looks to the sky before looking straight ahead. He pauses, waiting for Aurek's permission.

Then he nods.

"I'm sorry," he says.

There is a whooshing sound, and the sword begins to fall. Without meaning to, I close my eyes; I can't help it.

They fly back open when I hear screams, a bullish bellow of anger, and a thud behind me. I jerk upright and turn.

Lief is on his back, knees bent under him, his one eye wide as he stares at the sky.

There is an arrow in his chest.

I turn and look out to see Merek standing on the roof of a merchant's house, bow in hand, another arrow already nocked.

"Run," he screams, then turns his bow on Aurek.

Chapter 26

I stare at Lief, waiting for him to move, groan, or even blink. But as I watch, a dark stain blooms beneath him, thick red liquid spreading along the wooden platform.

But he can't be dead; we thought that before and we were wrong. He's Lief. He's . . .

I move toward him, and something smashes down where I was, sending shock waves through the platform and making me stumble. I turn and see a golem, faceless, lifeless, raising a club high over its head to strike again. I roll aside a split second before it crashes into the dais, sending splinters of the wood through the air. I scramble back, and the golem swings again, and I move, until I've fallen off the dais and onto the ground, breath forced from me as I land on my back.

For a horrible moment I can't breathe, can't move, can't even hear, staring at the clouds racing overhead as my chest feels as though it's collapsing in on itself. Then I manage to gasp, and air fills me, and sound returns. Roars and clashes and shouts, and my panic rises. I roll again, under the dais, trying desperately to untie my wrists. I move my fingers, slow and sluggish from the cold, and feel something attached to the rope, some kind of cylinder. I need to free my hands or I'm dead.

Beyond the platform, feet move, back and forth, from this angle strangely indiscernible from dancing, until one of the pair nearest to the dais hits the ground, blood spilling from his lips. He reaches out, his knife still gripped in his hands, toward me. Then he jerks, and I see steel glint as it's pulled out of his back. I meet his eyes as he dies, see them dull. I shuffle toward him like a worm on my stomach, turning until I hold the knife in sweating fingers.

I saw and saw at my bindings, guided by touch alone, no idea whether the blade is cutting the rope at all, as all around me people fight. I see the feet of the golems as they move amongst the crowd, see people scatter before them. Above me, there is a crash as something hits the dais again, and I saw faster.

Finally, I feel the rope start to give, and I tug, a thrill moving through me as the rope snaps and my hands are free. At once I twist and grab the cylinder, covered in paper, my fingers trembling as I unwrap it.

A single vial of a bright white liquid.

And wrapped around it, a note in my own childlike writing. A note that says *I love you*.

Everything falls away—the fighting, the screams, the golems— as I stare at the first thing I ever wrote.

He kept it all this time. And the vial. It's the Opus Mortem. It has to be.

But I watched as he crushed the last two beneath his boot. I watched him do it.

Except here is one, somehow secreted away and given to me, deliberately, in the moments before . . .

I remember the way he looked out into the crowd, and then the nod of his head.

He knew what was going to happen.

Then the wood above me vanishes, peeling back with a shriek, and the sky appears again briefly before two of the golems are there, hands reaching into the hole they've just made. I stuff the vial down my bodice and grab the knife, once more escaping the crushing blow of a club by the skin of my teeth. Their clubs slam again and again into the wood as they destroy the executioner's platform in a bid to end me.

I roll out, and a man in Aurek's livery, armed with a short sword, lunges at me. I sidestep, just as Hope taught me, and slash at his back, causing him to cry out. I kick him in the back of the legs while he's still surprised, sending him to the ground before dropping and slamming the hilt of my knife into his head.

When I turn back to the dais, Lief's body has disappeared, and as I bend for the fallen sword of the man I've just knocked out, I see a shape beneath the dais—it's him, fallen through the holes made by the golems in their attempts to get to me. The sight of him there, like a broken toy, makes it hard to breathe for a moment, until an arrow embeds itself in a post level with my eyes and reminds me that there is a battle raging.

I look around, scanning the fighters at first for Aurek, who has seemingly vanished, then for Merek: a pang of fear when I can't see him, either. The entire square is filled with fighting, men in the black tabards of the Sleeping Prince fighting people in everyday clothes with swords, knives, sticks, whatever they have to hand, or have stolen from others. I recognize the faces of people I know amongst the crowd: Hobb wrestling with a man before lifting him and throwing him through a window, Ema battering another guard with what looks like a butcher's mallet, malice lighting her face.

On the other side of the destroyed dais, Hope is fighting, whirling like a dervish, a short sword in each hand as she battles three of Aurek's soldiers, a snarl at her lips. As I watch, her sword slashes out, and one of the men falls, his throat spilling crimson. I see the uncertainty in the others as Hope stalks toward them.

Ulrin has taken on one of the golems, but even he is no match in size for the might of the clay creature, and he's losing ground. Then there is a flash of green, and Stuan appears from nowhere with a blazing torch, which he thrusts at the golem. With a flare of emerald fire the golem goes up in flames—someone has brought Errin's firewater—and Ulrin pulls its own club from its grasping hands and smashes it around its head, felling it like a tree.

He meets my eyes over the crowd and nods, and then his eyes widen and I duck instinctively. There is a breeze across the top of my head and I spin, lashing out, and my sword bites into the thighs of a soldier. As he falls to the ground, I stand again, and move, but a hand grasps the hem of the dress and pulls.

I stumble and drop my sword as I try to stop my face smashing into the ground. I reach for it and the hand tugs, moving from dress to my ankle and pulling me back vital inches from the hilt. I roll onto my back as the soldier tries to drag me toward him, half climbing me in the process, his eyes wild, his teeth bared. I sit and punch him in the face, forgetting to keep my thumb outside my fist, moaning as the impact wounds me, too.

He doesn't let go, fingers digging into my calves, and I cry out again, trying to kick him away. I grab a fistful of his hair and pull, and he punches me, catching my jaw. My teeth click together and my head rolls back, but then he lets go and I'm free. When I look again at him, blinking away the stars in my eyes from the blow, there is an arrow in his throat. I look around for the shooter but can see no one, so I haul myself to my feet and grab my sword.

No sooner is it in my hand than two more soldiers run toward me, and panic starts to mount; I'm not good enough to take on two men at once. I back up, sword raised, as they close in.

Then Nia is beside me, her skin glistening with sweat.

"Sorry we took so long," she says. "Got a bit held up."

"Just fight," I breathe, choosing an opponent and lunging at him. There will be time for clever chat afterward.

Though neither of us is especially skilled, we're an even match against the shopkeepers-turned-guards that Aurek has black-mailed or coerced into his service, and soon enough they start to flag. I'm gaining ground, preparing to strike, when something hits me, making the right side of my body explode in pain and sending me flying into the air before I crash back down, landing badly. But the first thing I do is pat my chest, checking the safety of the vial, the relief at feeling it whole rushing through me.

Nia screams, and so do the men, as the golem swings indiscriminately. Its club piles into the head of the man I'd been fighting, killing him instantly, and his friend flees.

Nia rushes to me and tries to lift me, but I cry out. "Ribs," I

352

gasp, sure the blow has broken at least two of them. Nia glances over her shoulder and then moves me anyway, causing my vision to white out.

"Get up," she shrieks at me, passing me a round green bottle. I bite down on my lip and stand, whimpering at the pain, and throw the bottle at the golem. It does nothing to deter it, but we both watch as the firewater soaks into the golem. "Here," she calls to someone, ducking as the golem swings at us, and then Stuan appears. He hands the torch to me and I throw it, even as my chest screams in protest. But it does the job, and the firewater catches, burning so fast and so hot that in seconds the golem is turning pale, and cracking. We all move back as it stumbles and weaves, until it finally explodes into dust, covering us all.

Stuan grins at me. "Was it like that when you did it?" he asks.

"I didn't have the firewater," I say, but manage a smile back.

"Look out!" Nia cries as a new soldier rushes in to take the golem's place, leaping forward to fight him with the ringing of steel against steel. "Get out of here!"

Stuan takes my arm, pulling me toward the shadowy labyrinth of alleyways that lead away from the square. Each step, each breath is like a dagger to the chest, but I push the pain away, try-ing to ride out the dizziness, crossing my arms over my chest. As soon as we're out of the thick of it, I draw him to a stop, needing to pause for just a moment. "Where's Merek?"

"I don't know. He was supposed to free Errin."

"Supposed to? Where was she?"

"In a cage, just behind yours. Gagged. I think he wanted her to watch you die."

"Did Merek get her?"

He shakes his head. "The Sleeping Prince went straight for her. He didn't even try to fight, just used some of the golems as cover and went for her. I didn't see what happened then; I was trying to get to you. Watch out!"

A man flies at me from the left. I barely register the three stars on his chest before Stuan has spun around, reaching across me to stab him in the heart.

"Thank you."

He shrugs, and bends down to take the man's sword from him, offering it to me.

As soon as I take it, I know I won't be able to use it; it would be too heavy even if I wasn't injured. I drop it to the ground.

Stuan looks at me, and then pulls a knife from his belt. "You can't be unarmed," he says.

"Again, thank you." I take it.

"Where do we go?" he asks.

"After Aurek," I say.

"Do you know where he'll be?"

There's only one place he could have gone. There's only one thing that might save him now, and he'll head straight for it.

"The castle," I say. "He'll have gone for Silas."

It's time to finish this.

Stuan peers around and then nods at me. "Now," he says.

It's hard to move because of both my chest and my skirts, and I'm soon urging Stuan to stop again while I slash panels out of the dress so I can move. I use some of the panels as a makeshift binder for my ribs, as Stuan nods his approval and helps me tie them.

"Wait," he says, shrugging his cloak off and throwing it around me. "It's not much of a disguise, but . . ."

"Thank you," I say for the third time.

Then we keep moving, him in front and me behind, scanning everywhere for golems, soldiers, or bowmen.

Even this far from the action, we come across the dead and injured, killed while fleeing or pursuing. I feel horribly grateful when I don't recognize any of them.

"Tell me what happened at the caves," I say as Stuan jogs, and I stumble, toward the spectre of Lormere castle above us. "Who was lost?"

"Breena," he says softly. "Trey. Serge. Linion."

I think of the soft-eyed woman who could hit a target every time with an arrow and the loyal men who camped for moons in the mountains to keep watch over the children of Lortune. Linion, whose nephews were there.

"It would have been more, if not for you."

"What?"

"You calling Merek back meant he was behind us all. While he was catching up, he caught sight of more men on their way to join those at the caves. He realized it was an ambush and raced to warn us, so we lay in wait for the reinforcements at the mere, and dropped down on them. They didn't know we were coming."

"And the children?"

"They're safe. We took them to the rendezvous point."

"What about Lief?"

"What about him?" Stuan asks.

I shake my head, still not wholly sure of my thoughts. "Never mind. Let's go."

When we get to the main gates of Lormere castle, they're unlocked, and unmanned, the first time I have ever seen them thus, and it sends a chill through me. Beyond the path leading to the main keep, the castle is in darkness, silent and still. This far from the town, the sounds of the fighting have faded, and the night feels as though it's waiting. Wanting.

Stuan and I exchange a glance and begin to creep forward.

Almost instantly, three of the golems loom out of the night, no clubs in their hands, but vicious axes. They attack at once, their lack of eyes no hindrance as they swing the blades so fast the air whistles in their wake.

"Run," Stuan bellows, darting around them. "I'll hold them."

"Don't be stupid." I run, too, sliding through the legs of the nearest one, wincing when the ax of another smashes into those same legs seconds after I'm clear. The damaged golem falls to the ground, a huge chunk of clay missing from both legs, but that doesn't stop it as it grips the earth and pulls itself after me, eyeless face pointed at me as though smelling me.

"Go," Stuan screams. "I've got this." He does as I've done, drawing the attention of the golem closest before doing as I did and dashing around the third. When the ax strikes it, I do as he says and move toward the castle as fast as I can. Behind me I can hear the sound of turf being pulled up as the broken golem tries to pursue me, but I don't look back.

I enter Lormere castle alone, armed with a knife, and the last vial of Opus Mortem.

Chapter 27

Inside, the corridors are colder, somehow, than it was outside, and horribly quiet. The carpets, laid so long ago for Helewys, are dusty, small clouds blooming under my feet as I walk. There are icicles hanging from the window ledges and the unlit candelabras; the walls are bare, and blackened from smoke. The castle feels as though it's been abandoned for centuries.

At the end of the passageway, I stand still, trying to choose which way to go. To my left, the passage to the ruined north tower is a black maw, and I shiver as I look down it. It seems unlikely that Aurek will have gone there. Where, then?

He's taken Errin to control me, I know that. He'll want Silas with him, too. But Silas wasn't down in the dungeon—Lief said so, and I believe him. Where would Aurek have imprisoned Silas after the fire?

My feet start to move before I understand where it is they're taking me.

The door to the west tower is open, and I slip through it, my heart beating hard behind my broken ribs. I move like a ghost, silent as the grave as I climb the stairs toward my former prison. I pause outside the old guards' room, listening, but when I hear nothing, I keep going.

As I round the spiral staircase, I see a faint glow coming from my old room, and then Aurek's voice, demanding that someone hurry up.

I draw a deep breath, clutching the vial in my hand, and take the final three steps.

Aurek turns at once, though I've made no sound, and moves faster than anyone should be able to, grabbing Errin by the throat and ripping her away from the bed, where she was tending Silas.

Silas lies prone, and the first thing I notice is his feet, the skin black and dead-looking. The Nigredo. His eyes are closed in his waxen face, and his breathing is shallow.

"Twylla," Errin gasps, drawing my attention back to Aurek inching slowly toward me. There is a small clay doll in his hands.

Beside him Errin stands, pressing a knife against her own heart.

Aurek looks down at his hands, and then at mine, where I clutch the vial.

"Trade?" he asks, a smile curving his lips.

I say nothing, trying to think of what I can do to get Errin out of here.

"Give me the vial in your hands, or I'll make her kill herself." Aurek's voice is level and pleasant as he comes to a halt by the bureau.

"Don't," Errin says. "Don't."

I look at Aurek, his head dipped as he watches me from under white lashes.

"You have to die, Twylla," he says. "You know that. But Errin doesn't. There's a piece of parchment on this simulacrum. It instructs her to hold the knife to her breast, and to plunge it into herself at my word. Give me the vial and I'll remove the instruction."

"Don't listen to him. He'll kill me anyway," Errin sobs.

Aurek lashes out, backhanding Errin. Her head flies back, hitting the wall with a sickening crack, but she doesn't fall. To my horror, she stays on her feet, snapping back into position, the knife never moving from its place over her heart.

"Harder," Aurek commands.

She whimpers as she pushes the knife into her dress; I see the material gather, then tear, and see the edges darken with blood as it pierces her skin. Droplets from her nose start to join it, and when I look at her, I see the despair in her eyes.

"You heard what I said out there," Aurek says, his voice crooning now, his eyes fixed on me. "What you are. What you've always been."

"A scarecrow queen," I reply.

"Just so. A puppet with no real power. An effigy."

"What are you, then?" I ask. "A relic. A throwback to a bygone era. An echo from a long-dead world."

His mouth loses its soft smile as the corners turn down, marring his otherwise perfect face.

"Lief betrayed you," I say, watching from the corner of my eye as Errin's mouth falls open, the blade in her hand temporarily forgotten by Aurek.

"It doesn't matter," Aurek says even as his brows knit together, contradicting his words. "It was always just going to be you and me in the end."

He looks at Errin. "Stab yourself. In the heart," he adds, and it's almost an afterthought.

"No!" I scream as she draws the knife back.

I fly at her, knocking her to the floor, sending the knife skidding under the bed. She throws me off to go after it, crawling across the floor, and then his hand is in my hair, tearing it from my head. I reach instinctively to make him stop, and he uses his other hand to pry the vial from my hands before throwing me down.

I look up as Aurek holds the vial to the light. "Mine," he says.

Then there is a rushing sound, and an arrow appears through his lower arm as if by magic.

He drops the vial and I lurch forward to catch it, just as in the commune with Errin.

Aurek howls, his shrieking filling the room as he turns to see who shot him.

Merek stands in the doorway.

"That's my crown," he says.

Aurek gapes at him. "You."

Then I move.

I fly to my feet and slam the vial, glass and all, into his open mouth.

Using all of my weight, I shove him backward, pushing my palm under his chin and forcing his teeth together. I hear the crunch of the glass, and he tries to open his mouth, clawing at my hair and eyes, blood bubbling from the corners of his mouth.

I hear the sound of a struggle behind me, Merek forcing Errin to the ground perhaps; of metal hitting the floor, and then something else, but I can't see. Aurek struggles, pushing into me, so I allow him a little way before I use his momentum to slam him back into the wall.

His eyes fill with disbelief and he renews his struggles, but he's getting weaker, even as he claws my face and tries to kick me. I can feel the cuts left behind but I don't let go, pinning him, holding his mouth and nose until he swallows.

At once he stiffens, his eyes rolling back in his head, and he slumps forward, sending me staggering back under his weight. He lands on top of me and I shove him off with a pained grunt, the crown falling from his head and rolling under the bed.

He lands with a thud, his eyes closed, his face still.

I look up at Errin to see her still struggling to get free of Merek.

As I approach, her body goes wild, trying to get to me, but I avoid her grasp and slip the sword out of the sheath at Merek's waist.

I look down at the Sleeping Prince, sleeping once more, and for a moment I wonder if I could leave him like that. Have him sent far away.

But one glance at the unconscious man on the bed, and the sound of my friend sobbing in Merek's arms as she tries to carry out his last instruction, is all I need.

I raise the sword high over my head, my ribs screaming at me.

Then I bring it down, severing the Sleeping Prince's head from his body in a single stroke far easier than it ought to have been. The wound doesn't bleed; the cut is clean, as though he were one of his own golems. As though he died a long time ago. Even as I watch, he starts to collapse in on himself, his skin beginning to look papery and thin.

Errin goes limp in Merek's arms, and I drop the sword to the floor, holding out my arms to her. She flies into them the moment Merek releases her, and we sink down next to the Sleeping Prince's corpse. Errin squeezes me and I gasp.

"Are you injured?" she asks, pulling back to look at me.

"Broken ribs," I say. "You?" I look down at her chest.

"Flesh wound."

Then she remembers Silas. She moves from me to him at once, sitting beside him and stroking his white hair.

Merek's hand appears before me and he pulls me up, placing an arm around me and helping me limp to the bed.

"I can take care of him," Errin says, looking at us through eyes that brim with tears. "I don't mind. I took care of Mama for so long. I can care for them both if I have to."

"No," Silas whispers from the bed.

"You're awake." Errin's voice quavers, and I watch as she swallows, pressing her lips together before speaking. "Now, there's no point in arguing, because I've decided. It's all going to be fine."

He opens his golden eyes, and I'm astonished to see how pale they are, drained of brightness. "Please, Errin. Please just kill me."

"Don't say that."

"I can't live like this," he says.

"And I can't lose you, too."

He tries to lift a hand to reach for hers but can't make it an inch off the bed before it falls limply back and he sighs. Errin's face crumples, and she collapses, pressing her face into his chest. Silas turns his gaze on us.

362

Please, he mouths.

Beside me, Merek slips his hand into mine, and I stare into Silas's eyes.

Can there really be no way, no antidote for this . . .

Errin's shoulders are shaking silently as her hand reaches for Silas's, her white fingers twining with his black ones. It doesn't seem fair, that he should have to suffer so much to create something that stops others suffering. But as Errin said, everything has an opposite and—

"Wait—"

Everyone looks at me.

"The Opus Mortem is the reverse of the Opus Magnum, yes?"

Merek nods, and then his eyebrows draw together.

"Adding my blood to the Opus Mortem is what made it so deadly to Aurek."

Errin stares at me with an unreadable expression on her face. Then she nods.

"So the blood—my blood—is the opposite of a philtersmith's blood, yes? They cancel each other out?"

Errin sits up, all of her attention fixed on me.

"What would happen if I added my blood to the Opus Magnum?"

Merek stiffens beside me.

On the bed, Silas opens his eyes wider. "I thought you looked different," he says. "You're cursed."

I nod.

"Well, if that's the case, adding your blood to the Opus Magnum will curse you further." He lowers his gaze to his feet, then back to me, as if to demonstrate his point.

I ignore him and turn to Errin. "Help me make sense of this. My blood, plus the Opus Mortem, is enough to counter the Elixir. And therefore the opposite would be my blood, plus the Opus Magnum, to make a new kind of Elixir." I look at Silas. "One that might work on you."

"You don't know that," Merek says.

"She's right," Errin disagrees.

"I know you want her to be," Merek replies.

"It's not worth it," Silas says. He stares at me, at my hair and eyes. "You don't know where it will strike next."

"It'll only be the once," I say.

"Once is enough."

"Listen to him," Merek implores, turning me to look at him and taking my shoulders in his hands. "I know you want to help, but—"

"Do you have the vial of Opus Magnum you made?" I ask him.

His face becomes pinched and he shakes his head.

I shrug him off my shoulders and hold out my hand.

He looks past me at Errin, his face thunderous. Then it softens, and he bows his head, reaching into a pouch at his waist and pulling out a vial. He hands it to me silently.

I look around for something to cut myself with, my eyes landing first on the sword I beheaded Aurek with. I inhale sharply when I see Aurek's body is missing; for a moment I wonder if he's risen again. Then I see the outline of dust; at some point Aurek's corpse has quietly desiccated, becoming the dust it should have become over five hundred years ago. I turn away and spot the knife Errin had, in the corner of the room.

"Wait," Silas says as I pick it up. "You don't have to do this."

"I know."

He nods. Then he looks over at Errin. "If this doesn't work, I don't want to live. Please, I know I'm asking a lot, but I don't want this to be my life. I don't want . . ." He pauses. "For the last few moons, I've been here, in this bed, with him bleeding me, as and when he saw fit. No control. No choice. If it were just being weak, then . . . it would be different; I could live without the use of my legs. But I can't live wondering what happens if someone else finds me like this, and takes me for their own use. I don't want to be used again. I don't want to live a life where it's possible, and where my body isn't my own." He looks me in the eye. "You know what I mean. Promise me."

"I promise," I say.

I uncork the vial, cut my left thumb, and add the drop of blood to the Opus Magnum. It turns bright red, at the same moment Merek whistles. Errin and Silas stare at me.

I look down at myself. "What did it do this time?" I turn to find the mirror, and catch sight of something bloodred out of the corner of my eye. "Oh," I breathe, pulling my hair forward. It's red. Not the auburn of before, but an unnatural, deep crimson.

I look at Merek and he smiles, a soft, full smile. "Your eyes are red, too."

"How?"

He shrugs. "How on earth would I know?"

I look at Silas and Errin.

Errin's eyes are so wide, and so full of hope. She looks at the vial in my hand. I exhale slowly, and pass it to her. Gently, she cradles Silas's head and lifts it so he can swallow the liquid. He drinks it down, and all three of us stare at him, scrutinizing him for any sign of an effect.

As we watch, the deadness in his skin begins to fade.

Errin starts to cry, huge, heaving sobs that sound agonized. Again she buries her face in his chest, clinging to him. And when Silas lifts a perfectly healthy hand and places it on her head, she lets out a sound akin to a howl and launches herself on him.

He struggles to sit up, and then they're kissing with absolute recklessness. She pins him to the bed, her legs around his waist, and he wraps his arms around her, kissing her as though he's drowning. When she moans softly, I feel my own skin heat, and I look down.

I'm surprised to see my hand in Merek's, unaware it had happened. He squeezes lightly and then bends, picking up the crown—his crown. Then he pulls me out of the room, and I close the door behind us.

We walk down the stairs in silence, then through the corridors, dim now that dusk is falling. How has a whole day passed? Has it really been just one day?

When footsteps rush toward us, Merek pulls me back behind him. His expression is panicked, but then it clears as Hope, Kirin, Stuan, and Nia, hand in hand with the white-haired woman I remember from the Conclave, come rushing toward us. Kata, alive and free.

"Her ribs are broken," Merek shouts as they descend on us, causing them all to halt so suddenly I let out a giggle, and then a yelp as my ribs jar.

"The Sleeping Prince?" Hope asks.

"Very dead and gone," I say.

Hope beams, a full smile, and reaches out to cup my face. "Well done, child. Well done."

"Is Errin all right?" Nia asks.

"She's fine. She's with Silas. In the west tower."

Hope lowers her hand and makes as if to go, but Merek stops her.

"I'd give them some time to reunite," he says tactfully, and Hope's mouth falls open. Nia and Kata snicker behind her.

"You found the alchemists, then?" I say to Nia.

"We'd all but won when the last of the golems fell," she replies. "We made one of the guards tell us where the alchemists here were being kept, and went to free them." She beams at her wife, who smiles back. "There are still those held by the Lormerian nobles . . ." Nia adds with a frown.

"By now the other cities will have risen up," Merek says. "We should send men—people—to support them. Have the surviving nobles brought to the castle for trial. Send messengers to bring the children home. See what's needed to get back on track. To start again."

"Your eyes have changed again," Nia says. "It's a bit better than the white. But still creepy."

"I think they look fantastic," Kata says, her gold eyes glinting, and we grin at each other.

"Why don't you all go on to the Great Hall?" Merek says. "Down the corridor, left, then right. We'll join you there soon."

Stuan bows to him, and Kirin winks at me, and the five of them do as he asked. Merek tugs on my hand and leads me out of the castle, until we're standing at the top of the stairs that lead down, and eventually out of the castle grounds.

The wind has risen, whipping my hair around my face. I reach up to smooth it back, catching sight of the newly scarlet strands. I pull a few around so I can see them.

"Rubedo," Merek says. I look at him to see his skin has flared a shade remarkably similar to my hair. "That's what your curse should be called."

"Why?"

"It makes sense." Merek rubs the back of his neck, not meeting my eye. "Like Nigredo, but Rubedo. Red. I decided the white curse should be Albedo."

"When did you decide that?"

"When you were ignoring me at the commune."

"Rubedo," I say. The curse of my blood.

Below us in the twilight Lortune looks peaceful, though I know it can't be. Shops and houses are in ruins; blood and bodies litter the streets. Somewhere in the square, Lief's body lies, and I don't want it left there for the crows. He deserves to be taken to his family's mausoleum, to lie with them.

"What happened?" I ask. "With Lief? He helped us, didn't he? I saw him nod to the crowd before—"

Merek's face slackens for a moment, then he rummages in his pocket. "It's better if you read for yourself," he says as he hands me a small sheet of parchment.

I had no choice, it begins. Addressed to no one in particular.

I had no choice. Ymilla told him you were all here. I'll do what I can to protect Errin, but I can't protect Twylla. He plans to execute her, and he'll have me do it. It will be tomorrow. Midday. The men on the West Gate of Lortune are Rising Sympathizers, as is the owner of the book binders on the town square. Get there before dawn, and wait. Do what needs to be done. Tell Errin this is me fixing things. And that she was right, I was raised better than this. This is me trying

to be a better man. Tell her I love her, and to tell Mama the same.
And tell Twylla I'm sorry.

That's it.

I look up at Merek, to find him watching me closely.

"Is this all?" I hold up the piece of paper.

"Yes. I found it in Errin's lab."

"That's how you were there, waiting. That's why you shot him."

"I would have shot him to save you anyway," Merek says. "But . . . yes. I assume that's what he meant by 'do what needs to be done.' That he was prepared to pay any price."

"So does this mean he was with us, in the end? Is that what you think?"

"I think he regretted a lot of things," Merek says slowly. "From the beginning. I think he thought he was cleverer than he was, and by the time he realized he was in too deep, it was too late, and he did what he could to ease his conscience without risking himself, or his mother."

Typical Lief. I sigh, wrapping my arms around myself.

"He didn't tell Aurek I was alive and working in his employ," Merek continues. "He told us how to get out of Lortune. He refused the Elixir when it was offered to him. And he gave us the Opus Mortem recipe. Who knows what else he did, quietly, to undermine Aurek."

"That doesn't make up for all the things he's done—all the people he hurt."

"Perhaps not. But I think he was trying, in his own way."

I think of everything we went through together, me and Lief: His coming to the castle. Our being together. His betrayal. His alliance with Aurek. And now I'll never know the truth of him. Perhaps, on the King's Road, he was trying to get me away, not hurt me. Perhaps the reason he hit me at the commune was to stop me from fighting and getting hurt. He gave me the Opus Mortem; he gave me back my note to him. He gave up his life, knowingly, to help us. Yet no one will ever know the whole truth, and he died a villain.

I sigh again, and look back down at the town.

"There's so much to do," I say quietly, not aware I've spoken aloud until Merek nods. "As well as everything here, there's Chargate, Monkham, Haga. The whole country needs to be put back together. I don't know where you're going to begin."

Merek lets go of my hand and moves in front of me.

"Twylla," he says, but I shake my head.

I know what he's going to say and I don't know if I'm ready for this. I still don't know what I want. I'm attracted to him, yes. But I'm not ready to be his wife. Or anyone's wife. I might never be.

"I told you that you were the queen Lormere needed," he begins.

"A scarecrow queen, Aurek said," I counter. "A puppet. I can't be queen."

"You have to be. It was always going to be you."

"Merek, I'm not ready to marry anyone."

Merek frowns. "Who said anything about marrying?"

I stare at him. "But you just said—"

"That you're the queen Lormere needs. Not *my* queen."

"I . . . I don't understand."

"Technically, I gave up my throne to Aurek when I hid. I abdicated. And you just killed him. Which makes you queen by right of conquest." He holds the crown out to me. "You won the throne. It's yours."

My heart beats like a drum against my ribs, but the pain is nothing. "But you're the prince—you're the king . . ."

"Not anymore." He smiles. "Twylla, you've been queen in training since you were thirteen. Before that, you were preparing to spend your life taking on the sins of every person in this country. And over the last four moons, you've raised and led an army into war. You're the right person for this job. You're the *only* person for this job."

"I don't know how to rule. What if I don't want to rule?"

He gives a short laugh. "Remember that night, in my room, at the commune? I asked you what I should do after I won back my crown, because I didn't know. But you did. You already had a plan for Lormere, for all of us." I open my mouth to protest, because that was different, it was hypothetical, but he holds up a hand to stop me. "And do you really not want to rule? Truly? Because in the commune, every time someone referred to me as 'king,' you pulled this face." I watch as his eyes become stony, and his mouth a sullen line.

"I did not." My gaze drops to the crown in his hands.

When I meet his eyes again, he's smiling. "Oh, yes, you did. You might not have realized it, but I saw it. And given that you've defeated two of the last three monarchs to sit this throne, I'm not fool enough to take you on with those odds."

"The castle is ruined," I say stupidly.

"Then build a new one. You have a council to advise you; Hope, Nia, Kirin, Silas, Stuan. You won't have to do it alone."

"Half of them Tregellian. That's never been done."

"Twylla . . . Do you want to be queen?" His voice is soft, neutral.

I stare at the band of gold now dangling from the tips of his fingers and think about what it would mean. Not just to me, but to everyone in Lormere. The things I could do . . . The country we could become . . .

"Yes," I say, my voice steady. "I do."

When he holds the crown toward me again, I reach out, and I take it.

It's cold in my hands, lighter than I'd expected, too. For some reason, I thought it would be heavy. When I look closer, I see it's a little scratched, and there's a dent in one side. I rub my thumb in the small recess and look up at Merek. "What about you?"

"I'm going to ask Errin if she'll take me on as her apprentice," he says. "I want to learn the apothecary's art. And more about alchemy—even if I can't perform it, I can learn the theory. I'd like to study the texts the Tregellians have kept locked away. Then I plan to petition you for funds to build a school of medicine. Maybe two schools. And I wouldn't mind a place on your council, if you'll have me."

He gently takes the crown from my hands and places it on my head. It's too big, and it slips down until my ears hold it in place.

"Kirin was a blacksmith," he says. "He can adjust it for you. Maybe spruce it up a bit."

I laugh, because it's madness. He can't be serious.

Merek Belmis kneels. "I offer you my fealty, Your Majesty. I swear to serve and protect you as your most loyal subject until the day I die."

"Get up," I say, a high note to my voice.

He stands, and takes my hand and kisses it.

"I love you," he says simply. "Always have. Always will. But more than that, I'm your friend for life. No matter what you decide about your future. Even if you decide to rule alone. Even if you elope with Stuan."

I laugh again, the end twisting into a sob.

"You're going to make an incredible queen," Merek says, wiping away a tear from my face. He kisses my hand again and then walks back into the castle, leaving me alone.

I look back up at the castle, blackened and filthy. Such a dark, terrible place, the stones themselves seeped in sadness. I'll raze it, I decide. Start again. Build everything from the ground up.

It will take time, I realize. Castles can take years to build. Countries can take decades to recover. There's so much to do.

But I have time.

I adjust my crown, tilting it back so it rests at an angle.

I have time.

Acknowledgments

Firstly, the biggest thanks go to my agent, Claire Wilson. Writing can sometimes be a scary, lonely business. If you're lucky, you have a Claire, who cuts through the impossibility and makes everything exciting and achievable. Also, I'm pretty sure she'd be useful in a zombie apocalypse.

Thanks to Rosie Price and Sam Copeland at RCW, too, for stepping in to support me.

As ever, huge thanks to the usual suspects at Scholastic UK, in particular my editor, Genevieve Herr. I've had the best time creating this world with you. Thank you so much for your guidance and patience and insight. And editorial comments. I didn't even know how to spell *fnarrrrr* before I worked with you, and now I don't know what I'd do without it.

Thanks to Jamie Gregory for yet another beautiful cover. One day I hope my stories live up to his art. Thanks to Rachel Phillips for being consistently brilliant.

Also thanks to Lorraine Keating; Lucy Richardson; Olivia Horrox; Fi Evans; Sam Selby-Smith; Pete Matthews; the sales team; the rights team; and everyone else who has worked hard on my behalf behind the scenes, throughout the whole series. Thank you.

The YA community—online and off—have, over the last three years, become the best coworkers I could ask for. I don't know what I'd do without Sara Barnard; Holly Bourne; Alexia Casale; and CJ Daugherty. My continuing sanity over the past year is largely thanks to them. I also owe thanks to Catherine Doyle; Katie Webber; Samantha Shannon; Laure Eve; Alwyn Hamilton; Kiran Millwood-Hargrave; Anna James; Nina Douglas; Rainbow Rowell; Leigh Bardugo; Lucy Saxon; Jade from Bloomsbury Non-Fiction; and Lucy Lapinski for a lot of fun and support and laughter over the past year. Thanks again to Emilie, the Stu to my Nick. I'm over being a vampire. Don't believe the hype.

Thanks also to the following, who have continued being brilliant throughout my writing of *The Scarecrow Queen*: the Lyonses and the Allports; Sophie Reynolds; Denise Strauss; Emma Gerrard; Lizzy Evans; Mikey Beddard; Franziska Schmidt; Katja Rammer; Neil Bird; Laura Hughes; Adam Reeve; my brother, Steven; Auntie Penny, Uncle Eddie, and family; my sister, Kelly; and Auntie Cath and Uncle Paul. I love you all so much.

Over the course of the series, I've built up an amazing reader base, who make every day a joy, with their tweets, comments, art, photos, and general existence. Thank you all, for buying my books and for loving my stories, and for your constant, vocal, and brilliant support. Very particular thanks go to Sofia Saghir; Sally-zar Slytherin; Steph (eenalol); Holly (The_Arts_Shelf); Aimee (Geordie_Aimee); Marian (Witchymomo); Sarah Corrigan; Stacee (book_junkee); Mariyam (ohpandaeyes); Chelley Toy; Lucy Powrie; Kate Ormand; and Christine (xenatine), who have all given so much love to the Sin Eater series, and to me. I hope so much you like *The Scarecrow Queen*. Thank you for seeing it through to the end, and I hope you stick around for what happens next.

Final thanks go to my nan, Florence May Kiernan. Thanks for everything. She never knew I'd written a book—let alone a trilogy. But she'd be super proud. Especially because I got plants and poisons in there.

Melinda Salisbury lives by the sea, somewhere in the south of England. As a child, she genuinely thought Roald Dahl's *Matilda* was her biography, in part helped by her grandfather's often mistakenly calling her Matilda, and the local library's having a pretty cavalier attitude to the books she borrowed. Sadly, she never manifested telekinetic powers. She likes to travel, and to have adventures. She also likes medieval castles, non-medieval aquariums, Richard III, and all things Scandinavian.

She can be found on Twitter at @MESalisbury, though be warned, she tweets often.